Cold Blooded VI: Red Horizon

(The Nick McCarty Series)

by

Bernard Lee DeLeo

Cold Blooded VI: Red Horizon

(The Nick McCarty Series)

by

Bernard Lee DeLeo

*****

PUBLISHED BY:

Bernard Lee DeLeo and RJ Parker Publishing Inc.

ISBN-13: 978-1535092517

ISBN-10: 1535092513

The unauthorized reproduction or distribution of a copyrighted work is illegal. Criminal copyright infringement, including infringement without monetary gain, is investigated by the FBI and is punishable by fines and federal imprisonment.

Chapter One

Summer Camp Revisited

"Emily Waterson," Nick repeated after cutting another razor slice along his strapped down victim's stomach, evoking more muffled screams. "Powder our friend a little, Johnny."

Gus moved aside to allow his friend past with the bleach spray bottle. After the application, Nick waited five full minutes of burning agony for the man on the gurney down in his underground facility near the Carmel Valley house he gave to Johnny Groves. Nick nodded at Gus who washed the blood and bleach away, adding some salve.

"We don't like to waste time, Conrad. When I remove your gag I better hear the answers to every question I can think of about your buddies Les and Burt. I told you we already know who they are and who you are. Being strapped in our hell room made no impression on you. Now that we have the 'you can't torture me' and 'I want my lawyer' out of the way, you need to understand the rules of this interrogation, little buddy."

Gus removed the gag from Conrad's mouth. Nick gave him a sip of water through a straw as he gasped for breath around it. Conrad Al Sabi, a Saudi national worked for the Kingdom. Ever since 9/11, Nick had known with sixteen terrorist bombers and the mastermind being citizens of Saudi Arabia, it wasn't rocket science to conclude the Wahhabi cave dwellers fomented the attack. The failed kidnapping of Emily Waterson, Jean and her friend Sonny had uncovered at summer camp, represented a direct tie back to the Kingdom. Nick planned to solve the mystery with Conrad.

"We are buying up real estate!" Conrad sobbed and gasped, working feeling into his mouth. "I...I have my orders. The conglomerate of Wahhabi investors in the Kingdom sent us to buy land in remote sites. The other land purchaser died… in Washington state. A compound built there acted as a training center… to…to establish a Canadian conduit into America. It was located near Onalaska… but it was mysteriously destroyed."

"I believe we had the pleasure of making that compound extinct, right guys?"

"Yes, Muerto," Johnny replied. "We salted the earth on that operation."

"I am cursed of Allah! You three are that 'Unholy Trio' set of murderers." Conrad made a grave error and paid for it immediately with pain.

When Gus removed the gag this time, Conrad knew better than to make judgement calls from a position of representing an Islamist sect Nick felt should be exterminated. "I assume now you realize calling American patriots murderers because we confront you chicken-shit throat slitters will get you punished."

"Yes!" Conrad cried real tears with great wracking sobs. "I…I will tell all! I know you three. It is rumored your 'Unholy Trio' was behind the ocean liner massacre."

Gus moved between Nick and Conrad as his scalpel poised for a return trip. Nick gritted his teeth and nodded at his old friend. "Slow learner. If you mean helped execute vicious shithead pirates, and their enabling Iranian backers, hoping to endanger thousands of innocent people on the cruise ship 'Starlight of the Seas' then yep… that was us. I learned some new interrogation methods from a very unique patriot in our sister group, the Monster Squad: Lynn Montoya Dostiene. We killed until the ocean ran red with Muslim murderer blood. You're blessed because you'll be one of the few who ever knows anything about that very successful black op. You won't live to tell about it anyway. The interesting part is that the Kingdom knows about the 'Starlight' op. It makes sense. The

Kingdom finances most everything of a terrorist nature all over the globe."

Realization dawned on Conrad with Nick's words – he would not be surviving the interrogation. He saw in his captors' eyes his only reward for cooperation lie in no further pain. Al-Sabi closed his eyes. "Saran Al-Kadi is my boss. Saran marked Emily Waterson for kidnapping by those two dolts. I hope you tortured them to death!"

"I didn't have time," Nick said. "Stay on topic or you can make up for my missed opportunity. We know Emily's Father is Bret Waterson, a state senator. What's his role in all this?"

"He…he has begun blocking our land acquisitions in California as if he either knows of our ambitions or he is being fed information from a different source. Al-Kadi felt we could gain an upper hand by snatching Emily as proof we could touch them at any time. Dealing with the senator through the Les and Burt idiots, we hoped to negotiate his daughter's release once we made clear what he needed to do."

"I'm unclear as to the importance of one state senator," Nick remarked.

"The bastard… I mean… Waterson organized grass roots, massive anti-Islam and Sharia Law demonstrations. His petitions on the Internet drew signers in the hundreds of thousands. His popularity increases on a daily basis. We have no defense against his accusations… except Islamophobia and xenophobia. Our counter moves weren't working. He could well run for governor. Saran felt we needed to stop him any way we could, but his personal life and record are… exemplary."

Johnny scanned through myriad avenues connecting Saran Al-Kadi to numerous groups tied to 'The Muslims of the Americas'. He brightened suddenly, pointing at his screen. "Johnny Five comes through again. He contributed huge sums of money to our deposed traitor: Senator Diane Cameron. Perhaps now would be a good time to build a further file on Cameron and imprison her."

Nick sighed. "I wish. She made a deal we can't break to avoid being hanged from the nearest tree until dead. I should put a bullet through her head, but I can't get Paul to sign off on it yet. He makes the point we need a definite time space for our own security. He's right of course, but every time we get inside a plot out here, it has Cameron's fingerprints on it. I wonder if this thread would be enough for him to okay bringing her to room temperature."

"Forget it, Muerto," Gus said. "You've already sanctioned one sitting United States Senator. I don't think adding a retired one would be good either. Do you think Paul knows about Senator Ambrose?"

"He knows," Nick answered, still gauging how much good Conrad could do them to further any knowledge of this particular ongoing fact finding mission. Every time he looked at the man while thinking of all the tragedy and heartbreak he had authored, reality intruded on the side of violence. "Where do we find your buddy, Saran? Be careful how you answer, Conrad. I'm not in the mood for playing sixty questions… or two for that matter. I'll light you up."

"I don't know where he is. It…it's the truth."

Nick grinned. He gestured at Gus. A moment later, the squirming Conrad wore his gag again. "Let me tell you another thing I may have forgotten to mention, Conrad. I have a sixth sense for lies."

Gus and Johnny enjoyed that admission.

"My friends are laughing because they know I don't give a shit whether I'm right or not about my sixth sense. I have a feeling, and I'm going to teach you what happens when I have a feeling."

Nick cut Conrad's ball-sack. Bleach was applied, and no one questioned whether or not Conrad planned to add something to the discussion or not. He literally danced in place, begging for relief with high pitched muffled whistles of excruciating pain filled cries. Nick dumped water with baking soda over him. No one touched Conrad's wounded area.

"Please... give me something for the pain!"

"If you don't start talking, the pain you feel now will be like a long lost friend when I start again," Nick said.

"He... he's in Sacramento... please... If I-"

Nick motioned for the gag.

"An estate... near Pilot Hill! It has sixteen acres of land and... and three residences on the property. Al-Kadi uses it not only for a home when in California. He... he uses it for a dispersion area for cells planned around the state. Everything... everything is there. Identity forgery facilities, underground training complex where any weapons training can go unnoticed. It only has one access road on Plum Drive. I...I have been there many times. I can lead you to the rear access road where-"

"Give us the address," Nick ordered. "Do so quickly."

Conrad rattled off the address with Johnny checking everything from ownership to threads leading to suspicious front groups. Nick used a wooden stirrer to apply analgesic salve to Conrad's injured parts much to Gus's amusement as Nick made faces of distaste. After nearly ten minutes, Johnny smiled and nodded.

"It is an incredible place exactly as he described. A shipping company in Los Angeles owns the property. They are an offshoot of a corporate entity tied to 'The Muslims of the Americas'."

"Yes! I can lead you-"

Nick gave him a hotshot of death in the neck. "No thanks, Conrad. I'm sick of you already, but you were helpful enough to get your relief from pain. Besides… someone in authority would want to use your ass. I don't want to see you over my shoulder someday. I have enough problems as is."

Nick waved as the shot robbed Conrad of motor function and life, the startled look on his face fading to grim acknowledgement of death. He shrugged at his friends. "I know… I know… with patience who knows what we could have gotten. These asshole invaders trigger my barf reflex with their crap. Hell… if I gave a damn… they'd be the injured parties. We're practically escorting them into the country. Islam births new atrocities every day, and we're still bussing them in to protect them from themselves. Really! Let the mongrels eat each other alive in the sand. I don't care!"

Johnny came over to put a hand on Nick's shoulder. "I hear you, brother. Cala and I are done with Islam. We can worship God in our own way. We do not need to be even innocent worshippers of such an unrepentant and silent host of tragedy. It matters not about this worshipper of death. What will be our next step, Muerto?"

"We don't know how many banditos Al-Kadi has on the site of this sixteen acre place," Gus added. "I know you believe in 'One Riot, One Ranger' but we have to be realistic if success is a goal."

"When you have a Muslim horde problem, and you don't have any other choice, who you gonna' call?" Nick paused for effect. "The Monster Squad! I'll call Paul. We need official backing for this. If we get it, he can call Denny Strobert. I'll call John personally to prep him. I don't even know if they're available for an op like this so soon after the 'Starlight'."

"Issac still wants a part, Muerto," Gus said.

Nick noticed the uneasy stance his partner stiffened to while talking about his copilot on the 'Starlight' op. "I thought Issac wanted to return home to St. Lucia and buy a business."

"He's like us, Muerto. He can do more than one thing. We can fly him back here in no time. Issac wants to continue the helicopter training he's already completed, in addition to his skill at piloting a boat."

"I admit it," Nick replied. "Issac interests me. What's his angle in all of this? St. Lucia, named by the French, absorbed by the English in war, and carries on with English common law. They're a sovereign nation now. What does he want with throwing in with us on black ops? I'm sure he understands the dangers, especially when I paid him off after the 'Starlight' op. I explained how close we came to being blown to kingdom come by the Iranians."

Gus chuckled with a helpless hand gesture. "He thought we conjured up the F-18 Superhornets when the Iranian jets arrived. Issac was lost. He watched the F-18's dust those Iranian Migs and barrel roll over us in triumph like a six month old puppy with a piece of steak. I explained as I know you did that we were seconds away from death when they arrived. Issac loved the adrenaline rush. He also loves the money."

"Yep." Nick and Johnny unstrapped room temperature Conrad into a body bag for Cala the Cleaner to prepare for burial at sea in pieces. "Nothing wrong with pursuing the money trail. Issac does his job. He didn't panic either. I'm thinking he would be a good candidate for flying lessons on a larger scale than helicopters. It's good he went back home for a while to see what he can stir up on St. Lucia. We'll call him if something arises we could use him for. Let's put Conrad in the freezer. I need to get home, write another thousand words while I sip a couple, and call Paul. If he's interested, I'll call John. I'm glad since we had a joint venture you've adopted the Johnny tag, Kabong."

"I love that 'Short Circuit' movie. I make a much better Johnny Five than Harding does. I like Johnny better and so does Cala. Done deal."

"Fine," Gus replied, "but lose the 'Johnny Five' declaration."

"Blow it out your clown ears, Payaso," Johnny told him. "Johnny Five tones down for no one, minion of the T-Rex."

"Don't start that again. Tina doesn't like that tag."

Johnny gave Gus a hand flick. "Yeah? So what's your point? T-Rex doesn't consider our feelings when she goes postal on us for something. She keeps calling Muerto, Gomez. We're not the Addam's Family, although Muerto calling her Cousin Itt suits her pretty well."

"We can take it. She can't, and then I have to hear about it at home."

"Tina's caustic, Payaso," Nick said. "She does suit you very well though. You have to admit, Kabong, Tina was on her best behavior on our pirate cruise mission aboard the 'Starlight'."

"Sure, because it is very difficult to whine about a royal suite aboard the most luxurious ocean liner on the high seas. Plus… she didn't have Payaso to torture. Without her life's work aboard of annoying Payaso, T-Rex couldn't fill her time with the usual mundane things such as whining, ordering Payaso around, and beating him with a stick."

"She does not beat me with a stick," Gus insisted, listening to his friends' humorous appreciation of his interactions with Tina.

"I bet those days sailing on the Valkyrie were like heaven without T-Rex," Johnny kept hammering away as they loaded Conrad into the freezer.

"I admit steaming around in a gunship as lethal as the Valkyrie eclipsed anything I ever did before. Tina would have hated it – no doubt about that. We destroyed an Iranian battleship. Good Lord in heaven, where does a tugboat captain get to do that."

"Amen to that," Johnny said, shoulder hugging Gus. "I think we are all coming down a little from the 'Starlight' op. Go and do all your networking chores, Muerto. We grabbed Conrad early. Gus and I will be over later to find out how the 'Monster Squad' feel about another joint effort. Does it really matter in these times if Paul and Denny get involved?"

"It does. We can't do what's necessary to safeguard America without these internal battles, Johnny. All of it should be in the open with every citizen involved, coupled with border shutdown, and no immigration passes from anywhere in the Middle East. That ain't happening, so we're stuck with putting Band-Aids on each potential atrocity without ever attacking the cause. I'm game, because I damn well will not ever allow Sharia Law or Islam to dictate my life. I will kill until I have no bullets, no killing implements, and I am dead. As you two know, I will make my passing legendary."

Gus shook hands with Nick in double grip passion. "I'm in all the way, brother."

"As am I," Johnny added, joining the three way handshake. "I want nothing more in this life than to die with my boots on, at the side of my friends, as Dan did. He may not have had us at his side when he took out that piece of shit burglar, but we were with him in his head, along with his lost mate."

"Exactly right, Johnny. I'll call when I make arrangements one way or another for our buddy, Al-Kadi. If we get the 'Monster Squad' involved, this alteration in Isis plans is going to get real bloody."

"There is no choice in that. This hive must be dealt with, Muerto."

"I know, but we have to take some added steps to get backing or risk ending up on Harding's Monster Squad Island. We're in the middle of a silent war against an enemy so stupid they blatantly put their messages of pedophilia, honor killings, and female genital mutilation on public forums such as YouTube - yet they're funded, enabled, and whitewashed by a growing number of liberal dolts in this country. We may not ever be able to correct all of their traitorous mistakes." Nick shrugged with a sigh of acceptance and tightlipped purpose. "We could just accept it all as it comes. With me... that will never happen."

"Yes!" Johnny pumped a fist. "I was absorbed into this plague because I felt helpless to react as an individual. No more! Everything happening within Islam is blasphemy! To put it bluntly: peace my ass! At least I am finally part of something that can defend civilization in spite of a vocal part of our citizens who would rather be chained as chattel."

"I change every time we do an op like the 'Starlight' or gather in a blight on humanity like Conrad," Gus admitted. "I'm never giving up this chance to thwart whatever plot of one world order our idiot leaders splice together. We are not all the same. I want to barf when I hear about the rest of the world. Stay where the hell you are. Make things right or bend over and let them pork you in your own damn countries... idiots!"

Nick smiled. "Great... we've solved the world's problems. Let's split and meet later where we can return to the day by day grind of actually eliminating our enemy. Yes... I know it's still a 'Whack-a-mole' solution with no end in sight, but we only have one dog in this hunt: America. Since we all agree this Islamist Trojan Horse plague can only be stopped on a minimal basis at this time, let's concentrate on what we can do. We protect Emily and her Dad first and foremost. That can only be done in one way - wasting anyone fomenting plans against state senator Waterson's family. I have a bad feeling about the Pilot Hill pack. If I convince John and his crew to take a hand in this, I think those dogs plotting

14

to carry out any kidnappings in the future will think twice. I doubt many of them, if any, will survive this operation."

"I will bring Cala. Sometimes your words upset me, Muerto, and the only solution is Harding's professed saviors, the Bud and Beam brothers," Johnny stated with a straight face. "Cala will be my designated driver."

"Good thinking, Kabong," Nick said. "How about you, Payaso?"

"I'm in. Tina and I will walk over."

"You're making the T-Rex walk?" Johnny went through a series of first class outraged mannerisms. "You'll be hogtied for the remainder of your tortured life. Get on your knees like the penitents and saviors of civilization. Perhaps by prayer, she will spare you. We will all mourn your passing if she doesn't, my friend. Surely you know better than to make T-Rex walk, Payaso."

"Very funny, Kabong," Gus replied. "First off, we walk all the time together. Secondly, no one will either suggest or coerce such a thing from me. I'm not speaking to you again unless you apologize. Tina and I get along fine. Never presume to know another man's marriage."

"I apologize," Johnny said, hanging his head in a sorrowful manner. "I should never presume to know what T-Rex will do to you next. How is the writing going, Muerto?"

"Dark Interlude is a hit according to Cass. I've already started the new Diego novel. I wrote a couple thousand words this morning before anyone interrupted me. I haven't titled it yet though."

"You usually pick a title while you're outlining," Gus replied. "Will it be about our 'Starlight' op?"

"No. I figured I better put some time between Diego and a cruise ship caper. This one has my 'femme fatale' Fatima luring

15

Diego into an unforeseen professional gang heist. The gang works out of Issac's St. Lucia Island. It again has all the ingredients of a James Bond type interlude in the Caribbean, with Diego's faithful companions, Jed and Leo."

"Yes!" Johnny pumped a fist. "Thank you, Muerto! Leo will not let you down as a character. You must find a way to work in my talents in real life with this fabulous character you have created."

"You mean like sucking up, and kissing ass," Gus asked.

"Don't be a hater, Payaso."

Nick took a few moments to enjoy the interaction before gesturing for calm. "Let's stick to basics guys. We still have to puzzle out the Mother Ship, Jay Parks told us about before the 'Starlight' gig."

"Damn… that's right," Gus said. "With all that's happened, I forgot about Parks. He's fish bait. What he told us about his boss Fernando Carone should have been on the top of our list from the time we landed after the 'Starlight' op. A Mother Ship off of the Channel Islands near San Luis Obispo? I have to hand it to you, Muerto. You don't forget anything."

"Payaso's right. Did you get a call from your friend Neil about our execution of Jay Parks' 'banger crew, Muerto?"

Nick nodded. "Yeah… Neil knew it was the magnificent three that did in Jay's crew the moment he was summoned to the crime scene. They called an all hands on deck for their discovery of a dozen dead bodies to every precinct from here to Salinas. Naturally, the FBI, DEA, and every local cop had a theory. Neil asked me, but I answered in the form we have agreed on."

When Nick didn't go on, Gus threw his hands up in the air, frustration plain on his face. "What form, Muerto?"

Nick held out a stopping gesture with his hand. "Easy, Gus... sorry... if Neil asks me about involvement I tell him 'oh God help us, that's terrible'. He knows we killed the gang. I'm turning him to the dark side."

"Yeah, you have," Johnny agreed. "Will you please shelve the shocked features, Payaso? We need Neil in the know without making it obvious to everyone in existence. That he goes along with our needed operations is a big plus for us."

"This doing right crap is draining," Gus replied.

"Doin' right ain't got no end, Payaso," Nick stated, to much amusement at the 'Outlaw Josie Wales' movie reference from his companions.

* * *

I saw the Nick number on my iPhone. "Nick?"

"Yeah... it's me, brother John. I have another crappy caper to run by you. Paul signed off on it, but I wanted to call you before it trickled down from Denny."

Yep. That's what real professionals do. I hadn't talked to Nick since we split up after the 'Starlight' gig. "It's good to hear from you, Nick. We have free time. Send the specifics. Count on us for the dance. Is it a party or a prom?"

"It's definitely a prom date. We're planning on a possible full dress excursion with music, but only as a last resort."

I tried muffling the laughter Nick invoked. I knew he spoke of a 'Ride of the Valkyries' type date. "Understood. I'll prep our dates. This will be an exciting dance. We'll need them to bring all their moves. Good stuff, brother. Do you think we'll ever get to bow out of these formal functions?"

Nick paused. "We get older and meaner, Dark Lord. It would be a natural thing if our dates lapsed into more conservative

17

calm form, but I have no hopes of such a welcome respite happening to our party persona style, my friend."

"That's how I figure it too with the party leaders we have now. Let me know, brother."

"I will. Until then." Nick disconnected.

"Who was that," Lora asked me. She and Al had moved closer so as to eavesdrop on my conversation, with Lora pretending she hadn't heard Nick's name.

"Death and destruction."

Lora sighed. "So soon? I figured after the cruise, trouble would be at an end for a while."

I remembered Muerto's phrase he used often now. "Doin' right ain't got no end."

"You stole that line from Nick," Al said.

"Nick appropriated it from a movie called 'The Outlaw Josie Wales'. He's found another nest. We either handle it or prepare for some other catastrophe to happen. He'll be sending me the details. Nick already has an okay from Paul Gilbrech. That means Denny will be calling to make it official. It's Friday. Let's go have dinner at The Warehouse. Maybe Denny and the crew can meet us."

Lora sighed. "Great. Another Monster Squad night out. Did Tommy give you the weekend off from the Bay Poking sessions?"

"Yeah. Tommy wants me to do ground and pound on weekends. The fight with Costigan is still up in the air. Besides, the Rock doesn't like ground and pound. Neither does Berserker. Whichever one wins the rematch will be mandated to fight me. I have to train now for both."

"Is Lynn mad about not being allowed in on the training?"

"No," I answered Al, refraining from making the sign of the cross and saying thank God. "Lynn's busy tracking people with Clint for their FBI contacts. Lynn has been getting back into the serial killer manhunts again. Clint and Lynn helping keeps Sam and Janie on our side. They came through for us with all the prisoners we needed watched during the 'Starlight' mission. In addition to their help, they relieved us of all but a couple prisoners Denny wanted to keep. What about dinner?"

"I like it," Al said. "I love being around all of you. Jean and Sonny are depending on me to keep them informed. We have our own message drop. Don't worry, Dad. We don't discuss anything coming or ongoing. They like hearing about anything to do with Lynn."

"I'm for dinner too," Lora said. "Will you be inviting Claude Chardin? He went out on a few training sessions with you, didn't he?"

"Yeah. The prick enjoyed the hell out of watching Tommy poke the crap out of me. He even took a turn. Claude liked the background part he played in the 'Starlight' gig and the money. His contacts in Dubai really helped. Denny told me he really liked having him along in the AWAC surveillance plane. His insights and observations during the Iranian Migs encounter kept Denny calmer during what was the most dangerous part of the gig. I'll ask him to come along tonight. I'd like his input on whatever names Nick sends me."

"Good. I like his wife. I hear Claude and Nick hit it off too."

"Like peas from the same pod. Nick knows Claude was turned from the dark side. Claude would like a more active role in our outings together. He has bills to pay. I'll bring him in on this latest one if I can."

My iPhone dinged. It was Denny. "Just the guy I wanted to talk to. I take it Paul talked with you. Nick's sending me an invitation to the dance."

Denny sighed. "Good. You're familiar with part of it."

"Give me a chance to go over the invitation. You can have dinner at The Warehouse with us later to discuss the invitation. I'm asking Claude in too."

"Good idea. I'll call Claude. I already have Nick's info. I want to test Claude's knowledge as you do, I'll bet. I like something else Nick mentioned as an alternative to a full 'Ride' too."

"I'll look forward to reading the invitation. That was my plan with involving Claude," I answered. "I'm spreading the word for six. Is that okay?"

"Yes, but I'll be there earlier if Alexi wants in too. I like having Alexi, Claude, you, and me at five for a private chat if that's okay."

"Sure. I'll be there."

"Until then, DL," Denny said. "Claude let me know how much he liked your training sessions. It's nice of you to invite your new friend."

"I will smack your smart-mouth into next week, Spawn."

"Sorry. Did I say that out loud? I'll see you at five."

"Yeah." I disconnected. I pointed at Al. "Are you sure you want to get into basketball? Lynn already told me she wants to coach with me on the sideline with her."

"I want to do it, Dad. Being involved in any sport with Lynn as the coach psyches me. Sonny wants in too. We're lucky we can play coed leagues still. Will Lynn have a problem coaching boys too?"

20

"Crue and I mixed it up a little on the court. She plays very well. We went over basics and patience with the kids. She'll be fine. Clint will be helping too, especially during practices. They have Clint Jr. to raise. You know he'll be wanting to play sports."

"With all the babies born at the same time, I could probably coach my own team of 'Little Monsters'."

Now that was funny. The visions of Al running herd on Monster Squad offspring threw my imagination into overdrive. "Hold that thought. It will probably come true someday."

"Next summer, can I go to summer camp with Jean and Sonny?"

I had heard about what went down at the last Jean and Sonny summer camp excursion. I knew Lora didn't know anything about it, but I had a feeling Al did. "I don't know about that."

"What's the harm, DL," Lora asked. "Jean and Sonny are great kids. I don't mind if Al tags along with them."

I smiled at Al while Lora went to the sink. She did her hands clasped, contorted feature, pleading action. Al obviously knew I had been told about the last summer camp happenings involving kidnappers, kids near death, and Nick's execution of the two kidnappers.

"I guess that would be okay. I think for a treat like summer camp with friends, even though it's in the future, it should be good for at least a month free of Beeper."

"It's Justin Drew Bieber!" Al was not pleased. She pulled the Bieber out on us at the worst possible time… which for me was anytime.

I crossed my arms in a grinning wait for her decision.

"That's blackmail!"

"Oh no! Not that! Take it or leave it, Princess Beeper."

"I'll take it... but there will be blood!"

* * *

Nick hit dead center on the targets with the throwing knives. Using both hands, Nick completed underhand tosses with enough power to sink the blades to the hilt while turning from his position facing away from the targets. He grinned at his pupils, Sonny and Jean, who were staring at the target in open mouthed wonder while Rachel laughed.

"Much like you throw a fast pitch softball, it becomes a matter of hand placement with eye coordination." Nick repeated the throws, one after another, in more deliberate fashion. "After stationary target accomplishment, I'll rig a moving sound type target. When you two can hit a moving target underhanded while facing away from target, your training in knives will be done, except of course for constant practice."

"You hit targets with the knives dead center when your friend gave them to you, Dad."

"I have a talent for remembered physical action, whether it is a killing stroke with the hand, sighting in a sniper rifle, or throwing expertise with the knives. My life depended on... say it with me, kids... planning, projection, and perfection."

Jean and Sonny had repeated the mantra with him on cue. They knew better than to ignore their teacher's direction. Nick stepped away. "First, take turns using your right hand in a softball fast-pitch type motion. I bet you two understand why I made you learn to fast pitch a softball with both hands now."

"It would have been more exciting if you had explained why, Dad," Jean mumbled.

"Part of training begins with unquestioned steps attaining expertise. I went into training with Lucas Blake after my being in Delta Force for years. I learned within a week, Lucas knew more about survival and combat tactics than I had learned in all the years leading to my working in clandestine operations. Casey Lambert, Clint Dostiene, and I were selected as operatives from nearly fifty applicants from all branches of the service, alphabet soup agencies, and law enforcement. Naturally, our language skills, combat experience, and demeanor had much to do with it. Lucas Blake refused to pass the unqualified. Part of why he got out of the training end had to do with his uncompromising knowledge of what it would take to stay alive in the business. He kept getting orders to tone his instruction down because he had the lowest number of applicants passing of all trainers. What do we learn from that, kids?"

"To be the best, you must train like the best," both kids repeated the training cliché Nick instructed them in after learning they wanted more than a neat game to play.

"That's the key," Nick said. "I want you both in as many sports as is physically possible. Competition hones your skills and drive."

The doorbell rang. Nick gestured for everyone to remain where they were, including Rachel and Quinn. "It's probably either or both Gus and Johnny with their mates. I need to conference with Gus and Johnny, so I'll send Tina and the Cleaner back here with all of you, unless Cleaner wants in on the op we're going to do. I'm not sure if there would be a need for her on this Pilot Hill excursion."

"She's doing great with the piloting your new helicopter," Rachel said. "How in hell did you get a UH-60M Blackhawk helicopter by the way, Muerto?"

"Lots of money, and the backing of the CIA Director," Nick answered. "What you should be asking is how in hell did I ever buy my own hangar at the airport."

"Knowing the amount of money confiscated like a black clad Robin Hood, I already know the answer to the hangar

23

financial origins. The Blackhawk, on the other hand takes practically the hand of God, especially with the armaments procured and stored in said hangar."

"You have been paying attention. Laredo helped me with Paul's backing. I provided the money, so once permission from the top came down, I obtained the Blackhawk. Laredo helped refresh my training. I have to let our friends in. Keep practicing, kids."

Nick went out to the front entrance with Deke tagging along. The whole gang awaited his arrival. He opened the door with Deke heeled at his side. "Hi. Come on in. I've been conducting practice sessions out in the back if you'd like to join Rachel out there, Tina. If you want in on this new op, ask Johnny if you have his permission, Cala."

Cala laughed with appreciation while hugging her husband. "Johnny wants me with him in all things, Muerto. Will this involve helicopters?"

"It could involve a copiloting job if you're interested."

"Oh yes! I am so there, Muerto! The music will be involved, right?"

"Of course, although I have a quieter ending with another idea I'm thinking through."

"I'll leave you all to it," Tina said. "Can I stop in the kitchen for wine, Gomez?"

"Rachel already has your glass and a bottle of Beringer's ready for tasting, T. The kids are providing some very entertaining knife throwing exhibitions. They're practicing new tricks."

Tina pointed at Nick as she backed away toward the knife throwing target range. "That is highly disturbing, Gomez, but I suspect you already know that."

"Indeed I do, Cousin Itt."

On the enclosed deck above, Nick poured Deke a beer while Gus poured rounds of Bushmill's Irish Whiskey. "I don't know if this op will be officially sanctioned. Paul's working on it. He'll go down protecting us if it doesn't get official approval. I would like to avoid any involvement with him, but if we salt the earth it will have to be sanctioned. They'll scramble jets to take us out otherwise. John told me already they have to have an okay from high above or the 'Ride of the Valkyries' can't happen. The Monster Squad did a couple with tentative okay fom Denny and would probably do them without permission, but John's agreed it's not a good idea. The jets have to be grounded during a black op or they could be launched on us, especially on American soil. I've looked over this place they have and it is a gorgeous place. We certainly don't want to blow it into atom dust. Anyone want to guess what I have in mind?"

"You're thinking confiscation! Can something like that be done?"

"Sure it can, Kabong," Nick answered. "We could build a helicopter pad on the premises. The confiscation may require some creative alterations in ownership though. It could be a halfway house paradise between us and the Monster Squad. It's nearly sixteen acres. We could hangar a couple of helicopters there and maybe even one of those Harrier jets that can take off straight up."

"Those take maintaining same as the Blackhawk will. I have been studying with all the material you gave me on our UH-60M," Cala said.

"We would have to employ a crew at the Monster Squad Hangar, or our local Monterey Regional Airport, for serious maintenance. I serviced helicopters and jets during a CIA gig overseas. The regular maintenance has to be done religiously, employing intricate checklists. Since we already have the hangar at Regional, housing the beginning of our air fleet, we can split duties with the Monster Squad for any quick response aircraft we keep in the Pilot Hill Hangar. When we need something major done to the

25

Blackhawk, or whatever else we can procure, we'll have to do so under Laredo's supervision at possibly a military facility. We can get the more involved overhauls done through Denny Strobert or Paul at a military base. Denny managed to get the 'Sea Wolf' and 'Valkyrie' turned into combat ships. I'm sure we can keep our quick strike force on the down low if Laredo can oversee servicing at Regional, or the Monster Squad Hangar. I'd like to confiscate this place in Pilot Hill as a secret launch area for wiping out Isis nests we find. I know we can get the clearances. Think of being able to leave from there, under the radar, for a hit within range, and be back in a time frame without suspicion."

"Pilot Hill's over three hours away though," Gus pointed out. "We'd still be stuck flying out of Regional to get there. You have over ten acres where John lives."

"Can't do it there, Payaso. The locals' heads would explode if I built a hangar on my land in the Valley," Nick replied. "The first time a helicopter or anything else left my place, I'd have everyone from the PD to the National Guard going over our interrogation and storage facility. You're right about the connecting part. We'll have to puzzle that part out, depending on the mission. I love the idea of owning that place though in Pilot Hill. It doesn't get a lot of snowfall because it's a couple of hours down from Lake Tahoe. I like it for another safe house we can use as an armory too, along with doubling as a launch site."

"You really have embraced John Harding's Monster Squad, Muerto," Cala stated. "Gus has said you hated working with anyone. Now, we are becoming an army."

"John started out with only Lucas and Casey in the North under Strobert. They have a network now with Alexi Fiialkov watching the ports and streets, police on the pad for quick reports or cover, and a much larger force of killers. We've seen them in action. They can be counted on. This underground terrorist war keeps expanding, thanks to the idiots in government importing the bastards, or leaving the borders wide open for them to stroll in. For the first time ever, I'm not sure we can avoid a serious war on our soil. Like I told Gus once – I don't like being hunted, and definitely not in my own land."

The four sipped from their drinks quietly for a moment before Johnny broke the silence. "Have you considered anything else with the Channel Islands' Mother Ship near San Luis Obispo? You mentioned Fernando Carone after our interrogation where we initially extracted Al-Kadi's Pilot Hill location. When do you think we should move on him?"

"Before he recruits another bunch of 'bangers to pick up where the crew Jay ran left off. He's aware of the huge gang fight leaving his 'banger explorers dead by now. Fernando may or may not believe there's a more organized crime syndicate here establishing a presence. When a guy like Carone believes he may be getting challenged, he might send a few pros here to soften up the situation. We may have to do some detective work before we move on the 'Mother Ship'. If he sends pros, they'll be thinking to look for other 'banger types. They'll be leaning on local punks and frequenting seedier hotspots in the area, hoping to get leads on non-existent threats."

"Where would you go for that, Muerto?"

"If I was an out of town thug, I'd check in Salinas first, but then I'd have a drink at Carbone's on Lighthouse in Monterey," Nick answered. "They wouldn't expect to find anything there, but they'll probably stay in Monterey, even though they'll be looking for connections in Pacific Grove. Carbone's is one of the top rated 'Dive' bars in the area. It's a great bar. Chasing unknown thugs would be a waste of time. We'll take turns checking the place for the next week. Believe me. When the pros don't find any leads, they'll hit Carbone's some night soon if they haven't already. I'm hoping since Jay's crew's bodies were only found at the abandoned warehouse a short time ago, it will take Fernando time to decide about a follow-up check."

"Do you think Jay called Carone about the foiled roller rink heist?"

"I doubt it, Cala. I'm sure Jay and his buddies figured just like we heard before they met the Unholy Trio – they planned to terrorize me and the kids on their own."

"Okay, so we take turns having a few at Carbone's," Gus said. "What then?"

"We'll have to take them at their motel or outside the bar. We'll have to be discreet."

"How will you know if we find them, Muerto? They won't have nametags."

"I'm surprised at you, Johnny. To think you don't believe I'll be able to pick them out in a crowd is very hurtful."

"Are you going to the bar every night?"

"Nope. We'll take turns with our cams. If it's not my night, I'll be here at home with my iPad handy for live streaming. I'll do the first few nights to establish a presence."

"This sounds awfully flaky for the number one assassin in the world," Gus kidded him.

"You'll eat those words, Payaso, when I find our pros."

"Let me go tomorrow night with Tina. She and I haven't been out on a Saturday night for quite a while. This Carbone's sounds interesting. We'll take a cab there and back."

"If you find the pros, Payaso, just have the T-Rex eat them," Johnny said to much amusement.

"When do you think we'll get permission to start on the Pilot Hill mission," Gus asked, ignoring Johnny.

"Paul authorized at least a week of satellite surveillance," Nick answered. "We can't attack on a quiet basis without complete plans of the house and all information we can see from the surveillance. I want this place more than I want to reduce it to ash. That will take patience."

Johnny put a hand on Cala's. "Have you kept track of Jay's crew who they did put in jail? When they get free, they will be unpredictable."

"Neil claimed they'll be in custody awaiting trial. He'll update us if they get free on bail," Nick answered. "You can rest assured they will stay quiet for a time. We have their names and the addresses they're staying at. Let me give that some thought. We don't want to piss off Neil, but those guys in police custody could be in contact with Fernando on a daily basis depending on how scared they are. All calls are monitored so the pros won't contact them unless they get out of jail."

"So naturally we wouldn't want to wait for those two to get out of jail, right?"

"Are you second guessing my sixth sense, Payaso?"

Gus smiled. "Yeah. I think you'll need to wait until those guys get out of jail and reveal the pros when they make contact. Have you considered the lawyer aspect, Muerto?"

"Damn it!"

"Heh…heh… forgot all about lawyers passing notes, huh Muerto?"

"Cala! You've only had one sip. We need a driver. I'll splice into the 'bangers' lawyer. We'll go get them as the 'Unholy Trio'. Gus is absolutely right. A lawyer bought by Carone will have passed the info to his boss and the pros. My bad – let's hit the laptops and find out who represents these punks. We go tonight, take him in a safe zone, and bleed him dry. Thanks, Gus."

Cala had pushed away her drink. "Yes! Cleaner to the rescue!"

Chapter Two
Mother Ship

Lance Botorf relaxed in his chair of omnipotence. The chair brought him good luck. It was a state of the art chair. It tilted, vibrated, and practically put him on his feet when he needed to stand. Maury told him just now how valuable his simple report had been, cementing in his huge payday on this case. It was a simple interaction. He reported to a guy comically named Biff, who acted as the intermediary to the guy Lance already accepted an envelope of money from. This was the way it was supposed to be. It had been a simple matter to get the boys out on bail. They would be released tomorrow morning. The men he had dealt with stayed locally at a motel in Pacific Grove. The only thing left in what he needed to do was get the charges reduced to petty theft with the DA's acceptance. Done deal. He sipped his drink with the pleasurable feeling of success. He had bills to pay with a wife who couldn't accept a simple office romance, and a couple of kids who looked at him when he took time to see them as if he arrived from off planet. One moment he watched the movie he had put in, and the next he had three black clad figures in front of him, one with a clown face. He was deathly afraid of clowns. The clown leaned in suddenly close to his face. Lance passed out.

* * *

"Oh for God's sake," Gus mumbled.

"Nice one, Payaso," Nick said, while taking Botorf's pulse, shaking his head mournfully. "He's gone. Oh my, Payaso, that was just... disturbing."

Having been around Nick long enough to know a prank, Gus began slapping Botorf into consciousness, ignoring the hoots and hollers from Nick and Johnny of outrage over his brutal treatment of the prisoner. "C'mon, Lance. Wake the hell up, you pussy!"

"I never thought to see the infamous Payaso in his natural state like this, Kabong. He is truly a vicious entity of brutality."

"I must agree, Muerto," Johnny carried on the banner of outrage.

"Fuck you two!" Gus managed to get a slow shivering ascendance into consciousness from Lance. "Wake up, Lance! If you fade on me one more time, I will cut your dick off and stick it down your throat!"

"I will save you from the bad clown, Lance." Nick waved Gus away. "To make sure my partner Payaso doesn't get his hands on you, we need to straighten a few things out. Why don't you talk us through your defense of the two young gangbangers named Nano Calista and Doug Morgan? Did you get them a release date already?"

"Tomorrow... at 10 am. How did you get into my house? It has-"

"Shut up," Gus told him. "Who paid you to represent those two turds? Remember this, Lance: you hate clowns. I hate lawyers. If you don't want me to play with you, we need answers."

"I...I can't disclose anything about the case or who pays me."

"Yes, you can, Lance," Nick said, "or we're going to torture you until you do. We need a demo, Payaso. Lance needs to do the dance electric."

Gus stun-gunned Botorf for a short but pain filled moment in his groin area. He jackknifed off his chair into a fetal position on the hardwood floor. Gus kicked him in the side, leaning again into the gasping Lance's face, while pulling the man's shirt to get him closer.

"I will light you up for ten seconds next time! Your dick will retreat all the way into your chest."

"Biff… Cantor… and Ray Genaro! Oh God… I'm dyin'!"

"Not yet, Lance," Nick told him, patting his face. "Where can we find Biff and Ray?"

"At… the Sea Breeze motel. Who…who are you people? How can you be doing these things? I'm just a lawyer hired to represent two defendants. I have to do my job."

Nick grabbed Lance's chin in his previously gloved hands. "We know what you are and what you've been doing. We checked. You're a good lawyer, but your moral compass sucks. Here's what will happen. You're out of it. You got those two punks off. Stay the hell away from this now. If you call anyone to warn them or you have anything to do with mob business, we'll be back. They won't get us, but we will get you."

Gus jammed a sleepy-time shot into Lance's neck. "Did I tell you guys I hate lawyers?"

"Yeah. I think you've mentioned it a few dozen times, Payaso," Nick replied. "So much so, Johnny and I are outlawing you from mentioning lawyers. You got burned one time in conjunction with the legal system and you've been raw for a decade. Make the sign of the cross and move on, brother."

Even Gus chuckled at Nick's reprimand. He shrugged. "I admit it. Lance will be out for a while. Should we tie and gag him too?"

"I'll fix him for waking up in a weird place. You guys pick up everything and get the Cleaner into position in ten minutes. Don't leave as a couple. Split up on returning to the Ford. Keep

Cleaner moving around the block. I'll be along shortly and meet you all out front."

Gus and Johnny moved to do Nick's bidding. Nick shouldered Lance and took him into his bedroom. Nick stripped him of everything but his underwear. He positioned Lance in a relaxed position on his bed, covers over him. He then gave Lance an eternity shot in between his left foot 'this little piggy went to market and this little piggy stayed home' toes. Nick checked over every moment the 'Unholy Trio' had been in the house. When satisfied, Nick watched for headlights from Gus's Ford SUV to move slowly down the street in front of Lance's house. He ran out and slipped inside the rear passenger compartment, holding the door closed until they were out of hearing from anyone on the street. Nick closed the door quietly then.

"Shit!"

Gus's exclamation from the front seat drew an inquisitive glance from Cala. "What's wrong, Gus."

Gus did a thumb gesture backward at Nick with his left hand, never looking into the backseat. "Muerto killed the lawyer."

Silence, multiplied by Nick's neglect to refute Gus's claim, confirmed it. At the first red light, Cala turned toward Nick. "Did you kill the lawyer, Muerto?"

"Drive, Cala," Nick ordered. When the SUV was moving again, Nick spoke," I couldn't leave an unknown at our backs. He made his choice. I made mine. Sure… we could have all done barbeques and birthdays together but this is reality, kids. We leave no one at our backs to cause problems."

"Did you at least give him last rites, Muerto," Johnny asked.

It was many moments before any of them could speak, including Cala, who parked alongside of the road. She pointed at her husband accusingly between gasps of air. "You…you got that from Jess and Dev. I…I remember when they told us John Harding wanted to make the fighter called 'Dragon Hands' see Spongebob with a squeezing death grip in their match. Jess told Dev to give the Dark Lord an exorcism, and Dev complained because he had only recently memorized 'Last Rites'. Very humorous, my husband."

"That…that was good, Kabong," Gus stuttered out.

"In answer to that," Nick replied finally, "no, I didn't. Like Dev… I don't know last rites. I will learn it and the exorcism ritual for no other reason than pronouncing it over the Dark Lord when he goes astray."

"I'll learn it for you, Muerto," Gus promised.

"May I remind you that I didn't make a joke of lawyer Lance expiring? The moment I admitted to killing him… all there's been is laughter. Cowboy up. We need to collect Biff and Ray. We need a decoy, Cala."

Cala pumped her fist without looking away from the road. They were already headed toward the Sea Breeze motel. "Yes! Cala the Cleaner strikes again! I don't have a uniform. Hey… I could approach like a hooker with bored expression. When they claim they didn't ask for a hooker, I'll pretend interest, claiming I'll do anything not to make it a wasted trip."

"Damn… that's good, kid," Nick said. "Chances are they won't be around on a Saturday night. If they are, that ploy would work. We have your back but I will let Johnny have last word."

Johnny sighed. "I see your heart's into it. I cannot oppose what my love wants to do. I will be backing her. I doubt there will be very little protestation once they see her prostitute actions. The only problem will arise when they ask about her connection to the motel or who could have sent her. What if they're gay?"

Cala's snort of unhappiness shut Johnny up before he began again. "Okay… it doesn't meet all our criteria other than surprise. We will be nearby. I will be at Cala's side no matter how they take our alterations. We need to focus. Stopping will get us nothing. Once inside though, Cala will need some cover story."

"I believe you're right, Johnny," Nick admitted. "We're overthinking this. Cala gets sultry enough to answer the door and the moment the door gets unlatched, I'll throw a flash-bang into their room, hold onto Cala, and then jog inside to find out what we can about the operation. The big deal in this will be making sure we have both Biff and Ray present. Otherwise, we'll have to hunt them down."

"Enough talk," Cala said. "I am ready. I am no Snow White. Let's get this done so we may find out where Biff and Ray found out about the gang in this town. Then, it will be a decision as to when we hit the Carone's Mother Ship, and how."

"Muerto's in charge, my love," Johnny reminded her. "You are sounding a bit like the T-Rex. We don't want that."

Cala gasped as the others enjoyed Johnny's comical upbraiding. Cala giggled. "I did… didn't I? She is very forceful. I thought to emulate her somewhat but maybe I am going too far."

"We like your input, Cleaner," Nick said. "You don't have to tone down for us, but it would probably be to Johnny's liking if you sound like yourself rather than like Tina. I've been getting too wild lately. The moment we're working on a plan to take a couple guys, I start thinking about grenades and flashbangs. The Sea Breeze isn't the Hilton, but I'd rather not damage one of their rooms with exploding devices. I'm becoming careless. I'll take surprise to another level with Cala."

"How do you mean, Muerto," Gus asked. "For once, I didn't think the flashbang was such a bad idea."

"I have FBI and CIA credentials along with being a United States Marshal. I'll have Cala get them to open the door – then, I'll arrest them with you guys there to make the restraining arrest. They'll think they're being detained by the regular federal authorities. We move them to our interrogation facility without any disruption in the Sea Breeze room décor, or in public displays of mayhem. It's a win/win situation."

"I like it better than your other ideas but it will be more dangerous," Johnny said.

"Oh, step up, Johnny Five," Cala joked with her husband. "Once Muerto has the drop on them, they will believe they are really being arrested. I could probably measure them for their disassembly and deposit in the ocean while we are transporting them."

Johnny threw his hands into the air. "Allah... spare me... I have created a monster."

"All in favor of arresting these dastardly gang enablers." Nick raised his hand. Gus and Cala followed his lead with Johnny slowly raising his. "It's unanimous. Although they won't understand why they're blessed, the Sea Breeze Motel will be pleased with our operation."

"Finally, a lead on mission for the Cleaner," Cala said excitedly. "Let us go quickly before Johnny Five finds some way to derail Cleaner's first black op. Is it too soon for renaming our squad... maybe Cleaner and her Unholy Trio?"

Nearly five minutes passed before anyone but Cleaner could move. After many attempts to stem the amusement of the Unholy Trio, Cleaner sighed and walked out.

* * *

Biff Cantor refilled Ray Genaro's drink glass and then his own. They played gin rummy, the stakes minimal in terms of

37

money, to pass the time until they could get a meeting with the gangbangers Fernando had marking territory in the Monterey area. He and Ray teamed doing jobs for Fernando Carone nearly four years ago. Carone paid them very well. Biff and Ray acted as competent intermediaries between Carone and the public, never allowing the law or the people they dealt with get close to Fernando. They lived aboard 'The Tempest', Carone's Mother Ship for 'Panga Boats' to dock with and do business. 'The Tempest', a luxurious two hundred forty foot super yacht, acted as both a gambling pleasure cruiser and Panga boat dock for trafficking in anything from drugs to girls marked for transfer to Middle Eastern ports.

Biff and Ray originally acted as Los Zeta Cartel enforcers in the East LA area before Fernando Carone bought their contracts. They lived like kings now, killed anyone or anything Fernando pointed at with displeasure. They handled all expansion details, including collections, once gangbanger trade annexed an area's business with protection and extortion rackets. Fernando assigned one of his craziest gangster run crews to the Monterey area. After losing contact with Jay Parks, the leader of the gang, Carone waited impatiently for accurate word about his holdings in the area. With only jumbled news paraphernalia about a drug war with many dead, Fernando sent his best men down to find out the truth.

"Lawyer say Jay dead, so what we meetin' with the punks for, Biff?" Biff's partner, a black man no one messed with in East LA since Ray reached puberty, sipped from his glass with a nod of satisfaction.

Biff, a medium height, thin, mixed race broker of pain and death, smiled at his partner. When anyone needed finished off, Biff made the kill shot. He lived for the sight of death. "You know Fernando. We do everything until we get it done in detail, including burying Jay's two jailed idiots in the desert. Remember… we nice as pie until we get them alone where we can find out what the fuck went wrong. One minute Jay's crew 'bangin' and extortin' – next... all but these two are dead."

Ray nodded. "Fernando looked worried when he sent us. Fernando never worried... ever. Somethin' bad here, partner. Rocky cliffs, bustin' big waves crashin' against the rocks, foggy salt smellin' nights, and no threat in sight. What's that all about, brother? We can't whack nothin' to make anything right here. I say we collect the garbage, bury them in the sand, and go tell Fernando the area toxic."

Biff chuckled, sitting down in relaxed manner with drink in hand. "We don't get paid to bring fairy tales back to the man. He find out... it'll be us eatin' sand. Tell you what, brother... now on... we go slow... step by step. The lawyer say the 'bangers don't know what happened to Jay and his crew. They damn sure can explain better than him about what the hell happened to them."

"Yeah... I hear you. I-"

A knock at the door startled them. Embarrassed, Ray shoved away from the table. "I got this. You got me wantin' to kill somethin'."

Ray looked through the peephole at a beautiful, mini-skirted woman in her early twenties with long black hair. She looked up at the inspection peep hole with a sultry pose and smile. Ray chuckled, turning to Biff. "Hey, blood... you order a hooker?"

"Nope." Biff walked over to glance through the seeing-eye peephole with interest. "Damn... she fine. She don't belong here. What she doin' knockin' on our door?"

Ray grinned as another soft knock sounded. "Don't know. She can't be here entrapping us. Maybe Sea Breeze has connections. They ought to at least have her in one of those sexy maid uniforms."

Biff snorted. "I'm good with finding out. Want me to meet and greet?"

"Yeah... I'd probably scare her away," Ray replied, moving out of sight.

Biff unlocked the deadbolt on the door and opened it. He eyed the woman with undisguised lustful notions. "Hey, baby doll – you lost?"

She reached over to run a slim hand over Biff's cheek. "I don't think so. Fernando said you two might like some entertainment. I can make the time pass for you and Ray in ways you two never dreamed of."

All suspicion left Biff's features at the woman's mention of Fernando and Ray. "You know who I am too, baby?"

"You bet I do, Biff honey. Fernando told me not to come in unless you and Ray asked me."

"Damn... you hear that, Ray?"

"Hell yeah, brother." Ray moved from his place of concealment to stand next to Biff. "You are one fine lookin' piece. Did Fernando tell you we like the rough stuff, baby. He know-"

A dead eyed man whipped around the doorway with a silenced MP5 machine pistol pointed at their faces, his finger hovering over the trigger with almost a caress of desire. "Move a finger and I blow your faces off with one burst! Interlock your fingers behind your heads and carefully kneel on the floor. Miss a step and this will be an execution rather than an arrest. Now, ladies!"

"Fuck!" Ray watched the woman stifle amusement and scamper around behind the man he could tell was a killer. "Do what he say, Biff! He wants to pull on us. I tol' you this fuckin' place is jinxed. We in it now."

"What's this all about, officer?" Biff interlocked his fingers behind his head as did Ray. He switched tone of voice to cultured confusion. "May we at least see some identification? We have done nothing wrong."

"Oh, yes Sir, I'm sure this is a misunderstanding," the dead eyed man said. "Once you have knelt and are restrained, I will show you badges from both the FBI and US Marshal's Service. I am US Marshal, Nick McCarty. Kneel now with care, gentlemen."

Ray began to get suspicious. "He's a killer, Biff. There's-"

"Kneel or die!" The man claiming to be Nick McCarty looked a split second from murder. His finger closed on the MP5 trigger. "Ever see that TV show 'Justified'? That's the kind of US Marshal I am. I don't give a shit whether you kneel or die."

Ray saw instant death in the man's eyes. He interlocked his fingers and knelt as ordered with Biff following his lead. Two men came around the entrance with professional ease to restrain their hands behind their backs. They were then helped by the two new arrivals to their feet. They were shown both identification from the FBI and the US Marshal's Service as promised. Ray relaxed slightly.

"It's the law, Biff."

Biff searched the trio's faces, who were professionally patting them down, and confiscating everything they had on them. The little whore in the mini-skirt brought in a bag. She searched through the small room, bagging anything of an electronic nature. "This don't look good, partner."

"We want our lawyer." Ray cursed himself for their smartphones and electronic tablets. They got stupid. No way should he or Biff been found with anything other than burner phones. A happy thought crossed his addled mind in a brief streak of relief. "Where's your warrant? Are we under arrest? You can't just take whatever you want. We'll have your damn badges!"

"All of your questions will be answered shortly," the man named Nick answered. "Once you're in interrogation you can speak with anyone you want to call. Are we ready, Cleaner?"

"Yes, Muerto. I will be right back." The woman hurried off with the bag in hand. A Ford SUV drove into the Sea Breeze parking lot. It turned with doors opening automatically for them.

"Here's our ride. Let's go. This way, gentlemen." The US Marshal guided Ray, with Biff following at the prompting from the Marshal's cohorts into the SUV.

Once inside the vehicle, driving away from the motel, the large black guy with the man claiming to be Marshal McCarty approached them with syringes in his hands. Ray began to battle, only to have the MP5 pressed to his head.

"Go ahead and fight, Ray. It won't matter."

Moments later, Ray and Biff lost consciousness.

* * *

"You were exceptional today, Cleaner," Nick complimented Cala as he strapped Biff into place on a gurney inside the nightmarish Carmel Valley interrogation room. "Your suggestion of using a supposed gift from Fernando of a hooker was perfect. The performance you acted out netting Biff and Ray without tearing apart the Sea Breeze elevated you from minion to valued soldier of the Unholy Trio."

Cala took the compliment with a squeal of delight, embracing Johnny. "I am Cleaner Cala, soldier of the Unholy Trio. Yes! Thank you, Muerto!"

Nick shrugged. "I can't turn ten year old Jean away from this business. I've given up trying to figure out the attraction. With Jean, it was seeing bad guys being dealt with violently, instead of running from them. I suspect not being at the mercy of your whacko male family members turned you to our dark side, Cala."

"You know those cretins very well, Muerto," Cala replied. "They would still kill Dimah and me at their first opportunity. The only thing stopping my honor killing monster relatives is that they will have to face violent men. The cowards have been raised to think all men will allow them to do anything they want to do to women considered their chattel. Johnny has been training me. I will not ever lower my head in deference again to them. I do not know how dark I am inside, Muerto, but it is a good darkness. I know what is right and what is wrong."

"That's the key, Cleaner," Gus said, patting her shoulder. "Until I met Lynn Montoya Dostiene, I didn't know if any woman could embrace what we do. She's so far above what I think of as cold blooded killer mental skill, I don't even compare with her. You have the mental outlook to be as deadly and as cold blooded about what we do even now. You surpass her in the hands on skill level, Cala."

"Really, Gus? I do?"

"Her husband Clint told us she can't clean anything. She would leave a murder scene without a backward glance. Only Nick is better at you in crime scene cleaning, and you learn at an incredible rate, both on the ground and in the air, Cala. We're lucky to have you. You're like Nick and Johnny. Nothing bothers you about this bloody business."

Cala's features revealed her disgust. "You are right, Payaso. Cutting up vicious bastards, who would kill countless innocents, for disposal does not bother me at all. I am not affected by the sight of much blood or the cutting. Naturally, I did not know this until being with all of you. I will be the Unholy Trio's 'Cruella Deville'. She is amazing. Did you watch the cutting Lynn did on the gangbanger she called 'Darla'? Oh my… that woman was fast with a blade, but could not hold a candle to Lynn."

43

"I saw the video, and it is as you describe it, Cala," Nick agreed. "I hate to say this, but I think Jean will be just as proficient. She loves the knives."

"Cala is very good at martial arts, as Lynn is," Johnny said. "Even if caught alone somewhere, she will surprise the cave dwellers."

Biff and Ray began to groan. Cala ran around to start the eerie music and begin the black light show of the walls shining torturous images beyond description. The Cleaner and Unholy Trio watched in anticipation as Biff and Ray awoke to a nightmare. Biff impressed Nick with his grasp of the situation.

"We're fucked, Ray!"

"This is… some kind of new scare tactic," Ray answered. "No one can do this to us! Keep it together! Hey! Anyone here? Okay… you've made your point. Let's talk money."

"This ain't about money, bro," Biff said. "We're dead. They didn't strap us on these gurneys in a room like this for the hell of it. They knew Fernando and who we are. We're fucked."

Although they had to be careful, the Unholy Trio donned their costumes with Cala recording the interrogation. They approached the gurneys with rehearsed ease. Nick patted Biff's cheek before speaking through the voice altering mask. "Hi there, Biff. You've been given to the Unholy Trio. We want to know everything you know about Fernando Carone and his Mother Ship, 'The Tempest'. You are right. You and Ray are in a nightmare of pain. I sense you understand the importance of telling us everything you know. Otherwise you'll be experiencing this."

Nick moved over to Ray's body. He sliced down from his sternum to his groin with the scalpel. Ray screamed as his intestines bulged. "Apply the magic ingredient, El Kabong."

Johnny moved into view next to Ray's body and poured bleach along Ray's evisceration. Ray stayed conscious for only seconds of hell before he passed out. By then, Biff gasped, howled, screamed, and begged as Ray's body relaxed into momentary coma-like stillness. Nick moved into view in his Muerto disguise.

"I see in your face you recognize the fact you won't live, but you could die comfortably. That in itself should be a comfort. I can supply you with a painless death, or you can watch your buddy, Ray. He'll give you a preview of the way you'll go unless I get detailed answers to all of my questions. Do you understand the consequences of playing with us, Biff?"

Nick noted the open mouthed stare of horror highlighting Biff's features. He smiled. "C'mon, Biff. Use your words, buddy."

Biff focused finally on Nick's masked features. "What... what do you want to know?"

"We know your boss Fernando wants this area under his thumb for drug, extortion, and even human trafficking. We want to know every detail of the operation, including Panga boat exchanges, guards, weapons, and Fernando's presence on board. Leave nothing out. I will let you talk because we know many details already. Choose your words carefully, Biff. If you don't match what we already know perfectly this will be a bad day at black rock for you, pal."

"Ah... what do you know?"

Nick chuckled which came out as an evil Darth Vader sounding amusement. "That's for us to know and you to find out. Start talking."

* * *

Biff relaxed backwards with a loose bodied movement indicating complete capitulation. He gave them everything about Carone's ambitions in the area, including the fact no one had been sent yet to replace Jay's exterminated crew. Biff began to sweat as he explained how Fernando recruited him and Ray in East LA from their enforcement job with the Zetas. He wanted to fuck these assholes over somehow. Ray's torture unnerved him in a way he didn't think was possible. If he could hold back something before they gave him a hotshot it would be worth a gamble. After he told them about the sleeping quarters for Fernando on board 'The Tempest', along with the number of guards watching the boat during the night, Biff fell silent. He pretended trying to think of something else he left out, repeating a detail about Fernando's party habits he'd already mentioned.

"Not bad," Nick stopped him. "I think maybe you earned a sleepy-time shot, Biff. I-"

Cala had been watching Biff closely. She rushed over to Nick, who approached Biff with a syringe Cala knew meant death. "Wait, Muerto! Biff is lying... or withholding a critical fact. He's sweating although he is naked. Do not trust him. I have a feeling."

Shit! Biff wrestled around in his bonds. Sweat stung his eyes. He glanced at Nick, who watched him with a smile. His ploy was dead and he knew it. "I...I forgot one thing."

"You didn't forget, Biff. Cala caught you. Nice one, Cleaner. I think a couple of incisions with a little bleach should get you on board."

"Dickerson! He...he's a lead cop Jay mentioned as being impossible to buy off in Pacific Grove. Fernando has a hit on him to take place tonight! Please... I'm sorry... I...I thought maybe-"

"Maybe nothing," Nick cut him off. "Who did Carone hire and where's he staying?"

"I don't know where he is... honest to God! His name's Fenric Ballesteros. He's a pro. The contract is for tonight. That's all I know!"

"Do you know him, Muerto," Gus asked.

"I know of him. He's amongst my Rogue's Gallery of guys to watch out for. I saw him in Cairo nearly three years ago. My old boss Frank Richert wanted him tracked for possible sanction. Frank had an address for him in Cairo and knew who his target was. I found his target first - an official with the Saudi government visiting Egypt on official business. Then I found Fenric casing his target. Frank aborted the sanction. I have plenty of pictures of Fenric from that time. Carone's becoming a real problem. He wants the Monterey area under his thumb; but why? I can understand sending in a group like Jay's crew to do some exploring for opportunities in the Central Coastal Area. It makes no sense to start assassinating local cops."

Nick turned again to a terrified Biff. "You can still earn a quiet, painless passing. Why the hell would your boss send a damn professional to kill a local cop?"

"Fernando figured to establish a presence with gang contacts as a screen... you know... to give the locals something to bitch about. We did it in the Southern California area, but Homeland Security tightened operations down there because of the ports. We...we had sweet Panga boat ports in all the small coastal cities."

"Keep going," Nick said. "I want to hear everything concerning this floating operation."

"Like Fernando says... we need a key cop in the area we establish a presence in, along with a gang like Jay's under our control. We can use the gang to distract from any kind of port activity we have going on. The drugs are only part of it... but I guess you know that. Fernando could move anything: weapons, women, drugs, even explosives."

"You're beginning to bore me." Nick moved on Biff with the scalpel when he paused.

"Wait! Give me a minute! I...I have to get this straight. With one or two key cops in our control, we can own an area, moving anything we want in and out of the port. The gang causes just enough of a problem with small shit on big transfer days to allow our cop contacts to recommend big police attention away from what we're doing. The best is it never ties back to us. It...it's worked so far... until now."

"That's a steep step to get from small time chaos to killing cops," Nick replied.

"Not if a pro does it random like," Biff explained, seeing the scalpel in Nick's hands begin to rise from his side. "Think about it... a pro like Ballesteros breaks in, kills the family, takes shit like a burglar, and gets out without leaving a trace. The cops go on a useless manhunt, looking for someone with a grudge against Dickerson. Fenric is long gone before they even discover the scene."

Nick's mouth tightened into a thin slash. "You left the part out about Dickerson's family being murdered too."

"C'mon... sorry... I figured you would know Fenric would have to kill the whole family... random... bloody... and violent." Biff began to hyperventilate watching Nick. "Please... for God's sake... don't cut me! I told you everything! I'll make this right! The Tempest isn't at sea all the way down near San Luis Obispo or the Channel Islands. We're anchored five miles west of Point Lobos. That's good info, right? The coordinates are on my tablet in a note file marked Point Lobos."

Nick backed away with iron control, thinking about Neil and his family. He gestured at Gus. Without another word, Gus gave both the comatose Ray and the relieved Biff hotshots into eternity. Cala sized the two bodies with cold calculating purpose before turning toward Nick.

"Helicopter, Muerto? We have freezer room if you want to store them for now."

48

"Let's store them, Cala. This really brings Neil into our business bigtime."

"It saved his life, Nick," Gus stated. "Did… you know… ever kill a family to cover a sanction?"

Nick grinned, knowing it would be stupid to act outraged at the suggestion. "No. I would have figured a way to take Neil out in some other form, probably like I did in Senator Ambrose. I'd use ether on anyone in the house who might waken. Then I'd simply stick him with a heart attack shot or cut off his breathing. It leaves the coroner looking for clues about a guy dying in the midst of his family without any sign of break in."

"That was a great tip to get the exact coordinates for The Tempest. Nice catch, Cala," Gus said. "What do you have in mind for stopping Fenric, Muerto?"

"We'll need to recon Neil's area, making sure Fenric's not keeping lookout on the house at this time," Nick replied. "We won't be looking for him. That would be a waste of time. We'll concentrate on the target. He'll come to us and I will stop him somehow. If he's not casing the area around Neil's home, we'll slip the Dickerson family out. I'll take their place."

"What if he is watching Neil's house," Johnny asked.

"Sucks to be him," Nick said. "It looks like you're our driver for the evening, Cleaner."

"I know Neil, his wife and their kids. I would kill this Fenric myself," Cala stated.

"Not necessary, but you will need to calculate space in the freezer," Nick replied.

"I will do so happily, Muerto."

* * *

Fenric Ballesteros watched the Dickerson household with the calmness of an experienced killer from early in the day. Enjoying the commonplace family activities as they moved about their lives without a care in the world touched the only part of Fenric he cared about. Killing meant an end with monetary stability. Feeling the everyday actions of a busy family who smilingly skipped around happily inside their pathetic lives without a clue thrilled him in an indescribable way. It made the tedious prep work actually exciting and the killing just a mundane action.

Fenric smiled in anticipation. He found Mrs. Dickerson to be quite the tasty morsel. Clueless wives could be a wonderful addition to any crime scene. For the next few minutes, he imagined the unimaginable acts he would engage in with the cop's wife. Ballesteros couldn't decide whether to keep the cop alive to watch or not. Fenric made disparaging gestures, even as regret in the thought plagued him. Some things would need to be unscripted. The killing of Dickerson's family would need to be haphazardly violent. If a rape opportunity presented itself, Fenric would be ready. The suddenly appearing flashing lights at his back stabbed reality into his consciousness. *Fuck. What the hell could this be?*

A dark figure approached Fenric's vehicle with slow care. Not knowing how many cops might be in the Ford SUV, Fenric decided on feigned ignorance, hoping to dissuade the cop with a lost persona. He rolled down his window with a smile of helpfulness, secretly cursing the time and opportunity window missed.

"Hello. Did I do something wrong?" The Taser needles shot into his chest blanked any random thought. The one who shot them into him watched with a grin until Fenric lost consciousness.

* * *

"Nope." Nick also answered the question to himself, *and you won't be doing wrong... ever again.*

The Ford drove alongside with side door popping open. Nick deposited Fenric inside. He then got into Fenric's vehicle without a backwards glance, following the Ford away from Dickerson's house. He activated his networked com unit.

"Did you get that interaction, Kabong?"

"It has all been digitized, Muerto."

"Good. This worked out very well. Fenric had no idea he might be in danger from any outside source. That helped immeasurably. We spotted our boy. We had a plan. We engaged. We have Fenric in our control. It's Miller time," Nick joked. "I can handle it from here if you three want to call it a night or day."

"I'm in to the end," Cala said. "I know this monster would have killed them all without a thought. Johnny and I will sleep later."

"Me too," Gus stated. "The 'Starlight' gig soured me on the milk of human kindness. Like Cala said, Fenric no doubt had a kill mission in mind."

"I have researched everything about this creature," Johnny added. "He is suspected of heinous acts no human being should be taking on as a so called job. Do all assassins think in this way, Muerto?"

Nick hesitated. He shrugged. "Mostly… we're psychopaths. I would have never taken any job with a family involved as collateral damage, but I know it happens. You're right though, Johnny, assassins don't question their employers for the most part. We see targets. We kill targets. Very seldom do we get into the morality of contracts."

"Will he talk, Muerto?"

"Sure, Cala. Fenric will talk easier than anybody we've had for interrogation. Once he wakes on a gurney in our funhouse,

Fenric will cooperate for anything we have to offer. Look... we have no conscience, no loyalty, and no compassion."

"You do, Nick," Gus said with solemn emphasis.

"I could pretend for you, Gus. Unfortunately, my inner dark side doesn't disappear at will. Harding calls his people the 'Monster Squad'. He differentiates his crew between Monsters and Snow Whites. Consider me in this way. Depending on the circumstances everyone is a Snow White to me."

"I'm well aware of that," Gus replied. "I also know loyalty strongly influences every one of your actions."

"That is so, Muerto," Johnny agreed.

"Let's leave the morality lessons alone for now. Take us to the Funhouse, Cleaner."

"Yes, Muerto."

* * *

Fenric ached all over. The application of Taser needles until he passed out affected his short term memory. He kept his eyes shut while quietly taking stock of his physical attributes. Cursing himself internally without showing any outward sign, Ballesteros concluded his limbs as well as his head were restrained with straps he could not slither away from. He thought for a moment as to his choices, wondering about who or what he could barter away to keep his life. It was then three men approached, dressed in black, one with a vicious clown mask, and the other two with black silk face masks. A woman accompanied them, dressed in black, with a red eye mask and a red headband. One of the black silk masked men checked the video camera mounted directly behind the four. He nodded at the one at the other end of the line, who came forward with a water glass and straw. Fenric drank with hard to pretend thirst.

"We know you were staking out the Dickerson house," the man said, stripping off his mask. "I'm-"

"Nick McCarty! Oh sweet Jesus! You killed Felix Moreau. Listen, Nick... I don't have a contract on you. This is business, compadre. My employer doesn't even know you. I'm here for the Dickerson family across from where you snatched me. I would never have taken a contract on you. Sure... I would shoot you in the back of the head if I saw you. I damn well wouldn't go hunting you. I heard you took down the Frank Richert Cartel inside the NSA. How can I make this right?"

"You can't, Fen," Nick answered. "I'm willing to forget you were going to hit the target bought and paid for by Fernando Carone. It's nothing personal. It's just business. You know reality, brother rat. You're not walking out of here. Let's get the finances out of the way first. Cleaner? Come over and scope this out."

"Yes, Muerto." Cala streaked into position, staring at Fenric. "I'm ready."

"This is 'The Cleaner'. She's a living lie detector. We'll need all your bank accounts first. Please don't play make believe with us. We'll keep you alive for a time until we confirm everything. Then, I'll give you a peaceful, painless death. God help you if we don't get the truth or your account information doesn't check out. In that case, I will give you a glimpse of hell. My other compatriot, El Kabong will be using his satellite uplinked laptop to transfer your funds first. Begin quickly, Fen. You have ten seconds to comply with your account locations and numbers for transfer. We'll get to the rest later."

Fenric recited in precise terms everything McCarty asked for. He observed for over a decade what can be done to a man in interrogation. The choice was clear – he either gave them everything they wanted or they would torture him until he did. He recognized McCarty immediately. Fenric had laughed when watching reports and videos of the 'Unholy Trio'. Never did he think to cross their paths. Unlike other observers to the videos, Fenric knew they were not fake. The Middle East idiots, he had watched the destruction of an Isis cell in Ohio with, claimed it was a fake, vowing to find the filmmakers responsible. Fenric told them, 'Allah help you if you do'. Carone had hired him for a simple kill in quiet Pacific Grove. If McCarty wanted Carone, Fenric would help him. He didn't know if Carone knew about McCarty or the Unholy Trio, but if he had sent him into their hunting grounds without telling him, Fenric wanted him to pay for it with his life, as he himself soon would.

* * *

Johnny nodded at Nick after finishing transfer of accounts from Ballesteros's holdings into their own offshore accounts. "It is done. He had nearly five million as he claimed."

"Very good, Fen," Nick said, turning to Ballesteros. "You may have guessed we want the guy who hired you. Fernando Carone put the hit on our police friend and his family. We know where he is and what his plans are. You were to kill the Dickerson family tonight. Is that correct?"

"Yes. I will help in any way I can for you to get the bastard who put me in your sights. Our kind do not have friends. Why make this personal?"

In most instances, Nick admitted to himself, Fen was right. His career as a writer, and moving to Pacific Grove as a base, changed him. Then, along came Rachel, Jean, Deke, and now Quinn to cement the change into place. He knew explaining it to Fen would be a useless exercise. "Shit happens. I never took a contract on a family. I don't hold that against you, but we were never the same kind. We need you to confirm information gathered from two of Carone's other henchmen."

"Of course," Fenric agreed, relaxing his head back while staring up at the horrific ceiling. He smiled. "This is a very nice setting, Nick."

"Thanks, Fen. I'm glad we won't have to introduce you to some of the room's more nightmarish implements."

"I appreciate the chance to buy an easy death. Some of us would have tortured me simply to hear me beg for death."

"Do you have any family? I will send them most of your money."

"Thank you... but no, I have happily been alone. Keep it... hey... now that you mention it, I had to be a homeless bum in New York City once to cap a mobster. His name was ah... Willie Fangona. Anyway... I scavenged on the streets in front of Fangona's apartment building, trying not to get rounded up by the cops. A woman who worked the Salvation Army pot on the corner started giving me coffee and donuts when I'd walk past. She always smiled and said, 'good morning, I have something for you'. I'd tell her I didn't need it, and she answered the same way, 'of course you do'. Give the Salvation Army whatever you want to, Nick. Would you do it in my name too?"

"Sure, Fen. I'll have to wait a while though."

"No problem. Thanks."

Gus brought over his tablet with the schematics of Carone's yacht, including variations of where Burt told them Carone spent most of his time. Fenric looked over everything carefully. He also named the hotel he was staying at in Monterey.

"The hotel keycard's in my wallet. It looks like you have everything I could tell you. He likes hanging out on the bridge. The three times I have met with him in person, Fernando took the meeting on the bridge, dressed in a ridiculous white captain's outfit like he was on the 'Love Boat' or something. He keeps a skeleton crew of about fifteen on board all year. They're handpicked cartel killers, with other skills for crewing a yacht like The Tempest, and handling the Panga boats with whatever transaction's going on."

"Good info," Nick said. "I'm surprised you ever met with him."

"Yeah... not too smart. I was getting careless. I should have retired with my money but I'm a psycho. Sooner or later I would have killed someone... just for the hell of it."

Nick chuckled. "We don't retire well. What would you like? I have a hotshot of heroin or I can give you the usual instant mix."

"Oh man... give me the H. That would be great. You guys really do some nice work. I saw the Ohio Isis cell video with the guy dancing around in front of the hangar before you blew it to hell and gone. The Middle East fruit-loops I was stuck with at the time thought it was fake. I knew better. Well... good to meet you, Nick. Shoot me up, brother."

"I'll see you soon, brother." Nick gave him the heroin death dose.

"I hope not... ahhhhhhh...," Fenric's eyes closed as he smiled a final time. "It's going to be hot where I'm..."

Nick unstrapped Ballesteros, allowing the fading assassin to lie without restraints in the final moments. "Fen went with his boots on. We'll need to go collect his stuff before we call it a day. I think it may be a good time for Ebi Zarin and his lovely wife to get decked out in traditional cave dweller Islamic garb for confiscation of Fen's earthly goods, at least his electronic ones."

"Good idea, Muerto. Maybe we will be done in time to watch the sunrise at Otter's Point," Johnny said.

"With a bit of Irish?"

"Of course, Payaso," Johnny answered. "We had a very good day and night. I am glad Fen decided to cooperate, even though I didn't get to do a movie."

Cala grasped Nick's arm before he and Gus lifted Fen into a body-bag. "Did you think of letting him go, Muerto?"

"Not for a second," Nick answered. "He would have killed all of us at the first opportunity. Fen wasn't a lost puppy we were putting down at the pound. He was a top echelon killer. We don't forgive and forget."

"You spared Johnny."

"I needed Johnny. Also, he didn't kill families. Besides, I liked him."

"I was recruited as a soldier of Allah," Johnny added. "They wanted me to be a murderer. We were not being persecuted. A few of the believers asked me when I hid out in their mosque why I was a terrorist. They did not dare ask anyone else, but I seemed more open. I told them I served Allah to keep Islam free. They would whisper, 'but we are free here'. The longer I stayed, the more disillusioned I became. I became angry with the quiet believers who said nothing. I asked them why if they thought what we were doing was wrong... then why did they not speak out. They were too frightened. I grew up in a small village. Sharia Law was meaningless there. I learned the true face Sharia Law shows in secret, with honor killings, female subjugation and mutilation, stonings, murders, suicidal death on a whim while Islam's leaders live like kings."

Johnny drew Cala into his embrace. "I will die before I allow such blasphemy here. If Cala is approached even one more time by her idiot Kader family, I will hunt them down like the jackals they are. I will do El Kabong movies of each death."

"Count me in," Gus said.

"El Muerto will be at your side, Kabong. Let's get Fen in the freezer. I think we'll have a short time to enjoy the beach before we have to move on Fernando. It's the weekend. I'll pack a bag and bring Jean, Quinn, Rachel, and Deke with me."

"Until we deal with Fernando, maybe you should drive everywhere," Gus suggested. "We're not even sure Carone wouldn't have added you onto Fen's hit list."

"Those 'bangers will be out this morning in spite of their lawyer's unfortunate passing," Johnny reminded everyone. "I think Payaso is right, Muerto. It may be dangerous for you to walk around. What about your new ascendency to number one assassin in the world?"

Nick shrugged while they placed the Fenric bag on the gurney for transport. "There's a bunch of notes on my drop, some from my fellow assassins. Apparently they figured rightfully I was no longer taking contracts since ending Frank Richert's NSA power grab. Since learning the fate of Moreau, I'm getting very popular. Moreau's old employers are a bunch I'd like to deal with for one reason: to get into a position to put a bullet through their heads. There are Saudi potentates with numerous wives who would rather a professional assassin murder their wives. I swear to God... sometimes... I feel like doing a hit list through the Saudi royal family. Their money funds chaos throughout the world, along with the shitheads who follow that murderous cult of Islam: Wahhabism. I admit I'd take a hit on a Saudi royal family member in a heartbeat."

Gus stopped the procession. He pointed a finger at Nick. "That means you've been recruited to do exactly that. You're warming us up for the trigger. Bad Muerto... bad."

Nick shrugged. "I was offered a million dollars to take out a Saudi royal prince. It's flaky by a source I'm unfamiliar with. It's just one of many I've gotten since suspicions were confirmed by Felix's handlers. They want to adopt me too. I don't answer the drop e-mail unless it comes from our close personal contacts. I've lit up the 'Dark Web'. Every suspicion about how Felix met death has been gone over in significant detail there, with me as the star."

"What name do you go by on the 'Dark Web', Muerto," Cala asked.

"Terminator," Nick answered with a grin. "I know Gus introduced Rachel and Jean to the tag long ago. It's a game. So many departments scan me, measuring prosecution, it's funny in a way. I hope they're actually paying attention to the real enemy."

"I remember a time when your tag on the 'Dark Web' was funny," Gus said. "After the first time you helped me rescue my brother and friends, I knew the Terminator tag was absolutely accurate. It has proven true in every single op we've ever taken. I don't talk Muerto out of various venues of course. It doesn't mean I don't know all he's done. It means I trust him to be on the right side of every single action in his name. He has been, and I trust he will be so until we end this. The more we talk, the thirstier I get, and the more I desire that damn cold beach. Plus, I get to watch Kabong dance with the goofy birds."

"I shall dance the dance of birds in flight," Kabong said. "Especially, since I will bring them special treats today."

"One of these days we'll watch the birds cluster about you in those waves you've drawn and then you'll simply disappear on their upward flight."

"The birds love me, Payaso. Don't be a hater."

Chapter Three

Carone

Quinn laughed in Rachel's arms as she held him aloft to watch Johnny throw bits of bread into the air, surrounded by a flock of beach birds hovering for snacks. Jean, Sonny, and Deke maneuvered around him while staying far enough away to keep from interfering with the feeding. Deke in particular acted entranced with the bird feeding as always, staying slightly behind Jean's leg, while peeking at the chaotic scene.

"I don't think Deke ever will get used to the flying rats," Gus said. "I swear… every day we accompany the birdman from the sand out here, the swarm grows in numbers."

"You're probably right, but the kids love it as much as Johnny does," Nick said. "There's so many now, I keep expecting them to attack like in the Alfred Hitchcock movie 'The Birds'."

"That movie is creepy," Tina added. "It gives me chills watching him. I'm like Gomez. I keep waiting for them to start poking his eyes out."

"The birds know him so well now, if he ever comes to the beach without food, they will surely attack," Cala remarked.

Jean pointed at an approaching vehicle. "Police car, Dad."

Nick sighed while taking one last long sip of his spiked coffee. He didn't look around. "Is it slowing down?"

"Yep," Rachel answered while playing with Quinn as she glanced toward the street. "It stopped. Neil got out. He's waving."

Gus took Nick's cup. "I'll be back."

Nick trekked to where Neil waited. "Hello, Officer Dickerson. How may I assist you?"

Neil gestured at the squad car. "Let's talk in the car, Nick."

"Do you want me in the front or the back?"

"Very funny."

Inside the vehicle Neil waited for Nick to begin the conversation. Nick kept smiling. "Aren't you going to say something?"

"I texted you the details. What else would you like?"

"A professional assassin contracted by a mobster living on a 'Mother Ship' was sent to ace me because his boss, Fernando Carone, wants to build a port connection for illegal trafficking. You found him before he did it. Want to tell me how?"

"Can't. I only told you about the hitter because until I get Carone shut down, you'll be in danger. Those 'bangers being released today, Nano Calista and Doug Morgan, were part of Jay Park's crew. Carone sent them all in to test the waters for his port plot."

"Their lawyer, Lance Botorf died yesterday too. His secretary found him early this morning. It seems he died in his sleep. You wouldn't happen to know anything about that, would you, Nick?"

"Why ask me that, Neil? I've went over the details of everything you should be concerned with. Let's focus on going forward. I can't watch for all the 'bangers who show up in town, hoping to create extortion rackets and drug outlets. You know now to be observant when strange hoodie idiots frequent the town. We'll move on Carone as soon as possible. He's dangerous in more than a few ways."

"You saved my life again. I know that. Calista and Morgan have already been released. Is there anything else you'd like me to do?"

"Nope. We're good right now. I may ask you to keep an eye on my homestead soon. Gus, Johnny, Cala, and I will be traveling into the Tahoe area for a time. It's undecided whether I'll be taking my family or not."

"I can do that. What's with calling Groves, Johnny, and did you three cartoons draft Cala?"

"We've been collaborating with another team in the San Francisco Bay Area. Their leader's named John Harding. Johnny loved that robot movie, called-"

"Short Circuit... Johnny Five?" Neil took a moment to enjoy that piece of information. "That...that's good stuff. I've seen John Harding fight in the UFC. Is it the same guy?"

"The very same, and Cala requested a more active role. She's taking piloting lessons. Cala also has a few other impressive skills."

"Things seem to be heating to a boiling point around here since you all went on that ill-fated cruise. Did you partner with Harding's crew on that action? I read where it was heavy combat with pirates."

"It was heavy combat with Iran backed Isis assholes. There were no survivors... at least on their side. I have a morning's relaxation to get back to, Neil. Thanks for letting me know about the two 'bangers being released."

"No problem. They gave us an address in Salinas. It's a known gang hangout. I'll text it to you. They had money for a taxi, so no one met them when they left. I didn't know if you'd want them followed or not. Now that I know about Carone, maybe I should have."

"We'll stay alert. Until Carone's taken care of, we'll have to be on guard 24/7. See you later, Neil."

"Until then." Neil gave Nick a small wave before getting in his squad car.

Nick rejoined his crew, relating to them the news about Calista and Morgan. Johnny had finished the bird feeding. Jean and Sonny were walking along the coastal path with Deke as Nick sat down. Gus indicated he had the kids on com. "The cops found the lawyer already. I warned Neil to be on his guard until we fix the Carone problem."

Rachel handed Nick a refilled Irish coffee. "We're lucky to have Neil."

"Or he's lucky to have us," Gus replied. "Nick's already saved his bacon numerous times. He's on the pad."

"There's only so much he can do. He knows many times we have actionable intelligence about national security problems. Grace left a text wondering about fallout after the 'Starlight' at sea action. I'll let her and Tim know about our Carone problem. It would be interesting to know if the DOJ has ears on Carone's ship, Tempest."

"What's on for the rest of the day, Muerto," Johnny asked.

"I'm thinking a cruise possibly tomorrow. With The Tempest parked only five miles off of Point Lobos, we could empty the freezer, and see if we can spot Carone's pleasure craft."

Gus leaned forward in his beach chair with an earnest look. "I've studied pictures of Carone's super yacht. It's magnificent. Is there any way we could confiscate it, Muerto?"

"I don't know, Gus. Mostly, we can't spend what we do have without attracting the attention of our government. We have the money to buy one or custom make one of those super yachts. To stay under government radar we had to get special permission to get a helicopter through government channels beginning in the CIA Director's Office, and that was with us paying for it. It's the money that will be our undoing. I can talk to John Harding. They have an escape island. If we could pull it off, John might let us build a pier to accommodate it."

"It's a waste," Tina said. "You cartoons would turn it into a battleship anyway."

"Stay out of this, T-Rex," Cala said. "It would be beautiful going on cruises in our own yacht. By the way... who are you calling a cartoon?"

"Oh... I forgot you've become a cartoon too," Tina retorted. "What was it they call you... Clammy or Crabby... something like that?"

Cala giggled. "Good one, T. Let's do it if we can, Muerto. Think of having our own super yacht. Gus mentioned it's 240 feet long. Doesn't that take a lot of professional crewmembers?"

Gus nodded with a sigh. "That's the drawback. Most are automated to a point they nearly run themselves. A full crew would probably be about seventy members and more, depending on if the yacht can be chartered to the wealthy or not. On a stationary 'Mother Ship' that moves only rarely, a skeleton crew of around fifteen would be about right. Maybe crewing with John Harding's people would be close to the only way we could go on a cruise safely. Even if we hired Issac on a permanent basis, we would need a lot more people. Vetting them to sail with us would be nearly impossible. I could train all of you, but we'd still need Harding's people too. It's probably a bad idea."

"Don't discount it yet. I'll talk to John and see what he thinks," Nick said. "It would mean an armed assault on the boat against nearly twenty killers. I had planned a full on kill mission. I would mine the ship to blow. After the explosions, we would move in for weapons free destruction until nothing was left. An armed assault to take the ship would mean a bloody battle or my getting on board with some form of toxic gas after everyone is asleep, depending on sentries. I would have to kill them first from long range before going on board with the gas. It would be a tricky mission for one guy."

"You and John mined Port Chabahar together," Johnny said. "The Tempest is a three decker nightmare to assault, especially crewed by killers. I think it's a bad idea, Muerto."

"Did you just insult me, Johnny?"

That drew laughter from even Rachel. Gus was the first to speak. "When Muerto went on board to end Jason Bidwell and Max Stoddard, he rigged the whole thing by himself, including the interrogations. After that gig, if Muerto says he can do it, he will. If the sentries are roving around the inside of the yacht instead of standing watch, they'll be tough to spot."

"I'll talk to John. As you pointed out about the crew, we may not have enough able-bodied people to sail a yacht the size of The Tempest. What if we took care of the crew and flew on our own crew of professionals to sail the yacht to 'Monster Island'. They wouldn't know what happened to the crew. You could captain your new vessel to the island then, Payaso. I can use CIA people through Paul to make 'The Tempest' under a completely different registry. We'll create a dummy corporation to be the front desk owners of the yacht."

"Damn, Muerto… that's brilliant," Gus admitted. "Talk to John. We'll need him on board for this. We'll need a well-built docking facility. They may already have one built for their own boats. A 240 footer would require a dock far larger than even their 'Valkyrie'."

"No harm in finding out. I'll call John today before we empty the freezer and go hunting for The Tempest tomorrow. Can you prepare our fish food for tomorrow morning, Cleaner?"

"Of course, Muerto," Cala answered. "Johnny will help me. We'll be going now though. We need some sleep. Although Johnny has only had one coffee, I am designated driver for Payaso and T-Rex too. Let's go lushes. We must prepare for our cruise."

"Don't you be issuing orders, Nurse Ratchet! Kabong? You need to keep 'Crabby' in line. She's been hanging out with you cartoons too much."

"My love," Johnny said, taking Cala's hand. "Don't aggravate the T-Rex. She will take it out on Payaso and he'll whine all day tomorrow."

"You are right. I am so sorry. Please take your time joining us at the humble Groves mobile," Cala replied, waving at Nick and Rachel. "See you tomorrow, Muerto."

"Viper? This is Payaso," Gus called out on his com unit. "Return to base."

"Understood, over," Jean replied in his ear.

"They're on the way back. Nice morning." Gus handed his com unit to Nick.

"Yep. It was a good one, Gus. We'll be a bit busier tomorrow. I'll let you know later how John feels about our boat plans. Would you like to come along on the cruise, Cousin Itt?"

"About as much as I'd like to be put in a closed box full of Tarantulas, Gomez."

"A simple no would suffice, Cousin Itt," Nick replied.

After their friends left, Nick and Rachel relaxed for a few moments while sipping their Irish coffees. They knew it would not take long for Jean, Sonny, and Deke to return.

"Your horror show dance card sounded full, Muerto," Rachel shifted the sleeping Quinn slightly in her arms. "I'm glad you've joined with Harding's crew on some of this terrorist crap.

66

With all of you sharing threats and information, maybe there can be a lull in this insanity. I figured after the pirate combat and destruction of Chabahar, it would at least give the Muslim horde pause for a couple months."

Nick thought about Rachel's words for a moment. He didn't want to blurt out some feel good talking point to a wife who had spotted for his sniper's nest in combat. "I've given up trying to decipher what our government leading idiots have in mind for us peons. They import terrorists under the guise of human rights in the tens of thousands, positioning them all over the states... I guess so they'll be ready to massacre us during their final uprising. They constantly try to take away our Second Amendment rights, the only protection we have against them and the invading Islamic plague they're importing. They use laws they passed without our representation to intimidate anyone standing in opposition to their tyranny. They steal the money we earn, the money we save, and the money they confiscate from our bankrupt Social Security retirement. Worst of all, they give our confiscated money to illegal aliens, terrorist imports, and professional welfare cheats."

"Damn, Muerto... we should run you for President. If you'd stop killing people for a few years, your checkered past might dip under the radar."

"Very funny. See, this is why I never answer you with anything other than sarcasm or humor. When I answer you seriously, I get disrespected and discounted."

Rachel muffled amusement with her hand. "Discounted? You mean like a reduced price Muerto where we only get a couple dollars for a discounted Muerto?"

"You're mean!"

* * *

Deke sniffed over a varmint hole under the rocks as Jean and Sonny came into sight of Otter's Point Beach where the coastal path paralleled the road. Jean smiled over at Sonny. They could hear Nick and Rachel laughing.

"What do you think they're laughing at?"

Jean shrugged. "Who knows? They could be snorting over anything. Dad's sharp funny but Mom's catching up to him fast. Mom spotted for him on the cruise in the fight with the pirate boats. I can't wait until he can take us out shooting again. We did real good, both with the range finders and the rifles."

Jean held the range finders she had taken on the walk with them. "What did you think of using these? Pretty neat, huh?"

Sonny nodded. "I liked the target shooting lessons a lot. All the calculations in the range finding was heck of cool too. Think about your folks on top of the ship with your Mom calling out targets and your Dad killing one pirate after another from that distance. I-"

An engine revved in the direction of Lover's Point along Ocean View Blvd. They watched a Camaro convertible roar into view at twice the speed limit with the top down. Three guys with black hoodies and sunglasses occupied the front and rear seats. The two not driving hung over the door frames on the passenger side. Slowing to a stop a distance down the road from the kids, the car occupants watched the Otter's Point beach for a moment with the driver pointing. The Camaro began approaching again at a fifteen mile per hour pace. Jean didn't wait. She tapped her com unit.

"Incoming gangbangers, Dad! Metallic dark green Camaro convertible!"

"Understood! Get down, Viper!"

"Understood!" Jean crouched, pulling Sonny down with her and gesturing Deke to her side. She moved into a comfortable position, where she could stay in sight of Nick and Rachel's position on the beach. Sonny crouched next to her with Deke joining them, his head poking in between to see what held their attention.

The kids watched as Nick scooped Rachel from the beach chair with Quinn in her arms, and physically put her in a position next to the rock wall where she could not be seen from the road. Jean sighted in the Camaro with the range finders as it neared the spot opposite where Nick had placed Rachel and Quinn. It brought the occupants into crystal clear clarity. She tapped her com unit as Nick retrieved their beach bag, taking it with him to the wall near Rachel.

"They have those funny looking machine gun things, Dad!"

"On it. Thanks, Kid. Stay down."

"Understood." She looked over to see Sonny had his knife in hand, ready to streak down the path toward the beach. Jean put her hand over his. "Don't, Sonny. We would only die rushing down there. If bad things happen, we have to stay alive… to get the guys who did it."

"Jesus, Viper… do you think those guys can get your Dad."

Jean smiled, watching Nick move along the rock wall away from Rachel and Quinn. "They don't have a prayer."

* * *

Nick's chair tipped over after talking with Jean for only a moment. In the next few seconds Rachel was in his arms, with Quinn held tightly at her chest, and then against the stone wall bordering Otter's Point. "Is Jean okay?"

"She's fine. Stay here, Rach. Don't move." Nick handed her the Glock 9mm handgun from the bag he hurried over to retrieve. "You know the drill. Stay still until you have a target. Call the cavalry."

"On it." Rachel shifted Quinn for access to her iPhone while staying in control of the Glock.

Nick moved below the wall to a spot twenty feet beyond Rachel, nearly to the rocky outcropping on the left of the beach, acknowledging Jean's weapons warning. He waited, visualizing Ocean View Blvd. Nick calculated the angle he needed to adjust when he made his move to fire. The curb along Ocean View, near Otter's Point's rock wall, poked inches up from the dirt, separating the curb and wall. Nick closed his eyes while readying his .45 caliber Colt. Hearing the Camaro's deeper throated exhaust throttle down to idle, Nick twisted upwards from his position, instantly acquiring targets.

The first hollow point .45 slug smashed into the first hoodie's head, hanging over the passenger side front door frame, splattering blood and brain matter as it exited. The second went through the rear seat passenger's head. When the cringing driver, who had dived down on the seat straightened to punch the gas pedal for a hasty escape, Nick was standing next to the Camaro on the driver's side. Nick pistol whipped the driver and reached in to shut off the engine, but kept the ignition in the run position. He hit the switch for the convertible roof, closing it.

"Everything's fine, Rach," Nick called out. He smiled when a hand waved over the stone wall.

"Cleaner's coming down the street with Payaso and Kabong, Dad."

"Good! You and Sonny can join your Mom and Quinn. Pack up. We have to get away from here. Keep your eyes open for anyone jogging or stepping out of the surrounding houses."

"Understood."

Nick opened the driver's door. He shoved the unconscious driver over the gearshift into the lap of the dead passenger, continuing to force the man down into the space between the seat and dash. By then Gus stood at the passenger door, yanking the still alive driver's hands behind his back. Johnny handed him a plastic lock restraint which Gus used on the driver. Johnny handed Gus a syringe to make sure the driver didn't wake until they needed him to.

"Give me a hot shot too, Johnny. I'm going to try and question the driver on the way. If I get lucky, we'll fix him for a quick deposit with the rest."

"So much for nice mornings," Gus said, giving the driver only a partial shot. "Johnny and I will take Rachel and the kids home. We'll join you right after we tuck the family into the saferoom. You can ride with Cala driving to horror house. Are you okay with riding next to dead men, Cleaner?"

"Did you just insult me, Payaso?"

Cala's indignant reply earned a moment of humor as Nick dived into the rear and Cala took over driving duties. Nick waved at his friends. "Thanks, guys. Viper may have saved our asses. She warned me from down the pathway we had trouble on its way. See you both in a little while."

Johnny clasped Cala's hand for a moment and then moved on to take care of Rachel. Cala sped off toward Carmel Valley immediately. "How did Rachel take it, Muerto?"

"With 9mm in hand," Nick replied. "After our time on the run, nothing much bothers Rachel."

He continued shoving the body in the back down between the seats. "Next place in the road where you can stop without much traffic, I'm going to yank the live one back with me."

"Just ahead," Cala replied, driving to a spot off the road, nearly barren of traffic on the way toward Lighthouse Avenue.

Nick got out quickly, ran around and ripped the live hoodie from under the seat. Cala waited with the rear door open for Nick to shove him into a sitting position on the rear seat. A moment later, Cala drove away from the roadside again. Nick fixed the man into the seatbelt. The hoodie absorbed the blood from Nick's pistol whipping, where it had coagulated to glue the material at the side of the man's head. Nick buckled him in with his hands already restrained at his back. He slapped the man into groaning consciousness. The man's eyes blinked as his head swayed from side to side in pain. Only after a few more minutes of groans and moans did the man start trying to form words.

"What the fuck you do me for?"

Nick used his stun-gun on the man's groin, causing him to jackknife upwards with a scream. Cala giggled, keeping the vehicle steadily moving. "No stupid questions. I'll keep it simple for you. The next bad answer or stupid question and I will toast your nuts for thirty seconds of hell. Do you understand?"

"Yeah… yeah… don't zap me!"

"First. How did you know to find me at Otter's Point beach?"

"My boss knows all your hangouts. He tell me you and your friends are always at the Point in the mornings. He say cap your ass and anyone with you there. I picked up Calista and Morgan when they were let go. We came after you the moment they got released. Man… nobody say you was a killer, blood. Can't you let me go? I ain't in this killin' shit."

"What's your boss's name?"

"Carone… Fernando Carone."

"Did he call you personally?" Nick knew if the minion with him said Carone called him personally it would be a lie.

"No, man… Carone call nobody. He get his boy, Hector, to call me from his boat. They anchored off the coast some place."

"When Hector told you to bring Calista and Morgan to kill me, did he say why?"

"He tol' me you a local fud, stickin' your nose in Carone business. He don't know you a killer. Who the fuck are you, man? Carone never give up when he got a problem. He send King Kong and Godzilla to get you if he have to."

Both Cala and Nick shared amusement over their captive's declaration. "What's your name, homeboy?"

"Jarrod. Let me go, man." Jarrod saw in Nick's eyes he would not be living past the day. He shook his head more in self-loathing than outrage. "Shit! I knew it... I tol' Calista this was bad Juju."

"I can help you to the other side without pain," Nick replied. "I have only a couple more questions. Were you a member of Jay Park's crew?"

"No... a guy named Biff hired me to drive. I used to 'bang in Salinas, but the money with Carone was double anything I ever got. All I had goin' was to follow instructions. Biff and his boy Ray in town too. They killers. You best pray they don't find out what you done. They mobbed up down in East LA for a cartel in one of those Flamingo countries."

Nick put a comforting hand on Jarrod's shoulder. "Ah... thank you for your concern. I hope Biff and Ray weren't your besties or anything. I already guided them into hell earlier."

Jarrod's eyes widened, staring at Nick in shock. "You did Biff and Ray both... man... what the fuck are you... the reaper?"

"Wrong movie," Cala giggled from the front. "He's Muerto, the Terminator."

"Oh shit!" Jarrod's chin dropped to his chest. "We fucked with the Unholy Trio. I...I seen those videos. Please... don't do me like those guys."

73

Nick injected Jarrod with the hotshot Johnny gave him before they split up. He watched Jarrod stiffen with eyes wide before slowly relaxing into his smiling journey to hell. "You earned a quickie, homeboy. Say hello to Biff and Ray for me. Tell them no hard feelings, it was just business."

Jarrod's eyes closed for the last time, his mouth trying to form a last response.

"I think the cruise tomorrow will be very important," Cala commented.

"Yep. We have to get after this Carone guy. We don't want him to have a chance to send King Kong and Godzilla after me."

* * *

Rachel lay on her side, panting as Nick stroked her side lightly, causing her to shudder. "What did you do to me?"

"A little of everything."

Rachel turned in his arms, pulling Nick in close to her. He kissed her with the tenderness of a lover's care. "God... I love you."

Nick continued his light touch along Rachel's side, the sheen of sweat coating both partners an indication of their intense interlude. "I love you too, baby. I am sorry I didn't call you after our beach combat session. I should have, but I needed to help Kabong and Cleaner with our room temperature cruise passengers for tomorrow. I lucked out and caught Jerry. He took the Camaro with short notice on a weekend day."

"I know. I didn't mean to sound like I needed an apology earlier, but apology accepted and thanks for the penance. Gus remembered we were waiting in the safe-room, so it was only an hour in the vault. Jean and Sonny of course relived every aspect of the event. Do you think they could have killed us all before you stopped them?"

"It depends," Nick said truthfully. "Their choice of car with altered exhaust sound would have probably triggered a look and put me on alert. Because of Jean's warning, I was able to get you armed and undercover with Quinn. That's golden because I could focus on the bad guys."

"You sure did that. I'm glad it was still early in the morning and the joggers weren't all over Ocean View Blvd. Would you have called Neil if some of the weekend runners or gawkers had witnessed it?"

"Maybe. I needed to find out how deep the shit pile was that left us in the target zone on my beach. I'm not giving up Otter's Point, even if I have to kill every 'banger and thug from the Monterey Peninsula to Salinas."

Rachel brushed her lips over Nick's shoulder before hugging him. "I'm glad the kids went out like lights tonight. The day long strategy session, morning combat, and afternoon knife throwing contests wore Jean out. Sonny was dragging too when I took him home. Quinn's been eating well so he's finally sleeping easily. You sure put our small space of alone time to work in a pleasurable cause."

"I enjoyed it as much as you."

"Want me to make you something to eat? I know you didn't have much chance to get a meal today."

"No. I don't feel like it." Nick rolled over on his back.

Rachel moved atop him, stroking his cheek. "Why, what's the matter. You should have worked up an appetite."

"I don't know what it is but I can't taste anything but tuna fish right now."

Rachel gasped, smacking Nick on the side of the head while he tried and failed to suppress amusement over his sexual innuendo. Rachel began chuckling after a moment. "Not funny!"

"You're laughing," Nick pointed out. "It's funny because you know it's not true."

"You'd tell me if I smelled, wouldn't you," Rachel asked, climbing over him and pinning Nick's shoulders. "I don't smell like fish... do I?"

"Hell no. It was a joke, Rach. You're wonderful in every way, baby. Don't start obsessing."

"Do women really... you know... smell like fish?"

"Some do."

"I'm not trying to be naïve but what do you think causes it?"

"Bacterial infection mostly, Rach. Don't get into the specifics. I repeat – I was kidding."

Rachel shook his shoulders. "Okay, but were you ever with a woman that... did smell?"

"Yep."

"Well... what did you do?"

Nick hesitated for a moment before pantomiming uneasiness at his being with a woman exhibiting possible bacterial problems. Then his voice went into robotic bass voice as if issuing orders in his brain. "Abort... abort! Danger... Will Robinson... danger. Abort!"

Nick's abort order solution amused Rachel to the point she rolled off of Nick and onto her back, with both hands over her mouth, stifling laughter while her feet drummed on the bed. Nick reversed positions, angling for something other than hygiene jokes. Rachel pushed on his chest, noting the reversal.

"I don't want you to go on the cruise today. I have a bad feeling."

"Have it in about twenty minutes."

* * *

"At least we deposited the fish food early." Gus steered The Lucky Lady toward coordinates which would bring them in sight of the Tempest but not suspiciously so. "You must have worked all night on the prep, Cleaner."

"Johnny and Muerto helped me." Cala watched Gus closely. He pointed out wind speed, direction, currents, and brought them into perspective with smoothing the boat's ride. Cala was training to be his backup ship's pilot in case they couldn't get Issac Leon flown in on a mission because of the time frame. "We finished in the early evening after Muerto dropped the Camaro off at Jerry's job for its rebirth."

Gus chuckled. "Jerry's a magician with the vehicles. I've seen a coupe he's worked over. Every newer one has to have a complete work over from another at the wrecking yard so it will have a completely different electronic ID. We've been sailing together for a while now. How do you like driving a boat?"

"I love everything we do," Cala said. "Training to do so many different deadly and exciting things makes every day a new adventure."

Gus sighed. "Yep. That's what happened to me when Nick brought me in on the cross-country jaunt to save Rachel and Jean. When we settled down in Pacific Grove after it was over, Nick was right all along, I couldn't let it go. I talked him into the hit in the sand we nearly died a half dozen times finishing with the whole mess following us back here. Muerto enjoys the missions and always prepares for the worst, but he turns feral when someone crosses him. Rachel hates the Salvatores. That's a given. Because of how he feels about Sonny, he won't ever harm them, but he'll make them wish they were never born. If it weren't for Sonny though, the Salvatores would have been fish food long ago."

77

"Yes. They are very lucky to have Sonny. He has already saved their lives numerous times. I doubt Rachel's joking when she claims they would adopt Sonny after making him an orphan."

"You have that right," Gus agreed.

"I am like you, Payaso. I am an adrenaline freak. Johnny knows and he likes having me with him all the time."

"You and Issac are very important to us. Both of you have faced certain death with us. Trust is a huge factor. Neither of you have shied away from anything that we've needed done."

Nick joined them on the bridge. "Johnny and I are done with cleanup. How long before we sail into sight of the bad guys?"

"I'm thinking about fifteen minutes," Gus answered. "Did you ever get a chance to talk with John?"

"I called him while delivering the Camaro. Lucas was with him. They loved the idea. They left the planning phase to me. I told them we'd be looking over the Tempest today. We already have the plans for the ship and the most likely spots to find Fernando. We're not taking prisoners unless something unexpected happens. It would be a bad idea to leave behind witnesses."

"Agreed," Gus said, as Johnny slipped next to Cala, kissing her neck.

"Muerto has a great idea for pirating the Tempest," Johnny said.

"I thought if John and I could get aboard where they take the Panga boats inside, we could secure the area for our boarding party. Once we have control of the lower hold, we could make an all or nothing assault on the bridge, especially if they aren't aware they have been boarded. The main part to scope out today is the Panga boat hold, where they can actually bring them inside the Tempest. Lucas said if we can get the Tempest in one piece, he'll put together a professional crew for transfer to 'Monster Island'."

"What about the docking facilities?"

"Already done, Payaso. They envisioned one day having a fleet there. Best of all, it's a deep water pier facility. We have got to go see this island," Nick stated. "I think we should all sail to the island. It has over twenty-nine acres off the coast of Washington. John told me they have a new compound built in addition to the already beautiful mansions that originally came with the island. Strobert bought a fortress of weapons and early warning radar gear. They already have a landing zone. I want to tour the place. That's for sure. It sounded like a great home for the Tempest."

"Washington's even colder than down here. Why didn't they get an island in the Caribbean? There's lot of them."

"Leave it to you, Payaso, to start whining about a place you don't own, or are even a part of yet," Johnny kidded him.

Nick smiled through Johnny's critique of Gus's complaint. "John can lock down the island tight. In addition, it's close to the United States coast and reachable with a strike force by helicopter if someone decides to invade it. California doesn't have any good private islands for sale. Alcatraz and Angel island are about the only ones around and they weren't for sale. Besides it's cold on them too."

"I was just curious," Gus said. "After hearing about the pirate action Harding's crew engaged in overseas, I considered asking Issac to look around near St. Lucia for a place where we could sail to and own. We have a fortune. We can buy in to 'Monster Island' and own our own Caribbean retreat too. There have been more than a few attacks by pirates in the Caribbean."

"We'll take it under consideration," Nick replied. "It wouldn't hurt to have Issac look into it for us. We'll need a place to revamp and reregister the Tempest though right after we capture her. As to your personal 'Pirates of the Caribbean' adventure, even John gets cover for pirate action from Denny Strobert. Keep track of current events. If anything forms there looking like a larger developing problem, and I could present the op to either Paul or Denny without making them look like fools, I'd do it."

"You know, Muerto, this pirate plotting by the sneaky Payaso makes me suspicious." Johnny peered into Gus's face in comical fashion with Gus finally giving him a push away. "Just as I envisioned. The happily married to the T-Rex, Payaso, loved his time alone on the 'Valkyrie'. He's looking for a mission to get away from his honey-bun."

"Shut-up, Kabong!" Gus kept his eyes on the sea ahead while his friends enjoyed the discomfiture Johnny's suspicion provoked.

"It would mean time away," Nick said. "I'm not allowed to go gallivanting around the globe, leaving Rachel on her own with Quinn and Jean. If we had an island sanctuary to operate out of while pursuing occasional pirate baiting excursions, I could talk Rach into a Caribbean Island stay, especially if we made it luxurious enough. Let's concentrate on the Tempest for now."

"How come Muerto gets a free pass when he admits to being under restraints by his wife?" Gus glanced accusingly over at Johnny, regretting it immediately as he could see his friend had been waiting for just that reaction to Nick's words. "Don't do it, Kabong!"

"Muerto never speaks as the great and all powerful alpha dog of marriage, complete with jewels of advice he never practices himself. Whipped dog is what you are, Payaso. You want pirate adventures so you can escape your collar for a while."

Gus's mouth trembled as he snorted lightly to keep from showing his amusement at Johnny's accurate perception. "That's… just mean. Get your range finders out. The Tempest should be in sight very soon. I'll do a wide angle curve around it when we come in sight. Get your com units in. Stay with me, Cleaner. I'll show you how to judge a curve at the farthest distance from a target we can get without looking as if we're on a surveillance mission."

"Great!" Cala kissed Johnny before he and Nick left the bridge. "I will be on the pirate mission with you, my love."

"Yes, you will."

Nick and Johnny left and Cala moved again into position. "They can see us too though, right, Gus?"

"Yep. Their radar can spot us on approach too. We're dressed out on the surface like any other fishing boat or cruisers out for a day on the ocean. It's not foolproof. If they get suspicious, I'm sure they have high tech range viewers the same as we do. There's nothing they can do about it. My Lucky Lady is listed as a fishing trawler and rent-a-boat. The boat registry is solid to a dummy corporation we have professional credentials for. It's not tied to either Nick or I. Fernando would have to find the Lady in port and stake us out to track her back to us."

"They could get worried and decide to make us disappear," Cala pointed out while tracking Gus's movements in relation to the digital panel. "You and Muerto made an Iranian patrol boat disappear."

"True, but if Fernando wants the Tempest to stay where it is, he wouldn't make any wild decisions concerning unknown civilians. You're right to worry though. Carone could do exactly that. Believe me when I say he wouldn't stand a chance. Nick has enough firepower on the Lady to take on a combat ship."

"Yes, but then we will lose the Tempest."

Gus shrugged. "The Tempest would be nice, but if it meant losing any of you, I'd blow the ship to hell. There she is."

Cala looked out on the left horizon. She grabbed the digital range finders Gus kept on the bridge, sighting in the Tempest. "Oh my... it's beautiful. Uh oh... they have guys on the top deck watching us. You were right about the radar, Gus."

"We'll only be able to make one pass so we don't tip them off. I'll take the Lady further out as if we're making a wide-"

"Gus! They've launched a boat out of the side hold. There are half a dozen men on board. What should we do?"

"I'll turn away. They don't know how fast the Lady is. I doubt if Nick wants company. It seems unusual for them to intercept us." Gus began turning the Lucky Lady to a course gradually parallel and then in the opposite direction.

Automatic weapons fire from the 'Panga' boat smashed into the water alongside the Lady. A second afterward, Cala saw the gunman's head explode. The man at the wheel tried to turn but his brain matter coated the inside of the small bridge in the next instant. The boat slowed into a circle with the dead man's arm draped over the steering control. She smiled as two more died in the same way. The two survivors dived down into the boat's interior. More rounds pierced the boat from bow to fantail, blowing pieces out of the hull until it began to tilt, bringing out the last two men alive diving for the ocean. They didn't make it, their bloody corpses hitting the water instead.

"I guess our surprise visit will not go undetected," Cala remarked.

"Muerto doesn't like to be hunted," Gus replied. "We'll head for home. Nick will get permission for satellite surveillance to see if they pull anchor and steam for parts unknown. He probably should have done that to begin with, but I think Muerto wanted to test them. If they're that touchy about any boat within sight, it makes a big difference in whatever plan we'll have to create for boarding."

"I wonder what Carone will think of what happened to his Panga boat crew." Cala continued watching, shifting her view to the Tempest once again as Gus held course. "Some men have come out on the top level with weapons."

"Muerto better not hurt my ocean liner."

"Huh?"

Gus smiled over at Cala, holding the Lucky Lady steady. "Wait for it."

The armed man on the top deck of the Tempest in the middle of his companions suddenly pitched backwards, his weapon falling over the railing. Cala enjoyed the aftermath of the dead center shot. The dead man's companions scrambled down into the ship's interior.

"I think the ship's fine, but it will need a cleaning," Cala observed.

* * *

Nick, with Johnny trailing, entered the Lucky Lady's wheel house, his silenced M107 .50 caliber sniper rifle still in his hands. "We better go home, Gus. Our experiment didn't end well but at least we know our planned assault needs a far more subtle approach than we hoped."

"You could have waited until the Panga boat reached us," Gus replied. "Maybe they were out here to issue threats to stay away from the area."

"Maybe they were census takers for the Neptune Society. Carone already has too much information. He knows the Lucky Lady and registration which we figured on. In one scenario, we could have done a wide sweep and anchored for a while as if we were enjoying the day on the ocean. An immediate challenge like today's action means they have far reaching detection on board and someone watching at all times. They'll either move location which we'll track, or hunker down and go nuts trying to perceive what the hell happened today."

"You sure turned their water off, Muerto," Gus replied. "As you say, we have facts now that were not in evidence."

"At least we have the Lady's registration cloaked to a point where Carone will have to send minions into town once he finds out where the Lady is ported. That will tell us more too. We have surveillance coverage all over our docking area. Carone's already after my ass so fooling around with him today won't mean much in the way of added danger if he does link us to the Lady. Besides, I feel better now. If the prick would have shown his face anywhere on deck, we could have assaulted the Tempest at our leisure, and tracked it while the crew came to grips with their headless leader."

"I watched for Carone, Muerto," Cala said. "He did not even peek out above deck."

"Johnny was spotting for me. He didn't see any sign of Fernando either. Paul knows I have to get Carone. He's already supported my request for full on satellite surveillance we can tap into. If the Tempest moves, I want to know where. If they land a helicopter on the yacht, I want to know where it goes when it leaves. I'll call John when we get home after having a sip on my deck in honor of the poor lost souls in today's boating accident."

Nick's remark provoked instant hilarity as Gus increased speed for home.

Chapter Four

Tempest Collaboration

"I want you, Harding!"

The shout from the entrance drew the attention from my party crowd, but only barely. When I get the Monster Squad together for a dinner date, the only matter even a little entertaining would be a frontal assault on The Warehouse. The families enjoyed an earlier dinner and an extended enjoyable time of jokes, sporting talk, and no mention of Monster business. Claude Chardin and his wife seemed to love every moment with our very strange group of deadly killers, and our earlier meeting hour before dinner proved informative. I knew a handful of the most dangerous people alive stood near me at the end of the bar away from the entrance. I had two stretch limos bring us all here. One took our families home after the more jovial part of the night. We Monsters sipped drinks together now: Lucas, Casey, Denny, Laredo, Clint, Lynn, Tommy, Jess, Dev, Jafar, Samira and Lynn's minions – Silvio Ruelas, Gus Denova, and Quays Tannous. Our guests, Alexi Fiialkov and Claude Chardin, listened to everything in play concerning Nick's new information on Saran Al-Kadi's compound at Pilot Hill.

The Warehouse, an Oakland PD cop bar, was our informal and sometimes formal hangout. Because I became predictable in also meeting some famous names in the UFC fight circuit, we kept getting interrupted at annoying times like these. Everyone had been waiting for me to finish my description of the black op we'd have to do on Al-Kadi's compound, and a new wrinkle Nick introduced about confiscating the place. I could tell Claude knew the names I mentioned but waited until I finished to add his knowledge of the subject. There were a few police officers working the gaming section while sipping beers on the house at Alexi's treat. We had reserved the bar but no police officer was turned away, with or without family. My Monsters chuckled and snorted in amusement at the people interrupting our evening. Our wonderful waitress Marla began walking over to confront them but Alexi took her arm, shaking his head.

"It's about time the entertainment arrived, Cheese." Lynn smiled at her deadly mate, Clint. She lived for my annoying interruptions.

"Damn... what is this a 'Black Lives Matters' protest," Tommy muttered for our group to hear. "Did you shoot one of my people in public, DL?"

That of course provoked hilarity which did nothing for calming our visitors' attitudes. Jess and Dev bumped fists with Tommy.

"Good one, T," Jess said. He turned to me with massive black hands on hips. "What have you done, DL?"

Lucas Blake waved my personal jokesters off. "Don't start that 'Black Lives Matter' shit in front of me. I can't even read the news without getting violent images of a rooftop, my sniper rifle, and the next BLM human roadblock in my sights."

"Lucas! I'm surprised at you - a black man, not wanting to embrace those race baiting thugs claiming to speak for all us po' black folks," Devon said in fake outrage.

Then it was on. Lucas went for Dev with Casey conveniently holding Lucas back. Jess grabbed Dev in the same hold me back posture as Lucas and Dev danced around, motioning at each other in 'come on and get some' type gestures. It was very funny and their playacting distracted our annoying visitors so much they simply stood at the entrance watching. They pulled all the clichés out for their fake verbal duel.

86

"You ain't black. You white in your head," Dev said.

"I'm bad, black, and got a job so I don't have time to go out pissing off other blue collar working stiffs trying to make a living!"

"Uncle Tom! You nothin' but a 'House Negro' eatin' with Jim Crow!" Dev stabbed an accusing finger at Lucas.

"Listen, Topsy. Get out of my face before I show you what happens when Snow Whites need Marine attitude adjustments!"

That was too much for Dev. I think the 'Topsy' tag got him. His infectious laughter broke Lucas out of his role, and soon he was braying with Dev and the rest of us. When I saw the group at the door begin moving toward us, I straightened to move forward and meet them with my hands out in a placating posture. We had real business. The leader of half a dozen relatively well dressed black men in their twenties all in dark suits, bowties, and sun glasses stood in a triangle as if they were swallows flying home for the winter to Capistrano.

"I'm John Harding," I told the leader, who was a bit larger than me in every way.

"We did not appreciate that minstrel show your houseboys put on for our amusement."

Uh oh. I spun only just in time to catch a flying Lucas with murder in his eyes and on his brain. Tommy, Jess and Dev joined me. "Easy Gunny. These aren't BLM's. Let me find out what they are."

Lucas pointed at the leader, his features a sudden mask of dead calm. "You call me houseboy or minstrel again, Farrakhan's turd, and I'll snap my fingers like this."

Lucas snapped his fingers.

The leader grinned in the usual condescending manner most of us were familiar with when looked on as ignorant jerks by the more enlightened amongst us. "What happens then, old man?"

In the next instant Lynn materialized at his side as if beamed there with razor sharp knife at his throat. "When Pappy snaps his fingers again, I slice your throat, and we kill everyone you walked in with. What we joke around about with each other in a private party has nothing to do with you, ass-wipe. Speak every word from now on as if your life depends on the content because it does. Say you understand."

The man looked at death. Luckily, he recognized it. I didn't plan on any more interventions. I was hoping Alexi was placating our Oakland PD friends in the gaming section. His companions I could tell were less than enthused with the situation. "I…I understand."

Lynn patted his face. "Good. Don't forget. My reminders won't go well for you."

I took a deep breath. "Okay then. You wanted to see me. How may I help you?"

"I am Mohammed Knowly of the Nation of Islam. Your group of-"

"Careful!" I could see the end of life smile on Lynn's face. Lucas was straining to hold onto control at my side. "You apparently didn't understand Lynn's warning clearly enough. Stick to the point you came here to make. I thought you guys all wear red bowties."

"Never mind our dress, Harding. Your group has been terrorizing the Muslim community. We've been informed of your intervention to take Amara Nejem from her rightful family, and you have a woman preaching hatred against Islam in public: Samira Kensington."

"Amara is part of our family now. She's going to college, learning skills, and is a personal assistant on movies with Director Dostiene. Amara couldn't be happier. As for Samira, she's here now and can speak for herself."

Sam slipped forward through the grinning Monsters with a smile and Jafar at her side. He wasn't smiling. "I'm Samira. If you mean that I speak of Islam's subjugation of women, you are correct. Islam needs reformation. I do not consider myself a Muslim any longer, and your sect believes in the extermination of white people. Even true Muslims don't go that far... yet. I have looked into the hatred long enough. I only speak now when asked, and I am honest in my admission. Women are not chattel to be abused. I have a daughter now, and I will kill anyone who tries to treat her as they do other women under Sharia Law. Why are you self-important toads really here? Amara Nejem and I are not slaves. We are free, happy women."

"There you have it, Mr. Knowly," I said, when Samira's introduction caused momentary silence. "Did we cover everything? This is a free country. If you and your friends don't like it, maybe you'd better move to a country with Islam's brand of Sharia Law slavery, if they'll have you."

"You represent the Oaktown Cartel. I've come to challenge you."

When the laughter died down I took another deep breath. "I don't think you understand the rules of the Oaktown challenge, Mohammed. If I win, Oaktown absorbs your group. I can't speak for the others but I don't want your Nation of Islam toadies. As I understand it, you don't sell drugs, or do anything else against the law. We only stop gangs terrorizing communities. You're free to live any way you wish on your own, including hating anyone who doesn't match your skin color or beliefs. As long as you don't act on that hatred, we won't ever have a problem."

"If I beat you in the cage, you will hand over Amara Nejem, and stop Samira Kensington from blaspheming Islam. If you win, we will forfeit twenty-five thousand dollars."

"Okay… now you're pissing me off. I don't own Amara. My associate Lynn will slice you into little pieces if you touch Amara. If you ever threaten Samira Kensington or Amara, we will erase you and your crew from the face of the earth without a trace. That said, why in hell would I need to fight you? In addition, even the Muslim hate groups like 'The Muslims of the Americas' don't recognize the Nation of Islam. They're a cult to us, and they think of the NOI as a sub-cult. I don't see them reaching out to you bunch. What do you want and why should I care?"

My dismissal of his objective ticked him off.

"So, you are afraid to face me!"

"You better cool that talk, brother," Dev told him, trying to ease a public confrontation from ending in a killing. "John explained we're not in the slave trade and we protect our own. Even if he agreed to fight you in the cage and lost, you wouldn't get Amara or silence Samira. We have no beef with the NOI community. Why… oh… I get it."

Dev turned to us, his confused companions. "It's the Nejem family. We hit them hard without a follow-up. They must have decided to get the NOI in on the situation. Talk about snakes out of different pits."

"The Nejem family requested our help in rectifying this outrageous situation. Amara was promised in marriage to a true believer. It is her duty to honor that contract," Knowly said.

"Are you stupid?" Tommy and I had faced off with NOI members before. They're a bit like the black Klan, but instead of simple separatism as the Klan practices, the NOI want the white race to disappear. Usually, they stay inside their own community with the race hatred stuff. "Dev just explained you're not getting

Amara. John and I have worked together for years in Oakland. We've seen your communities taking care of their own. Live and let live. Back out of here and forget the money the Nejem family promised you. Yeah... I'm certain there's a payoff for this dumb move, but you can't spend it if you're dead."

"Besides, Betty," Lynn decided to throw gasoline on the cooling flames, "you couldn't beat the Dark Lord in a cage-fight with a baseball bat, pussy. Hey... that's an idea. Why don't-"

"Don't say it, psycho!" Tommy's intuitive hunch as to where Lynn was going with her insult generated amusement. He turned to Knowly, who was seething under Lynn's verbal smackdown. "I'll tell you what, John will fight you straight-up for twenty-five thousand if you want to get your ass kicked that badly, but you won't be getting anything else."

"Or... if you're smart," Jess added, "you'll walk the hell out of here. Grab your prayer rugs for getting down on hands and knees and thank Allah you're still alive."

"What'll it be, Huckleberry," Tommy asked. "We have real business to attend to."

"How much did the Nejem family offer you, by the way?" I wanted to know for future reference.

I could tell the way his features went blank for a moment he never thought we'd question his motive, but Tommy knows nearly everything has a money origin. I wanted a figure to determine if we needed to erase the Nejem family or not.

"Fifty-thousand, brother," Jafar stated. He had been working his iPad. He has clearance to use any assets the FBI or CIA offer. Hacking into financial institutions isn't one of them but Jafar knows his way around.

"How… you cannot access our financial records without a warrant!" Knowly neared the sanity demarcation line. "I will report this!"

"No you won't. Put up or shut up," Tommy demanded.

"I will beat you to death in the cage," Knowly stated, pointing at me. "Then, I will work with the Nejem family to destroy your organization of criminals."

Tommy sighed. "Tomorrow at nine in the evening. Do you know where we hold the cage fights?"

"I know it. You will pay for these blasphemies tomorrow night, Harding." Knowly backed his crew out the door.

"If those idiots weren't tied into the Islamic death cult and racist bullshit, the community ideals they have of hard work, two parent families, and belief in God could turn around any inner city problem in existence," Lucas said. "Knowly called me a houseboy. I want you to beat him until he cries for his Mamma, Recon."

"I'll make a note. Let's get a drink. I need the brothers to wash down this episode of stupid people walking." I led the way back to our place at the bar, waving the all clear sign to the three Oakland PD officers. They waved back and returned to their dart game. Marla had my drinks ready. I drained my Beam brother and half of brother Bud. "Oh my… that's much better."

"A baseball bat, Psycho? Really?" Tommy wasn't letting Lynn's adrenaline rush negotiation alone without an accounting.

"Oh calm down, Snow White Sands." Lynn gave him the wave off. "We need to start charging a penalty for the number of times these posers claim they're going to beat Cheese to death in the cage. I need to direct an award winning documentary of the fight tomorrow night with the title 'Before Bragging About Beating John Harding To Death In The Cage, Watch This'. You'll need to bloody him, Cheese. Tommy let you out of poke drills this weekend. You need the work in the cage".

"Ah… I think there may be a little more to this." Jafar held his tablet for us to see. "Knowly is a Northern California MMA Heavyweight Champion – twenty-three wins, no losses. He fights under the name Black Jihadi. Alexi would know more than I do about it, but I think Knowly's angling to get into the UFC. So far, all he has is a few local TV appearances. It may be how the Nejem family interested him in making this about Amara and Samira."

"Jafar's right," Alexi agreed. "If Knowly beats John handily in a made for YouTube video, he could catapult into the upper levels of UFC with one appearance. Do you still wish to do it, John?"

"Sure. This at least takes the mystery out of Knowly's annoying visit."

"I will arrange all the specifics for tomorrow night. I'll call Earl and 'Rique for security. Do you wish to bar the politicos?"

"Nope. I know the betting's good with them in the house. We'll have tight security, right Gus?"

"Yes. I will call in the Asian Crips to work the outside area," Gus Denova said. As acting Godfather of the Oaktown Cartel, our absorbed gangs did our bidding.

"You can bill it as Hard Case versus Black Jihadi the MMA Northern California Champion too," Tommy added. "You have other business too with Nick's newly found nest between us and Tahoe."

"It's good business for us and the country. If we hit the compound in a precise killing manner, Nick has it in mind for us to confiscate it. I've seen the pictures. The surrounding acreage looks like a mountain paradise. The compound has hot tubs, huge rooms, fireplaces, and only one way in, or out, by road. Muerto's thinking helicopter pads, and possibly an airstrip. It would mean being able to launch at least a helicopter strike without anyone knowing where it originated."

"I want in on the assault. A luxury mountain retreat would be a terrific escape for a few days, especially if we could fly there," Lynn said, with everyone else echoing her sentiments.

"I'll fly the mission to get a piece of that," Laredo said. "Traffic into the mountains toward Tahoe is the pits in the winter. If it's not blizzard type weather, either me, John, or Jafar could fly there. We could have a Monster Christmas in the snow at our retreat."

"Agreed," Lucas said. "This op took the bad taste of Knowly away. You must be thinking stealth insertion on the outskirts of the compounds acreage."

"Exactly," I replied. "There's a bunch on the grounds right now, including this Saran Al-Kadi. Can you get us satellite surveillance 24/7, Denny? It's vital to know their routes around the compound in case they have anything booby-trapped."

"I'll get it started tomorrow morning," Denny agreed. "There could be a treasury of info in a place like that. You're not thinking of using an EMP bomb on it, are you, Cheese."

Silence, crickets, clinking of glasses in the background. I shrugged as amusement set in at the Spawn of Satan reading my mind. "Yep. That was exactly what I had planned. I figured on a blackout when we reached assault positions with Agent Tonto. Between our super-dog and night-vision gear we could practically walk in and shoot everyone in the head."

"Could you at least consider an info gathering mission? I'll fly with Laredo and Jafar. With Nick's crew and Tommy, Jess, and Dev, we can have all the backup we need, including land vehicles on the main road waiting in reserve."

"We don't want to rebuild the place after the assault, Spawn," Casey said. "The good part of John's assault is possibly holding the mayhem and destruction to a minimum. Uh oh... I just thought of a drawback to the EMP bomb. I'll bet a great place like that has everything wired on computer controls, with apps for turning on lights, hot tubs, music, and even fireplaces. Maybe we should take a chance on Denny's more circumspect plan of attack. We'll send the minions in to take the first hit."

"That's just mean, Case," Sylvio complained.

"He's only kidding, right Case?" Quays' brow furrowed when Casey grinned instead of answering. "This... after we went shoulder to shoulder with you into Chabahar, waiting for Iranian jets to turn us into dust particles."

"Calm down, my fellow minions," Gus Denova soothed. "The Monster Squad has an assault crew and we aren't it. I'd step up and take the first hit though to have a chance at the mountain retreat vacations. We're only a short jump to that small air field at Lake Tahoe too. We could cruise there for a night at the casinos."

"I like your thinking, Gus," I told him. "Let's wait for a couple days of satellite surveillance before we decide. It may be Al-Kadi's crew are complacent in their hideaway. Nick told me Al-Kadi won't know how we accessed the location. We'll have to be ready for anything though. Paul contacted you and confirmed the kill mission, didn't he, Denny?"

"Yes. It doesn't mean we can't make room for prisoners. I'll take care of them. It's a black op though on USA soil. We're contractors with the CIA. It wouldn't take much of an investigation to trace our roots. We've been lucky so far with the threats we've handled on US soil. The nitwits in DC know how close we came to an atomic bomb hitting China Basin on board Alexi's tanker. I know how stupid the rules of engagement are. Paul Gilbrech is the best CIA Director I've ever worked with. He got those Iranian jets splashed before they wiped the Monster Squad and Unholy Trio out after Chabahar. Paul wants this Al-Kadi and the rest of his Isis shitheads removed from this dimension. He's trying to rig us a silent approval of operation where we can move as a contracted strike force with congressional backing."

"All the more reason this expansion of strike bases we can launch from makes sense," I added. "If we could get an exception made for our operations on US soil, it would be much less difficult to move on a target. I saw your facial expression when Saran Al-Kadi was mentioned during our discussion before dinner, Claude. I was hoping you knew him."

Chardin nodded. "I didn't say anything then because we were meeting with your whole team now. I needed to think through the complications that may arise for me. Al-Kadi tried to have me killed in France. I stopped taking contracts from the Saudis. Whether rogue elements of the government initiate these branches of Islamic murderers or the plague is systemic, the fact is they fund nearly everything from behind a curtain of payoffs to political figures all over the world. As I've explained previously, that 'Arab Spring' bullshit was the last straw for me. I can tell you this much, once Al-Kadi knows of your team, he will stop at nothing to destroy you and your families. That is why I needed time to decide. I am in with you on this. I see you are committed to fighting these bastards by any means available."

"We protect our own too, Claude," Denny said. "I have an idea for a way in without blowing the place apart. It carries some danger of course. If you're interested, I'll call Nick and see if he likes the idea."

"I do not care about the danger part. I only care about protecting my family once Al-Kadi knows I am involved. What is it you would have me do?"

"You know of Nick McCarty's elevation in 'Dark Web' lore to the number one assassin in the world since his killing of Felix Moreau. It would be a bold move if you and Nick arrived at

Al-Kadi's compound at the front door. If you two could get inside, I believe the distraction would be enough to enable the rest of our assault team to enter with a minimum of destruction."

Wow. Thinking it over silently, Denny's idea seemed not only plausible, but perfectly suited for the op if Al-Kadi's curiosity could be stirred by the arrival of two world class assassins. I kept my mouth shut because Claude needed to make up his own mind. I could tell from the faces around me, I wasn't the only one who liked the idea.

"What you describe would be very bold," Claude acknowledged. "If Nick will join me in this, I will do it. You do know once Al-Kadi knows it is me on his doorstep, he may tell his men to open fire."

"If Dead Boy's with you, he'll shoot them in the head before they can aim," Clint said. "We'll be in position as a strike force to move quickly if something goes wrong. Lucas will have a sniper nest picked out with full view of the main house front. You have to be careful with Dead Boy though. He'll sneak a grenade in and our vacation retreat will be a pile of rubble."

Clint's warning provoked much amusement.

I think the Nick and Claude approach fits. "Denny's plan works for me as well. If we can get Nick and Claude inside before the men frisk them, they can hold the entrance until we double time inside. Then it may get wild. I'd like to gas them through their ventilation system like we did the mobsters that time in Tahoe, but if Al-Kadi does have guards, it would be nearly impossible to do it without discovery. Then we'd be back where we started with a shootout at the 'Okay Corral'."

"We'll stream the satellite footage and make a final decision after reviewing what we get," Denny said. "Now, that aside, why the hell do you need to fight Knowly tomorrow night?"

"We have to keep the Nejem family and their plots in our sight," I replied. "Knowly saw a chance to snag some money and get a shot at making a splash in the UFC. The Nejem family turning over fifty grand for him to put a whoopin' on me goes beyond suspicious. I wonder if a few of their representatives will show at fight time."

"This is my fault," Denny admitted. "If I hadn't turned Daddy Nejem and his crew over to the police after he answered my questions, this wouldn't have happened. I thought with the video and audio evidence he wanted to kill his own daughter he'd be in lockup for at least a year."

"Don't worry about Amara," Clint said. "Lynn and I will make sure she's safe. We'll take her to the classes she has over at the college. Maybe we'll spot some suspicious guys paying too much attention to her. The fight will be a key place to start looking tomorrow. I wonder if Papa Nejem is stupid enough to attend the fight. After what Lucas did to him, he'd piss his pants if he saw Lucas. I'll take sniping duties if you want to attend the fight inside, Lucas."

"Hell yeah! Thanks Clint. I'd love to see that woman beater again. This time he goes on a cruise. Amara doesn't have to know. Better yet, Jafar can practice his helicopter skills. He can fly us way the hell out over the ocean so I can drop Daddy into the drink alive."

Lynn in particular enjoyed Lucas's final solution for Mohammed Nejem, Amara's Father. "I wonder what he thought would be accomplished by this fight. He knows John won't be the only one he has to contend with. His demands for a challenge smack of stupidity so deep as to be laughable. I'm thinking there must be more to this – a diversion maybe."

"Case? You take sniping duties," Clint said. "Lynn's right. Nejem would know we'd all be at the fight in anticipation. I'll stay at the house with Dannie, Amara, and Clint Jr. Lynn needs to be at the fight. Achmed? I want video of Lynn stirring the Farrakhan dupes into a rage."

"Will do," Jafar agreed.

"I'll handle the sniping," Casey added. "I should have been spelling Lucas in the nest anyway. Do you want the minions to back you at the house, Clint?"

"Did you just insult me, Case?"

Hilarity ensued.

* * *

Oh yeah! I smelled the perfume of desperation, excitement, and fear. When politicos and rich celebrity types mix with gamblers, street goons, and mobsters, they create an ambrosia of anticipation which permeates the cage battleground. UFC fights in the spotlight of giant video screens, howling thousands, and filtered air conditioning acted as a tame entertaining background; but this sheet-metal warehouse surrounding still awakened my origins with a splash of violence unattainable anywhere else. I was home.

Our entry into the fight night building went without incident. Although a large crowd filled the upgraded cage facility, security from Earl and 'Rique, along with Alexi's force, provided enough presence to keep interactions at a quiet drone of gambling exchanges and fight talk. Jack Korlos, Alexi's right hand man now, led my corner crew to the cage with my Monsters in the background, assessing the crowd. Out of nowhere, a phalanx of bow-tied dupes blocked our way to the cage with some weirdo in front, featuring some inner rage he must have been whipping into life on the sidelines. He spiked a fist at me, I imagine as a gesture. Unfortunately for him, Jess planted the idiot with a right that probably broke his jaw.

Jack Korlos stepped out right away. "Don't know what you assholes have in mind, but it won't work. Get out of the way or the crew with John Harding will make this your last night on earth."

Devon Constantine waited three seconds before wading into the small mob, throwing posers to the side as if they were bowling pins with forearm blows and elbows to maim and kill. "Back the fuck off. We're the non-lethal warning. The people following take lives. What the hell are you posers doing blocking our way?"

"We...we're showing solidarity with Reverend Knowly," one of the posers said, holding his arm where one of Dev's elbows probably fractured a bone. "Allahu Akbar! We-"

Lucas streaked forward and smashed the speaker's face in, propelling him to his back out cold. "Anyone else with a catchphrase best keep it to themselves. When I hear that particular one I get violent. Get the hell out of the way pussies!"

That was the end of an entertaining distraction. The small mob, already in fearful disarray, moved back with my Monsters searching visually for hands reaching, or out of sight. Lynn in particular wanted to arrange some pre-fight entertainment. Any Knowly goon who didn't move back far enough in Lynn's perspective received a bitch slap to increase the spacing. One recipient reached to grab her blouse. She cut him in a downward slash nearly impossible to follow. He gripped his wrist in horror, fleeing the building. I didn't get involved. My Monsters lived for this stuff. In a moment more I stepped into the cage with my corner crew, anticipation building with every step. I smiled across at my opponent, who had been following my progress from the entrance. Knowly stupidly thought the usual intimidation tactics would chill my confederates. He knew better now. Knowly smashed his gloved hands together.

Korlos checked his watch a few moments later. He signaled us to the cage center. Knowly and I waited for Jack's usual pat-down for unseen weapons or chemicals on gloves. Jack had added on his own an inspection for chemicals after Marko Hristov, The Assassin, tried to blind me in the cage. I killed him, but Jack never forgot the added check now. Knowly endured the inspection without looking away from my face. I smiled. I never did get into the gnarly stares of death. Time enough for intimidation when the blows start landing. Jack recited his pre-fight warnings and rules.

"That's it, gentlemen. I expect you two will at some point put me in a position to do a final calling of the fight. Don't force me to use my sap. No one dies in the cage tonight. Am I clear, John?"

"Yeah, Jack." I tried to show some outrage at being singled out for my prior transgressions but I simply shrugged in compliance. Knowly apparently didn't know about that part of my cage past. His features showed it.

Jack motioned us back with the crowd roar growing for the fight to begin. "Nod, if you're ready, gentlemen."

We indicated readiness. Jack signaled us to start. Knowly was no dummy. He didn't know me other than my YouTube videos. Those obviously made him reluctant to rush in on attack. No such hindrance slowed my opening. I ran straight at him, right arm cocked for a haymaker. Knowly jutted into a side pose to counter my attack. I dropped at the last second to the mat, lashing a pile driver roundhouse kick to my favorite target at the back of his forward knee. Oh my, did that blow change the fight vista. Knowly screamed out in pain, hitting the mat on his back. I scrambled to full mount and pounded him with forearm blows, body shots, and general mayhem until Tommy called out time from my corner. I rolled away to my feet. This was, after all, a training session. I don't give a crap about Knowly's MMA Heavyweight Championship Belt. I'm a 'show me' type of guy. Violence, pain, and brutality define me. I don't pretend to be something I'm not.

My complete wipeout of Knowly silenced the crowd. In the dead still of the cage, Knowly writhed from side to side before realizing I was waiting for him on my feet. Jack didn't like it.

"Damn it, kid," Jack whispered at me from where he stood next to me. "What the hell do you have going here... a training exercise again?"

I held my gloved hands in formal defensive position. "I'm surviving, Jack. Tommy's calling the shots. Complain to him."

Jack stifled his amusement. "Okay... I got it."

Knowly finally figured out he needed to get up or pretend he was out cold. He stood, to his credit. With hands held in stolid defensive posture, he moved towards me, jutting out respectable jabs, kicks, and combinations. I measured his responses and power, countering with form. My counterpunches utilized combinations and speed. I took nothing for granted. Knowly was big enough to take my head off if I got cocky. Knowly began accumulating a bit of confidence so I blasted a left hook counter to his overhand right that I misjudged and nearly ended the fight. He stumbled quickly backward against the cage, his face a mask of pain. The round ended with me following him there with left jabs and short rights.

It's dark beyond the well-lighted cage and front seat area. I didn't bother wasting my time looking for Nejem family members. I knew my Monsters would be taking a Nejem family census during the fight. I sat down in my corner while Dev and Jess applied wet towels and salve. Jafar gave me a drink and Tommy gave me directions for the next round. Lucas, I knew had a seat behind my corner. I could hear him yelling 'Recon'.

"I see you're not playing with this guy," Tommy said. "Stay covered. He's had a bunch of knockouts to his record. Can you take him down for some hold work?"

"Sure, but a guy that big will have to go down like he did in the first round. I'll have to buckle him, T. If I miss the takedown, he could smash me with an elbow to the top of my head. He felt the left hook. I'll nail his ribcage with another and take him down."

"Good plan, DL. I see Jack's not happy."

"We'll be hearing it from the crowd too pretty soon. Too bad. We didn't ask for this. Besides, he insulted Lucas. If I don't get payback, Lucas will make my life miserable."

"Take your time," Dev said. "Screw the crowd. I liked your work last round. He's fast and you set him up for that left hook perfectly. A little harder and Jess would have been nagging me to give him 'Last Rites'."

"Don't make him see SpongeBob, DL," Jess added as I stood. "That's gross."

"There are Nejems in the audience, brother," Jafar said. "They are not happy. Daddy Nejem's one of them. Lucas walked by him and spilled a beer on his head. It was very funny. A slight altercation followed. Two more Nejems were knocked out by Casey and Lucas when Daddy's four companions wanted to rumble. They sat back down."

"I'll bet. See you guys in a few." I waited for Jack to signal us to start. Knowly looked a bit too confident for a guy who just got his ass kicked. If not for the fact that Jack Korlos was the referee, I'd suspect the fix was in.

Jack started us. I went to work even more carefully. I pounded Knowly's arms with blacksmith type precision and patience. He threw the right. I nailed him with the left to the ribcage again. This time, it dropped him to his knees. I measured him and shot a knife-hand strike to his left temple. It spilled him sideways, nearly unconscious. The crowd howled for blood. I worked as Tommy directed. Knowly didn't know yet I was playing with him. He struggled gamely, trying to glance upward while writhing inside the myriad submission holds I locked on him, but then released. It bugged me a bit, wondering what the hell he kept searching for. I-"

"Roll, Cheese!"

I reacted instantly to Lynn's scream at the cage. I heard something hit the mat where I had been a split-second before. I held a hand over my eyes to shield the lighting as I looked upward in time to see a dark figure in the rigging above. A shot sounded. The dark figure in the rigging pitched out of his nest silently to the floor below. I crab crawled to the spot I heard hit. I plucked a tiny dart from the mat while Knowly tried to get to his feet, still groggy from the naked choke I practiced on him before the dart incident. I took the dart to the cage where Tommy took it from me.

"Be right back," I told him. I scrambled around between Knowly and his crew as he regained his feet. I saw Gus Denova, Casey, and Lynn move on the corner crew.

"Hey, Betty," Lynn called to him from his corner. Casey covered the crew. "Best if you kneel and say your prayers, pussy. Lucas told me to tell you not to worry about any more payback. He's pissed though because Nightshot here nailed the prick in the dark right between the eyes. Denny and Lucas have the Nejems."

I heard Casey chuckle in the dead silence after his killing of the dart shooter. No one in the crowd moved. I smiled at Knowly with a hand wave acknowledgement to Lynn. Knowly searched for escape no longer available. Alexi stood near Tommy on my side of the cage, motioning Jack away. "It looks like it's just you and me, Mohammed. Tell me how you came to this dirty business and I kick your ass but let you live. Dummy up, and I kill you right here in the cage."

What made Knowly an MMA Champion surfaced in a mean faced determined look. "The fifty grand was to make sure we had a shot at ending you, Harding. The Nejem's didn't want you beat. They wanted you dead. I plan to complete the contract no matter what."

I heard Lynn's cackle behind me. "Take my advice, Betty. Get on your knees and pray. Cheese has a soft spot for Christians."

"I ain't no fuckin' Christian! Allahu Akbar!" He charged.

I leaped to land a flying knee square on his charging face, smashing it to pulp. He dropped as if hit by a sledge hammer in the side of the head, spurting blood from his ruined face. I could see he could still suck wind at the mouth so I turned him to his side. I motioned at Jack to call the fight. He did, while beckoning to the medical team Alexi employed now on a regular basis. They entered the cage from my corner with collapsible stretcher/gurney. While they began triage on Knowly, I walked over to where Lynn and Casey entertained the Knowly crew of bow-tied idiots.

"Thanks, Nightshot. Good call, Lynn."

"We knew something was up," Lynn said. "We watched the Nejem bunch like hawks. They started glancing into the rigging above between rounds. So did we. What do want to do with these other pussies?"

"I think I'll let Denny have them. I don't know what we could get out of them. We have no choice with the Nejems."

"Agreed. See you outside. Lucas, Denny, Sylvio, and Quays have the Nejems. C'mon, Nightshot, let's get these clucks ready for transport while Earl and 'Rique are busy mooning over your handy-work."

"On your knees with fingers locked behind your heads, boys," Casey ordered. "Drop now or I shoot you all in the head. You've heard of James Bond, double zero designation with license to kill, right? I'm double ought Nightshot. I have the same license in reality. Don't test me."

Knowly's crew dropped. He grinned at me. "We're even again, brother, from the ocean save."

"You know you weren't on the pad for that, brother. We're hitting The Warehouse after this mess is over."

"Amen to that."

* * *

We arrived at The Warehouse in style after shipping the bowties, dart, dart-gun, and dart shooter with the police. The minions escorted the Nejems to Pain Central for a debriefing on Sunday. We picked them up at Pain Central in the limo with Jafar driving after the deposit in our holding cells. The Warehouse was Saturday night busy, so we snuggled into our corner at the very end of the bar with Marla already serving shots, beers, and wine for Lynn and Samira. It was only after jovially clinking glasses to my survival that I noticed the hulking figure at a table near us with bowler hat and two companions dressed in dark suits and ties. He grinned at me. It was Rock Costigan, the UFC Heavyweight Champion, in my damn bar once again. Lynn of course noticed. She notices everything.

"Well damn, Cheese," Lynn whispered to me with Clint chuckling at her side. "Aren't you just a font of entertainment tonight? I didn't get to kill anything at the fight. Let me slice these three bozos into bite-sized bits for deposit later."

It dawned on me how in sync with her I felt. This Rock Costigan was beginning to annoy me. Lynn noticed. She gripped my arm with fervent passion.

"Oh Cheese... please... let me do 'em. Clint will help me clean up afterward. He does anything I say since he made me clean a milk spill off the kitchen floor this morning."

After raucous enjoyment of Lynn's ownage of Clint, I shook my head. "I'll handle this, but not until I throw down one more Beam brother."

My telepathic barkeep, Marla, had already refilled my Beam brother. "Bless you, sister of The Warehouse sanctuary."

She laughed, waving and returning to where Alexi nursed a beer.

I sipped my Beam half down, drinking in the ambiance of the bar, my Beam brother, and the Monster family around me. Then a voice pierced my brain, obliterating the moment.

"Do you have to get drunk to talk with me, Harding?"

Even Lynn choked on her wine at that remark. Rock's blurting stupidity silenced our merriment. I noted it drew tenseness amongst the Oakland PD patrons near enough to hear his words too. I turned while standing away from my barstool to face his table. Maybe it was the Bud and Beam brothers, the earlier escape from death, or the Monster rising. Who knows? All I knew at the moment was the bullseye I'd had on me all day annoyed the hell out of me. I planned to share.

"I've fought tonight. I've had a couple of shots and beers. I don't need drink or anything else to kick the living shit out of you, poser! If you want me, we don't need no Las Vegas meeting place. I'll take your life right outside this bar, Betty. Get on your fucking feet and let's do this right now!"

One of his behemoths who thought he had a card to play jutted in front of me as I moved to Rock's table. Oh baby. I planted him in between the tables with a left uppercut that nearly severed his head from his shoulders. You could hear a pin drop in the place other than the attractive music playing in the background. I leaned on Rock's table with both hands.

"Repeat the insult, Rock. If you do, or don't take my challenge, I'll drag your ass outside where I can end you for all time."

Tommy rocketed in, annoyingly for me in that moment. "Easy, DL. Don't do this here. Let's take this down a few octaves. C'mon, John. We know this game. Let me handle this."

I stared at my brother for a long moment while straightening away from the table. I nodded. "Okay, T."

I turned to Rock with blood in my eye and a grin of anticipation. "Say one word of disrespect and I kill you. Say you understand so when I do it, all of us within earshot will know I warned you… Betty!"

"I understand," Rock replied, knowing he was out of his element completely. He was in a universe of reality we all thought he had learned when he faced us in the hotel room before the 'Starlight' mission.

I slapped his buddy into consciousness and plucked him off the floor. I stuffed him, groggy and bleeding, into his seat. I jammed his cloth napkin into place over his busted mouth, following it with his hand. "Don't move from this chair."

Turning to the very quiet Saturday night crowd, I took a deep breath. "Sorry about that folks. Just a little misunderstanding. All tabs are on me tonight, so eat, drink, and be merry."

Applause and whistles of appreciation brought the room out of its silent binge and restored the Saturday night festiveness. I brought Tommy over a chair because there was only one extra at the table. We sat down with the Rock.

"You coming here instead of contacting either me or Alexi Fiialkov was ill-advised to say the least," Tommy stated formally. "Our group aren't video gamers playing 'Call of Duty'. You found that out in New York. What could possibly be so important you had to come here? I've already figured you had a hand in stirring the Mohammed Knowly group into action along with the Nejem family. That's how you knew to find us here."

Rock nodded his head in recognition Tommy was right on all counts. "I do know your group's rep. I figured you'd learn I bought in on tonight's fight as one of Knowly's backers. I came here to tell you I had nothing to do with the dart-gun guy. When one of my men called and told me what happened, I came directly over here."

"Okay," Tommy replied. "Getting mixed in with John's murder would have been a stunt you would never pull, so I'll grant you that much. Did you have much contact with the Nejem family?"

"No. They wanted to know if I was interested in buying in on the fight through Knowly's people. I only heard they were financing the fight, asking if I'd consider giving Knowly a boost into the UFC ranks if he beat Harding. I agreed to help him and... I put ten grand on Knowly to win."

There's some good news. Tommy and I exchanged grins.

"We don't have the results back yet on the dart they used, but if it's poison as we suspect, the police will want to talk with you. It would be best to go speak with them first and get ahead of this," Tommy advised.

"I'll do that." Rock noted my Monster Squad eyeballing him like a big juicy piece of prime rib. "We'll leave now. I know you've heard the UFC plans on making it mandatory for the winner of my fight with 'Berserker' to fight you. I'm working to make sure that doesn't happen."

"I don't blame you," Tommy replied. "We're aware fighting in the cage under the Las Vegas lights will be different than John plucking your heart out in the parking lot. Backing Knowly cost you ten grand. Don't approach John anymore. You have my number and Alexi's. Call one of us if you need someone to contact concerning fights. Is that clear?"

"Yes. May we leave now?"

I stood, gesturing the way was clear. Rock and his men filed past the Monster Squad, eyes on the door. "Thanks, T."

"It was nothing. I didn't think our Oakland PD bar should be the scene of a triple homicide. Otherwise, I would have been interested in seeing you mulch the Rock out back. I hope they let us know about the test results soon. I imagine that will make Crue's interrogation tomorrow interesting."

"It couldn't have been anything but poison. If Crue and the guys hadn't spotted the Nejems looking up, I'd be dead. They wouldn't have plotted the dart-gun guy episode to drug me. Jack would have stopped the fight. They wanted me dead. We'll find out tomorrow. Let's have a drink. I'm not overdoing it either. There's too much going on around here."

"Agreed." Tommy followed me over to the bar.

Denny had slipped in during my Rock encounter. "The dart was tipped with enough curare to kill an elephant. The police have all Knowly's crew in custody as accomplices to murder, including Knowly, who won't be discharged from the hospital until morning. Since it was attempted murder on a federal agent by the Nejems, whom I've had listed on the terrorist watch list, we keep them. Two of Daddy Nejem's men are here illegally, of course."

"I'm betting Daddy gives me a name. He didn't finance this hit himself or initiate the plot," Lynn said. "One thing – no one bothers Amara with this crap. Daddy and the boys are going bye/bye. I remember Nick mentioning a problem with Cala's Kader relatives consorting with terrorists. I'm wondering if we don't have a similar situation. These bastards have a network, which is why we should be shutting off all flow of the cult into our damn country."

"Paul and I harp about just that at every closed door meeting. We don't know why the hell we can't convince these idiots in DC to listen. We have proof of every nightmare imaginable concerning terrorist infiltration and motives. No one listens. We only managed a few concessions on the ports after the China Basin incident."

"Sooner or later we won't be able to kill them fast enough," Clint remarked. "The Nejem family will not be part of the new Caliphate when our idiot representatives allow it to happen. They leave the earth tomorrow. Period."

"If we're taking the Nejems on a final cruise, we better poke Mellow Yellow for his training session," Tommy said.

"I have the weekend off." Thoughts of the Bay wiped away my buzz in a heartbeat.

"Sorry, DL," Tommy replied, not sorry at all. "The heavyweight championship will be on the line. It's the banana suit for you tomorrow."

"Shit!"

Chapter Five

Game On

Daddy Nejem gave us the name of his backer before we could take him from the holding cell. The surprise he named Al-Kadi, the guy we planned a mission on, did not seem to faze Denny. "I don't see any sticker shock on your features, Den. Do you know something we don't?"

Clint, Lynn, Denny, and I joined the minions this morning at Pain Central. The Nejem final cruise would follow the interrogation, but there wasn't any reason to call in the others on a Sunday. Tommy would join us at the dock for my torture session. Right now, we were busily recording everything Amara's Father knew. When he began repeating himself, I stopped him.

"Thanks. That will do for now." I helped him to his feet, guided him into the interrogation room where the minions already prepared Lynn's tools. He began to struggle when I placed him on our specially outfitted gurney.

"What are you doing? I have told you everything!"

"Yeah... about that," Lynn said, walking in with Clint. "We don't take kindly to terrorist woman beaters trying to kill one of our own. Therefore you, my little guppy, will be showing your companions down in holding what will be happening to them if they don't remember some very interesting information."

Mohammed Nejem began crying as Lynn inserted her needles. I didn't blame him. I flicked the switch for video feed to our holding cell screen. We didn't know how much his three companions knew, but the technique worked so well, it was worth a try. Besides, as Lynn stated, we aren't much of a 'forgive and forget' bunch. I didn't like the attempted curare dart murder attempt.

Lynn stroked Nejem's face. "Ah… isn't that cute. Daddy cries real tears. You tried to kill my brother and my adopted daughter. I'll teach you what pain really means. You can set the example for your buddies down in holding."

Dr. Deville, doctor of podiatry torture supreme, spent the next half hour with Mohammed Nejem during his last moments on earth before a blood vessel popped in his head. After we removed Nejem from his restraints, the minions and I stripped him for his final cruise. Once we set aside the body-bag, we journeyed down to holding where all our guests were crying. It reminded me of the movie where the Kurds captured these Isis supposedly bad dudes. The only thing they did with no one touching them was cry for their mommies. That's how our guests were. They began screaming when Dr. Deville arrived. She shushed them with a gesture.

"I see you enjoyed Daddy Nejem's adventure movie. I hope you boys thought of something really sweet Daddy didn't tell us. Otherwise, I'm going to have to inspect some feet."

"Yes! We know something he didn't know," one of them with a full black beard shouted, wiping away the tears. "He…he did not know one of the people funding Al-Kadi. We learned of him from the men who had a safe-house in Ensenada before we came into the States from a container ship. His name is Fernando Carone."

"Where can we find him?"

Blackbeard broke into sobs. "We…we don't know. He lives on a superyacht along the coast, dealing drugs, and girls. May Allah strike me dead if I lie!"

His buddies wailed in sync with him as if we cared.

"Oh shut up!" They quieted immediately upon hearing Lynn's order.

"Usually, I'd go for the gold on these goons," Lynn said. "I remember Nick extracting a name before the 'Starlight' gig."

"Good memory," I replied. "Carone was the name Nick mentioned. He has a 'Mother Ship' in the area somewhere by San Luis Obispo."

Denny, who had been quiet all morning, spoke in a soft voice of urgency. "Let me take these guys. We can learn a lot about this Ensenada safe-house."

"Uh... no," I said. "We'll take each one to interrogation. They will explain every stone and bush surrounding the Ensenada safe-house and how they reached there, right boys?"

A chorus of affirmative sobs wailed until Lynn shut them up once again. "Well, Den... there you have it."

"Fine." Denny sighed and started toward the steps. "Bring them along. Let's keep them apart so we can make sure they deliver the goods for us to compare."

Lynn clapped her hands together. "Line up boys. My minions will escort you all to our holding room where our figurehead leader, Captain Blood, may question each of you alone for later story comparison."

"I heard that," Captain Blood called from the stairwell.

* * *

We admittedly took our partying out to sea with us. Jafar practiced his captaining skills with Samira as his copilot. Lucas joined Casey, Tommy, Dev, Jess, and the minions after our bad guy fish feed. Tommy let me off with a forty minute banana suit poking. Clint stayed home for the day with his son doing research, so Casey stood in as my shark watch. I was damn good in the water considering my fight the night before. I could tell Tommy was pleased, partly because of my performance, and partly because of the new insulated gloves he used in the poking drill. They eliminated the sting when I whipped around perfectly for a pole strike with knife-hand stroke. Lynn, on board with us alone, joked and fished with Dev and Jess for the first time.

My satellite secured line phone beeped while we were sipping and fishing. It was Nick. "Hey, brother... I was going to call you after we fed the fishes to compare notes on a guy."

Nick chuckled. "Achmed already put your near death experience on the line to me. Damn, John, I hope you're sipping a few in celebration of cheating death."

"I sure am. It was a close one. Nightshot Casey put one right between the dart-man's eyes in the dark."

"Damn it!" Lucas grabbed the satellite phone. I had us on speaker. "Don't say anything more, Dead Boy. Casey's head's so swelled today, he can't even wear a ball-cap."

"Give me the phone, Ahab," I ordered with a sigh. Casey and everyone else were enjoying the exchange. "Nick and I have business."

"Fine! One more Nightshot line and I smash the phone over your thick skull!"

"Understood," I replied. "You still there, Nick?"

"I...I'm here. What guy did you want to compare notes on?"

"Fernando Carone."

"Oh boy... this can't be good. He's the one I'm calling you about."

That straightened my ass up along with everyone else. I hit all the high points, explaining how we learned of Carone. Nick did

115

the same in short order, along with his idea about yacht confiscation which had my companions barking in pirate talk for Nick's amusement. We Monsters enjoyed Nick's decimation of an attacking boat crew from Carone's Tempest.

"If their radar warning system works well enough for them to know we're in the area and they're paranoid enough to fire at a civilian listed fishing trawler, what did you have in mind for an approach. I'm thinking the only way to get control requires destruction."

Nick hesitated for a moment before revealing his thoughts. "I'm thinking you and I helicopter drop from the Stealth about a mile and a half away. Once we get aboard, we assess the situation. If we can take over the ship without a massive assault, great. If not, we send it to the bottom of the sea."

"Recon! Don't you and Dead Boy hurt my superyacht! Good plan. Don't think for a second I'll let you exit the Stealth with grenades, Dead Boy." Lucas caused much amusement as Nick went silent. "I knew it! Why do this if you're going to blow the shit out of it at the first indication of a problem?"

"Oh... I don't know, Lucas," Nick replied finally. "I was hoping John and I could survive this op. The grenades were to make sure that happened."

I raised my hand. "Show of hands. All in favor of Nick and me surviving in case we have to use grenades raise your hands."

No hands. Only snickers.

Nick chuckled. "No one raised their hand, did they?"

"Not a one, the pricks. I like your approach though. It's a long swim, but would pretty much guarantee an undetected arrival. I can't think of anything better. It seems we need to confiscate our new superyacht before going after Al-Kadi."

"Agreed. I wouldn't want to leave too much time go by in case he's in constant contact with Carone. These assholes networking like they're doing makes me wonder how many money sources they actually have. We know the damn Saudi's are funding a lot of this crap. In addition, they own most of our top politicos lock, stock, and barrel. I'm wondering what the hell has to happen before we get to actually stop these bastards."

A chorus of loud agreement followed Nick's statement from my crew. "Probably an event like the atom bomb on a tanker running into China Basin, or them blowing Boston Harbor to hell and gone."

"Damn it! I can't pull back and let something like that happen," Nick muttered. "I guess if they keep stocking our American swimming pool melting pot with piranhas from the Middle East, sooner or later our leaders will get what they want – a conflagration or Sharia Law. They've certainly stocked more upper level administration positions with Sharia Law advocates. Ever wonder where all the outrage went when the feminists disappear during any talk of a woman's position under Sharia Law and Islam? The Gay Movement is a joke. They're executed under Sharia Law... yet they are also silent. I guess the pictures and video of our ambassador in Benghazi, raped, tortured, and burned for hours, didn't convince them of Islam's other than peaceful intentions toward the Gay Movement."

"We hear you, Muerto," Lynn said. "I've dealt with the Middle East cave dwellers enough to know when they come calling, I give better than I get. The Gay Movement is a laugher just as you say. I guess they plan to burrow into the underground after they help lose the only nation on earth where they had real sanctuary. The one I'm curious about is the new transgender bullshit movement. They'll disappear under Sharia so fast, no one will even notice. They'll have to go back to pretending in their own bathrooms during dress-up time in the dark."

Lynn struck a comical cord with that one. We Monsters don't permit men to go into women's bathrooms when our kids and wives are in there. God help the guy in a dress going in to share the bathroom with Lynn. He will be a woman after that experience and won't have to worry about the right biological equipment. His will be gone.

"I will call you once satellite surveillance of our hoped for mountain retreat and superyacht give us some definition on a final approach to both. That was a disturbing deal with Carone's minions attacking you at your beach with the kids around. We can't have that, brother. We'll kill them all. I'll talk with you soon."

"You Monsters watch your six," Nick said. "I'm getting the itch of violence. It happens whenever I figure I haven't killed enough people."

"Amen to that, Nick." I disconnected. "I love Nick's idea about the superyacht at our new island sanctuary. I hope it works out that he and I can save the ship during mission op."

"You damn well better, Recon," Lucas barked. "It's written in script now. You and Dead Boy must pirate the Tempest and bring her into the fleet. That's an order."

"Blow it out your ass, Ahab. If Nick and I get into trouble, the grenades will fix the situation real quick and we ain't dyin' to preserve the superyacht so the rest of you better be very attentive when Nick and I get aboard."

"We'll have to be close and steaming full bore," Lucas said. "Otherwise, the only suggestion I have is an attack by Stealth once you and Nick secure a landing zone. Then we can plunk armed people right where we need them instantly."

"I like it, Lucas. We'll have to go full helicopter assault on this one. I say we sail on the 'Valkyrie'. It has the helicopter LZ's we need for doing this. I'll text your idea on to Nick. I'm sure he'll be on board with it."

"Damn… this collaboration with Nick is getting freaky good," Lynn said. "I have to plan another directorial action down in LA with El Kabong. He has fresh ideas and knows how to get them across to me at the right time. The new season of LA Bounty Hunters will be in production soon. I hope Nick can spare him for a time."

"If we pull off the confiscation of Carone's superyacht Tempest and Al-Kadi's compound at Pilot Hill, we'll have some valuable launch sites. I bet those two guys have a couple of nice offshore accounts to share with us too. We'll have the budget of a small country soon."

"We'll have to create some discreet defensive systems on board the superyacht, Recon."

"I know, Lucas. Carone probably has some good systems already. We know his radar is first rate. It's a nice touch it can launch Panga boats from its interior. We'll have our own 'Mother Ship' although the Valkyrie with the helicopter launch pads and RGM-84 rocket array is already a battleship. We're approaching superpower status, Ahab. I think we need to get you an admiral's uniform."

"One more ship and I think we need to attack Saudi Arabia," Lucas replied in character.

I threw a line in the water again. "I'm beginning to believe we should do just that. We need to watch them closer. Maybe we could find proof of something horrendous we know they enabled. We could hit them hard under the same circumstances as we did Iran."

"Well… aren't you the cutest thing," Lynn said. "Put that talk on the back-burner for now, Cheese. I need to direct a real movie before I'm put to death by my own country."

I took a deep breath. "I'm glad we're networking with Nick. He has a knack of turning over rocks and revealing new leads to threats and people. Dangerous times, my friends."

"It's a dangerous time for Carone and Al-Kadi," Lucas stated. "I see a bad moon rising for those two and everything they own."

"As Dead Boy would say – absolutely," Casey stated.

* * *

"I told you, Cracker." Jean smirked at her partner in crime.

Sonny's mouth tightened into thin lipped frustration. "I didn't doubt you. I told you we should take this to your Dad."

"I have to see this through. We're good together, Cracker. We see things no one else does. Dad's into some big ops. He doesn't have time for this small stuff."

"Small stuff? This is an extortion ring," Sonny hissed. "They're collecting money for protection. These three guys are small time hoods, pretending they're connected. That doesn't mean they're not dangerous."

"We spotted them in the market near the school," Jean whispered. "Keep your voice down. There's no question these guys are shaking down the owners for money. Our next step is to get the owners together. We have all the evidence to bring these guys down. The only part to fill in is testimony. Once the owners know there's no mob behind these guys, they'll testify against them. This is our case."

Sonny watched the three men, dressed in three piece suits, with dress fedoras. They looked very impressive. He and Jean followed them. They had the license plate number for their Lincoln MKX. From that, Jean had used Nick's satellite uplink laptop in the safe-room to learn the address they listed. It seemed to be a small time operation with thug type, heavy-handed threats. Three drive by shootings listed in the news happening at businesses on the thugs' list convinced the business owners to pay for protection. The three entered the last restaurant on their list while he and Jean moved behind the building's edge they were conducting their surveillance from.

"Hello there, you little twerps!" Rachel grabbed Jean by the ear, shaking her. "What the hell is wrong with you, 'Daughter of Darkness'?

"Ow!" Jean looked around sullenly, seeing Nick and Gus, with John and Cala behind them holding Quinn. Sonny had jumped into a defensive stance. He relaxed with shoulders slumped. "We may as well wear clown clothes with signs saying 'Stupid is as Stupid Does', Cracker. The entire band of cartoons snuck up on us."

"I can't believe this! When your Dad told me he had something to show me, I thought it would be a nice surprise. Instead, it's my two ten year old charges following dangerous thugs on the Sunday night they're supposed to be at a movie. Did you two even go inside Lighthouse 4 movie-theater when I dropped you off?"

"I can't believe Dad ratted me out."

The innocent observers restrained amusement until then. The 'ratted out' tagline generated a laugh-out-loud moment until Rachel turned on them with hands on hips. "You knew what they were doing all along, didn't you, Muerto? Don't think for a moment I'll forget this you Unholy Trio nitwits. I'm really surprised at you, Cala."

"What? I didn't do anything." Cala pointed accusingly at Nick. "It's Muerto's fault! He called it innocent fun. Besides, we've been tracking them. No one was in danger."

"So why wasn't I told about it?"

"You are too close to the T-Rex. You cannot be trusted with information from the inner circle," Cala stated, shifting Quinn into a human shield with a squeal as Rachel moved on her.

"Give me Quinn. I'm going to show you an inner circle… of birdies, when I clock you upside your head, traitor!"

"Calm down, hon." Nick only regained the ability to initiate coherent speech a moment before. "We could never have fooled Jean if you'd known from the beginning."

"Dad's right, the traitor! I read you like an old Diego novel," Jean remarked, enjoying the attention shifting to Rachel. "Cracker and I have the goods on an extortion team. We were ready to move on them when you ruined our surveillance gig. These guys will get away with it now."

"What exactly were you and Cracker going to do," Nick asked, taking Rachel's hand. "You both know we're in dangerous times right now with my alter ego."

"It started out as a game. We saw these three suits taking the store owner into the backroom where we stop for an ice cream when you allow us to walk Deke with the com units in. Hey… you've been bugging us! You rigged our com units to transmit even when we don't activate them, didn't you?"

Nick waved off Jean's waving finger. "Think of it this way, doody. If something happens to you like a stray bullet from a drive-by, what do I tell your Mom… whoops?"

"But…but we have them. You can't stop Viper and Cracker now!"

Nick pointed at the store. "Just watch."

Three police cars drove to the curb a couple of car lengths away from the front of the store without lights or sirens. They had a perfect viewing when Neil and his partner stepped away from their car with the others following suit. It was all perfect until the three emerged from the store. At the first shout, the one in the middle with sharkskin suit and deep gray fedora yanked a mini Uzi from inside his custom suit. In a flash, everyone saw the cops had not drawn weapons, unsure if it was anything but a dress-up con. No one saw him move. The loud bang from Nick's .45 Colt sent a hollow point slug into the man's forehead from seventy-five feet away across the street. Gus and John immediately pulled everyone against the building side. The police drew weapons, pointing everywhere. Neil kept his sidearm pointed at the remaining suits.

Once the two suits were handcuffed and the coroner called, Neil gestured at Nick, who was peeking out, making sure he wasn't shot by the good guys. "C'mon over, Nick."

Nick turned to Gus. "Take everyone home, Gus. I'll see you all on the deck sometime soon, I hope."

"Will do, Muerto."

"Sorry, Dad," Jean said, hugging Nick.

"We'll talk about it later, Viper. Good instincts as always, Sonny."

"We really weren't going to confront them, Sir."

"I believe you. I'll see you all at the house." Nick kissed Rachel. When he saw Neil watching, Nick proceeded like a convict walking the 'Green Mile' death row final jaunt to the electric chair.

"Knock it off," Neil ordered. "You're killing me here."

"No," Nick pointed out, "they were about to be killing you here."

"Thank you for our lives. We should have treated this situation with more respect," Neil stated. A heartfelt echo sounded from the other police officers. Neil turned to one of the veteran officers. "Take over, Bill. I need to speak with Marshal McCarty."

"Sure. Nice shot, Nick."

"Thanks, Bill." Nick followed Neil away from the scene.

"Jean and Sonny really did this on their own?"

"John, Gus, and I took turns monitoring them. Jean scoped the protection con guys using my satellite uplinked laptop. I have a program to see anyone's keystrokes from the moment it's used. She used it during the time I had to have her in the safe-room with Rachel, Quinn, and Sonny during a time I was away. We looked into it. It was my decision to allow her and Sonny to play detective. The moment the kids gathered enough evidence to get these clowns to plea out, I called you. Rachel didn't take it well. The kids have been using deception to do their surveillance with Rachel as the unknown enabler. I had no clue the chumps were packing machine pistols though. I'll be hearing about that when I get home."

Neil chuckled. "The kids did damn good. Can we keep the police arrest as quiet as we can without documenting our rookie approach?"

"Of course. Do you need my Colt?"

"We already have the Colt on file. Keep it. Did you get any video of your intervention on behalf of cocky cops, Deadshot?"

"John filmed it. I'll send the file when I get home along with my report. For the record, you approached the guys with hands on weapons. It wasn't a situation calling for all of you to descend on the scene with guns ready to fire. I'm glad none of your crew threw a shot off in my direction. That was very nice restraint."

"Thanks for the charity support," Neil replied wryly. "I'm hoping we can get the two survivors to cop a plea. Their Uzi carrier being black could have some impact on the case with the usual criminal enablers who seize on anything to make us reactionary Nazis."

"Yep. The only way the police are ever in the right nowadays is if they die in the line of duty." Nick smiled. "We were doing a cartoon movie when one of our perps decided to pull the 'Black Lives Matter' card. Payaso pulled off his mask and got busy on him. John and I of course expressed outrage at his brutality."

"I'll bet. I've seen you testify. You're the best in any court testimony of facts I've ever witnessed. If it hadn't been for your main witness Dan dying before the Kensky case, I'm certain the jury would have convicted him with your testimony. I saw the way you ate Kensky and his lawyer's lunch in front of the media outside the courthouse. If Kensky had really known you, he would have confessed again just to get put in prison for life."

"That would have been disappointing," Nick replied. "I'm glad Gerald was freed to make a new life for himself. He had dreams, needs, desires, and passion."

"Right. How many hours did he have to enjoy all those wonderful treasures of freedom?"

Nick shrugged. "He had what seemed an eternity to ponder his transgressions. Gerald paid his debt to society in a way he never dreamed possible."

Neil's features contorted in distaste. "I've seen your Isis videos. Yuck. I'm glad you're not doing those in our town. You three cartoons are together so much, someone would put two and two together. We received calls about gunshots early in the morning right after I talked with you at the Point. Did I miss something?"

"As it turned out… yes. It was a thread going somewhere I haven't had a chance to brief you on. I'm working on making the morning's adventure a onetime occurrence. We learned about a Kingpin of crap is off the coast causing gang, drug, human trafficking, and terrorist problems. I believe any bleeding back into Pacific Grove already happened with the calls you received. No other trace of that event will come to light."

Neil took in a deep breath. "I remember when the only criminal activity in the 'Grove' was an unruly tourist once in a while."

"I have it on good authority these incidents will be on an upswing because of our importing terrorists on a stupidly steady basis. California politicos rival any terrorist enablers I've found. I'm networking with another under the radar group I mentioned to you. They stopped a terrorist attack using a tanker to ram China Basin with an atomic bomb aboard."

"You mean John Harding, right?"

"He's the one. We'll be collaborating to get rid of the offshore threat. I know you're like me, hoping for authorities to waken from their naïve sleep of idiocy. Since they refuse to do so, we're on our own to confront these assholes. I am going to make their life miserable until we hopefully live through this politically correct nonsense where we have to commit suicide to appease the cave dwellers."

"Amen, brother. I'll call you if I need you at the station. Your report would be great as soon as you can send it."

"Will do. Watch your six, brother. I can't be watching your back every moment."

"Ouch," Neil muttered, walking away with his head down.

* * *

Nick heard laughter coming from upstairs as Deke greeted him. "It sounds better than I thought it would, Dekester. Did you intercede for the Daughter of Darkness?"

Deke muttered an under the breath humming grunt while burrowing his head into Nick's lap as his human master crouched near him.

"I bet no one thought to give my dog brother a beer... did they?"

Deke went wild in place, all four paws marking time, with tail wagging so fast it blurred to the human eye. Nick roughed his head with amusement. "Okay, lead the way. I-"

Deke streaked up the stairs before Nick could finish a thought in words. He grinned and followed Deke upstairs. In his enclosed balcony, family and friends watched the Jean show as she pantomimed one of her teachers at school who had recess duty during the week. She walked, talked, and recited clichéd lines so well, Sonny couldn't breathe, he was laughing so hard. Jean wound her act down as Nick entered, going to the bar and pouring Deke a beer in his bowl.

"I'm glad this latest ten-year-old's surveillance gig ended today. What have we learned today?"

"Never trust my Dad not to rat me out to Mother Gorgon?"

"Why you little turd!" Rachel went after Jean, but then returned to her seat without initiating an attack when Jean crouched behind Deke. "How did it all go with Neil, Muerto?"

"Very well. I told him John recorded the event. I'll be sending him our files on Jean and Sonny's case. He said there would not be any repercussions. I even got to keep my Colt. I won't have to testify unless one of the accused makes a scene at the station." Nick paused, putting a hand on Jean's shoulder. "I recognize your impersonation. I've met that teacher with the Full Monty of liberal ideology you were disrespecting at the PTA meetings. I don't know what she's capable of in a classroom. I hope she's sticking to covering the subjects she's assigned to teach. Public schools are getting weird."

"I know kids in her class," Jean said. "Ms. Nazari teaches the five pillars of Islam. She encourages prayer rugs and beads! I thought teachers couldn't teach religion in school."

127

Sonny regained his voice at the reality message Jean imparted. "Ms. Nazari is in charge of recess. She doesn't like Jean."

"I make fun of her in ways she can't get back at me for," Jean admitted. "I do stuff like I was doing when you walked in. She only realized I was imitating her when the kids started laughing."

Nick took a deep breath, looking longingly at the Bushmill's bottle. He remembered making a Nazari family member his reentry into the Company when he killed Sheik Abdul Nazari in the sand. Rachel came over and poured him a drink from the bottle in spite of his reservations. "Relax at the table with us, Muerto. I've gotten over the unknown surveillance operation under my own nose. Gus and John explained you three cartoons were watching out for the kids. This Nazari bitch pisses me off too. She seems to think she's in an Afghan cave. Insisting on wearing a headscarf, of course, even in the classroom, Florence 'Islamic idiot' Nazari isn't teaching kids… she's indoctrinating them. Jean drives her crazy which is the only reason she isn't grounded until turning eighteen after hatching the protection racket, gang surveillance plot with her Igor."

Nick sipped contentedly while listening to Sonny's denials of being in thrall to the 'Daughter of Darkness', much to the amusement of his audience. He sat down at the table next to Rachel, glad his two thousand word goal in the new novel wasn't hanging over his head. The new scenes with Fatima entrapping Diego, Jed, and Leo in a Caribbean gang plot unfolded on Nick's keyboard in less than two hours during the day.

"What's the ramifications of Viper's assaulting Florence each day? I imagine she's a new convert, having married a foreign Islamic national, right?"

"Oh yeah," Rachel answered. "She's one of those wild-eyed newbies, dedicated to screwing the rest of us female nonbelievers. Jean can tell you. I've arrived at the school in an attractive dress for working at the Monte Café, only to get the beady-eyed stare of retribution. You know how well I take to that. The first time, I didn't give it a thought. The third time she eye-balled me, I went right into her face."

Nick smiled. He could tell Rachel had imbibed a couple glasses of wine. It appeared Cala was again the designated driver for the others. "Okay, Rach... are you going to tell us what happened or do we have to beg?"

"I told her I don't appreciate you staring at me like I was some kind of freak. She thought about playing the Islamophobia card, but thought better of it when I jutted a finger into her face and told her I'd bitch slap her into next week if she pulled it on me. Flo the Islamist mole runs when she sees me. I'm at fault for Jean's behavior. I told her Flo has no right to push religion in a public school. Jean, knowing all the unsavory facts about Islam, challenges Flo on a daily basis. Flo would like to make Jean disappear. Instead, knowing she's in the wrong, Flo has quieted her proselytizing to moments when Jean's not around. Unfortunately for her, the rest of the kids have begun adopting Jean's attitude toward Islam. I think they've talked about Flo to their parents. The parents have reinforced Jean's take on Flo and complained to the principal."

"The principal toned her down, Dad. She still goes nuts but she mutters on her own where we can't hear her. I'm glad I don't have her for a teacher. Watch this, Dad. I can do her perfectly."

Nick stopped her with a gesture. "Flo has it coming, I'm sure. Her indoctrination program against school policy is something we'll fight against. I don't like you making fun of adults unless they're in on the joke like we are. Like your Mom says, Flo's an Islamic newbie, enflamed with her new calling, willing probably to sell out her country, and indoctrinate kids to her cause. I won't soft sell the danger you kids already know about from this cult. I don't sugarcoat anything. When someone believes in something against all logic and common decency, we step back and allow them to proceed on their discovery phase into reality, especially with the death cult. Flo may learn the hard way about her place as a woman in Islam. Because of the Kaders, you kids know of the dangers. Only one pseudo religion preaches the decimation of other races and religions who do not believe in their cult worldwide, while carrying out genocide in reality."

"Do you believe in God, Sir," Sonny asked.

"I sure do. I do not believe God wants us to kill or maim everyone who doesn't believe as I do. The God I believe in doesn't want us to mutilate, subjugate, or stone women for indiscretions. My God doesn't want pedophilia to become a man's right. I can freely believe in anything without annoying other people." Nick grinned at Jean. "My God also doesn't want me to allow a child under my care to be a bullying shrew either."

"You said when Mom and I forced you to help the cop by the side of the road a long time ago, that we forced you to do what's right, and sometimes you didn't know what was right anymore."

"Arrrrghhhhh... I've been pierced to the heart by my own words, although mutilated to fit Viper's storyline. Let me put it this way – I don't want you making fun of other people in front of me. We all make mistakes in judgement. I've made so many, I don't even think about them anymore. I'm sure Gus has them all catalogued though. Restraint is the key to adulthood, Viper."

"Restraint is the key for sissies."

Nick stifled a laugh while Rachel gasped, staring at the ceiling in frustration. "I know your Mom agrees with you on many counts. One of the reasons charter schools are so popular is because of just this type of nonsense. Politely and quietly handling these incidents through the school authorities usually results in changes as you've already noted with the other parents complaining."

Jean grinned at Rachel, who gave her daughter a quick negative head shake. "C'mon Mom, tell him."

Nick refilled his drink. "Tell me what?"

"Nothing really. Her husband came over this past week to the school with her. He's the whole package, full black beard, kufi skull cap, and pajama robes. I thought Flo was a nitwit but her husband takes the cake. This guy traipsed around with his hands clasped behind his back eyeballing everyone. He came over to us when I dropped Jean off for school. He said his name was Majd Nazari and his wife felt uncomfortable around us."

"Mom said, 'tough titty said the kitty, but the milk's okay'," Jean broke in while giggling. "A bunch of people around us started laughing. It looked like his head was going to explode. He started forward but Mom lit off her stun-gun. She told him to go hump someone else's camel."

Jean's delivery and storytelling flair reduced the room to wild amusement for a few moments. It was only then Jean noticed Nick wasn't laughing. "Dad... it's okay. Ms. Nazari came over and clutched onto his arm, begging him to come along with her."

Nick turned to Gus. "See what happens when we don't have escort duties, Payaso."

"Yes," Gus replied wryly. "A tense situation gets handled without a killing."

"Very funny. I'm not amused with the 'Beard' showing up to intimidate."

Rachel, like Jean, saw the cold blooded killer flow over Nick's features. "Hey... did you just insult me? After all we've been through, I would figure you'd assume I can handle myself. Flo saved his ass. I had my pepper-spray in the other hand. One more word from Majd, and I would have sprayed him and her until they dropped, after which I zap until all movement stops."

Nick grinned and nodded. He sipped his refreshed drink. "There's too much Islamist intimidation crap going on. This place is beginning to resemble the idiot European Union nations that don't have armed citizens, importing the Islamic plague into their midst. Their own citizens, terrorized daily by these assholes, have actually begun knuckling under to the lunatics. They have Islamic No-Go zones now, where police have to ask permission to enter. Did you bunch know the French allow these troglodytes to burn nearly a thousand cars of citizens on New Year's Eve since the 'Arab Spring' bullshit. Laugh now, but I'm rethinking my stance on mimicry. We're not the French. We don't surrender our identities and culture to a bunch of Islamic throat-slitting cowards. You're lucky Nazari didn't have you arrested for a hate crime, Rach."

"Cala and I are with you, Muerto," Johnny said. "It is a mistake to laugh this plague off. They will continue to infiltrate our country like locusts, destroying everything in their path. I wish I could have seen you frighten away the bearded pussy, Rachel. He surely would have tried to humiliate you."

"No one intimidates or humiliates me, Johnny," Rachel replied with calming tones. "I understand the threat. I also knows it's related to the upswing in missions against terrorist ghouls you guys have been involved in. Let me make this clear – I don't care how many innocent Islamic dupes there are. I adhere to the old cliché: go to bed with dogs and wake up with fleas. I'm not ready to execute Flo and Majd, but I don't plan on letting them threaten Jean or me."

"A woman in one of those burka things walked by me yesterday," Tina said. "I was dressed a little for the warm day in something Gus likes to see. She muttered 'disgusting', thinking I didn't hear her."

"I stopped Tina from grabbing her by the throat," Gus admitted. "I was in the wrong. I'm beginning to believe we need to

132

intimidate them. The ones who don't like our culture need to get the hell out of the country."

"Just so we're on the same page and we don't stir the 'Daughter of Darkness' into a rampage," Nick said, "I want to keep the Nazaris in our purview at all times from now on. I don't like what I'm hearing. Lately, when I don't like what I'm hearing about the Middle Eastern contingent of our citizenry or illegal aliens, I get violent thoughts. School just started. Let's cool this conflagration until we gather more information on what the Nazaris are trying to do. I detest the indoctrination aspect and that is exactly what the new crap with 'Common Core' is trying to institute."

"I'm in for the walk to school," Gus said. "It will be interesting to see whether this Majd guy begins showing in the mornings with his wife. Deke's been neglected anyway. He needs to make the jaunt over to the school."

"I wish to come too," Johnny said. "The Cleaner will accompany me in case we have any trouble from Flo."

"Yes! I will handle Flo," Cala agreed.

Nick leaned back, hands gliding over the close cropped hair at his scalp. "This will not be escalated to a war at the elementary school. It's a nice walk. We're going to look like a parade with all of us going. That said, anyone wishing to accompany us to school is welcome, but with reservations. We don't want confrontations at the school, especially now since I had to cover for Viper and Cracker with a killing."

"Oh… that is so wrong!" Jean stood with hands on hips. "Cracker and I investigated a dangerous situation. We assisted in a police matter. We should get a medal for shining a light on those leg-breakers. Also there's no way the police get a conviction without our evidence."

"True," Nick agreed, "but you need to confer with me about any surveillance gigs you get interested in. As to the school problem, I'd like you to stay away from Flo. Let's cool things down. We'll try the live and let live response for the time being, okay?"

Jean shrugged. "Okay, but the Nazaris bother me because of all the things I know about Islam. It's not a religion... it's 'Murder Incorporated'. We're just kids but we can read the headlines. The Muslims keep killing people all over the world. They remind me of when we were on the run from the gangsters trying to kill us. You stopped them. You didn't do it with understanding and giving them the keys to the Kingdom. I'll stop messing with Ms. Nazari but I hope the parents keep complaining."

"I never thought I'd see an actual pirate attack," Sonny added. "Those people were going to hold that mammoth ship and everyone on board for ransom. It's not wrong to blame Islam. They would have killed any number of people to gain control of the ship. People cheered when the attackers were destroyed. None of them cared who or why it was done. I want them to fear us. The Unholy Trio is the best!"

Sonny's declaration quieted the adults.

"We had a lot of help from John Harding's crew," Nick said. "You two are the most mature ten year olds in existence. We'll take the Nazari situation one day at a time. For now, thank you for not messing with her. I have a feeling the first time she annoys her Muslim man, she'll learn the other face of the true believer."

"How soon do we go on the Tempest," Gus asked.

"Very soon," Nick answered. "As to our attack plan on the Tempest, I have only a vague outline to take control of the superyacht without sinking her. The success of saving the ship for ourselves to use is not a foregone conclusion. It will depend on weather, resistance, and my ability to get on board with John

Harding from the ocean. Only then will we be in a position to assess the chances of capturing the Tempest in one piece. It won't be a walk in the park. In the end, we may have to sink the ship or damage it beyond repair. One tool on the list the government feels we need to pursue is Carone's tie to Al-Kadi. Paul wants information from anyone we can capture and interrogate. The money backers are becoming more predictable and in plain sight. After the Tempest is secured one way or another, we'll have to move on Pilot Hill before Al-Kadi learns the fate of Carone."

"Agreed," Johnny said. "Do you wish for a plan of attack on the Nazari husband?"

"No. I don't plan to overreact to Majd. There are too many people involved in these altercations at the school with the complaints already made about Flo. I'm not sure there's any real danger to Jean and Sonny. The Nazaris may be the typical couple for all I know. I'll do a background check and learn if Majd is a citizen by birth or by marriage to Flo. We'll be closely observing anything of a threatening nature. Jean's not a newbie. She knows better than to discount anything or ignore it. We can't change school policy so what Flo gets away with will have to stay between her and the principal."

"I know you have to do this Tempest thing, but what do you think is really going on with a connection between Carone and Al-Kadi," Rachel asked.

"Money for Carone. My guess is Al-Kadi's backers set Carone up with the Tempest to provide an endless money supply to fund Al-Kadi's Pilot hill operation. The Tempest is a perfect transfer station for terrorists moving through Mexico from Central America. Those Panga boats can drop them anywhere along the coast for Al-Kadi to hide and train at Pilot Hill. We should be able to learn how extensive this network is with the capture of the Tempest. Homeland Security and the FBI can do their jobs with investigating once we have proof of what's happening. I admit we're in the dark concerning the range of this. We'll at least know if we've stopped this before it spread across the country. Pilot Hill may be their starting point for a Muslim No-Go zone where they can try to build underground armories and hide infiltrators in remote places. Think of a network of hidden conclaves able to store munitions, weapons and an army of trained fighters throughout the nation. If we discover what plans they're formulating, we may be able to finally interest our idiot leaders in stopping the Islamic Trojan Horse from rolling over us."

Nick shrugged in a blame me gesture. "Yes… I know none of this should be discussed in front of the kids. It will probably cause them to do more stunts like this extortion gang surveillance gig. I'm hoping they learn as they get older to bring me in as the last arbiter on anything they plan. As to the Nazaris, they need to be monitored in any way we can. We'll do it somehow without stirring more trouble for the school, including watching their financials, behavior in public, and of course any threats they make. Threats get them a one-way ticket to the House of Horror."

"You can trust Viper and Cracker," Jean stated. "We'll get to work on the undercover assignment right away."

Rachel slapped her hands over her face in comical fashion. "We'll have to chain her in the bedroom. You're my early warning system from now on, Igor."

"No way do you coerce my minion into ratting me out! Don't listen to her, Cracker."

"Minion? Really? I'll do it, but only if she's plotting something dangerous, stupid, or both," Sonny said.

"I'm thinking this partnership is over."

"If your Dad hadn't been watching our backs, the partnership would be dead for real," Sonny retorted. "I better get home. I have another undercover gig watching my parents. They've been huddling together formulating some new scheme. I think it's just a real estate 'house flipper' plot."

"I'll walk you home and give the Dekester another outing to get rid of the beer he inhaled." Nick smiled at Deke jumping around, having heard the magic word walk. "Are you coming, Viper?"

"I guess so."

"I shall drive all the lushes home." Cala stood, patting Johnny on the shoulder. Would you like us to send Neil the files and do the Nazari background check, Muerto?"

"Sure, if you don't mind. I-" Nick's phone beeped. He saw it was John Harding. "What's the good word?"

"We're heading your way with the Valkyrie tomorrow. I snagged the best underwater communications gear around. It's much better than the ones we had in Chabahar. We're thinking tomorrow night for our approach."

"We'll be ready. See you then." Nick disconnected. "The Tempest op is a go for tomorrow night."

"Issac arrives tomorrow morning," Gus said. "We'll need him if we get the Tempest in one piece. He'll help me get the ship north to Monster Island."

"We can leave him aboard to watch our ship with a professional crew until we get done at Pilot Hill. We'll move it toward Monster Island though after we search for any trackers they may have on board. John may want to leave the Valkyrie with the Tempest once we get to another anchor spot."

"Do you think they'll try and recapture her?"

"We'll know once Cruella Deville interrogates Carone. Until then, we take nothing for granted. I want the ship reregistered and named the moment we get control, depending on damage. Do you have any other ideas of what to rename her? Lucas suggested 'Ranger'."

"Yeah, I liked Lucas's suggestion. He told me on the USS Ranger Aircraft Carrier they used to play the Lone Ranger theme song, the William Tell Overture whenever they met with another ship or ported. We could add it to our 'Ride of the Valkyries' and 'Jaws' theme."

"Not bad, Gus. I'll suggest it to John."

"I was thinking of Infidel's Revenge," Johnny said.

Nick chuckled. "We may as well blow it up ourselves."

Chapter Six

Monster Pirates

The full face masks incorporated GPS digital programming and wireless communications. Nick and John swam fifteen feet below the surface toward the Tempest with steady flutter kicks. The dry-suits were thick enough to provide comfort in the cold water. A towing pod with negative buoyancy controls streamed behind the two men, strapped to each man's waist belt. It carried weapons and munitions along with Kevlar vests. They had tested communications after rappelling from the Stealth helicopter nearly two miles from the Tempest. With communications established and working on the masks, they maintained silence to make certain their communications did not get hacked into accidentally. The sliver of moon peeked from the cloud cover only intermittently, which suited their needs perfectly.

Nick enjoyed the long kick to the Tempest, never until now doing a dive with equipment as technologically advanced as he and John wore. The midnight hour they started the dive at provided a pitch blackness in the slightly choppy water needed for the approach. Only their surfacing bubbles would be visible. The crewmen would have to be maintaining a watch with night-vision equipment and be in the exact right spot to see their surface bubbles. He and John would remain below the water until moving within fifty feet of the Tempest. They would then gauge their approach. Satellite feed of the Tempest confirmed the Panga boat door closed which they expected. Agreement had been made to board the Tempest by way of the plush fantail deck with ascending ladder stairs. No guards had been spotted in the video feed. With an advanced radar system, Nick figured correctly they would monitor their radar gear day and night with a rotating watch, but would feel they had no need of an actual deck watch.

Although carrying double tanks to make certain of staying underwater the entire way, Nick and John used less than one attaining their agreed upon surfacing distance. The drawback with the full face masks was communications. They broke silence only after circling the ship, watching for any sign of crew or passengers moving around on deck. Satisfied the very chilly night confined the crew and passengers to the ship's interior, the two men slipped aboard on the lower fantail deck, silently pulling their pod on the deck. They stripped off their gloves first to open the pod. Nick retrieved the silenced MP5 from the pod, keeping watch until John stripped off his gear and pulled on the Kevlar vest. John took over the watch while Nick readied himself, including equipment pack. Nick stuck two grenades from a small bag jammed into the end of the pod into the pouches in his pants he wore under the dry-suit.

"You sneaky prick," John whispered as he put on his com unit and pack. "Do you want the upper or amidships deck?"

"I'll take the upper," Nick replied. "Should we try communications with the Valkyrie?"

"Let's wait until we secure the decks. We'll have Gus steer the Valkyrie toward the Tempest at full speed then. If they have the radar station monitored, we'll kill anyone coming on deck until help arrives. Jafar's on line with latest satellite feed info as well as jamming equipment. Our jammer will probably work on everything but their ship's radio."

"I'll turn on the jammer the moment we get into position. Ready, Dark Lord?"

"Ready, Muerto. Let's go get some. Try not to stumble around like a boot camp."

Nick chuckled. "Aye... Captain."

Nick led the way to the upper decks, both men angling away from the deck lights. John would have watch over the main and amidships deck while Nick would secure the top deck and provide backup for John. They climbed silently with their extra 9mm clips for the MP5s secured inside Velcro straps fitted on the Kevlar vests, marveling at the swimming pool on the main deck. It was nearly 1:30 am. The ship's interior only showed minimal lighting through the glass ports and doors. Nick crouched in a spot near the rear railing next to the hot tub where he could control the entryway while also watching the lower decks. He noted John doing the same thing.

"Ready to rumble, DL. I'm turning on the jammer."

"Call the Valkyrie now, Muerto. Let's get them coming our way. It would help if there was a bit more cover where you are. I have some nice deck furniture down here."

"I guess I'll have to shoot before they shoot me."

"That would be wise."

Nick activated his com. "Achmed?"

"Here, Muerto."

"Tell Payaso to head toward us at full speed."

"He's on with you. I've turned on the network."

"Full throttle as of now, Muerto," Gus said. "Issac and Cala are with me on the bridge. Laredo's in the air with the Stealth. Do you want him to land your backup yet?"

"No. John and I need to scare our hosts so they're ducking inside while backup arrives on top deck. Did you copy that, Ahab?"

"Got it, Dead Boy. We're ready."

"I'll follow the Valkyrie until you give me the go ahead, Muerto," Laredo said.

"Understood," Nick acknowledged.

Gus counted down distance as he sped toward the Tempest. When he reached the two mile distance mark, Nick heard the alarms go off inside the ship. Moments later, two men ran out on deck, weapons in hand. Nick fired single shots into both men, followed by a kill shot when they collapsed on deck.

"Two down."

"Only one so far here," John replied.

Nick grinned as the theme 'Ride of the Valkyries thundered over the waves so loudly from the Stealth and Valkyrie that the Tempest reverberated with audio vibrations. He could hear John humming in his ear, unable to resist. "Oh yeah!"

Three more ran into sight near the top deck hatch, one with a rocket launcher. Nick's MP5 burst stitched through the launcher and across the man's head. Knowing his burst in the dark revealed his position, Nick dived to his right while hitting the second man dead center. The third man fired an AK47 at Nick's shifting position so close Nick felt the displacement of air by his ear. Nick's return fire turned the man's face to red pulp. Making sure no others were following on the trio's heels, Nick crab crawled to where he could again cover both lower decks. A full scale gunfight erupted on John's amidships deck.

"Talk to me, DL!"

"Stay where you are, Muerto! I'm taking sniper fire from the lower deck!"

"On it!" Nick rolled to a position where he had line of sight covering any gunman that could fire onto the second deck.

For the first time since coming on board, Nick thought of rolling a grenade into his top deck entryway and leaping down to join John. His hand fondled the grenade as he watched the lower deck for attackers. He spotted the man trying to maneuver along the outer lower deck railing for a shot at John. Nick's single shot

9mm hollow point slug tore the front of his face off, leaving him screaming on the deck for his brethren to hear. Nick popped in a new magazine, deciding it was time for explosives. He reached for the grenade at his waist.

"We're coming in, Dead Boy! Don't you use any of your damn grenades!"

"Shit! Get out of my fucking head, Ahab! I have your back, DL. Talk to me."

"All good, Muerto. I have cover. You chased a bunch directly to me. I have six dead bad guys here. I couldn't cover the lower deck. Screw Ahab. If we don't get some respect shortly, blow the shit out of the upper entry. We'll land the troops in safety at all costs!"

"Understood. Stay down!" Nick saw another trio race to the lower deck stairwell.

He waited with cold blooded killer anticipation, a slight smile forming as the three became silhouettes on the angled ladder. Anticipating their hesitation as they approached the amidships deck, Nick glanced at the entryway he guarded, then calmly cut down across the men at neck level with a burst which nearly severed their heads. They tumbled down the ladder steps as the 'Ride of the Valkyries' became a wall of sound.

   * * *

I liked my amidships deck with plenty of items to form a barrier between me and my access point from inside the ship. I made my fort, layering everything I could in a formidable barricade between me and the interior hatch. I could keep an eye on the amidships hatch and still watch my back which was slightly exposed to the lower deck. As the Valkyrie tripped their radar, one of the Tempest minions ran out with AK47 in hand. I shot him and waited, hearing Nick's silenced rounds over me. It was then all hell broke loose.

143

A group of guys with automatic weapons streamed through the hatch, firing as they came. I picked my spots, shredding each one while moving behind my barricade. Some prick below me popped out and fired on my deck blindly. I put Nick on him and he was screaming seconds after a comical exchange with Admiral Ahab about damage to his yacht. I thought we secured our spots very well until I glanced behind me at the diagonal ladder from the lower decks. Three men had crept to the upper ladder level and one of them was taking aim at yours truly as Nick told me to stay down. A medium burst from above cut their throats. I liked watching the bastards tumbling back down to the lower deck as examples of what would happen to any following them. I kept humming the 'Ride of the Valkyries' as Laredo deposited our other warriors on Nick's upper deck with a virtual universe of sound. It was a good day to be a Monster.

* * *

Nick ran to the hatch access on the upper deck as Laredo hovered over it. No matter what feelings Lucas had on the matter, he planned to grenade the interior of his level if confronted by anymore resistance. No more faces showed as figures rappelled to his deck. Within seconds Casey, Lucas, Johnny, and Clint with Tonto in his arms were down on deck, ready for action. He glanced up to see Lynn behind the .50 caliber machine gun wave at him. Nick waved back as the 'Ride of the Valkyries' pierced his senses.

"Hey, Dead Boy," Clint greeted him as Tonto ran over to check him out.

"Damn good thing you didn't ruin my superyacht," Lucas said. He reached with professional touch to Nick's neck. "You're bleedin' son. The boys have it now. Let me take a look."

Nick reached with his left hand along his head, face, and neck while keeping control of his MP5 slung in firing position. His hand came away bloody. "It can't be much, Lucas. I think my ear got nicked. You know how they bleed."

"Hold the fuck still while I check. Yeah… you're missing a piece of your ear, Muerto." Lucas clamped a suture tape in place at the notch, which adhered to the dry skin on the undamaged ear. "You're good to go unless you'd like to pussy out. I can have Laredo lift your sissy ass out of here if you want."

Nick and everyone else on the network enjoyed Lucas's dress down. "I'm good to go, Ahab, you unfeeling prick. Are you good, DL?"

"Your execution of the three on the ladder ended that avenue of attack, Muerto. Payaso has the Valkyrie in position on our fantail with Lynn's minions covering both lower access points. Laredo, with Lynn on the fifty will watch our six. Samira is spotting for her. We're good to do the compartment taking of the ship."

"I'll send Lucas and Casey down to you. Johnny and I can work our way down to you with Clint and Tonto, making sure we don't have anyone left on the upper deck. From there, we'll all take the compartmental search and destroy with Tonto in the lead."

"Excellent. Let's do it."

Lucas extended his hand. "Give me the grenades, Dead Boy."

Nick grinned. "Kiss my ass, Ahab. You heard your orders. You and Casey reinforce DL."

Lucas smiled, waving as he and a chuckling Casey moved to the ladder. "I have a long memory for disrespect, Dead Boy. Watch your six."

"I'll see you shortly, Admiral."

Nick turned to Johnny and Clint. "Ready boys?"

"Yes, Muerto!" Johnny edged forward but Clint put a restraining hand on his shoulder.

"Let Tonto take point. He'll give us an indication by stopping with a grunt. Be ready to fire support." Clint motioned Tonto ahead on point with a hand gesture wavering downward.

Staying low to the deck, Tonto streaked ahead through the open hatch. Nick saw him reach the middle of the large one room observation deck, growl, and leap over the plush couch seating. Three men popped from behind their cover, trying to aim at Tonto streaking to the side. Clint, Johnny, and Nick fired a burst into the men Tonto had forced out. They then ran over to fire a certainty kill shot into each while keeping an eye on Tonto.

"The admiral won't like all this blood," Nick said.

"We'll worry about Admiral Ahab later," Clint replied. "It's a good thing you didn't charge in here, Johnny."

"I see that. Tonto is the best. He knew to scramble to the side away from the firing line." Johnny maneuvered amongst the other furniture on the observation deck, checking for anything out of place.

Nick looked down the inner ladder to the amidships deck landing. "Tight space with no line of sight. I don't like it. We need to flush any birds out of the bush. Hold on to Tonto, Clint. Watch this."

Nick tossed one of his grenades noisily down the ladder, where it hit the landing, one of the bulkheads, and then slid into the room. "Grenade! Fire in the hole."

"What the hell? I told you not-" Lucas's verbal onslaught ended with shouts, screams, and gunfire.

"Guard the ladder, Johnny."

"On it, Muerto."

Nick gestured an amused Clint to follow him. He led Clint and Tonto to the outside ladder to the amidships deck where a gun battle raged. "I think the little birdies left the bush."

* * *

Lucas, Casey, and I kept watch behind my fort waiting for our cohorts to clear the upper deck. Muffled bursts of silenced MP5 fire announced Nick and company had found some Carone soldiers above us. I heard Nick's 'fire in the hole' shout and Lucas's enraged retort a second before chaos reigned inside the amidships level. Four men rushed the hatch into our line of sight, firing as they ran. Our return fire cut them down, leaving our outer deck quiet once more. I smiled at Casey next to me.

"Dead Boy! You are on my shit list for that stunt," Lucas shouted up at Nick who was waving from the ladder.

"He loves that grenade trick," Casey muttered.

"The trouble with Muerto is we'll never know whether he pulls the pin or not," Lucas retorted.

"Who cares?" I earned an immediate slap to the back of my head.

* * *

"We're letting Tonto go down the ladder inside, DL, with us following," Nick announced over the com unit after rejoining Johnny at the inner ladder. "Hold your fire, guys. That goes double for you, Admiral."

"Blow it out your ass, you disrespectful piss-ant!"

"Understood," Harding acknowledged, enjoying Nick's verbal shot.

Clint crouched next to Tonto, pointed downward, and made a circle with his finger in front of the dog's eyes. Tonto leaped to the amidships landing, only touching the ladder steps twice. He jetted into the interior with his human companions on his tail. Tonto scooted along the deck, alternately leaping over or under the luxurious setting's furniture. After a complete search of the room, Tonto returned to Clint. Nick retrieved his grenade.

"We're clear," Nick said. "Want to jump in the hot tub before we secure the boat?"

"Hey, Sylvio," Clint said. "Take the minions into the main deck interior and flush the bad guys toward us."

"Still not funny, prick," Sylvio said. "We have seen no lights or movement inside, but it's dark. We have our night-vision goggles on. Do you want us to board on the main deck?"

"No," Nick said. "Stay aboard the Valkyrie. Keep watch. Don't fire unless sure of your target. We'll work our way down and let you know when we clear the main deck. We'll need you guys to watch our backs while we secure the area below decks."

"Understood, Muerto," Sylvio replied.

Inside the amidships deck interior, the men stood near the ladder with backlit rock crystal staircase. Nick shook his head. "Damn… this is one beautiful ship. I don't know whether the grenade trick will work again."

Nick retrieved a canister from his pack. Lucas grabbed his arm. "What the hell you doin' boy?"

"Tear gas… military style."

"Are you out of your damn mind? We won't get that shit out of the furniture and bulkheads for years. If you pussies don't want to clear the lower deck I'll do it myself."

"We'll need a clearing on the landing for Tonto to proceed," Clint said. "I'm not fond of using him in a bind like this. I mostly figured to have him smell out occupants in the cabins."

148

"I can take the first hit like always," Harding said. "I agree with Clint. I don't want to risk Tonto."

"It's too narrow and circular." Nick put away the gas canister with a sigh. "I'll do it. Give me your vest, John. I'll put it over mine. Clint, Casey, and Lucas can follow me down for head shots. There's too much glass from the outer deck for an approach from there. They'll see us and open fire through the glass. They won't care about damaging the Admiral's new ship. If this was easy, anyone could do it."

Harding stripped off his vest, handing it to Nick. "He's right. Let's do this. We've iced these guys enough."

Nick put on Harding's vest over his. Laying the MP5 down, he retrieved his .45 caliber Colt. "The more time they have to screw around below decks, the worse our chances of capturing the ship in one piece. I need to get a prisoner so we know how many more guys they have on board."

Walking over to the spiral ladder down, Nick smiled back at the others following him. "Remember... I'm the one with a bandaged ear."

In the next instant Nick dropped down the spiral ladder, rolling painfully to the landing as AK47 weapons fire blasted into the stairs. Nick dived to the side, rolling once again into a shooter's crouch, firing at muzzle flashes. MP5 fire from behind Nick silenced the automatic weapons fire. Screams of agony echoed along the bulkheads. Johnny gave Nick a hand to his feet.

"Are you okay, Muerto?"

"Yep. They stitched the material on my Kevlar but I'm okay. Get some lights on, Johnny and check for a live one we can question. I hear some unhappy candidates."

Turning on lights as he circled the room, Johnny checked the bodies while Clint, Casey, and Lucas covered the scene and access points. The Dark Lord came down the spiral ladder with a smile as he checked his Kevlar vest covering Nick.

"They barely touched it, DL." Nick took it off and handed it to John.

"I have a good one, Muerto," Johnny called out as he helped a groaning man off the deck who gripped his shoulder in partial shock while staring glassy-eyed at his captors. "This one has a .45 slug through the shoulder but he can talk."

"Good." Lucas shot the screamer through the head. "This one took one through the nuts. He wouldn't be much good for anything other than screaming. This boat has a crew of twenty-two normally. Counting these guys we've probably killed about that many. Don't set the bleeder down anywhere that he'll leave a stain, Johnny Five. We've already done enough damage."

"Put him here, Johnny," Nick told him, pointing at an already bloody chair. "Silvio? We have the main deck secured. Come aboard and guard the other decks with the minions. See what you can find on our dead guys."

"Yes, Muerto."

Johnny guided the man into the seat. Nick took duct tape from his bag, He wrapped the shoulder wound until it was covered and sealed. Nick straightened from his task as everyone else watched the interrogation chair along with the ladder leading down to the lower berthing, kitchen and dining areas.

"Who are you people?" The man spoke with a heavy Spanish accent.

"I am Dr. Muerto," Nick said. "These are my companion surgeons, Dr. Ahab, Dr. Johnny Five, Dr. Nightshot, Dr. Dark Lord, and... ah... who are you again, Nowhere Man?"

"If you don't want me to have Agent Tonto piss all over your leg you'd better keep a civil tongue in your head, Dead Boy," Clint replied.

Nick chuckled. "Okay... those are the introductions. We need a couple questions answered."

"Give me something for the pain! Do you know who you are fucking with? This ship belongs to Fernando Carone. He will have your badges and careers for this travesty!"

"What's your name?" Nick smiled at the amusement the man's declaration generated from Johnny and Harding's Monster Squad.

"Paulo Riggs."

"Now, Paulo... do you really think we could possibly be DEA or some other federal agents? We just killed all your comrades. If you answer my questions I'll take away your pain. If you remain silent, I'll have to do surgery on you. Believe me... you don't want that. Where's Carone and how many more passengers are below?"

Paulo looked into Nick's eyes and saw his death. "I knew I should never have taken this fucking job. There are three women on board in the two cabins next to Carone's master suite at the end of the passageway. He has two Cartel hitmen as bodyguards. They're probably in the suite with him by now. The rest of us were ordered to repel boarders."

"Are the women part of the operation or entertainment?"

"Crew and entertainment."

"I like you, Paulo. If you've told me the truth we'll put you into the hands of a guy from the CIA. For now, I'll give you something for your pain." Nick retrieved a syringe from his bag and injected Paulo with it. In less than ten seconds, Riggs was dead.

"Ah… Dead Boy," Clint said. "You killed him."

"Sorry, Clint… was he a friend of yours?"

"We thought you were going to give him over to Denny," Lucas said.

Nick met his old friend's gaze with a grim set to his features. "No prisoners, Lucas. I don't care what Denny and Paul want. Anyone we leave alive at our back will be a danger later, especially Carone. I'll tell you what, if the women stay in their cabin until Kabong and I put on our black masks, I'll blindfold them for Denny. If they see our faces, they get an eternity shot. Can we get Lynn landed for the interrogation?"

"We're on with you now, Muerto," Lynn remarked. "Let me know when you get Carone secured and I'll be right down."

"Thanks, Lynn."

"Do you have any ideas on the lower compartments," John asked Nick.

"If it's like Paulo said we'll stick to our original plan and let Tonto sniff the people out. I'm thinking the grenade trick would be a good one for Carone's cabin. If it doesn't work, we can throw in a live one."

"I swear you have me on my last nerve with the damn grenades!"

"Calm down, Lucas," Nick urged. "You have to admit the unloaded grenade trick works pretty well."

Lucas shrugged reluctantly. "It's worth a shot."

Nick didn't wait. Taking his MP5 from Harding, he slipped down into the interior corridor running from one end of the ship to the other. Ready to take weapon's fire, Nick hugged the bulkhead until he was sure the corridor was empty. "C'mon down with Tonto, Clint. I think poor old Paulo was right. It looks like Carone

152

and his banditos may be hiding in his room waiting for an all clear sign he ain't ever getting."

Clint and Tonto, followed by John, Lucas, Casey, and Kabong joined Nick at the bottom of the decorative ladder staircase. Clint gestured Tonto into action. Tonto sniffed at every door, moving on while two men then searched the cleared room. With Lucas and Casey guarding for movement into the corridor, Clint, Nick, John and Johnny moved with Tonto, clearing each room, below decks kitchen, dining room, engine room, and every space where someone could hide or lie in wait. The work, tedious and at times nerve wracking, ended once again at the main corridor. Tonto showed no interest in any room until reaching the area housing the master suite.

Harding knocked on the door from the side that Tonto indicated first. The rest of his companions stayed tight to the bulkheads on both sides. "Hello in there. If you are women, say so. Then, stay in your room until we tell you to come out."

"Who are you," a woman's voice asked.

"Never mind that. Do as I say. Is there a man in there with you?"

"No."

"Where are the other two women," John asked.

"Next to me, the one before the master suite."

"Stay put." John moved to the next door, knocked and repeated his initial greeting. A woman answered and acknowledged another woman shared the cabin with her.

Automatic weapons fire shredded the center top part of the master suite door streaming down the corridor. Nick dropped down in prone position and fired an MP5 burst through the lower door center at knee level. Screams wailed in shocked agony. Nick's action drew general amusement from his companions as he rolled

153

again to the bulkhead. When the screams softened to sobs interspersed with cries of pain, John moved to one side of the master suite door with Nick opposite him with the grenade. When Nick had fired into the lower door, he had made a nice round hole by design that would accommodate his grenade.

"Hi there," John called out. "Come out with hands locked behind your head and you won't be shot."

"Fuck you! You'll kill us anyway… you bastards!"

Nick shrugged with a smile when John glanced over at him and mouthed. "He's right."

John grinned and nodded. "If you don't come out in thirty seconds, my companion will toss a grenade inside your cabin. It doesn't matter to us if you're alive or dead. We're here to arrest you, Carone. You and your men will be questioned. Otherwise, we execute you."

They heard hoarse angry voices inside, accompanied by the plaintive cries for a doctor from the wounded man.

"Ten seconds," John began counting down.

"I'm Carone! We are coming out!"

"Fingers locked behind your heads or we shoot you in the head."

The cabin door swung open. A medium built man with thinning black hair and a mustache walked through the doorway with fingers locked behind his head as ordered. The man behind him was much larger with a full beard. His fingers weren't locked. As they cleared the doorway, the second man pushed the first man aside, bringing a mini-Uzi to bear.

"Kill, Tonto!"

Tonto leaped before the man could get the Uzi down from his back, jaws locking on his neck, fangs ripping his throat out,

154

blood spurting in a cascade of red rain. Tonto's momentum jarred the dying man to his back where the dog ripped until certain of his kill. John had thrown Carone to his face, holding him there on the deck until Tonto completed his mission.

Nick kept an eye from a crouch on the other man, huddled into a fetal position, gripping his legs with small yips of pain and pleas for a doctor. Nick waited until Tonto moved off his kill, returning to his master's side with dripping jaws. He then went inside the cabin, securing it first with care, after which Nick killed the wounded man with another syringe from his pack. Nick tore the bedding from one of the beds and rolled both dead men into the bedding. After soaking towels in cold water, Nick threw one to Clint for Tonto and then swabbed the deck, leaving the towels to absorb the blood.

"Thanks," Clint said as he wiped Tonto's face. "It wasn't necessary though. I would have had Tonto wipe his face on Cheese as always."

"Thanks from me then." John dragged Carone to his feet. "Was that your dumb idea, Fernando?"

Carone remained silent.

"How's my toy, Cheese," Lynn asked.

"Very quiet, but I'm sure he's waiting for the proper motivation to be your good little helper," John replied to much amusement. "Come aboard, Crue."

"On my way. Sylvio has my mobile kit ready to go on one of the lounges amidships, so take Fernando to his interrogation site. Dr. Deville is on her way."

Carone's eyes scanned the smiling murderous faces around him. "Who…who is this Dr. Deville person? You cannot torture me. It is against International Rights Laws!"

155

"Oh… so only you Cartel lunatics and murderous Islamic horde frog hopping from one nation to another, can torture, huh?" John smashed Carone across the face with a bitch slap from hell. "Welcome to the new neighborhood, Fernando. I'm going to warm you for this meeting with the foremost torturer in the world today. She'll be angry, but in your case, I don't care. She will make you feel pain you thought impossible – pain so great you'll crack the teeth out of your head. You'll be able to make her pause by telling us every fact about how to get your untold fortune to put into our accounts, and every single detail about your terrorist connections. Then I'm going to ask Dr. Deville to take you to the undiscovered country of pain until you die!"

Nick smiled, watching the transformation flowing over Carone's features. Staring into the darkness of unendurable pain etched in John Harding's grim features, Carone broke. Having measured the hatred Harding compartmentalized for these Islamic enablers and their murderous horde, the chances of any plea for mercy would fall on deaf ears.

"Wait! I will give you everything! Take…take these numbers and account descriptions!" Carone began reciting his bank account numbers, passwords, and locations. Lucas grabbed John's arm, whispering in his ear.

Harding nodded at Lucas's input. "Slow down. We'll check. God help you if your info proves false. I will keep you alive as chum for the fish, feeding you to them one bite every few minutes for three full days until there's nothing left of you but your beating heart and open eyeballs."

Fernando repeated everything, although Nick was sure Jafar had begun investigating the financial leads from Carone the moment he overheard them on the network from the beginning of their open network access. By the time Lynn arrived in person for her Dr. Deville foot inspection, Carone had spelled out every aspect of their operation and his financial transactions. Only when he began repeating himself, and reached the end of his helpfulness concerning terrorist connections, did John give him a pop in the forehead.

Fernando shut up immediately. "How was that, Denny?"

"Achmed and I are working it, DL," Denny replied. "I will have confirmation within the hour. Relax if you can. We're here on the Valkyrie, including Laredo and the Stealth. He says he can launch again in minutes if you decide to put the ship down."

"We've adopted the Tempest," John said. "Call me the moment you get everything in order. I don't like this guy. If anything doesn't pan out I'm going to ask Dr. Deville to strip Fernando's sanity from him."

Denny sighed. "What about the women? They're still alive, right?"

"They're confined to quarters," Nick answered. "When we're sure of Fernando's information, Kabong and I will cover our faces to get them. We'll restrain, blindfold them, and transfer them to you where you will lock them down until transfer from the Valkyrie to wherever you want them. I want your word you'll do so, exactly as I outlined, Denny."

Silence until Nick's mouth began to tighten. John took a hand then. "We're all a little tense in this operation, Denny. If you don't agree with your word, I'm going in with Nick to relieve the little Tweety-Birds from life."

"You have my word... damn it. I should be able to get Fernando. You don't understand the capital we can-"

"One more word and even confirmation won't save him for a heartbeat!" Nick had his blade against Carone's throat. No one else moved.

"Say something stupid, Denny! I want to see Fernando, 'the butcher', Carone get it," Lynn called out. "We know what this bastard has done! None of what you say will matter though.

Carone's cut up kids in front of their parents, executed people at will who said one word against him, and killed whole underling's families at the merest slight he's felt. I obey the wishes of the Dark Lord. If he asks me to, I plan on keeping Carone screaming until morning light."

"Understood," Denny agreed. "Please let me have the women for transfer."

"We'll give it a shot. They better not give any hint of being involved. When we do a physical confirmation on Fernando," Lynn replied. "We will be asking him."

Denny sighed once more… as if his audience cared. "Fine. I'll talk with you soon."

"Are you ready, DL," Nick asked.

"Yep… I'm done coaxing answers. On the good side, Jafar figures we're fifty million the richer from the text I just now received. I don't want to wind up in jail, but God help the prisoners trying to get the Cheeseburger anyway."

Nick grinned. "We're not letting anyone put you in a cell, DL. Let's leave Fernando for the moment. I'd like to ask the only other ones alive a few questions. C'mon, Johnny Five. Let's go see about taking prisoners."

"On your six, Muerto!"

* * *

Nick tapped on the door Gus Denova and Quays Tannous had been watching. They were the cabins where the three female crewmembers remained in hiding. "Open the door. You will be blindfolded and restrained during transfer to American soil."

The woman in the first room gasped audibly enough to be heard outside the cabin. "You're nuts. Why the hell should I go along with that bullshit deal?"

Nick's affable request turned to dour threat in a split second of hearing the woman's condescending tone. "You'll obey every single order you're given from this moment on or I will break through the door and slice your intestines out of you while my companion pours bleach on them. Want a demo?"

The door flew open to reveal a late twenties blonde with no other attitude on her face other than survival. When she saw the two black masked figures with MP5s pointed at her, she dropped to her knees in begging tones, crying for mercy.

"Shut-up!" Nick restrained the sobbing woman, yanking her upright. Johnny added a hood after taking her digital fingerprint and a mouth swab for DNA testing.

They went then to the next door where Nick knocked and called out in comical voice. "Come out, come out wherever you are in there."

The door opened immediately. Both the women had 9mm handguns. Nick and Johnny fired simultaneously, instantly riddling the two women across chest and head from their positions at the sides of the doorway. Johnny repeated the fingerprint and DNA tests which would be repeated for all the bodies aboard the Tempest. The woman captive dived to the floor against the corridor bulkhead.

"That did not go well, Muerto."

"I half suspected it, which was the reason I had the minions watching these cabins. We have one here I believe will provide valuable information once Dr. Deville works her over. I doubt she's an innocent crewmember because there are no innocent crewmembers aboard this boat. We'll keep her separate of Carone until he's questioned."

Johnny helped the woman to her feet again, as Monster Squad members raced into the corridor. Johnny held up his hand.

"We're good, my friends. It appears the women were not so innocent as Paulo claimed."

"Bring her to my casting couch, Kabong," Lynn said. "I finished with Carone already. He confirmed everything he told us so we cut him some slack. His laptop, he kindly gave us all the file passwords for, catalogued all his dealings, including with the Pilot Hill bunch. Fernando did mention the female contingent. He likes the ladies… dangerous ladies. All three of the women are Cartel hitters. The blonde is his favorite. I see the two bloody brunettes so blondie's in the bag I assume. Her name's Senta Bulgar. She's from Albania. Senta is on loan from Al-Kadi. According to Fernando, Senta killed the heads of two Central American Cartels he passed her off as a prostitute to. Carone never bedded her. He's scared to death of her. He gives her anything she wants and has used her to handle the women transferred through his hands on their way to Dubai and Saudi Arabia as sex slaves."

Nick glanced at his companions, wondering if they were thinking the same thing he was. Harding voiced it.

"I'm reading your mind, Muerto. You're considering using your number one status with Fernando and Senta at your side for an intro into Pilot Hill."

"That's scary good, Cheese," Nick said. "I'm slipping if I can get read like a four year old playing five card stud. What do you think, Lynn?"

"Let me get a look at Senta, Kabong." Lynn walked over to their surviving female prisoner with features in neutral observance for the introduction.

Johnny removed the hood. Senta had been listening to the discussion of her real calling. She knew they would torture her to death no matter what she pretended now. She spit on the deck after looking into the eyes of another female killer. Senta made an error in judgement. She thought she had been captured by regular

160

federal authorities, in spite of Nick's threats. The woman in front of her looked down at the deck and sighed.

"Gently, Cheese," Lynn cautioned. "We need her face undamaged."

"On it." John Harding upended Senta as if she were a recalcitrant two year old. He lowered her slowly, with Senta cursing her heart out over her spittle. He forced her face directly into it, stirring and swabbing with gentle swirling motions to the amusement of his audience, ending the final wipe with her hair.

"Recon!" Lucas enjoyed the show even more than the others. "Now that's the way a Marine cleans the deck, swabbies!"

Lynn grinned at the sputtering Senta as Harding righted her, caressing the side of her head. "Oh good. Senta still thinks she's in charge of what happens. You'll learn to obey, my dear one. Soon, you will pray never to hear my voice raised in anger. I already own your pal, Fernando."

Outraged instead of thinking through her situation, Senta made a second, more egregious error. She spit in Lynn's face. "You will get nothing from me, Puta! Oh, I know how to handle bitches like you! I will die before ever helping your skank ass."

The men who knew Lynn fled backwards a few steps - not from fear, but because they could imagine what lie ahead of Senta at Lynn's hand. Lynn sighed with contentment while taking out a handkerchief to wipe off her face.

"Oh my. That was lovely. C'mon with me, honey. I think we need to get to know each other better. I like you already, sweetie. You're going to love me."

"That's what you think, bitch!" Senta tried to twist away from Johnny to no avail. "Why not take me on woman to woman? I'll stomp your stupid Puta ass into a bloody pool!"

"Maybe later after we visit Pilot Hill, sweetie," Lynn replied without raising her voice. "We need your face in one piece right now. Hey, how do you like the blade?"

"I love the blade, Puta. I know you'll kill me after I refuse to help you so what does it matter?"

Lynn laughed, a haunting titter of sound capable of freezing the hearts of lesser men and women. "Don't worry about that, dear. You'll help. In fact you'll beg me to help. I'm thinking my cohort, Muerto, will need a female on his arm at Pilot Hill. We'll be close friends by then, Cara Mia."

Casey shook his head as Senta passed him. "Sucks to be you."

On the couch set by the minions to be Lynn's interrogation tool, Johnny and Nick strapped Senta down with the binding straps found aboard. Nick took off his mask as did Johnny. Senta would never return to the general population of anywhere. Senta gasped.

"I know you! You're Nick McCarty! You killed Felix Moreau! Felix was a lover of mine. He mentored me. You bastard! He wasn't even on a contract in your way. I know the accounts on the Dark Web about the way he was killed are lies. No way, you ever came close enough to him to kill Felix with a knife. How did you kill him? You shot him in the back."

Nick shrugged as his companions enjoyed the exchange. "I would have. Felix was so easy a target, I hardly needed much effort to get him."

"Liar!"

Johnny smiled hugely in anticipation while retrieving Felix Moreau's last moments on earth from his iPad files. He brought it over for Senta to see. She watched her lover's death by Nick's hand with wide eyed shock. At Nick's last words while Moreau

162

faded into eternity, Senta struggled wildly against her bonds before realizing after a moment the hopelessness of her situation.

"It's nice to know Felix was loved," Nick stated with comical whimsy to the loud amusement of his companions. Nick patted Senta's restrained hand. "He died with his boots on, Senta. He was a murderous scumbag without a conscience but he died okay."

Nick's humorous eulogy enraged Senta but Lynn grabbed her in a painful pinch at the nose. "Don't bother. If you say anything else I may forget we're trying to keep you alive. I'm glad you know Nick. You'll be introducing him and me at the door of the Pilot Hill compound. Once we get inside with Al-Kadi, then we'll have some real fun."

For the first time, Senta smiled as Lynn released her. "I will never deceive Al-Kadi. You will see. I will say one thing now to please you, but I will betray you to him the moment we cross the threshold of the house."

Lynn clapped her hands in delight. "Oh… Cara Mia… when I get done with you, I would be able to use you as a campfire girl leader in a brown skirt uniform. No more talk. Let's get to my showing of the enhancements in interrogation I've contrived. I think you'll be impressed. Please hook Senta to my needles for her first lesson."

When Nick did as bid. He inserted the acupuncture needles at Senta's heels. Her feet had to be held in place by Quays Tannous and Sylvio Ruelas. Senta, for the first time, began to believe the people in front of her were not going to coax her into doing as they outlined.

"Wait! What is this? You can't torture me! It's illegal! Who the hell are you people? Assassins, torturers, cold blooded killers… what the hell is going on?"

"We're the Monster Squad and the Unholy Trio, baby," Lynn said, patting her cheek. "When the pussies in Washington DC crap their pants and don't know what to do about some cult of murderous assholes, they call us. We don't ask questions. They tell us we need to fix something and we fix it. Don't try to understand it all now, honey. I'll teach it to you in small doses until there's no doubt in what's left of your mind about who we are, what we plan on doing, and how you will help us."

"McCarty! I know you. Tell her! I will do as she asks. I see this is business now. I kill on command. I do as I'm paid to do. I'll help you get inside Al-Kadi's place... no charge. Let me live! I'll fix everything. Give me a damn weapon and I'll help you execute anyone you want killed! Tell her!"

Nick leaned over Senta, revealing a mirror image of cold, unfeeling, death that existed within Senta. He smiled after a moment of silence. "I see you do know me. I am a psychopath like you in many things. I've found I care about some part of reality. America is part of that reality. As you've already stated – you will say one thing now and another later. When Dr. Deville finishes with you, the psychopath inside will be dead. All that will be left is a minion of Cruella Deville who lives to do nothing but what she asks. I could claim you won't feel a thing but that would be a lie. Happy trails, Senta."

Chapter Seven

Monstrous Happenings

A half hour later, Senta needed splashed into consciousness as the three minute intervals of absolute agony, without any way to stop them, reformed her being into a template of pain. She tried to speak as Lynn leaned over her with a smile. All that came out was gibberish. Lynn chuckled.

"That was only a half an hour, Cara Mia. Wait until we get to hour three."

Senta screamed.

"Oh yeah... that's what I'm talkin' about," Lynn said, before Denny's voice pelted into her ear from the Valkyrie.

"Bronstein class frigate heading toward us at full throttle... ETA forty minutes," Denny stated. "Do you read?"

"We hear," Harding said from near Lynn.

"That boat has torpedoes," Nick remarked. "What's the assessment, Captain Blood?"

"Apparently, Fernando called for help before we got his communications shut down. Can you ask him about it, and if there's some way to send the approaching threat back to Mexico where I see it originated? I'd like to not have to make a Mexican Navy frigate disappear with all hands on board, folks, but I doubt it can be done any other way. Paul's in agreement."

"Oh, for God's sake, Denny," Lynn said. "Scramble a couple of jets and tell them to go back where they came from."

"Lynn's right," Harding agreed. "We have bases very nearby. Get them on an intercept course. They can warn a Mexican frigate off. Hell... we sold it to them I'm sure. They must know we can ruin their evening."

"The formal authorities dummied up the moment they were contacted and warned about an interdiction by federal agents on a ship in international waters. Rogue elements in the Mexican government have already refused all offers, saying the Tempest was under their control," Denny answered. "They think they can save the product and ship by a show of power. I'm betting they can't and we're not going to let them. I can't speak for you Monsters; but if Ahab and Payaso want the Tempest in the fleet stationed at Monster Island, something will have to be done about the inbound frigate. The other option is to take what we have, including the bodies, and go home. We can file an official complaint with the Mexican government later about their rogue battleship. I admit I love the idea of having the Tempest; but in order to get her, a sea battle with the Mexican frigate will be the only way possible."

"Oh my!" Nick made grasping movements to his heart as Denny ended his update. "Uh... would there be any chance the Mexican government, who also has an air force, would be willing to launch on us poor Monsters. What you're talking about is an act of war."

"As much as I love this damn ship already," Lucas added, "I have to agree with Dead Boy. How do we get out from under sinking a supposedly friendly nation's warship? At the very least this is an international incident."

"Shall we run then? I believe Paul can end all negative fallout from the event. This show of force to get the Tempest back confirms our suspicions that elements of the Mexican government enable piracy incidents here, and in the Gulf of Mexico, along with massive at sea transfers of drugs, weapons, and human trafficking. Paul hurriedly recruited key congressional leaders to list this as an official CIA joint task force with the FBI, Homeland Security, and the Justice Department. As representatives of the aforementioned agencies, Paul issued a warning that any action on the part of the approaching frigate would be looked on as from a hostile enemy."

"Why didn't you lead with that, Spawn," John asked.

"I admit to questioning whether I believe Paul can pull this off. If Mexico decides to back the actions of their rogue warship, we'll have to defend ourselves against whatever Mexico escalates to in the realm of warfare. I didn't want to soft-sell this. We could be looking at a Bay of Pigs or Benghazi sellout. It won't be Paul who does it. They'll be crossing him too if they yank our backing. We'll go with whatever you decide."

"We can fire the RGM-84 from the Valkyrie."

"Muerto's right," Clint said. "Once the frigate is hit, we can move on them with both the UH-60M Stealth and our Mi-24 attack helicopter for the finish."

Gus Denova brought Carone into the room at Lynn's order. He was openly sobbing by the time Gus forced him down on a chair. Lynn patted his shoulder. "Hello there, my little helper. You didn't do as well as I thought. I'm very disappointed in you."

Carone openly cried, his shoulders heaving. "I...I forgot! The pain was so bad, I forgot about sending the text to the contact drop in the Mexican government. You have to... believe me."

"What about the women and your personal assassin?" Nick watched Carone's face.

"I thought you had killed everyone but me, including the women." Carone's surprised features indicated truth. It was only then Lynn, Harding, and Nick moved from in front of Senta's delirious form. "Oh my God! I...I didn't know. Senta Bulgar is a killer. The officials... my contacts... Gabrielle Ruiz and Zepeda Osorio... they are ministers of Foreign Affairs and Defense."

"Is there any way to call them off," Lynn asked.

"I...I cannot. They delete the drop the moment it is used. I do not get a new drop until the following day... if then. I could try calling Al-Kadi. Perhaps he has a more direct line."

Nick shook his head. "We want Al-Kadi clueless for now. I have another idea. I saw the Panga boat in its stall. We have the XM25 airburst grenade launcher with EMP load. Let Payaso and I meet the frigate. For a lob shot I'd only have to be within seven hundred yards."

"What if they have it shielded, Muerto?"

"We'll run. I'll bring our XM307 too in case we have to hold them off. Payaso? Are you following this?"

"I'm on my way over now with both weapons. Issac has the Valkyrie helm. If we have to abandon the Tempest, Lucas will be with him as well as Cala. Can you find the controls for the in hull boat dock, Lucas?"

"On it. I don't think much of this idea. How close are they now, Denny?"

"They've slowed. We're bombarding them with stand down orders. Jafar is networking with Johnny. He should be receiving streaming positioning data now."

"I have it, Muerto," Johnny acknowledged, with tablet in hand. "I will go with you and Payaso. It will be the Unholy Trio on the attack."

Nick smiled. "Let's get going. See you all on the other side."

* * *

"Oh Muerto, this baby is fast as hell!" Gus maneuvered in an exaggerated approach pattern, zooming from far side to far side, varying speed and pattern.

"This will be close guys. They will open fire on us the moment we get in sight or slightly before," Nick said. "I'm glad you thought to bring my M107 too, Payaso. Johnny can fire the XM25 EMP round and use my range finders, while I keep an eye on any targets I can spot on the ship."

"You're nuts," Gus muttered while paying close attention not to repeat any movements. "I know how good you are, but hitting anything from this moving Panga boat is beyond even your Muerto death magic."

"Heh...heh. If we make the frigate dead in the water, the Unholy Trio will show the Monster Squad how to have a little fun."

"You do know we can hear you, right Muerto?"

"Uh oh. I forgot it was open mic night," Nick joked. "Yeah, I know, Lynn. Hey, Laredo... you have the Stealth ready to back us dumb-shits if this doesn't work, right?"

"Nope. Clint said we'd fire the RGM-84 using you guys as laser pointers."

General hilarity ensued for a few moments until Johnny indicated they would be in sight within seconds.

"Ready the XM25, Kabong. Hold her full speed for a broadside parallel to the frigate's starboard side, Payaso. That would be the frigate's right side and our left on approach."

"Fuck you, Muerto!" Gus smiled, listening to everyone on the line enjoying Nick's insinuation Gus didn't know the difference between port and starboard.

Search lights turned on, scanning the area as Gus paralleled their target inside the five hundred yard range going in the opposite direction. The frigate fired with 20mm cannon and .50 caliber machine gun fire with tracers.

"Fire, Kabong!"

Nick had found the machine gun turret with the M107 night vision scope. His six shot semi auto burst stitched through the machine gunner as if he were made of papier-mache while the 20mm cannon fire crept nearer. Johnny fired the XM25. The EMP airburst load exploded over the oncoming frigate with incredible effect. Instantly, the frigate cruised to a floating stop, bobbing in the water.

"Holy shit, Muerto! That was at least a six hundred yard shot from a moving boat. You, my friend, are scary good," Gus exclaimed, bringing the Panga boat around.

"Those tracers were getting too close and I couldn't tell where the guy was without the night-vision scope. Now we deal with that damn 20mm cannon." Nick moved behind their portable XM307 turret and obliterated the 20mm cannon emplacement aboard the frigate.

Johnny switched to 25mm airburst grenade rounds and fired at will while Nick swept over the bridge with 25mm rounds. Gus turned the Panga boat to move toward the Valkyrie. The frigate was ablaze. The ammo magazines blew then, turning the main deck into an inferno with survivors jumping overboard.

"It's all yours, Laredo," Nick said.

"Understood."

Gus retreated away from the fiery hulk with Nick and Johnny relaxing near him. They waited with anticipation for what they knew to be on the way. The faint roar introducing 'Ride of the Valkyries' echoed across the water, gaining momentum into a tumultuous, mind numbing horror for the frigate's surviving crewmembers. The AGM-114 Hellfire missiles hit the frigate, sending waves of heat, sound, and force across the Panga boat with Gus turning to stunt the effect. The Unholy Trio watched the

Monster Squad repeat wave after wave using everything aboard the Stealth, including the 70mm Hydra rockets.

"Holy God in heaven," Gus whispered. "We are very bad men."

"We're going back to the Valkyrie, Muerto," Laredo said. "All the bodies are on the Valkyrie for-"

"Mexican F-5 fighter on approach!" Denny wasted no words. "John's locking in by radar on the fighter with the RGM-84. It's only a few minutes away. What do you have left, Laredo?"

"Nothing, boss. Clint's on the .50 for all that will do. I have chaff to deter a first attack and then we're history."

A moment later, the F-5 zoomed low over the burning frigate debris before barrel rolling upwards. Nick detached the XM307 from its portable stand. "Grab the stand, Johnny. Laredo, fly over us!"

"Okay... nice working with you, Muerto."

"Hold that thought. Turn the boat toward the frigate, steady as she goes. Help me get this damn gun mount pointed upward, Johnny. We're going to run the F-5 into our flak fire. Yes... that's it. Gus, put her on auto and come steady me and the mount while Johnny fires the 25mm airburst."

Using life jackets, ammo boxes, and equipment bags, the three men turned the mounted XM307 into a surface to air launcher. Johnny shoved against one side of the mounting with the XM25 in hand while Gus steadied the other side and Nick.

"Incoming! Chaff fired!" Laredo flew the UH-60M over the Panga boat, releasing fiery chaff into the sky as the F-5 fired missiles.

The chaff worked, but the exploding missiles in the chaff rained deadly debris downward, nearly obliterating the Panga boat.

171

"Fire!" Nick held onto the XM307 for dear life while firing round after round into the sky of the oncoming F-5 fighter. Johnny did the same with the XM25.

The F-5 couldn't avoid the flak and airburst 25mm grenades. It blew in spectacular fashion. Nick, Gus, and Johnny cheered from their sinking Panga boat but the celebration was short lived.

"Uh oh," Nick said comically as the blazing F-5 fighter streaked directly at them. "Abandon ship, maties. Captain Blood! We're in the water."

The Unholy Trio dived deep for all the good it would do them if the jet crashed atop their boat. It didn't. The F-5 hit the water fifty yards in front of the sinking Panga boat and cartwheeled in flaming fashion until bursting apart at the seams, scattering debris for hundreds of yards. Nick, Gus, and Johnny swam to the drifting Panga boat with only small debris cuts and wounds.

Laredo flew the UH-60M over them, lowering a ladder as the Stealth stirred the waves. Gus climbed upward first with Johnny behind him. Nick retrieved his M107 sniper rifle and the XM25 from the Panga boat.

"Will you for God's sake get your Muerto ass up here," Gus yelled down at him.

Nick strapped his M107 over his shoulder while hanging onto the swinging ladder with the patience bred of being a psychopathic killer. The weight and bulk from the two weapons slowed Nick's climb. When he reached the open hatch, hands reach down to propel him upwards. Instead, he shoved the weapons one after the other to his frustrated cohorts.

"I'll be back." Nick descended.

"We can buy a new XM307 you moron," Lynn called out to him with a giggle.

Nick grinned but kept on to his objective, grunting under the effort of securing the nearly eighty pound load to his frame. The climb upwards this time took all of his reserves to reach the hatch where his friends pulled him in. Clint and Lynn dragged him inside against the far bulkhead while Casey secured the ladder and shut the hatch. Nick waved at Laredo.

"You're the best, Laredo!"

"If not for you cowboys, I'd be in Davey Jones locker. Let's go home, kids. That was one exciting adventure I'd rather not repeat. God knows we're lucky they didn't scramble more than one F-5."

"We have everyone, Denny," Clint said. "We're on our way back."

"I know I'm a day late and a dollar short, but when you see the fighter escort arrive, they're ours," Denny replied. "If it helps, they would have shot the shit out of the jet that killed you."

"Wow... what a comfort," Lynn said. "Okay, Muerto... thank you, but what the hell was that all about... dragging replaceable weapons aboard a combat helicopter?"

"We brought down a jet fighter with them, Lynn. What can I say, I'm superstitious."

"Good point," Lynn replied.

"I have to admit it, Dead Boy. Those were some well-done combat adlibs," Clint said. "That water's a bit chilly, huh guys?"

"Tha...that's an understatement," Gus managed with only a slight shivering stutter. "I hope to hell I can find something dry on the Tempest."

"Since we don't know what the hell Mexico will do about getting their F-5 splashed by us, I think we better crew the Tempest to Monster Island without delay," Casey said. "Should we dump all the drugs and keep the weapons, or turn it all over."

"At the rate the idiots in charge of our government are importing the Trojan Horse Muslim refugees into California, we'll need to confiscate the weapons on board so we can outfit a good militia when warfare breaks out," Nick stated.

"Damn… Muerto going all militia survival on us," Lynn replied. "I'm in. Maybe we should start training a militia. We have a lot of veterans who've seen combat. Between the Marines and Delta guys we have, a trained militia would not only be feasible but a damn good idea. From now on I vote we confiscate all weapons when we find these Muslim terrorist enclaves instead of turning them in."

"It's definitely something to think about," Casey said. "I used to think a militia was farfetched until the stupidity in government lately. Think about it. Importing a horde of possible terrorists while taking away our Second Amendment right to bear arms so the common citizen can't even protect themselves. Soon, we'll have Muslim refugee hordes rioting through our cities like they do in Europe."

"No," Johnny stated. "We will stop them, my friends. If not, we will all be dead with all our ammo expended. I like the militia idea."

They paused in the conversation as the roar of low flying jets went by, their trails showing in the clear night air.

"At least we won't have to worry about any surprises on our tail," Laredo said over the network. "As to your pow-wow about militias, we have been gathering both a Navy and an Air Force. Air support wins wars. The Valkyrie is a jewel because of the helicopter pads and RGM-84 rocket emplacement. I never thought I'd say this either, but it may be time to think about preparing for war on American soil."

"If it comes to that I know we won't be running to the island," Clint said. "That's why it will be important to secure the compound at Pilot Hill. If we did train an actual militia it would have to be done there. We'll need an airfield and definite helicopter landing zones with hangars for anything we have. I like the armed militia idea for one reason more than anything else – I don't want citizens dying while trying to fight off an enemy while outgunned."

"I know you've been listenin', Denny," Lynn said. "What do you think?"

"I think it's a damn good idea. I'm in all the way. From now on we take all the weapons with us, starting with the Tempest. The drugs will be enough to explain our interdiction, not that I plan on sharing shit unless Mexico gets involved. Don't forget we'll have two new enemies in the Mexican government if our evidence gets ignored by El Presidente and the rest of the cabinet ministers."

"We're two minutes out," Laredo said. "Light up my LZ, John."

"On it," Harding said. "I wish I would have been on the Stealth when the Unholy Trio splashed the jet. I think I would have hit it with the RGM-84, but too damn late to save any of you. That was a hell of an action sequence from the Stealth cams."

"LZ lit. Coming in. Hold her steady, Issac."

Issac laughed with Lucas from the Valkyrie bridge. "Would if I could, my friend. I have heard you old Vietnam pilots can land anything anywhere."

"Very true statement," Laredo replied, easing the Stealth down onto the bobbing Valkyrie helicopter pad. "How's it looking for a Monster Island run, Lucas?"

175

"We're shorthanded to drive both boats but I agree with what Case said. We need to move immediately. You know… I bet we could afford to buy a couple of combat jets. It seems we're constantly getting close calls with our missions, involving some jackasses with jets." Lucas paused for a moment before going on. "Nick? Weren't you qualified on fighter jets? I read it in your Delta file when you were transferred into my training group."

"Yep. That was a long time ago, Lucas. No one wanted me to fly jets. It was a skill paid for so I could possibly bail my team out on a mission because I had an aptitude for it. The Air Force flight instructors were none too happy teaching an uneducated army puke. Why?"

"We have John and Laredo qualified on jets. If we got you a refresher course would you add on to our qualified pilot reserve program?"

"Sure. I'm glad we talked this out. The militia idea has been drifting around in my head for a while now," Nick responded as Laredo settled the Stealth into place. "We already know out here the vocal contingent of Californians have bought into every liberal bullshit program on earth. They're waiting for the chains with bonged out brains and a stupid smile on their face. I'd like to reach the veterans from our area who would join us if we need an army to stop these bastards."

The combatants exited the Stealth with Johnny and Gus helping carry the lucky weapons with Nick. Cala ran over to grip Johnny's arm, leaning her head into his shoulder. John Harding, Lucas, Jafar, Denny, Tommy, Del, Jesse, and Issac welcomed back their friends. The minions had Fernando and Senta in control on the amidships deck.

"We heard we're crewing the Tempest to Monster Island," Tommy said to Gus. "Which one are you going to pilot?"

"It's decided already, T," Lucas said. "Gus and Issac will pilot the Tempest. I'll pilot the Valkyrie with Jafar and Cala helping. We definitely need more trained boat drivers for our naval operations. When do you all think we should leave? Denny and I are thinking the sooner the better if we want to maintain ownership of the Tempest. Anyone think of a name to reregister her under?"

"You're the admiral of the fleet, Ahab," Lynn said. "Pick a name."

"Well... I did a stint aboard an aircraft carrier back in the day in the Marine detachment between deployments: the USS Ranger. They've scrapped her but the name's a good one. Let's call her Ranger."

"I like it," Lynn replied. "All in favor say aye."

A chorus of ayes reinforced Lucas's pick for the new name.

"We'll have to make the Ranger into a ship to be reckoned with," Harding said.

"Of course," Lucas agreed. "I've been thinking about another addition to the Valkyrie since we're talking fighter jets. Do you think we could land a Harrier type jet on the Valkyrie, Laredo?"

Laredo took a second look at their spacing on the pads to any bulkhead type interference. "I think we could. The Harrier is way beyond the F-5 or its like in fighter jet qualities, especially if we get a later version with all the bells and whistle."

"Good input, Lucas," Denny remarked. "I'll get on it. I think we might be able to get a McDonnell Douglas AV-8B Harrier if we can fit it. Have you ever piloted one of those Harriers?"

"Did you just insult me, Spawn?"

Denny endured amused catcalls for a moment. "Sorry... let me rephrase... can we get it on the Valkyrie?"

"I think so, but we wouldn't know for sure without testing it out. It wouldn't hurt to have a jump jet like the AV-8B. It's a great ground attack jet with bombing capabilities. Lucas is wrong about the fighter jet capabilities though. It's not an air combat type aircraft. It wasn't designed for a dogfight in the air. It would be a hell of an addition to our air force whether it fits on here or not."

"I'm going to shower and find some clothes," Gus said. "They have a great bar aboard the 'Ranger'. Do we have cover until tomorrow morning to sip a couple and get some sleep, Denny?"

"I guarantee it, Payaso."

"That is an excellent idea," Nick stated. "I've been meaning to try out the Bud and Beam brothers with the Cheeseburger."

"I'll be with you on that one, Muerto," Harding replied. "We have to toast you on your first confirmed kill on the way to being a jet fighter ace."

"Without the Unholy Trio, I'd have been swimming with the fishes," Nick replied.

"Oh great!" Clint gestured at the skies as if seeking divine intervention as Lynn danced around clapping her hands. "Now... for the rest of the night we'll be tortured with Godfather Deville's lines from the entire series. She uses every line ever made popular in that damn movie set to annoy the hell out of me. Thanks a lot, Dead Boy."

"Calm down, Nowhere Man... leave the gun, take the cannoli."

* * *

Rachel met Nick at the door in an embrace, leaving no doubt of her missing and worrying about him, while juggling a sleeping Quinn in her arms. She released him after a moment to allow Jean to give him a hug and Deke to attack with full on head butting action. "God, Muerto! We've heard reports of drug operations, Mexican Navy and Air Force casualties, and high seas gang wars, not to mention piracy, helicopter assaults, and human trafficking. You look like hell."

"The master mariner and our guys fled the storms along the Northern Pacific Coast to no avail. We rode the Valkyrie through seas I thought we'd lose our landed helicopters. It got so bad one night, we played 'Ride of the Valkyries', and Gus went full throttle as if we were doing at sea combat. He brought us through it all. On the upside, we deposited the newly named ship in our fleet, The Ranger, at the deep water dock Denny had a crew of engineers build. She's a real beauty – a true super yacht in every way."

"How bad was the combat, Dad? It had to have been bad with the reports we saw on TV, even if they were twisted."

Nick shrugged while petting Deke. "Let's go in the kitchen. I want a Bushmill's and to hear about your adventures here in the 'Grove'. Did any ruling come down about my shooting of Jean's gangster?"

"All done," Rachel answered. "Neil called and said they accepted the plea deals. We've been steering clear of our newbie Islam bitch. The husband's been dropping her off as if she's in danger, which is exactly the scenario he's trying to build."

"She's tried to goad me a little at recess, but I've had Cracker with me at all times as a witness in case I have to kick her ass."

"Jean! Honest to God, Daughter of Darkness, I will kick your ass if you don't watch that mouth of yours."

"Sorry. Ms. Nazari gets away with doing all kinds of stuff none of the other teachers can do, especially concerning religion. It's a double standard when she can preach Islam, while no other religion can even be mentioned."

"I'm pleased you can use double standard correctly in a sentence." Nick sat down, drink in hand, with Deke lying across his feet. "It's a good thing we took everyone we could with us. We needed to move the Ranger right away. Having Cala and Samira with us helped a lot. If we would have run into a bad storm while journeying home, sailing both ships toward Monster Island... Mama Mia."

"Did you capture the Carone guy?"

Nick glanced at Jean. She smiled back, putting her chin in hands with elbows on the table, completing an intensely interested pose. "Yes, Daughter of Darkness, we captured Carone and a woman assassin."

"Really?" Jean had expected Nick to tell them there were no prisoners. "A woman assassin like Lynn?"

Nick chuckled. "No one's like Lynn. We'll be using them to help us gain entrance into a terrorist compound at Pilot Hill. They've been making it into a halfway house for Isis cell members."

"Why the hell doesn't the FBI and Homeland Security move on the compound like an army? How many will you be going against? Maybe I should start going on more missions with you," Rachel said.

"They don't want these guys in the news or in the courts. In truth, any action we take with them is legal. They're saboteurs without country or uniform. They're plotting the destruction of America on our soil. That means they can be executed just as the saboteurs in WWII were. We're not sure at any one time how many they have at the compound. Denny Strobert will be providing us with satellite surveillance of the place. On your last note, Rach, you did an excellent job spotting for me on the 'Starlight of the Seas' mission, but as we talked about in the past, Jean and Quinn will need one of us alive if a mission goes sour."

"I know… it's just I'm a bit jealous of Cala's ability to do what she's done – taking flying lessons, learning to crew a boat, cleaning crime scenes… oh, wait a minute… maybe I'm not that excited about her many talents," Rachel joked.

"Let's get the Daughter of Darkness raised along with Quinn and then I'll take you along anywhere I go. I've been asked to reacquaint myself with fighter jets. We're thinking about getting a Harrier jet if it will fit on the Valkyrie helicopter landing zones. I'm sure they're thinking of having one at the compound."

"You flew jets?" Jean, learning something Nick hadn't shared yet, dropped the cute pose, and grabbed on to his arm. "Who'd you shoot down?"

"Nobody. We were going on a mission in Syria to steal one of their jets we had heard the Russians installed an advanced tracking system on. I learned how to fly a MiG23. Our Delta team crossed into Syria through Turkey to Taftanaz Air Base. The report was false. They didn't have anything on their MiG23's so I stole one of their Mi-8 Russian helicopters and flew my team out before they knew what we'd done. The base was in an uproar because we made it seem as if they were getting hit by incoming rockets. The black op fun part started when we called out for help from the fleet in the Mediterranean Sea. I flew the Mi-8 onto the USS Eisenhower Aircraft Carrier. They sent their air-wing to meet my pursuers. It didn't end well for the Syrians."

"Holy crap, Dad!"

Nick, who never thought of his deployments, combat, or training as entertainment, realized for the first time he should be sharing it, in particular with Jean. He already had no doubt she would be in combat. "Sorry, kid. I tend to forget about my past as it becomes the past. In any case, we were flogged for using naval assets in the region for a black op. My CO was an old Vietnam vet. He told the Admiral who called him we were all on the same side, thank you for the assistance, and go fuck yourself if you think saving American servicemen is a tragedy. The Admiral laughed and said he'd take the heat from the morons over him. I heard they became best friends."

"How many past surprises do you have stored in your Muerto mind," Rachel asked.

Nick sipped his drink with calm satisfaction. "I don't live in the past. When you two trigger something from my past, I explain it. I have found a crew to collaborate with who are as monstrous as I am. They served America, kept on with what skills they could develop within their range as cold blooded killers, and we serve now to defend America. We will not defeat this Islamic scourge by pretending they don't exist and it's all a misunderstanding."

"So… if I said tell us everything… what would you do?"

"I'd tell you to go upstairs and get to work on your homework. You would of course be grounded for eternity. Your Mom and I love the passion you achieve your objectives with, but you scare both of us with the lack of foresight you show in achieving them. I'm not shy about answering questions about my past life, but be careful of what you ask for. Some things cannot be explained as if they were a trip to the county fair."

"Understood," Jean replied with grim acceptance. "I don't care much about flying stuff. I want to be on the ground, stopping bad people."

Nick smiled at Rachel burying her face in her hands. "Understood, Viper."

Rachel peeked out from between her fingers. "We're going to hell."

"Welcome to my world."

* * *

Nick happily walked Deke and Jean to school, taking extreme pleasure in the still gray skies, cooler ocean generated temperatures, and watching Deke hop up and down as he walked next to Jean. All was right with the world for a moment. He glanced over at Gus, his brother by another mother, with light hearted enjoyment. In that heartbeat Nick spotted the accelerating car in the distance. He threw the smiling and shocked Gus toward Jean.

"Protect Gus!" Nick pushed Gus toward Jean and Deke, only adjusting at the last second to what evolved. He saw Gus take Jean down, covering her with his own body and Deke sitting calmly at their side. Nick grinned as he drew his Colt.

Nick did not wait for gunfire. His senses, honed over the past missions, ripped reality into his ongoing perception of everything. Nick stood in a shooter's crouch, weapon aimed. The moment Nick saw the machine pistol appear at the rear passenger window, he fired a three shot group into the driver's head. The vehicle caromed to the tree enhanced side, opposite their walking path to the school. Nick noted the engine didn't rev as he approached the vehicle on a dead run. He killed everything in the vehicle, seeing surprised looks from the other occupants as he fired without hesitation into each head. *No one hunts me or mine.*

Nick reached in and turned off the key. He recognized the features of what was left of the faces belonging to the shooter's companions. "Aw… shit."

Gus peeked from his duty in shielding Jean, knowing he was the last defense if Nick failed. He eased the 9mm handgun from its side holster, ready to bring it to bear on anyone until his own last breath. "Nick?"

"It's me, brother. There's no use in Jean going on now. I'm calling Rachel. She can pick you, Jean, and Deke up. We have another Kader problem, Payaso.

Gus helped Jean to her feet while Nick kept watch, Colt in hand. "Are you okay, Jean?"

"Yep." Jean hugged Deke who remained vigilant at her side. "How many, Dad?"

Nick took a deep breath from his crouch. "Three. Please call your Mom. It would be better if she heard your voice first."

"Sure. I got this." Jean called home, laughed, and brought the phone over on speaker with both Gus and Deke at her side. "It's Mom."

"Hi, honey." Nick did not relax for a moment. "Little busy. It's the Kader show again. Please head here. I'll have Gus call Johnny to warn him."

"On my way."

Gus had his phone in hand, calling Johnny.

Nick stayed vigilant as he heard sirens approaching.

* * *

An hour later, Nick sat at Neil Dickerson's desk. Neil joined him with a folder, sitting down opposite Nick with a pinched look on his face. "First off, I'm glad you, Gus, and Jean are alive and well. Please don't think otherwise. That said, this new incident on the heels of the gangbanger shooting is going to be rough. Your friends in the US Marshal's Office confirmed for the DA that you have been targeted by the Kader family. I took this folder detailing the planting of explosives on your house. I explained how the Kaders were also tied into the Fontaine incident. I think if he could, the DA would order you exiled from Pacific Grove."

"I couldn't very well allow them to kill us," Nick said.

"I think the execution style killings in the car worried the DA, his words, not mine."

"Apparently, he doesn't know much about those MP5's they aimed out the window at me. They were fully automatic, Neil. We would have all been dead in seconds. I couldn't very well allow them to recover from the tree ramming and open fire."

"I told him. The fact all three had fully automatic submachine guns definitely made an impression. The DA thinks you can just shout halt and the whackos with submachine guns lay down their guns and surrender. I reminded him it would be much better to worry about where the hell those three came into possession of the guns."

"I'm concerned about that myself. I recognized one of them, Ishmael Kader. He's the only male Kader I've ever met who I thought was reasonable. There he was, in the backseat of the car this morning, getting ready to blast us with a submachine gun. That means Cala Kader's marriage to Johnny Groves set off the crazies in the Kader family. They refused my offer of a dowry, even though it was much greater than Fontaine's. Ishmael was the Kader family negotiator. When I talked with him last, Ish wanted no part of me. Did you have a chance to find out who Ish's friends were?"

"Yes. I'm sure their identities and background won't make you feel any better. They were accepted in the last bunch of Syrian refugees."

"Oh goody. It wasn't enough I had the family already here trying to kill me. Now, California decided to import them for me. Ever wonder if maybe our looney tune leaders want to be part of a new Caliphate the Muslims keep killing people all over the world to install?"

"I don't know, Nick. I meet people in this state all the time. I live near some very good people. They work blue collar jobs. They live a conservative life style – but they go out on Election-Day and vote into office the worst idiot leftists they can find to vote for, who don't believe in anything they do. I don't have an answer for it."

"Can you send me what you found on the other hired killers with Ish? Oh… uh… am I free to go?"

"Yes to both questions. I'll call if there are problems. I'll go with you to get your personals. How does Jean manage with the events like today on the walk to school?"

"Exceedingly well, my friend – frighteningly so. None of it is a game to her, but Jean's fearless. At least Rachel doesn't think I'm corrupting her.

"You could drive, moron."

Nick stood. When he thought he could repeat what Jean said earlier, in tone with the way she sounded, Nick took a deep breath. "Jean told me, 'if we avoid our regular routines, the terrorists win'."

The two men endured a lengthy appreciation of Jean's adlib.

* * *

The woman cried in muffled quietness. She had buried her husband, Ishmael Kader, that morning. Their two children slept in the adjoining room at the house of Ishmael's relative who was also now dead. A hand gripped her shoulder, causing a brief bark of surprise, as she turned to the person clutching her shoulder. The black masked figure made hushing motions, which she obeyed instantly.

"Hello, Aara. Do you know who I am?"

"Yes… you are El Muerto," Aara answered in whispered tones. "He told me you would come once he failed to kill you. He guessed who you were, but he could not convince his family elders to leave you alone. They threatened to kill us all for trying to escape the family. He sacrificed himself to save us, but Ishmael knew you would come. My husband foresaw his death in a dream."

"It's too bad Ish didn't call me. I would have freed you all from the Kader nightmare," Nick explained. "I have killed all the males in this house except for the children. The women have been sedated. They will awaken. I noted you were still awake. I liked your husband. He attacked me, my daughter, and my friend, after agreeing to stay away from me."

Aara nodded in sad agreement. "Ishmael told me I might barter for my family's lives if I gave you this."

Nick accepted the thumb-drive from Aara's hand. "In reality, I never would harm you or your children. I only allowed you to talk with me because I needed to warn you and the other women Kaders. Pass the word once the bodies of the male Kaders are found in the house. Plead ignorance to the police how such a thing could happen. Blame it on Islamists unhappy with the Kader's failure to obey Sharia decree. Count your blessings, find men for husbands outside Islam. Never mention anything about me ever. Here."

Aara accepted the envelope with reluctance. "I will never mention you again, Muerto. No one who has any sense of reality will ever speak of you again. I will warn them. I do not know if the women will heed my warning after your visit here, but I will tell them. Blaming extremists will be what I do when asked. If you post my husband's thumb-drive contents, the police will suspect the actual men responsible for all these deaths."

"The envelope contains a cashier's check on a bank in the Cayman Islands for five million dollars. Use it to help free yourselves from this Kader curse. Also in the envelope is an internet drop address. Contact me there with any information or problem you have. No one else will be able to access it. Once you use it, another will be issued to you. Each time will be untraceable. Keep silent about the money, Aara. Work in silence to help the others. Do not worry about the zealots who wish to wail in the streets. Leave them to their self-pity and grief for maniacal male mutants who terrorized them daily. They will be lost. I know each of your fellow Kader women wives has been mutilated... except for you. Ishmael was the only man amongst the male Kaders to refuse the atrocity. I am sorry for your loss."

Nick injected Aara with a syringe to sedate her until morning. He wasn't sorry for her loss, but he felt after learning how much Ishmael had refused to do under pressure, that his wife and kids deserved more. Plus, he now had an unexpected gift Ishmael meant for his eyes only. Five more mutants were brought to room temperature this night in the house of Kader. Nick had no doubt the sudden unexplained deaths would bring the authorities pounding at his door. He also knew they would be able to prove nothing in relation to his involvement. Nick had left his own clues amongst the dead, pointing to an Isis betrayal and claiming the deaths of the males as retribution for their disloyalty. Combined with the messages of outrage posted earlier on hacked Muslim terrorist sites, Nick figured to have enough misdirection to play ignorant at the Kader killings. *I'm not done by a long shot. This will be war as promised.*

Nick stayed close to the house fronts with mask on. Arriving at the street perpendicular to his targeted street, Gus drove to the curb and Nick entered the back. Johnny sat next to Gus with satellite imaging while monitoring the police band. Nick passed the thumb-drive to Johnny.

"Do a quick scan of this. We may be able to post it into the police website if the info helps distract from my Kader culling of the herd."

Ten minutes later as Gus drove along slowly towards Nick's house, Johnny removed his headphones. "Ishmael confessed to the attempt on your life as ordered by elders in the family and an outside group with Isis ties. He claims they would have killed his wife and kids if he had not went along with it. Ishmael spoke plainly he did not expect to survive the attack. I have found nothing yet expanding on anything that would jeopardize what you did tonight. In fact, once I go through the entire recording I will bounce it around and post it to the police."

"Maybe I won't have the cops beating on my door after all. There will be no more school walks. I'll be driving Jean and Sonny to school from now on. Deke will have to walk with me down to the beach for his outings. That was a very close call with the Kader hit attempt. Did Ish mention names, Johnny?"

"Yes, but three of them are now dead. They were in the house you relieved me of in-laws at and acquired this marvelous thumb-drive of proof. One other family name resides in New York. He was the one who sent the three you killed. Another interesting thread concerns the Pilot Hill compound of Al-Kadi. Although Ishmael didn't know their names, he said two other men sent from New York stay at the compound. The elders threatened his family, claiming the cell would take vengeance on Ishmael's wife and kids. By sending the two assassins to accompany the Kader relatives they left Ish with very little room to maneuver. He should have called me."

"Good Lord," Gus muttered. "The comedians make jokes about mother-in-law problems. This is ridiculous. By the way... no one talks of the moms. Where is Dimah's mom? Johnny, where the hell is Cala's mom? Do they ever speak on behalf of the children their husbands wish to sell into slavery and murder?"

"It is not a subject we discuss," Johnny admitted as Gus stopped in front of Nick's house. "Cala claims both mothers supported their husbands with the same vitriol and wailing support of anything destroying America. They have turned their own sons to the dark side. Cala tried to talk with her brother. He told her if he sees her he will kill her on sight. I have decided to relieve him of his life but Cala asked me to hold off from doing so for a time."

"Let me know," Nick said. "Dimah has expressed the same request. The males in the family get no special exceptions from this point on. Ask Cala if she would like us to teach her brother about shooting his mouth off down in the chamber of horrors."

Johnny grinned at Nick. "Yes. It will be as you ask, Muerto. Cala can take care of herself but I worry he will catch her unawares."

"We cannot lose the 'Cleaner', Johnny," Nick replied, getting out of the vehicle. "If Cala sees the brother in the chamber of horrors, she can ask him anything she likes once. Then, we'll know which way the brother will go. If we see any animosity toward Cala after he hears her plea to remember they have blood ties, we will try the hard way. After that, he sleeps with the fishes."

Johnny chuckled. "Yes, Godfather. Shall we meet at the Point after Jean and Sonny get to school for a discussion of coming events, complete with the Deke and the Irish?"

"Of course, dog brother. Will you be joining us, Payaso?"

"Yes, dog brother, if I'm allowed to come out and play by the infamous T-Rex."

Chapter Eight

Back to School

Jean sat with disgruntled frown and arms crossed in the front seat while Nick drove. Nick could see Sonny smiling in the backseat. Deke sat happily with his head hanging out the window, tongue lolling in the breeze. The decision to drive from now on to school did not sit well with Jean who openly preferred gun battles to peaceful transfer to the school grounds.

"You're getting to be a spoiled brat, Jean," Sonny stated.

"What?! Oh...my...God... Sonny Salvatore! You did not just disrespect me with the S word!"

"Yeah... I did. You deserve it, you little whiney wart," Sonny finished with a flourish. "Your Dad's trying to protect us. You were nearly killed the other morning. I care about you! I don't want you killed because you insist on being an idiot!"

Nick grinned. The two carried on conversations as if they were twenty instead of ten. He could tell Sonny's words about caring for her silenced Jean. He could see the myriad retorts she wanted to zing him with floating across the Daughter of Darkness's features. "Sonny's right, kid. You're not bait in a trap. Once I make sure the threat is gone we'll walk again together with Deke. Until then, it's not happening."

"You're going to walk Deke to Assassin's Beach this morning," Jean accused. "What about that?"

Jean's renaming of Otter's Point threw Nick off for a moment while unable to contain the amusement he would share later. "One day soon, we'll be walking old Deke to the beach, and you'll be fully capable of protecting the old Dekester with knife or gun. You can wait until those times come."

"Deke!" Jean's sudden teary eyed sob brought Deke across the seat into Jean's arms. After noting she wasn't in danger, he stuck his head out of her window.

Knowing he had crossed a future tragedy of age not to be dealt with, Nick shut up. The remainder of the short ride to parking the car near the school was completed in silence. When they were parked, Nick started out of the vehicle but Jean grabbed his arm.

"Don't, Dad. Sonny and I will be fine. C'mon Sonny." Jean kissed and hugged Deke before getting her bag from Sonny. "Bye, Dad."

"Bye, Kid. I'll be over to pick you both up after school. Your Mom's working the Monte today on the late shift."

He watched Jean and Sonny walk along toward school with Sonny hesitantly taking her hand. Nick smiled, looking over at Deke. "Sorry I mentioned your years down the road, my canine brother."

Out of nowhere a bearded man ran at Sonny and Jean. Sonny saw him coming and shoved Jean behind him. Deke yipped plaintively as Nick forced him down on the seat with a stern 'Stay' order. Deke slithered to the open car door. He slid down to the pavement. Nick ran a full speed sprint to the scene. The bearded man shoved Sonny to the sidewalk, reaching to grip Jean. Nick's charge upended and flattened the man whom he guessed was Majd Nazari. Nick resisted the instant reaction of snapping the man's neck. Instead, He revealed something Jean and Sonny did not know the extent of: his physical strength. Nick grabbed the easily hundred and eighty pound man off the sidewalk by his robe at the neck and belt, snatched him over his head, and body slammed Nazari to the ground. For a split second Nick forgot where he was, readying a killing stroke to the man's neck.

"Dad… behind you!" Jean's scream brought Nick around in an instant, Colt in hand.

Nick had only a moment to see the two coming at him before Deke smashed the leader to the ground, ripping him at arms, hands, and groin. Nick pistol whipped the man's partner to the ground, resisting the impulse to shoot him in the head. "Deke! Hold!"

Deke lunged across the man under him trying to writhe into a fetal position with screams of pain. Deke grabbed his throat, snarling wildly, and only calming when his victim stopped moving. Nick did a quick weapons search of the man he had pistol whipped, bleeding from the head wound, and groaning in shock. Nick confiscated everything he found into his windbreaker, including the 9mm Beretta pistol and wallet. He then stood and pointed at the pistol whipped man.

"Deke! Hold!" Deke left his first hold to grip the second in the same manner. Nick acquired a Glock 9mm, knife, and wallet from him in quick succession. He looked toward where Jean helped Sonny to his feet. "Are you okay, Sonny?"

"I'm good," Sonny stated with emphasis as he saw Nick point his Colt up through the man's throat. "Please… it's all good, Sir. Jean and I are okay."

"We'll go in the school, Dad. I'll call Mom and let her know we're okay."

The Terminator retracted slightly as Nick catalogued where he was, the details, and the oncoming sirens. He nodded at Jean, waving her toward the school. "Thanks, Jean. I'll see you kids later."

The gaping mouthed stares from the school crowd generated a perception not blending with reality for Nick. He realized there could be no violent endings for Jean's attackers at this time. Jim Amos and Rita Gonzalez moved to his side instantly.

193

Behind them, Ruth Gurkovsky secured the scene. Nick relaxed, seeing his three military background friends from a past flag incident at the school.

"Hey, brother," Jim said. "Can we help? Rita, Ruth, and I have decided to become the Nick McCarty backup crew here at the school."

"Your wife, Rachel, is a badass," Rita added. "We would have moved in on the scene the other day but she backed the beard here off without blinking."

"We saw the whole thing this morning, Nick," Jim said. "So did my kids."

"Thanks, Jim." Nick watched Ruth take Florence Nazari to the ground with attitude. By then, the police cars arrived. Nick took a deep breath as Neil Dickerson approached.

"How many dead?"

"Very funny," Nick replied, motioning Deke to his side. "I took everyone's advice and drove Jean and her friend Sonny to the school this morning, even though my daughter pointed out if we stop doing our normal routines, the terrorists win."

Nick had to pause as Jean's line drew avid amusement from everyone within earshot including the police. "They got out, walked toward the school, and Majd Nazari attacked them. Sonny stepped in front of Jean to protect her. Nazari cuffed him to the ground. He then grabbed for Jean. He didn't make it. Deke and I handled Nazari and his two buddies."

"That's exactly what we saw," Jim said. "My boys and I couldn't believe this kind of thing can happen outside a school. Ruth has this idiot's wife on the ground over there. She's a teacher although anyone who has a kid in her class would dispute that."

"He…he is a murderer!" Majd Nazari screamed in outraged falsetto voice. "McCarty killed five men last night! He makes war on innocent families!"

"I don't know what he's talking about. Do you know anything about five guys dying last night?"

"He's right, Nick. There were five deaths, but I received substantial proof it was an internal Muslim Isis problem. They apparently killed five Kader males for not following through on a Sharia edict to kill Dimah and Cala Kader. Also… I'll bet there's been a Fatwa issued by some clown in the Isis ranks on your life for helping Dimah and Cala. The other adults in the house were sedated and unhurt."

"We were defending ourselves!"

"By beating up on two ten year old kids," Rita asked. "You sick piece of shit! I hope you and that idiot wife of yours get sent to prison."

Ruth joined them as one of the other police with Neil took charge of Florence. "It looked as if these three planned to kidnap Nick's daughter. No other explanation makes any sense."

"You…you are all in this plot to kill us!" Neil gestured for Majd and his cohorts to be cuffed while Nazari raged on. "We will sue for this act of barbarism and discrimination."

Once they were handcuffed, joined by the sobbing Florence, Neil read them their Miranda rights. "You attacked a United States Marshal's child. Nick McCarty also has credentials with the FBI. You'll be charged in accordance with that attack. I'm curious how you could know about those killings at the Kader household since they are not on the news, or been mentioned on any police band."

Majd immediately shook his head in angry response. "I want my lawyer, as do my friends. I see what you are trying to do!

195

You want to blame Muslim murders on Muslims instead of the murderer right here with you."

"You idiots kill each other in whole scale slaughter overseas," Ruth said. "Why wouldn't authorities suspect Islamists to do the same here?"

"Racist!"

Ruth laughed. "You'll have trouble pulling that one off. We all saw what you did. My kid hates your wife. She tries to brainwash the kids with that Sharia Law bullshit. I hope you're pressing charges, Nick."

"I sure am. They attacked Jean. I will see this through. I believe they were attempting to kidnap Jean just as it looked. I'll wager Majd had a driver ready to load her and take off. Sonny jumping between him and Jean gave me enough time to reach them without having to open fire which I would have done. You and your buddies owe Sonny for every one of your stinking lives. If you had laid hands on Jean with your buddies, I would have shot you all in the head."

Neil made contact over his com unit.

"I have some men patrolling the area looking for anything out of sync, and yes, they'll be profiling. I'll have statements taken here so none of you folks are inconvenienced," Neil said after hoots of appreciation for Nick's declaration of death quieted. "Can you come to the station though, Nick?"

"Sure. I'll drop Deke off at home and reassure Rachel. She has to be at work shortly." Neil held bags for the weapons, labeling each as Nick informed him of whom they belonged to.

Nazari began to respond but Neil motioned him to silence. "Save your spiel for the precinct and your lawyer. Let's get them loaded, including the wife. Keep her separate. I want to make sure their stories don't get loaded together in the squad car. I don't think you understand how serious this is, Mr. Nazari. You've all brought firearms onto public school property. I'm betting none of you have a license to carry. I know Nick does. We won't need to do much for a conviction on the weapons' charges."

Florence Nazari began wailing as she was frog marched toward a squad car by a police woman. Many of the parents watching the drama stifled laughter as she was guided into the car. Majd and the men restrained with him shouted at her in Arabic.

"They're telling her to say nothing," Nick told Neil. "Ruth knows Arabic. She can back me up."

"Nick's right," Ruth agreed. "They must have been desperate to try and do this kidnapping or whatever in broad daylight."

One of the other police officers ran up to Neil, pulling him aside for a conference. Neil returned with a smile. "You were right, Nick. The driver waited too long in the area. He was driving one of Nazari's vehicles – a Honda SUV with the license plate covered. They surprised him, but he was armed."

"We have been entrapped! These men are my bodyguards! My wife and I have many enemies and our lives threatened."

"Lie to the infidel, huh," Nick replied. "Good luck with that defense. Did ten year old Sonny attack you? Three of you big strong dupes and a driver, all to capture one little girl. My... you must be very proud."

Neil tugged the now cursing Nazari toward a squad car with his other officers dragging along the other two. "See you at the station, Nick."

"I'll be there." Nick shook hands with everyone. "I am really sorry to have brought this business to the school. I suspect it has to do with a Homeland Security case I'm working right now for the Department of Justice. We believe the Kader family Neil

197

mentioned are involved. It seems their cohorts got them before we could. You all remember Dimah Kader. She's doing great now. She and Bill, her Marine, live on base so she doesn't have to deal with her family. Rachel and I will talk about putting Jean in a private school or hire a tutor. I don't want to endanger other kids."

"I can't speak for everyone," Rita stated, "but please don't do that. If not for Jean we would never have heard about that bitch, Florence, trying to brainwash our kids."

"Rita's right. We have to make a stand somewhere," Ruth added. "I'd rather beat these assholes than appease them."

"Same with me," Jim said. "We talked before this incident. We know they attacked you on the street and you killed all of them. Speaking only for myself... oh hell yeah! That's what I'm talkin' about. We didn't fight the damn war so we could give these bastards our country on the sly. We're at war! The sooner our idiot leaders understand that the better. It's an honor knowing you, Marshal McCarty."

Nick shook his hand again. "It will always be just Nick to all of you. If anything ever happens you're uncomfortable with, each of you have my number. Don't hesitate to call. My Justice Department cohorts and I have teamed with a group of federal agents in the San Francisco/Oakland Bay Area. We're forming a strike force to combat these threats. I hope all of you will be comfortable with relaying anything out of the ordinary in our area to me. We know because of the ports and coastal areas, the terrorist groups are establishing cells onshore and offshore. We believe they're trying to form No-Go enclaves on the coast under Sharia Law, and forbidden to outsiders, just as they have in Europe. We're going to stop them. I'll be dead before I allow anything like is happening in Michigan. We can't have whole Muslim armies with armories inside their mosques ready to move on orders."

"Yes! Finally! Someone speaking the words we know to be true," Rita said. "They keep repeating the same clichés about it's only a few radicals. Then, out of the blue, a San Bernardino rampage happens. The moment it ended, the dupes in the media immediately whitewash the terrorists as if they were the victims. Good Lord! We are so stupid!"

"Instead of prayer rugs, beads, and Sharia Law, we should be teaching our kids how and why America doesn't need third world diversity and bullshit terrorist Trojan Horses ferrying our nation's enemies into our midst so we can accept our own slavery," Ruth stated.

"Damn right! My kids will know right from wrong. I hear all the time 'you're black... we have to fight the man'. Like Ruth said – bullshit. They don't even teach kids anymore that only two percent of Americans owned slaves, and some of the biggest slave holders in the nation were black, like William Ellison. He even supported the confederate cause. The idiots don't even teach who brought black slaves to the Horn of Africa. The Arab slave traders brought them to the coast in the millions. They still operate there now. To me... the world only has one enemy... and it ain't the white man. We're all Americans! When do we get off the liberal plantation and start acting like it? I'm with you, Nick! My family will keep our eyes open. If we see something strange, we'll contact you right away, brother."

"Thank you. I can't tell you how good it is to talk with citizens who feel the same way as I do about this crap. I better get over to the station and make sure the Nazari gang gets locked away. C'mon, Deke. We better go let Rachel blast me for not phoning her within seconds of this Nazari incident. If I look beaten the next time you see me, it will be because I didn't talk fast enough. Bye for now."

Laughter followed Nick and Deke on the way to the car.

"You disobeyed a direct order, dog," Nick informed the unrepentant Deke. He hugged him. "Thank you."

Nick breathed deeply. He called Gus, giving his longtime friend the Reader's Digest version of what happened. "I'll be joining you and Johnny at the beach but it's going to be a little later. I have to take care of statements to put the Nazari bunch in jail. There's no doubt about a connection between the Kaders, Nazaris, and the Isis flakes who sent Ishmael and his buddies after me."

"I'll call Kabong. They tried to snatch Jean. Hopefully they'll get out and we'll deposit them in the ocean. Text me when you leave for the Point. Johnny will bring the satellite gear so we can check out this new Kader thumb-drive info."

"Nazari's wife is a cover. I'd be surprised if she didn't marry him so he could gain entry into the states. They'll probably allow her to leave if they free any of them. She should be charged as a co-conspirator in a kidnapping. I'll talk to you at the Point."

Nick drove to his house. Rachel awaited him at the door. "Jean told me what happened."

"Nazari knew about the Kader deaths last night. That's no coincidence. After I file charges and make a statement I'll meet Gus and Johnny so we can go over the names we do have. Take everything with you to work, babe – your 9mm along with the pepper spray and stun-gun. Keep your eyes open for anyone suspicious at the Café."

Rachel grinned. "Shall I profile?"

"You'd better," Nick replied.

"I already told Joe, Quinn's coming along with me so just watch out for yourself, Muerto."

"Will do. Keep the phone near at hand."

* * *

Deke pranced in front of Nick on the way to Otter's Point, his tail wagging at hyper-speed as he inhaled every scent, happy to be outside. Nick, on the other hand, observed every vehicle suspiciously, knowing he had been officially targeted. The need to remove the threats against him would involve Al-Kadi's place at Pilot Hill. The two men arrested with Nazari listed their residence as the compound. They would not be going anywhere for a while though. Nick could only assume the two men were the assassins mentioned by Ishmael. Gus and Johnny sat in their regular place with Gus spaced ten feet away from his friend, the infamous birdman of the beach. The swirl of flying rodents around Johnny as he fed them the last of his bread treats dissipated quickly once the feeding ended.

Nick let Deke off his leash to run at Gus and Johnny before swerving away for the hunt along the rocks of the deserted beach. Nick placed his beach chair in Gus's buffer zone separating him from the birdman's completed feeding. Each of them held out a mug for their ration of the spiked coffee Nick brought along in a huge thermos. He poured and sat, sipping the concoction while watching the calmer wave action of the day.

"I talked with the DA and Neil when I finished my statement. My statement combined with the other parents' versions of what happened at the school meshed well enough for the DA to recommend their transfer to federal custody. There won't be any deals. It was as I suspected – Florence married Majd to provide him entry into America. The other two have phony papers. I called the two FBI agents working out of San Francisco we met before the cruise. They were very interested in the Kader thumb-drive info and the fact Nazari's two friends were probably the assassins mentioned on the drive. Sam told me he and Janie would pass the information to John Harding's crew. They're coming down to take custody of both Nazaris and the two men. Neil will hold onto the driver for the time being. I'll probably have to deal with him later."

"Is it possible they might take their prisoners to visit Cruella Deville first," Johnny asked.

"Great minds think alike, Johnny. I asked them if they would be taking them to Lynn or if they could give them to us," Nick replied. "Sam told me if they can get away with it, they will do exactly that. I explained the connection between our Kader problem and the Nazari/Pilot Hill compound thread. They want to know how to stop the No-Go Zone infiltration too. Sam's worried they want to make a Dearbornistan size Muslim No-Go Zone with mosques housing armories, complete with training centers all along the California coast."

"Since you know there's a Fatwa that's been issued for your death, are you still planning to go with Fernando and Senta to the compound under the guise of offering your services as an assassin," Gus asked. "That seems like a suicide mission now."

"It all depends on how the training is proceeding under Lynn's guidance. I would not underestimate Lynn's persuasion ability. I saw those two once she did the initial introduction. They literally would have done anything she wanted already. She will have them trained for their scene. It will be my responsibility to use their introduction into Al-Kadi's compound to explain my status. I'll be able to find out if our cartoon Unholy Trio identities have been pierced. I admit I've been getting a little careless."

"Didn't you mention being offered a contract on one of those Saudi princes," Gus remarked. "Maybe you could use the contract as a way into Al-Kadi's confidence. You could ask him if he knew anything about the contract on the Dark Web and whether he would want you to go through with it or not."

"Not bad, Gus. It might get me a meeting with him while John Harding's crew establishes a perimeter. Get out the satellite laptop and check out if there is a mention of a Fatwa issued on my ass. See if you can find mention of it first. Then find out if I'm mentioned by name or reputation. Neil surprised me when he mentioned a Fatwa. I did a scan of the info along with you and I didn't see any Fatwa mentioned. I asked Neil about it. He told me because of so many attempts on my life lately, Neil figured that I'd been marked for death. I'm hoping it was a misunderstanding."

"No mention of a Fatwa for either your real name, or the Terminator, or the 'Mr. Robinson' name you went by in the Frank Richert days with the rogue NSA outfit. You could play this trouble with the Kaders and Nazaris as a courtesy to Al-Kadi, letting him know you weren't doing hits on his people. None of them are surviving this purge anyway."

"We have an extensive data mining program on the worst chatter spots. If they don't have any mention of it, then it's probably not out there. Good input, Johnny. I think we have to hope Sam and Janie can put the Nazaris and company into Lynn's hands. I'll call him just in case she does get the chance. I need to know if Al-Kadi wanted those Kader guys to kill me or if they were using Al-Kadi's compound as a base for their private business."

"Do you want me to check the Dark Web for any mention of the Saudi prince on there?"

"Yes. His name is Rabiah Al-Saud."

A few moments later, Johnny glanced away from his screen with a grin. "Isis wants him dead because he funds Al-Qaeda, their rival on the Arabian Peninsula. Rabiah has a price on his head and is in hiding. I believe you have found a legitimate item of interest to discuss with Al-Kadi, Muerto."

"Yeah, if I don't get shot first."

"Someone that can outdraw you, Muerto?"

"It's hard to outdraw someone with an AK47 pointed at your head, Payaso," Nick replied.

"True… don't let that happen."

* * *

Lynn watched the reality play acted out by her two new stars Fernando Carone and Senta Bulgar. I played the part of Al-Kadi, greeting the two, and asking why they brought an imaginary Nick along. The two rehearsed under pressure and strived to please in any nuance Lynn thought needed work. After their second day of training, the two could talk their way out of anything I tried to trick them with, using the information Jafar gathered on the operation at the Al-Kadi compound. They did so without hesitation or any sign of unease.

"Very impressive! I believe you two can fool anyone."

"Thank you, Director Deville," Senta replied instantly as taught with Carone echoing her a split second later. The couple stood with heads lowered and hands at their sides.

"I liked your rehearsal phone call to Al-Kadi, Fernando. You handled all the initial reservations he would have logically, by spelling out the danger. Your reasoning in moving the Tempest to avoid the Coast Guard was delivered with perfect inflection in your voice."

Carone repeated his thanks, never raising his head.

"Quays," Lynn gestured for her minion. "You and Sylvio escort our acting crew down to their cells. That's a wrap for the day."

"How did John do, Mistress?"

"None of your business, Quays," I retorted before Lynn could answer.

"Cardboard cutout perfection," Lynn answered to her minions' amusement. "If he were any stiffer doing this we'd need an interpreter to figure out his monotone delivery."

"Thanks, Lynn." I made as if to snatch at Quays as he and Sylvio pushed their captives out of the room. The two darted out only slightly ahead of my halfhearted grab. "They did very well. If Nick's going to have a chance on the inside of the compound, it will hinge on those two staying in character until Nick can get into a position to act. I couldn't trip them up at all."

"When's Sam and Janie due to deliver my new toys? You said they have as much to do with success as Carone and Bulgar. We need to move on the compound, Cheese. It's one thing to scare the crap out of those two murderous scum, but it's completely different letting them loose in the wild with Muerto's life in the balance."

"These four could be the key. Two of them are assassins sent from New York by that Kader family Nick's people have been having trouble with. The other two are unknowns. We'll separate the wife first. Her name's Florence Nazari. Sam told me she was ready to break nearly the moment the Pacific Grove cops handed her over to actual FBI agents. Nick told me he needs to know whether those two assassins were sent to kill him by the Kader guy in New York or if Al-Kadi was in on it too, in which case we'll need a new plan."

"I get it. You figure the woman knows a hell of a lot and I can extract a plethora of facts to trip our male contestants."

"That's the plan, Lynn. Once Muerto gets in for an audience with Al-Kadi, he can recon guard numbers, look-outs, and possibly trick the number of men billeted at the compound in the initial conversation. Nick's roving encounter with Al-Kadi may make the difference between our confiscating the compound or blowing the hell out of it.

"Not to mention when he's through with the initial introductions, I'm thinking Muerto will reduce the number of combatants significantly," Lynn replied. "We'll be able to get a handle on how receptive Al-Kadi is to an audience with Nick during the phone call we've been rehearsing with Carone."

Clint joined us with Clint Jr. in his arms. "Sam called. He and Janie have our new arrivals twenty minutes away. Achmed and I found out a lot more on the Nazari guy and his two pals from Al-Kadi's compound. C'mon out and have a coffee while I show you the folders I printed out on them, Cheese. I made you a tea, babe."

Lynn gathered the baby into her arms as she and I followed Clint to their meeting area. "How's my little man doing without his Mama?"

"Quiet, hungry, and the usual. He seemed to be very entertained watching my computer screen. The Parakeet is with Achmed. She sat between us with Mia in her arms. The babies laughed and giggled at each other the whole time. We put them in the playpen together. They handed each other toys, crawled over each other, and sat together with the finger foods we gave them to munch on."

"That's cute." Lynn held Clint Jr. so she could examine him closely. "Is your old man fixing you up with an arranged marriage, kid? Mia's pretty cute, huh?"

The baby nodded and giggled which surprised me, but not his parents. "He's already understanding some words?"

"Sure," Clint answered. "Watch this."

Clint peered at his son with a stern frown. "Naptime for junior."

"No!" Clint Jr. shook his head in the negative while cringing away from his Dad. "No!"

We were still enjoying that demonstration when we reached the meeting room. Samira's melodious but non-stop help, while pointing and commenting at Jafar's screen, paused as we approached. Jafar sighed in relief only to get a smack in the back of the head.

"I am only trying to help," Samira said plaintively as she sat down with arms crossed over chest.

"You have been annoyingly chirping at us for the last hour, Parakeet," Clint said. "Give your husband a break."

Samira gasped as Jafar enjoyed Clint's observation and request as much as the rest of us. She jabbed a finger in my direction which I expected. "This is all your fault I am now the Parakeet, Cheeseburger!"

"No… it's because sometimes you chirp without taking a breath for a solid hour," Clint refuted her charge. "Cheese labeled you correctly. Sometimes you have to be reminded that silence is golden."

"Lynn! Is this true?"

"Listen, kid… you know my abhorrence for cleaning anything. That fact catches up to me at odd times with a pointed reminder. I love you but you are a chirpy little bird at times. Calm down. You're the Parakeet. Big deal. Embrace it. Jafar is 'Achmed the Dead Terrorist'. Clint's been telling us how well Clint Jr. and Mia get along." Lynn placed Clint Jr. in the playpen where Mia's face brightened as she crawled quickly to her buddy. Lynn watched the two babies giggling and chasing each other around the playpen for a moment with a big smile. "I think it's time to talk dowry, Achmed."

Jafar nodded, taking a break from his screen to join Lynn next to the crib. "They do get along wonderfully well. Is that not so, Parakeet?"

Samira took Jafar's hand with a sigh. "Yes… they get along very well. I will try to be less chirpy. Will I lose the Parakeet nickname after a time?"

"Not a chance, my love," Jafar answered. "Sit down with us. We need to show Cheese and Crue the folders Clint printed out."

Samira became animated immediately in gesture, and tone, as she grabbed the folders to place in front of Lynn and me after we sat with our beverages at the table with Clint. "They are horrendous! The two assassins come from Karachi, Pakistan. They commit heinous crimes in the tribal areas as enforcers of Sharia Law when called in. Isis smuggled them through Mexico to be at Al-Kadi's command. He shuttles them across the United States to enforce Sharia Law Edicts upon request. They come into an area, kill the target in horrendous but anonymous ways according to how they are requested to do it. When they leave, the police have no proof to arrest the suspected ones who hired the killers. Isis has expanded their duties. How in the world did Mr. McCarty capture them?"

"Sam told me they tried to kidnap Nick's daughter near her school in broad daylight," I told her. "Nick and his dog, Deke, got them in unspecified terms along with the Nazaris. That they are alive for us to interrogate is a blessing."

"Dead Boy's enemies are my enemies," Clint said. "I say they go on a day flight over the ocean when we get done with them. I'll leave it up to Lynn about the Nazari woman, but the male mutants die."

"Agreed," I said. "Any idea how Florence latched onto Majd?"

"Typical liberal guilt trip," Clint continued. "Her maiden name is Florence Domki. She's Pakistani, born in a Pakistani enclave in Los Angeles. I found nothing on her parents. They run a dry cleaning business in LA, spent a fortune sending Flo to Cal State Berkeley where she met Majd Nazari on a student visa out of Saudi Arabia. She married him after graduation and never spoke to her parents again. Samira confirmed that fact by calling them to say she was a classmate from Berkeley trying to get in touch with Florence. Flo and Majd have been working the Islamophobia card ever since. He's a professional con-man with ties to every place the Unholy Trio has hit in their area. That Al-Kadi sent his two best assassins at Nazari's request on behalf of the Kader family makes this interrogation very important. Nazari is very good or very lucky."

Our door beeped. Samira walked over with me close behind, checked our surveillance cam screen and opened the door. "Hello, Sam. How are you Janie? I have Mia with me and Lynn has Clint Jr. Come see them in the playpen together."

"That's wonderful," Janie said, her face a serious mask. "I looked over the files Clint put together on our prisoners. I felt like taking them into the desert and shooting them all in the head. Let's see the babies. Can we get a little help transferring our Isis gang?"

"Sure. Come inside." Samira accepted the SUV keys from Sam. She led the way to where the playpen was set up. While the two FBI agents enjoyed the two babies' antics, Samira handed the keys to me.

"Lynn? Would you like to introduce yourself now to our guests?"

"No. Call the minions. Tell Gus to put them all into our holding cell together after a bathroom break. I want to read these files over more thoroughly before I decide what I want to do."

"On it. I'll help them."

* * *

Gus opened the SUV door with a big smile. "Buenos Dias, my friends. Welcome to hell. I, Gus Denova, will be your host. These are my other helpers, Quays and Sylvio. We serve your interrogator, Dr. Deville and the big guy here, the Dark Lord. Come out of there. Save your breath for the screaming later. We

209

will take you all to the most comfortable place you'll probably see again while living."

Sylvio fired an arc from this cattle prod. "Please don't make this a difficult journey. There will be time for all of that later. We try to be pleasing and polite while following our orders to transfer prisoners. You do not want to make this difficult. It will not go well for you."

The woman began wailing so loudly as the prisoners left the vehicle, Lynn came to the door. "Get her silent or unconscious, Sylvio. That damn screeching is upsetting the kids."

"On it." Sylvio used the cattle prod on Florence.

She did the dance electric for a moment before collapsing in a heap. Gus and Quays nailed the three others the moment they moved to interfere. Being larger, the men received an extended electronic hello. In moments, silence reigned.

"Excellent, my minions," Lynn gave final approval. "Bring them in when they can do so quietly."

"Should we warm them with the video montage, Crue," Gus asked.

"Definitely. I don't feel like starting from the beginning. Warm them to boiling point, boys."

I slapped and kicked them all into groaning reality. "Get to your feet, or I drop kick each of you through the door. The noise will upset Dr. Deville and she will order another dose of silence. This time my greeters will fry your asses for a full minute. You have ten seconds to get on your feet."

They made it in five, including Flo, who no longer believed this was a game. The terrified look on her face coupled with the arrogant rage billowing out from the others combined to make me think this would be an informative interrogation. Flo's whole life flashed in front of her eyes, I'm sure. One moment Flo worked brainwashing a classroom of kids, and the next, she's handcuffed while being led into a place that did not look like any jail she'd ever seen. After accompanying the minions to our upper holding cell, I took the handcuffs off with the key Sam gave me while the minions watched. We then took each one to the bathroom before returning them to the cell.

"You cannot leave me here with the men!"

"Being left with the men will be the least of your problems," I told her. "Don't worry. We'll be getting to you very shortly. We know who you all are. We have dossiers on each of you already, especially you two women burning mutants from Karachi. My associates have videos for you to watch, so relax and enjoy the viewing screen during your short wait. They will illustrate the most pain free ways to get through the next few hours. The first mutant who touches the woman will be zapped, taken from the cell and zapped until his dick falls off."

Flo screamed. "Don't! Don't leave me with them. They will kill me the moment you leave!"

I grinned. "Sylvio is a bit of an electronics genius. The room you're in is very special. Give our guests a demo, Sylvio."

A moment later all four crashed to the floor as the electrodes meshed inside the walls, ceiling, and floor electrocuted everything inside the room. The minions of course went nuts. They had spent many hours making our special holding cell.

"See. No one does anything inside the room without our permission. Enjoy the movie." I walked past minions with pumping fist. "Oh my God that was an incredible tryout for the room. You guys are amazing."

The three immediately stood at attention with heads bowed. "Thank you, Dark Lord."

I was still laughing when I reached the meeting room where they enjoyed a replay of our electric room's test firing. "I thought it would be a perfect test firing. I never dreamed it would be that wild."

"Clint is sure right about the men," Lynn said. "They do not leave the House of Pain except in proper fish feeding portions. How much of the file did you read before transferring them, Cheese?"

I sat down with them again. "Too much. Their specialty was woman burning in the outer tribal areas."

"Jesus… God in heaven," Janie murmured, putting aside the file handed to her. "Acid baths, wood chippers, amputations… how… how did you get these files?"

"We have hacks into the Dark Web with a data mining operation me and Achmed created with Laredo. It's how we first heard a rumor about the 'Starlight' affair. All the most heinous mutant Islamists sell their wares from simple assassinations to torture and honor killings." Clint paused, glancing over at Clint Jr. and Mia sleeping in the playpen. "The mutants will establish their Caliphate here only when we so called 'Monsters' are all dead with a thousand bodies surrounding us to burn for our funeral pyre."

"Janie and I are with you all," Sam stated. He held up the file. "Our prisoners were rerouted into Homeland Security special bureau collaboration with CIA. Yes. It's legitimate. After everything achieved to prevent loss of life in the hundreds of thousands at China Basin, Isis compounds, and the 'Starlight of the Seas' operation, we have cover to wage war… a secret war… but a war none the less. McCarty and his crew are a valuable asset to this strike team. His capture of these mutants, as you call them, will be one more reason amongst many to maintain this force under cover. Janie and I will go now. We'll write the transfer paperwork, cloaked in the collaboration cover I mentioned. Thanks for letting us see the babies. They're an incredibly good contrast to this day."

"Amen to that, Sam. I'll walk you out," Clint said. "Crue and the Cheese will take care of our transferees."

After the goodbyes were over, Clint left with Sam and Janie. I turned to Lynn then. "Do you still want to start with Flo?"

"Oh yeah," Lynn replied. "I watched Flo. We'll let the minions strap her down for interrogation. You and I will go in for effect, silently smiling at her. Once I get her rolling, we won't be able to stop her. I'll blend a word or two in for continuity. I've already jotted down a list of questions for her after she burps up everything she can think of concerning these goons and their Pilot Hill hangout."

"What should we do with her after this?" Even I didn't know what to do with a true toady who lives in thrall to a murderous cult.

"You've heard the term 'too stupid to live', right? That's how I feel about Flo," Lynn replied. Jafar, Samira, and Clint who had only then rejoined us, all expressed agreement with Lynn's pronouncement. "We've had incredible success with the acupuncture technique. She has parents in LA who even Clint thinks are legit."

"Lynn's right. Achmed and I went through their lives with a fine tooth comb. They're legit. They don't even donate to the Islamist front groups like far too many supposed American citizens of Muslim leanings. No one will believe anything she babbles once she leaves here. Hell, her mind may be gone by the time Lynn retrains her. It would be a good experiment in the dark side turnings Lynn has already had some success with. We can return her to the parents as a reformed American. We'll check on her integration back into society without the burka."

"That sounds good to me," I agreed. "I guess we better get started."

213

"I'll stay with the kids, Achmed, and Samira," Clint said. "Developing those files left a bad taste in my mouth. If you need anything in the Podiatrist Room, call out to the minions. Gus told me they're staying until after we have enough info to decide on our plan for Pilot Hill."

"You and Achmed did a hell of a job with the files. They even shocked Sam and Janie." I went to our intercom system controls. "Mr. Denova... please escort our female guest to be prepped for interrogation. How did the warmup go?"

"Exceptionally well," Gus replied. "We'll settle Ms. Nazari into position. She's a bit out of sorts at the moment. We'll make her drink some water before anchoring her to the table."

We purposely have the intercom on speaker for the inmates' enjoyment. Flo began screaming her heart out as Gus disconnected.

* * *

Although recovering from an electronic jolt to quiet her down, Flo's twisted features could not relax from utter terror. The minions, having strapped her securely onto the table with her feet in our special restraints, filed out of the room as we entered. Lynn wore her new interrogation costume: black slacks, black lab-coat, red-lettered nametag with Dr. Cruella Deville on it, and black exam gloves. Her blonde hair, tied tightly in a bun like a 'Nurse Ratchet' clone, contrasted with her very dark eyeliner and lipstick. I wore black jeans, black t-shirt, and black exam gloves.

When she first walked into a room with all of the 'Monster Squad' in attendance, we were struck dumb for a moment, before erupting in applause. Flo took one look and began hyperventilating as Lynn and I followed our agreed approach to the table. Lynn remained silent, stroking Flo's hair and cheek. She then traced one black gloved index finger over Flo's center, leg, and right foot, pausing at the little toe. Lynn then smiled hugely at the gasping Flo.

214

"Hi there, Flo. I'm Dr. Deville. This is my assistant, the Dark Lord. We are recording our examination and conversations. Would you like to tell us everything you know about everything or would you like to play 'this little piggy went to market'?"

Flo tried to speak but could only babble. Lynn folded her arms in contemplation. "What do you think, Dark Lord? Perhaps Flo doesn't understand she is no longer in the hands of the regular federal authorities."

"I believe she's terrified out of her mind, Dr. Deville. Pain might be the only balm for this malady. I could break a finger so she'll have something to concentrate on besides her predicament."

"No! Please...please don't hurt me!"

"What do you know about that, DL? Flo found her voice all by herself. We have some time constraints, so tell us what you know about Nick McCarty and why your husband tried with those other two mutants to kidnap McCarty's daughter."

"Majd heard about an assassin named Felix Moreau being killed in Salem on the Dark Web. Moreau..." Flo ran out of air for a moment, calming herself with pleading features aimed at gaining a moment's respite from her interrogators. "My husband knew Moreau was hired by... Isis to kidnap Emily Waterson and kill her if State Senator Waterson didn't agree to stop blocking land acquisitions by our representatives. I-"

"Your representatives, huh?"

One look at the murderous glare Lynn visited upon her and Flo began crying. Lynn took a deep breath. She patted Flo's cheek reassuringly. "Go on with your story. You're doing real well."

"I...I'm sorry. Moreau was killed by an assassin, rumored to be Nick McCarty. Majd remembered McCarty's name from my confrontations with his daughter, Jean. He tracked all of the news stories about McCarty killing relatives of the Kader family, first in defense of Dimah Kader, a teacher at the school. Majd immediately contacted the Kader family, learning McCarty killed many of their family members, including three sent by the family only a short time ago. Then… five male members of the Kader family were executed, supposedly by Isis operatives. Majd knew that not to be true. He informed our mentor, Saran Al-Kadi of what was going on."

"If the Kader family hired the assassins as we've heard, what could kidnapping Jean have to do with the Kader's wanting Nick dead?"

"I don't know the… details. The Kader family agreed with Al-Kadi to contact Sohail and Javid who Saran knew to be in New York. He used Majd to act as an intermediary. The Kaders were promised McCarty would die once he carried out an assassination for Al-Kadi on a Saudi prince financing Al-Qaeda named Rabiah Al-Saud. The Kaders agreed to Al-Kadi's terms, paying for all expenses incurred. My husband thought he could corner Jean away from the school on a pretense of meeting with the principal. He didn't know McCarty had driven her to school. He thought it the perfect time because Majd saw Jean and her friend alone."

"Why didn't he try to have you approach Jean, or at least wait until she was alone?"

Flo's facial features showed momentary annoyance at my question. "Jean's never alone. She also is a very irritable child. She suspects everything. Majd gets impatient. I tried to convince him I could coax her over to the street where our driver could have arrived in seconds to pick her up. I would wave at the vehicle as it left, pretending Jean had to go quickly, and then tell anyone who asked that she had an emergency at home. Majd became angry, insisting she was only a girl, and he would handle it. We would never have tried such a thing with either parent present. Jean's mother wanted to beat me up the other day in anger. I know now McCarty is a killer. He was about to execute all three men until realizing there were witnesses."

"Wow!" I chuckled. "If these idiots weren't so dangerous, they would be laughable, Crue. Al-Kadi thought he could enlist Nick, the now foremost assassin in the world, to do a hit on a Saudi prince by kidnapping his daughter? Oh my… we should enter you geniuses in the 'Darwin Awards' this year."

"Kabong told me a story about some idiot gangster who sent two hired guns into a restaurant to collect Nick for an assassination," Lynn added. "Nick went with them, his .45 Colt pointed at their heads, to meet the boss. He pretended interest in the assassination until finding out who the target was and then Nick killed them all. It's a wonder there are any Kaders left."

"We'll run it by Nick. If we can get your new acting converts to arrange the meeting with Al-Kadi together, using the pretext Nick had killed all the ones sent after him, but was interested in the job he tortured out of them, Al-Kadi might take the meeting without hesitation."

"But…but he didn't kill… oh…oh no! Please don't kill me! I will help! I can-"

"Shut your pie-hole, Flo! Let me think." Lynn walked around the table to my side. "I like it, DL. Nick's no fool. If there's a flaw in our thinking he'll find it. We're going to be busy today. My curiosity is aroused. We have three more Pilot Hill compound frequenters. Let's put our Flo in the holding cell up here and get started on the bad boys. I'll make sure Nick's journey into darkness will be as safe as we can arrange it."

"Agreed."

"You…you're going to kill my husband?" Flo was slow on the upswing.

"No, dear Flo, we're going to send your husband and his two scumbag friends to Disneyland," Lynn retorted. "Now, shut up while DL gets you on your feet. One more question – your driver,

Jack Gichki, was detained by the Pacific Grove police. Who is he and what does he have to do with your operation?"

"Jack is a close friend of my husband's. He does anything my husband tells him to do. They fought together in Syria."

"I'll pass that on to Nick the moment I get Flo into holding, Lynn."

I saw a slight smile flit across her face until Flo noticed I was staring at her. "If we learn bad things about Jack you should have told us I will ask Dr. Deville to skin you alive. We haven't done a filleting for a long time."

"And my knives are a little dull," Lynn added.

"I meant nothing by it! Jack is a stone cold killer. He was under orders to act stupid no matter who talked with him from the police, but to do what they said without question. That is the only way the police could have captured him. Jack will kill McCarty."

"Oh... DL," Lynn grabbed my arm. "Quickly! Call Nick. He's in danger from the big bad Jack."

Lynn and I enjoyed that one for a while, as I unstrapped Flo.

Chapter Nine
Pilot Hill Preliminary

"Stop here."

Neil smiled in the rear view mirror at his former prisoner Jack Gichki. He had asked to be let out at the Sea Breeze Motel as listed on the arrest warrant. "Stay out of trouble, Mr. Gichki, and don't leave town."

"Where are my friends?"

"As I told you, federal custody."

"What of McCarty? Has he been arrested for the Kader murders?"

"No. Mr. McCarty had an alibi and I received solid information the Kaders ran afoul of an Isis group."

"That is a lie! We both know the truth. McCarty killed them!"

Neil kept a professional tone and posture. "We're looking into all possibilities, Mr. Gichki. You drove a vehicle plotted to be used in the kidnapping of Mr. McCarty's daughter. If I were you, I'd stay away from Marshal McCarty."

"It would be very wise for McCarty to stay away from me. I will find my friends."

"You have the FBI Agent's card. Call in a day or so," Neil said. "Have a nice evening. Your court time is 10 am tomorrow morning. Do not be late."

"I will be there. I did nothing. I drove my friend's vehicle as requested. You should be pursuing the murderer McCarty instead of harassing and profiling Muslims."

"Whenever you Muslims stop kidnapping children from their schools, I'll pursue some other avenue of criminality. Until then, I'll be forced to keep arresting you actual perpetrators." Neil drove away, leaving Gichki cursing under his breath.

* * *

Gichki hurried to his room. He knew Al-Kadi would be waiting to receive word from Majd. Gichki played the dummy as instructed - open mouthed surprise at every question, and a shrug of the shoulders for an answer. Jack prayed he would get a chance to kill McCarty. It gave him pause that McCarty handled Nazari, Bhatti, and Kamboh like children. Jack would kill him from a distance.

He opened his apartment door. As he walked into the room, Jack felt something at ankle level and tripped. Falling forward to the carpet on his hands and knees, he felt the smooth surface of plastic. A knee, in the small of his back, drove him onto his chest and face. He felt the wire cut into his throat, severing everything in its path. Gichki choked, his blurring vision and convulsing body heralding Jack's last moments on earth. Tongue protruding from nearly severed head, the tension was released, allowing Gichki's head to drop forward to the black and red plastic surface.

* * *

Nick gathered his razor wire garrote from around Gichki's neck, carefully slipping it forward from under the dead man's head. "Perfect trip, guys."

Gus gathered in their trip wire from Johnny. Gus took digital pictures, fingerprints and a DNA swab for filing with CIA, where Gichki's death would be catalogued, but remain secret. His two friends wrapped Gichki in the black tarp and duck taped it tightly to make sure no blood escaped. They transferred the wrapped body to a large moving trunk on large casters. Nick had already packed Gichki's bags. The weekday patronage at the Sea Breeze was minimal. Gus drove his Ford SUV in front of the room. In moments, the three men packed away everything from the room, including the deceased. Johnny added the final touch. He resembled Gichki slightly. With ball-cap in place, hoodie covering it, and sunglasses on, Johnny entered the office to turn in his room cards, complementing the staff for their service. The woman behind the counter took the cards with a small smile of acceptance.

"Thank you, Mr. Gichki. We hope to see you again."

"If ever I am in the area, I will certainly stay here. Goodbye."

"Goodbye, Sir."

Johnny exited the motel office and entered the front seat of Gichki's Toyota Camry which Nick drove. "Did you leave a tip, Muerto?"

"Of course and Gichki was no cheapskate. It was nice of the Dark Lord to worry about us. I assured him we had not forgotten about our innocent driver. Neil's boss was the one who made the decision not to send the driver with the rest of the pack because Nazari claimed he had merely hired Gichki."

"Do you think we should have questioned Gichki?"

"Lynn milked the other four so thoroughly I doubt we could have discovered anything new. This way, Jack disappears without a trace, misses his court date, and when they come to collect him, the cops or whomever find his place vacated completely. Neil will be off the hook. The staff here will only remember a nice guy who left a big tip. Case closed. On to our Toyota Camry rebirth. Did Jerry say whether now was a good time?"

221

"He said he would be at the shop for the next few hours," Johnny answered. "Did you check the registration?"

"It's Jack's. Jerry may have to part it out. I brought his pay envelope. We have to hurry. Payaso will be whining if we leave the dead body in his new Ford very long. Cala doesn't have to hurry the prep work. No one will miss Jack. His friends will be dead. Lynn said she will handle all the reeducation points with Nazari's wife before they drop Flo back with her parents in LA. The first call will be to resign her teaching position. We'll go over and clean out her apartment tonight too. We may find some extra items of interest there. The rest of the crap we'll dump at a Goodwill Store. If all Flo the dip-shit has are different colored burkas we'll get rid of them too."

"You are thinking all four should disappear, huh Muerto?"

"I admit I'm as sick of the enablers as I am of the Islamist scum terrorizing the world. Flo embraces life as a slave, draped in a tent so no one ever sees her, enables any Muslim man to beat her, arrest her, throw acid in her face for any reason, or simply stone her to death. Flo has no rights and no clue, but she had no hesitation going into a public school to brainwash kids into a murderous cult. You tell me, Johnny. I have my thoughts on it, but I'm willing to go along with Dr. Deville and the Dark Lord. It will be easy to cover the disappearance of the others. Flo going bye/bye might attract a bit too much attention."

Johnny smiled. "We can always go get her later."

"Exactly, brother."

* * *

We worked Nazari first. Clint and I strapped him in after the minions brought Majd to us. We never took chances with strangers. Our ploys in the interrogation room sometimes produced humor, but we never forgot these prisoners' histories of violence. One misjudgment or loss of concentration could end in death for

222

one of us Monsters. A casualty away from combat always means an error made, especially here in the House of Pain. Lynn kills without thought, but errors happen even to professionals. If errors happen at Pain Central, two or three killers backed any play made. By this time most prisoners, after seeing Lynn's interrogation videos, beg to help us. Nazari wasn't one of them.

"Dead boy called," Clint said. "The very dangerous Jack Gichki sleeps with the fishes."

We spent a few seconds in humorous appreciation of Clint's Nick McCarty report. Lynn, a huge Godfather movie fan, loves anything related to the dialogue. Nazari didn't like what he'd heard. Apparently, Majd was a Godfather fan too. He understood the reference to his man Gichki being dead. I could tell he was stunned for the first time. I grinned at Clint.

"I think Majd thought his boy Jack could take Muerto."

"You lie!" Majd lost concentration. For a moment Nazari thought he was in an Isis meeting. Lynn zapped his balls with her stun-gun she always keeps with her.

Lynn waited until the screams and shock faded. She pinched his cheek. "We don't take shit from Isis Munchkins. Would you like to shoot your mouth off again?"

"How…how can you do this? Those torture videos… they cannot be real! Jack… he was the most dangerous man I ever knew."

"Against who? Most of you bad boys, like those two awaiting their turn in here, are all women killers." Lynn leaned over Nazari. "I'll bet your buddy Jack liked to knife little girls and cut the throats of shackled guys, huh?"

When Majd remained silent, looking away from Lynn, she started laughing. "I knew it. Clint. Show Majd how Nick fixed good old Jack."

Clint showed Nazari the pictures Gus forwarded to us of Gichki lying in a pool of his own blood. "On one hand, your buddy Jack is a lot luckier than you. He died quick. You won't be. I'll watch the baby while you two show Majd all the ways he's going to help us. Call me when you need me, DL. Let John and I take care of Sohail and Javid once you finish with Majd, Babe. They won't know much more than our big timer here."

"I'll think about it. Let me see what I can learn from Majd. I'll decide then whether to-"

"I will make a deal!" Majd twisted in the head harness. "I see you people will carry this game out to the end. Guarantee my safe return to Saudi Arabia and I will tell you anything you want to know."

"Oh my... you are a slow learner. Go on with the baby, Hon. Put in the needles, DL. Let's show Majd what's behind the other door that's not his safe return to Saudi Arabia."

"No!" Majd tried to make it difficult for me to insert the acupuncture needles into his heels. We redesigned the foot restraints each time we did an interrogation at first, but we found a combination of reinforced Velcro straps that easily held the feet immovable we were satisfied with.

I inserted the needles. Our needle clips now fit over the needles with thumbscrew tightness to our heat and electrical jolt machine.

"Wait... okay... I will tell you everything!"

Lynn patted his face. "Yes... you certainly will. Light him up, Cheese."

Normally, Lynn treated her patients in three minute intervals of hell. She gave Majd a five minute dose of hot foot hell after I stuck the pad in his mouth to keep him from biting his own tongue off. When Lynn finished with Majd, we knew a lot about his relationship with Al-Kadi. He also confirmed our suspicions about the Pilot Hill compound's purpose. Any imports from Carone's ship Tempest would be quietly handled through the Marina in Monterey. Infiltrators would be passed through Nazari's house and on to Pilot Hill. The weapons, drugs, and human trafficking were to be transferred back and forth in the same way. Al-Kadi trusted Nazari to run the operation as a middle man; but to our relief, Majd confirmed that Carone ran the operation from the ocean to Pilot Hill.

Clint joined me to transfer the nearly insane Nazari to a restraint chair. We needed to learn every detail about the compound from Sohail Bhatti and Javid Kamboh. They had lived there for a time. With Nazari completely under Lynn's control, we would use him as a confirming witness to anything his two companions said. Bhatti wanted no part of it. The minions had to zap him twice with the cattle prod to get him in with us. Sylvio gave him a full thirty seconds of the juice to get him on the table after he crashed to the floor trying to resist. I picked him up and jammed his ass down on the table finally. We strapped him into our rocket ship to hell. This murderer knew what awaited him. He believed the videos.

We all knew well what horrors Bhatti and Kamboh visited upon humanity during their putrid lives. Bhatti began crying when he saw Nazari in the observation chair. Apparently, Bhatti recognized the face of insanity due to torture. Nazari began yipping in short quiet barks until Lynn slapped him in the back of the head. Bhatti blubbered out phrases about being duped, led astray, blackmailed, threatened, used against his will, and finally at the end as we let him ramble the poor boy screamed out for his mama. Lynn and I recognized the jargon. Isis fighters captured by the Kurds begged in the same manner. Bhatti would get the same leniency those guys received from the Kurds. Lynn spent the next thirty minutes defining pain for Bhatti. No questions were asked and no quarter given. Sohail Bhatti began hallucinating after fifteen minutes.

"I think we have you nice and toasty now Sowhat." Lynn nicknamed him for our amusement. "Let's start with an easy one. Majd told us the names of everyone involved with this network between the ship Tempest and Pilot Hill. Most are already dead and others soon will be. What was compartmentalized according to him is the identity of the major Kader family member who sent you and your buddy, Java. We don't want to wait until Al-Kadi is in our hands. We want the name now."

"Yes… I will tell you!" Instead, Bhatti began to cry again.

Lynn gave him thirty seconds of electric sheep to count. "Save the tears for someone that gives a shit. Name, please?"

"Eliah! Eliah Kader…" Bhatti passed out.

"Did you get that, Clint?"

"I heard," Clint said from our meeting room with the kids. "I'll make the call."

       * * *

Nick answered on the first ring. He wrote on his upstairs deck. Jean and Sonny across from him did their homework. Deke sprawled over Nick's shoes while Rachel sat next to him, editing his already completed work. Quinn slept in a rocker between Rachel and Nick.

"Dead Boy… the man in New York is Eliah Kader," Clint said. "How are you doing, brother?"

"Five by five, brother. Thanks for the name. Do I have enough time to go see my friend in New York?"

"I'm afraid not. Although it appears your intro to Al-Kadi should go smoothly, he'll be getting suspicious because his connection to the Tempest is gone. Lynn has Fernando and Senta rehearsed to provide you with an Academy Award winning performance covering an emergency repositioning of the ship."

226

"Excellent! Let me know when you want us."

"Will do. Would you bring the family with you for safety?"

"They'll be fine here, but thanks. Is John orchestrating our positions during my visit inside?"

"Yep. Lynn's extracting final details on the compound from the two killers you sent to us. They lived with Al-Kadi for a time, so we should know all about his favorite places to hang out."

"That's very good news. If I'm familiar with where Al-Kadi would conduct a meeting along with where his men are normally positioned, I could get the drop on him and do some real damage inside."

"That's what we're hoping. Talk at you soon."

"Bye, Clint." Nick disconnected and started writing again, only to receive a Rachel bop on the back of the head. He turned with a sigh. "What was that for?"

"What the hell are you up to now? I heard references to New York and the Al-Kadi trip you've been planning all along with the Monster Squad. Secondly, what was the talk about the family being transported north for safety?"

Nick hugged her. "Concentrate on your editing. I already told you a Kader from New York ordered those two hired killers at the school. He may be the Kader kingpin we've been searching for. His name is Eliah Kader. Clint had good news on the Al-Kadi visit. Lynn has convinced Carone and Bulgar to assist me at the Pilot Hill compound."

Jean, who had been eavesdropping as usual became instantly animated. "Lynn is the baddest!"

"Lynn is the best interrogator I've ever encountered," Nick agreed.

"Are you certain you'll be able to trust what she's done once those two are beyond her reach," Rachel asked. "You'd be hung out to dry if they come to their senses at the door of the compound."

Nick shrugged. "Did you just insult me?"

Both kids and Rachel chuckled at Nick's mock outrage.

"Listen," Nick urged. "I will have the deadliest backup in the world ready to move if things go wrong. Besides… although I love the looks of this Pilot Hill compound confiscation, I would have no qualms about damaging it if things go wrong. I have a plan."

"A plan to get out of a compound surrounded by murderers?"

"Grenade."

"That's not funny," Rachel retorted.

"Do you see me laughing? The best diversions are messy. Besides, if I get an audience with this Al-Kadi, he's not going to allow me to get near him armed to the teeth. I'll need to make sure I have some diversion tools planted on one of my unknowing companions. We will cover everything from start to finish."

"I'd rather you Monsters simply fly in on your 'Apocalypse Now' ships and salt the earth. You buggers have more money than God. Buy some other damn place near Pilot Hill."

Nick smiled at Rachel. She blurted out the common sense, black and white facts without taking into consideration the Monsters. "First counter argument deals with all the electronic data and pipeline to other Islamist mutants across the country our federal agencies could act against legally with evidence. Think of us finding threads into huge Muslim enclaves like Dearbornistan."

Jean giggled. "You mean Dearborn, Michigan?"

"We're in a weird place as citizens, Viper," Nick replied. "The common citizen is labeled a xenophobic racist when we question our government's idiotic non-enforcement of immigration laws. The plot to induce two hundred thousand Muslim refugees into our nation is beyond belief, yet it is dropped on us with no recourse. The hard cold fact is Muslims do not assimilate into any nation they infest. They whine and cry to be allowed to escape their third world hell-hole, but insist on bringing it with them when they are granted sanctuary. They have infected Denmark and Norway to the point their protesters demand to annex parts of those sovereign nations as their own Muslim enclaves."

Jean's face twisted into an angry mask. "That's not right."

"You've already experienced life not right, kid. We learn and move on. We'll stop this threat, one way or another, and move on to the next. At some point in the future, we'll stop playing catch up and teach the troglodytes the meaning of war. Until then, allow us Monsters to tread water the best we can. We'll stay safe to the best of our ability."

"I remember in a time when Muerto was a cold blooded assassin his exact words describing an assassin in a novel were: 'one of the traits a world class assassin would have is the skill to foresee every possible scenario on a job. It would be idiotic to have him stumbling from one situation to another as if he were Peter Sellers in a 'Pink Panther' movie'."

"Okay... that's it, no more slinging my words in my face. I'm slowly regaining the edge to Muerto: cold blooded assassin. It isn't easy. I've been corrupted by civilian family members who didn't mind me risking my life for them, but I have to leave America at risk. How selfie of you, Rachel."

Rachel stood with hands on hips. "Don't blame your shortcomings on me, Muerto. You're the one who developed delusions of grandeur and decided you're bulletproof. Jean and I are simply left after your death to pick up the pieces."

Jean followed her Mom's stance in form and attitude. "Yeah, Dad!"

Nick chuckled. He leaned back in his seat and sipped the Bushmill's Irish next to him. "Good one. Do you two rehearse this stuff when I'm not around? I have a job to do you two are very familiar with. Hell, Sonny knows me as well now. I'm an abomination. I hold onto this family life with my fingernails. If not for Gus talking me out of retirement I'd probably be out at night full time with a mask and cape."

"You have a mask and cape, Sicko," Rachel reminded him, aware of Nick's penchant for steering a conversation by pretending moral and self-deprecating sensitivity. "I liked the 'I'm an abomination' touch – very dramatic."

"When do you have to go, Dad?"

"Soon. Clint said they're forming the last plans now depending on compound details from two men who lived there. The good news is it will not take long. Let's drop all this talk of future actions. I need to write another five hundred words in 'Blood Beach'."

"You named it?"

"You say that like it's a bad thing, Rach."

"I'm surprised but I like the title. It didn't seem like this time you wanted a title yet. I love the story so far. Diego and Fatima have some chemistry going on in this one."

"I like the title too, Sir," Sonny said. "You said it takes place in the Caribbean where there are a lot of beaches for sure."

"I think my title was better," Jean said.

"Caribbean Genocide doesn't fit the novel, Viper," Nick replied. "Genocide means murdering all the people of a particular race or religion like the Arabs wish to do to the Jews in Israel."

"Yeah but Diego murders all the bad guys," Jean persisted. "He's committing bad guy genocide."

Rachel stifled laughter at Nick's twisted look of frustration. "Bad guy genocide, huh? I have to admit I've been practicing the concept for quite a few years. The operation at the Pilot Hill compound will be one without mercy or quarter. So many terrorist activities from money laundering to infiltration and human trafficking pass through that place, I think of it as a blessing we stumbled on it in time. We may make jokes about places like Dearborn, but there's no humor in it if we're watching a horde of un-assimilating foreign infiltrators developing bases to wage war against America from within."

Nick put his head in hands for a moment before leaning back in his chair with his familiar smile. "We live the Chinese curse of living in interesting times. Sometimes the lack of common sense, logic, and even self-preservation stuns me into temporary shock. The only cure lies in missions like Pilot Hill, where something can be done no one else can do."

"Everything you get into, like at the school, sells another million novels in your Diego series," Rachel offered. "Your notoriety as US Marshal Nick McCarty has fired sales far beyond being a recluse in Pacific Grove. When you acted as a sniper backup during serial killer Kensky's capture, you were on the front page of every newspaper in the country. Severing his hand and foot off with two shots, coupled with your Delta Force training coming to light propelled you past your character Diego."

"I love writing pulp and walking Deke down to the Point with all of you. As you mentioned, we'll never need money. The book signings have been a source of entertainment I never expected. Adding in the real life stints I've allowed to seep into my public life are bound to cause us problems. I have a network of people around here from Carmel to Salinas who keep me informed when anything out of place shows up on the horizon."

"Then it becomes a red horizon, complete with blood slicks," Rachel quipped. "Speaking of book signings, are you planning to attend the one this coming weekend at 'Pilgrim's Way Books'? I would have thought you gunning down that guy in front of their shop also killed any chance of you being invited back. Apparently the news coverage of that event cemented an open invitation for you."

"I admit I forgot all about the signing," Nick replied. "This Pilot Hill hit takes priority over everything. The signing will be on Sunday. Pilot Hill may be over by then. Thanks for the reminder. I promised to do a 'Dark Interlude' talk coupled with some insights into the next Diego/Fatima paring in 'Blood Beach'. It may have to be arranged after I go on my New York Kader hunt. Johnny is so funny. When he found out I made you mobi files to edit on your Kindle of my progress in the novel, he asked to have a file copy too so he could track the progress of his character Leo."

"Uncle Johnny is so into his character, he keeps giving me plot ideas to pass on to you, Dad. I keep telling him it doesn't work that way," Jean said. "He keeps saying he understands but to mention them to you anyway. I think he wants to petition Leo into more novel parts than Gus's character Jed."

"Yep." Nick began typing again. "I'm certain of that fact. Gus has sensed it too. Those two banter back and forth about their imaginary parts every time we're together even though I haven't written anything new with either character. I'm considering an offshoot novel on the side with Jed and Leo engaging in a boating adventure where they agree to sail a group of mobsters to the Caribbean."

"Oh…my…God, those two will hound you into a coma writer's block you'll never emerge from," Rachel said.

"Don't tell them."

"Telling Momster not to reveal a secret is the same as telling a monkey not to eat a banana," Jean said, streaking for the door the moment Rachel twitched.

Rachel pointed at Jean. "You can run... but you can't hide. There will be blood."

"Mark my words, Dad. She'll cloak the secret in little clothes and hats with smiles and grins. When Uncle Gus and Johnny don't get the drift, she'll blurt the whole thing out to them with that sigh of frustration she does."

"I wish to remind you of something, Daughter of Darkness," Rachel stated with calm assurance.

Jean giggled but Sonny perceived intent and stared down at his homework paper. "What would that be, Momster?"

"You didn't take your phone or iPad with you to the escape route." Rachel snatched both items from Jean's side of the table faster than a cobra.

"No!" Jean rushed the table, only to confront the Momster in full parental mode. Jean smacked the snorting Sonny in the back of his head. "Why didn't you cover me, Cracker? I can tell you figured out what she would do."

Sonny straightened in his chair. "You're on your own, Viper. I don't take sides in McCarty parental authority disputes. I have immunity as long as I maintain neutrality, right Nick?"

"Absolutely."

* * *

Nick drove into the Salvatore's driveway the next morning. Sonny ran out the door. Inside of a second, he was sitting next to Jean in the backseat. Deke looked at him curiously from between the two kids. Gus sat next to Nick in the passenger seat.

233

"My Dad's coming out to talk with you, Nick," Sonny told him. "He and Mom are upset about the school episode. It didn't matter how many times I explained in detail what happened, he suspects there's more to it."

Nick shrugged. "There is. We're early. No big deal."

Nick walked to the door after shutting the car engine off. Phil Salvatore opened the door as Nick approached. Clarice waited just beyond the entrance, arms folded in her usual annoyed stance whenever Nick visited. Nick walked through the door with a smile and wave.

"Good morning. Sonny said you needed to talk with me."

"I called a school board member I know," Clarice said. "She told me Florence Nazari quit her job teaching at the school and won't be back."

"Well… there's some news to brighten my morning," Nick replied. "She never should have been given a teaching position there in the first place. She's an idiot. My dog Deke has more common sense than she has. Thanks for the update. I'll bring Sonny back after the kids do their homework."

"That's all you have to say?" Clarice flashed Nick her openmouthed, arm dropping stare of incredulity - a pose, Nick knew, would have earned her a bitch slapping, or stun-gunned, if Rachel had been with him.

"What more is there to say? Her husband and his friends tried to kidnap Jean in broad daylight. The authorities have all of them in custody."

"Florence was trying to introduce another perspective to the kids at school. She was an amazing teacher with fortitude." Clarice created an alternate reality on the fly without hesitation.

"You're good, Clarice," Nick replied. "You should write fiction. Flo tried to brainwash the kids about the death cult. That's about the only thing she was good for."

Phil and Clarice both gasped. "Death cult? Really, Nick? Those words offend. Islam is just like any other religion."

"No... it's not. If you're that damn ignorant about the world, Phil, just keep your mouth shut. If all you wanted to do was talk at me about the blessings of Islam and their poor misunderstood murderous horde, save it for one of your other politically correct nitwits. You can all drink the Islamist Kool-Aid together. You do understand you're coming to the defense of people who threatened Jean's life, right?"

"Sometimes Jean doesn't know her place. She-" Phil grabbed Clarice to quiet her, seeing cold blooded killer surface in Nick's face.

"Don't say anymore, Clarice."

"I'd advise you two useful idiots to not speak until your survival instinct kicks in. What's this all about? I know it can't be only because Clarice needed to spew her self-righteous phony crap at me."

Phil cleared his throat. "We...we're worried maybe this latest episode of yours will put Sonny in danger."

"From whom... peaceful Islam?"

"It's not a joke," Clarice replied with fists clenched. "Those people are dangerous. You've seen what they do overseas to people who cross them."

Nick chuckled. "I see now. You two aren't worried about the politically correct garbage. You're worried maybe the innocent and peaceful Muslims might think about turning their attention on you two. Don't. Call me if you see anything out of whack. I'll take care of it. Phil can tell you from experience what happens when you cross my path with violence in your heart. The school problem is solved. No one will be screwing around with either of you over that. I have to get the kids to school. Why don't you go and actually show up for work at the Passport Office you're supposed to be in charge of, Phil. It'll give you something to do. I don't care what you do, Clarice. Just do it quietly. See ya'."

The Salvatores kept their mouths shut as Nick exited their house, which convinced Nick they weren't completely brain dead. *At some point we will have to adopt Sonny or make him an orphan.* In the car, Gus was doing Phil impersonations which had the kids laughing and staring at him in disbelief. Nick had already been treated to Gus's hidden talent of mimicry. He had done Johnny in front of Cala to the point she cried real tears and begged him to stop.

"I see the Gusster has revealed his new bag of tricks."

"He…he is scary good! If I close my eyes, I'd think my Dad was in the car," Sonny said. The boy turned solemn. "How did it go, Sir?"

"Very well. We had a nice chat in alternate reality land," Nick replied while getting the car headed to the school. "I believe I calmed their fears, kid."

Nick's phone rang in the cup holder where he stuck it whenever he drove. It played the theme from the old 'Dragnet' TV show. "It's Neil. Can you get that, Gus?"

* * *

Gus, amused by Sergeant Neil Dickerson's theme song, answered on the third repetition of 'Dum da dum dum'. "It's Gus, Neil. Nick's driving the kids to school. He's right beside me."

"Can the kids hear me if you put me on speaker?"

"Yes." Gus straightened, holding the phone closer. "Give it to me straight. I'm listening."

"I…I have a hostage situation. A call went out to report a domestic abuse with kids on scene at Fisherman's Wharf in Monterey. They put out a distress call for help. My new partner, a rookie name Cheryl Rossdale, drove there because she was close to the Wharf. She's a hot dog, Gus. She's been keeping me apprised as I'm answering the call. They put her on crowd control. Two perps… one of them the husband… the other a friend, moved on the husband's wife and two kids while they walked along the wharf area. They've retreated to the buildings at the back of the Wharf near 'The Big Fish Grill'. The Monterey police have the area secured, but the perps are armed with automatic weapons. They have the wife and kids with bystanders ordered to the pavement in front of the restaurant. The negotiators are busily talking them down by cell phone. Cheryl's listening to everything. She believes they're going to kill the wife and kids along with bystanders. They're getting angrier by the minute because the idiots of course want guarantees of safe passage and no charges."

"Muerto and I have done some business on the Wharf. I think I know an approach. If I can get into position we'll need cover for taking the shot."

"This is bad, Gus. I have no dog in this hunt other than my hot dog partner. They didn't retreat into a building which set off my alarm bells. They're staying within cover between the buildings on the left side of the restaurant as you face it from the Wharf area. Cheryl says they fire a burst every few minutes to keep their hostages in place."

"On it. Stay tuned." Gus waved a very interested Nick down. "Let's get the kids dropped off, Muerto. I'll call Johnny and tell him to meet us at the 'Lucky Lady' dock. We have to take this one."

Nick drove without comment, watching with amusement as Jean and Sonny built their own scenarios from the one sided call they could hear. When they reached the school, Nick walked the kids to the door, exchanging pleasantries with his parental squad of

237

ex-military dropping their kids off. He maintained a smiling persona while plotting through his own speculation about what crisis project at the Monterey Fisherman's Wharf area meant in terms of action. Jean voiced with frustration what she perceived from the call.

"Dad! You're going out with the 'Trio'. What's happening?"

"Get in the building, kid. I'll tell you later. That's an order."

One look at Nick's face, Jean grabbed Sonny's hand and headed inside without another word. Nick grinned and jogged back toward where Gus had taken over driving duties. A huge Middle Eastern looking man planted himself in Nick's way with a seemingly innocuous crew gathering near him, past the school property's edge. Nick kicked him in the groin and ran over him to the car. Gus fired three shots from his silenced Glock 9mm that halted pursuit but didn't attract attention. In moments, they were headed toward the dock where Gus's 'Lucky Lady' was anchored.

Nick called Jean. The moment she answered, Nick launched into a verbally short update with cautions to keep inside school at all times. "I'll call when this other thing is done, Viper. Follow your orders."

"I have it, Dad. Be careful. Take care of Payaso and Kabong."

"Will do, kid. Talk at you later." Nick turned to Gus. "I guess the added surprise confrontation at the school has nothing to do with where we're going, huh?"

"Nope," Gus answered. "I don't know what the hell the school deal was."

Nick immediately called Rachel. He gave her the staccato version of what Neil requested, which was a vague perception created from Gus's side of the conversation. After he explained the short confrontation in front of the school, Rachel stopped him.

"Wait one, Muerto. I'm on my way to the Monte. Should I redirect to scope out the situation at the school?"

"Good call, Rach. Yeah. If you could stake out the school front and make sure there's no more cave dwellers haunting the place I would breathe easier while handling this other matter."

"On it. I'll call you from the school. Did you get a license number or anything?"

"No time, babe. I trust your instincts for noticing out of place vehicles and occupants."

"Okay... I love you."

"I love you too, my dear. I'll stay in touch about our Wharf adventure."

"If I find a car or van full of the mutants, can I drive by and shoot them all in the head?" Rachel's laughter as she hung up made Nick smile. He had put Rachel on speaker. Gus nearly drove to the side into a tree after her last question.

"Rachel's out of control, Muerto."

"It bothers me she didn't wait for an answer," Nick countered. "She'll drive around the school area and see if there's any reason for immediate concern. I wish I would have had more time to find out what that was all about."

"Maybe they just needed directions." Gus petted Deke's head as he jutted it between the seats. "I think Deke wanted some action."

"I don't want Deke getting hurt. I'd rather shoot them all. How's the ocean today, Gus. I'd like to make a couple shots without bobbing up and down like a top."

239

Gus checked his iPad for weather and ocean conditions. "Not good. It's going to be a bumpy ride."

"I may have to fire a short burst. It's risky, depending on their position. What do you think about me approaching from in the water? If I can reach the lower pier without being seen, I'd be able to take them out without risk to their hostages."

"I'll bet they're using that small room at the side of the restaurant. They would have a clear view of the harbor area and the restaurant front where they have the other people pinned down. Swimming over to them would be a suicide mission."

"You're probably right. Hey… what about the other side of the harbor cover along that small cliff? If you could drop me off there, we'll be so far away, my movements wouldn't draw attention or fire."

"I know where you mean. It's the tip of the finger of land with that big building near Breakwater Cove. You would have a clear shot. We can park on Lighthouse Avenue and go over the railing to that Monterey Peninsula Trail. Johnny and I can spot and watch your back. I'll call him to get your M107 out and our spotting scopes. With a solid nest, are you thinking of kill shots or wounds?"

"Good question," Nick admitted. "If they're using the room at the side I think they are, it will depend on the position of the wife and kids. I'm not anxious to blow the guy's head off in front of his kids, but I may have to. I'm not risking a shooting spree so the cops can take prisoners."

"Those .50 caliber hollow points make anybody they hit unlikely to do anything," Gus said, calling Johnny. A short discussion about needed tools and Gus disconnected. "He'll be waiting for us on the street with everything. He's already on the boat. He says the water's really rough today. The boats in the harbor are bobbing big time."

"Make sure you two have your FBI ID's handy so we can calm any hikers along the trail."

"Will do," Gus replied. "I hope you can wound them too. Otherwise, this will get tricky. You don't have a contact in the Monterey Police Department. Neil doesn't have the authority to request federal aid for another city's police situation. They have their own S.W.A.T. guys, don't they?"

"Yep, but they only shoot when given an order in the rules of engagement. I'm thinking Neil thinks I can pull this off and vanish like the Lone Ranger. I hope he's right. If we don't get a lot of foot traffic, I know a spot where we can drop down under a small cliff near Breakwater but out of sight."

"There's Johnny. He has Cala with him."

"Good. Another set of eyes watching foot traffic will be welcome."

Nick drove alongside the couple, who carried the equipment bag fitted for the M107 .50 caliber sniper rifle and their digital spotting scopes. The two entered the rear of Nick's SUV with a wave and smile. "There is never a dull moment with you, Muerto. Do you mind that I brought Cala with me?"

"No, we can use the extra cover. I see you brought along our HD camera, my dear Cleaner. Good idea. We'll need a close wide angle video of everything we can see on the pier."

"I will get it, Muerto."

Nick found a loop for emergency stops along the winding part of Lighthouse Avenue, near the spot he had in mind for his sniper's nest. He parked, leading the way left to a spot where the Monterey Peninsula Trail fronted an embankment with a huge tree at its crest. The four maneuvered over the embankment to the spot Nick remembered under the tree topped cliff. The four spread out slightly with Gus next to where Nick readied the M107 with Cala and Johnny on the sides. Nick allowed Deke to go along too. The canine companion instantly went into all out ecstasy while nosing around the rocks for small critters and new smells.

"You are right, Muerto." Cala used the range finders before shifting to her video camera. "This is perfect. We are nearly out of sight from the trail above. I see the Wharf clearly. I see the men! My video will be excellent."

"They're hanging out right where you thought," Gus added. "They have the big door to the side storage area open to block line of sight, but take turns checking their hostages down on the pavement in front of the restaurant. Those look like AK47's."

"Yep. That's what they are." Nick crouched behind the M107 mount where he had built a rock platform. Both men wore black hoodie windbreakers. "You see what I see?"

"They are high on some speed," Johnny answered. "Their whole bodies are vibrating slightly from it. I do not see the wife or children. They must be inside the storage room."

"They will blow a gasket soon," Gus added. He gave Nick wind speed, humidity content, and exact temperature. "Every third time they both come out at once from beyond the shielding door to check in both directions."

"Good call. The shorter one must be talking to the negotiator," Nick remarked. "His face is twisted in frustration. He also only has one hand on the strapped AK47 over his shoulder. The guy firing the warning bursts keeps both hands on. Okay... next time the weasels both pop out, I'm ready."

"I'll get Neil on the line."

Nick's index finger first pad touched the trigger gently as he settled his breathing to a whisper softness of calm. The temptation to kill them both ripped through him. He took another deep breath, smiling slightly. *Next time.* Both men emerged from the cover of the door, the shorter one shouting into the cell-phone he carried. Nick squeezed the trigger. The muffled sound of the muted M107 round caused a much louder chaotic shock on the pier as the .50 caliber hollow point slug tore through the man's wrist and shattered the AK47 stock he held. The force of the shot spun him screaming to the pier, pieces of weapon clattering around him. The companion dropped his phone, gripping the AK47 stock. A split second later, the same fate leaving his partner screaming on the walkway, pulped his hand and weapon.

"Neil!" Gus barked into the phone. "Both men are down and their weapons disabled. Tell the PD to move in if you can. I see the woman and her two kids running for the main pier. The hostages are realizing what happened and they are moving too. Nick has the two men in his sights still, but I doubt they'll be able to stand let alone do anything."

"Understood. Tell Nick thanks." Neil disconnected.

Nick waited until black clad helmeted police arrived on scene before he began disassembling his nest. "That went well. It's another beautiful day in the neighborhood. Should we send flowers to the hospital?"

"Only you, Muerto… only you," Gus said, shaking his head as Johnny and Cala enjoyed Nick's humorous rejoinder. "I'm surprised you didn't do a Kensky on them while they were down and blew their ankles apart too."

Nick grinned, remembering his maiming of Gerald Kensky, the serial killer up in Washington State. "I thought about it. This will be much easier to explain if I'm called in to make a statement. I'm hoping Neil will simply explain a US Marshal sniper was available and he asked me to assess the situation, where upon I kept in constant communication through the wounding of the suspects."

"That sounds very professional," Cala stated as the four trekked up the embankment to the guard rail separating the

Monterey Peninsula Trail from Lighthouse Avenue with Deke pacing next to Nick.

Johnny took the equipment bag and stowed it in the back of the SUV.

"I'll drive," Gus said. "You'd better call Rachel. She didn't update you on the school situation. I hope that doesn't mean bad news."

"Damn... I forgot... it's okay," Nick said, checking his iPhone. "She texted me everything was okay. I'll call her."

Rachel answered on the first ring. "I heard, Muerto. You did very well. The news crews were there in force with minute to minute coverage. Joe and I are watching it now. The reporters are interviewing the hostages. The woman and kids have already been transported from the scene. No one knows what happened yet. The ambulances have arrived on scene and the paramedics are headed down the pier towards the wounded. How bad?"

"Just a couple scratches," Nick answered. "Much less than they deserved."

"Yeah... I'll bet. Are you going to own up to this?"

"Only if I'm forced to. We're in contact with Neil. He'll let me know if I have to make a statement. If I don't have to deal with hurt feelings from the cops, I'll be good to go."

"I love you. See you after work. I guess you'll be picking Jean and Sonny up, huh?"

"I will do that. You didn't see anything of my school greeting party?"

"Not a sign. All was quiet when I drove around the school neighborhood. There's certainly not any people waiting in a vehicle for school to get out. Do you still have Deke with you?"

"Yes. I didn't have time to drop him off at home. He was his usual well behaved self. If it wasn't for those mystery cretins haunting the school this morning, I'd head to the Point with my crew for a celebratory beverage, and chance walking Deke with me to escort the kids. I won't though. It's too dangerous. Besides, I don't want to get called in by the cops half in the bag."

"A wise decision, Muerto. Call me if anything changes or you need a lawyer."

"I will. In today's world no good deed goes unpunished. I love you too. Bye." Nick disconnected.

"Should we stay in the area?"

I don't think so, Gus. Let's go over to my house. We can have coffee and snacks on the balcony."

"Payaso and I, the Kabong, will not have to drive," Johnny announced from the backseat where Deke stretched out across his lap with head in Cala's lap. "We can have a taste of the Irish without repercussions."

"I'm shocked. You two would drink in front of me after all I've gone through?"

"Absolutely," Johnny answered.

Nick sighed. "I feel the Diego series may need a death in the family. Poor Leo."

"That is very small of you, Muerto."

Chapter Ten

Preparations and Complications

US Marshals, Tim Reinhold and Grace Stanwick, ambled into the interrogation room where Nick awaited another round of ridiculous questions. "Hi there, my fellow Marshals. It's nice to see the two of you are still together. You're a saint, Tim. I didn't send for help by the way."

"You have friends in Congress and the Department of Justice, at least in the tier down from the idiots running the place," Tim said. "We've already talked with Neil Dickerson. He said you wouldn't let him fall on his sword for you. He is the one who asked you in on the hostage situation."

"Nice shootin' out there, Tex," Grace added. "I imagine you had the cartoons with you."

"I have no knowledge of what you speak Annoying Grace. As I've explained to the nice gentlemen in uniform accusing me of everything from out of jurisdiction to assault with a deadly weapon, I went in person with weapon to assess the situation. I recognized if something wasn't done immediately, the meth freaks were going to start hosing people down with their AK47's which were completely automatic and illegal. The thin blue line here looked uncomfortable about asking me all this stuff, especially after getting the toxicity report from the hospital on those two upstanding citizens. They're getting pressured from above somewhere. It's not like I killed them which was my first choice."

"They'll never use those hands again to pull triggers. That's for sure," Grace agreed. "We shut off audio and visual in this room. Tim told them if they want to be brought up on Federal charges, then just go ahead and ignore us. You're listed as a

S.W.A.T. sniper. Tim and I pointed out that you don't want any credit for assisting. Once we established Monterey's Blue can claim the takedown in any manner they wish, it was decided you are free to go. Tim and I also forgive you for not calling us on the Carone operation."

"I'm sure you've heard the rumors about how busy I've been. The operation you speak of had extenuating circumstances we're still in the process of handling. It was decided at the top of the food chain Carone and the threads leading from his organization would be handled by our special task force. I will update you two when it's over. Don't even mention the name again, okay?"

"Sorry, Nick," Tim replied. "That will be great. 'The 'Starlight' operation was incredible. Isis may not have been slowed down much, but you sure punched a hole in their enabler circuit."

"It went well. If I understand you right, I can walk out of here with you two?"

"Not exactly. The Assistant DA wants to talk to you. Her name's Emily Dorsett. She seems to think you need another five minutes of bullshit minutia after the hours you've already been through."

"If I can keep my name out of this, it will all be worth the lost time," Nick replied. "They made me check my iPhone though so I couldn't funny FaceTime with Jean. Let's get Em in here so I can get clearance to go."

"Okay," Grace agreed, "but hold onto your temper. Don't let Dorsett bait you, Nick. Tim and I talked to her for fifteen minutes and I still don't know what her point is."

"Ditto," Tim said. "Listen, nod, and let's get out of here, Nick."

"I'll try, Tim." Nick watched Grace walk out of the room and escort a thin young black woman with a pinched angry look into the interrogation room. Nick figured her age to be middle to late twenties.

She sat down opposite Nick while shuffling papers. When Nick didn't react she set the folders down, clasped her hands in front of her, and glared into Nick's smiling face. "I'm Assistant District Attorney Emily Dorsett. Do you know what these folders represent, Marshal McCarty?"

"No… but I have a feeling you're going to tell me whether I want you to or not."

Dorsett's pursed lips almost spewed out whatever actually reflected the vitriol going through her mind. What Nick couldn't figure out was why. He saw Grace and Tim giving him small head shakes. Grace in particular entertained him with oval mouthed pantomimes of no, no, no. *Game on.*

"You can make light of this if you like but these folders contain filings on behalf of your victims who are suing the city for twenty million dollars. Dominic Quale and Leo McKinley have a damn good chance of winning."

"No they don't." Nick took a USB flash-drive out of his pocket. "Can I borrow your laptop, Grace?"

Grace set her laptop in front of Nick with it open and running. Nick plugged in the USB drive. Nick narrated it, noting the meth-heads body language shaking with every movement. "You can also see the tall perp blasting away over the heads of innocent hostages forced to lie on the pier in front of the restaurant waiting to die. The shorter one holding the phone gets word he doesn't like on the phone from the negotiator. When the woman and kids were released she had been beaten and her arm was broken. The kids were manhandled and in shock with bruises and wrenched limbs. I know because I made sure to get a copy of the hospital report on the Mom and kids along with a drug screen on the two perps."

"Where did you get this video?" Dorsett's mouth went to instant torque.

"My associate filmed the entire incident. If need be, I have three eyewitnesses, two of whom hold FBI and US Marshal credentials. I explained all this to the police interrogators along with the fact I haven't made any of it public because I figured a trained poodle could get a conviction on two meth-heads threatening the lives of a multitude of innocent people with illegal weapons. My bad. They seemed satisfied when I wanted to hand over all credit to the Monterey Police Department. Didn't they explain all this to you?"

"They tried, Nick," Tim said. "Grace and I were in on the meeting."

"Dorsett here cut them off before they could get two words of explanation out," Grace added, causing Dorsett to spin angrily toward them. Grace gave her the wave off. "Don't bother, kid. You screwed up. I don't know what your angle is, but Nick's video stomps the hell out of it. Those two clucks will be going away for a long time. They ought to get the death penalty for what they did."

"Why… because they're black men?"

Grace slid in next to Emily with her face a few inches away from Dorsett's, so close in fact, something else crept across the DA's features: fear. "Listen to me closely, Nick's best friend and partner is black. He was probably one of the witnesses. What kind of crap are you pulling anyway? Are you auditioning for a leader role in the local 'BLM' mob or something?"

"That's not funny!" Dorsett stood away from the table.

Nick stood too. "Yeah… it is funny. What do you have in mind? As you saw in the video, you have proof to get those two making plea deals for anything up to the death penalty without a court trial. It's a win. You can take my copy of it. I have others in case you have something else planned behind all this."

"You maimed two men for life."

"They'll have to seek sexual gratification with the other hand in prison. Boo hoo. US Marshals Reinhold and Stanwick can tell you my skills encompass the ability to have blown both of their heads off, thereby saving the State of California millions."

"That's obscene!" Dorsett shifted her outrage to Tim and Grace, who were failing miserably to stifle amusement.

Nick walked over to her. "Listen closely. You've made an error in judgement. I'm wondering if you are even aware of the incident's facts. Did you simply see the two guys were black and think I shot them because of their color?"

"I...I... that doesn't matter. You shot without-"

"It does matter, nitwit! The guy's wife and kids are black, Em. Maybe you didn't care enough about them to read in fully on the case. You have the opportunity now to reverse whatever damage you've done shooting your mouth off without facts. Take the video to those dolts' public defender or ambulance chasing asshole that's representing them. It ain't likely you'll have to get through more than a few minutes. If they still have questions, let them know about the witnesses. If they're smart, they'll take any deal you offer. You'll save court expense, and the real victims' lives won't go through a lengthy court trial. I don't know what you've been thinking, but until you actually research all the facts within the prism of this video, shut the hell up. Can we go now?"

Dorsett gripped the table with both hands for a moment before using her right hand to wave them out. Nick let Grace and Tim lead the way. They accompanied him to pick up his personal things. That done, the three exited the police station.

"Can I hitch a ride home with you?"

"Of course," Grace replied. "Can you fill us in on the Carone operation?"

"I can't. It's another joint mission with John Harding's group. Even we don't know all the parameters of it yet. What do you think all that Dorsett stuff was all about? She talked like those guys' defense attorney."

"We weren't sure what she had in mind after the meeting we were present at with the police," Tim said. "Thank God you had the video. Is Carone dead?"

"No. He's in our custody."

"Meaning he's locked in a room somewhere awaiting death?"

"Possibly not, Annoying Grace. I'll let you know how it works out in the end. I'm trying to figure out what Dorsett could possibly gain by trying to railroad me with a bogus complaint. Did you hear any of the regular cops mention anything about me?"

"They wondered why you were being held and questioned at all. They saw your action as a win. You'll need to keep an eye on Dorsett," Grace replied. "Do you have enemies inside the Monterey DA's office?"

"I don't think so. Someone moved on the case real fast for the defense. Suing the city for twenty million seems like a ploy to get those two released. You know how fast the politicos start apologizing when anything happens to any minority, no matter what crime they commit. If the city settled, instead of prosecute for millions to keep the whole thing out of the headlines, I wonder if there's a connection to Dorsett getting a piece of the action."

"Plausible," Tim agreed. "I think Grace and I better meet with the police chief with your video. We may have to insist on you getting credit, but only as a mention about a US Marshal

251

sniper called in to assess and handle the hostage crisis alongside the police. That way Dorsett can't sandbag the video and allow the wrong outcome to surface."

"Thanks, Tim. That sounds good. Those two meth-heads had every intention of killing everyone they could. It makes me think I should have capped them both. It seems relying on a strong police response to insane accusations by the perps is a thing of the past."

"You had no way of knowing the DA's office would fold at the first hint of a ridiculous lawsuit," Grace said. "Tim's right. We'll get to the police chief and pin him down. Send me the video file."

"I copied it to your desktop when I plugged in my USB drive. It's labeled 'Hostage File'."

Grace checked her laptop as Tim drove. "Great. How did the mess at the school get resolved? When Rachel called to let us know about the attempted kidnapping I couldn't believe it. She said there was more to it but she couldn't talk about it on an open line."

"Same as with the Carone connection," Nick answered. "We're trying to get in front of this Isis wave. Right now, we're mostly playing catchup. We think this new operation will set back Isis operations on their heels. They want California badly as a base of operations. There's no denying that now. Al-Qaeda is also attempting to get back in the game. Just like overseas in the sand, the rabid dogs are tearing at each other whenever they cross paths. I have a plan I'm going to run by John Harding and his crew."

Tim arrived outside Nick's house. "We'll call with news one way or another within the hour."

"Thanks. I appreciate the backup today. I admit they blindsided me with their line of questioning about two wounded perps caught dead to rights. I will definitely be watching DA

Dorsett. I believe it's time for me to find a bit more information about her life, finances, connections, and interests. If she somehow screws this hostage case up, she'll be signing those two nitwits' death warrants. I don't plan on leaving two guys like that running around."

"Understood," Grace said. "Say hi to Rachel and Jean. We'll make a real visit soon."

"I will. Pay close attention to the suits' mannerisms and expressions. Something's fishy about this."

"Agreed. We're living in some damn strange times when two guys can beat women, manhandle kids, hose down a public tourist spot with automatic weapons fire, and then sue the city because they got shot doing it."

"You outlined it beautifully, Grace. Talk to you in a while." Nick watched them drive away with more questions than answers.

Rachel met him at the door. "I thought you were only going to be gone for an hour or so to make a quick statement. Then Neil calls and tells me they're holding you for extended questioning. Gus and Johnny went with me to the school for Jean and Sonny. They're all upstairs with Tina and Cala. The way Gus explained it, there shouldn't have been an interrogation."

Nick hugged Rachel, kissing her with a passion fired slightly by the black short-shorts and red halter-top. "Wow… you look very nice. Forget the other crap. Let's go have a drink. Did you see any sign of my greeting party from this morning? The cops took my phone so I couldn't call you to get an update or give one."

"No sign," Rachel answered as Nick also greeted the very happy Deke. "We repeated an area check for suspicious cars. You must have a problem when the cops want to put you in the back room to be beaten with rubber hoses for stopping two killers."

Nick took her hand, tugging her toward the stairs with Deke pacing at their heels. "At first the way DA Dorsett whacked me around, I thought it was because I shot two guys of the wrong race. The more I think about it, the more I believe there was something else prompting Dorsett. I told Grace and Tim I'd look into Dorsett's background. Without the video Cala filmed I'd still be in the box back at the Monterey station."

"Do you think it's politically motivated? You don't even know any of the Monterey politicos, do you?"

"No. Before you and Jean came along, I lived like a recluse. Only Joe, Dan, Carol, Jerry, and a few others scattered around the area even knew I wrote books. Frank would have sent more killer teams than he did if I'd gone overboard on publicity. I admit to getting a kick out of doing the public events now at the bookstores."

After the hellos floated around in good natured banter, Nick sat down at their spacious balcony table. Johnny and Gus already had their satellite uplinked laptops open while they sipped. Cala and Tina sat next to their husbands. Nick sat down with his Bushmill's Irish with Rachel on one side and Jean and Sonny on the other side.

"Grace and Tim will be checking with the police chief and DA if they can, concerning the circus event Assistant DA Emily Dorsett put me through. We have the joint mission at Pilot Hill coming soon. I don't want to be locked into a legal morass with the locals. Let's find out what's really behind DA Dorsett's outrage."

"She's black," Gus stated after going through the preliminary social page Google hunt. "Are you sure it's not just another race baiter ploy with the poverty pimp twins, Jesse Jackson and Al Sharpton arriving next to extort money from the city?"

"What would Dorsett get out of it though," Tina remarked. "Did you tell Dorsett your partner's black and his wife's black."

Nick's mouth tightened. "Grace mentioned it. I don't play the race card for anyone. I don't do that 'some of my best friends are black or fill in the blank race crap' to prove how politically correct I am. All my friends are Americans. That's as far as I go."

"Here we go," Johnny said. "Check your screens. It seems before getting her law degree, Dorsett worked as an intern for Senator Diane Cameron. She worked her way into a spot as assistant campaign director, rumored to have handled shredding all documents and e-mails tying Cameron to the Chinese influence scandal years ago. Check out all the pictures with those bosom buddies together at social functions in DC."

Nick and Gus studied their screens with interest. "Good one, Johnny. That's what I'm talkin' about. I could tell Dorsett was using anything to build the lawsuits Quayle and McKinley filed nearly the minute they were taken into custody. Di's out of office. Let's have a little hack party. I want to find out if Dorsett and her mentor have been communicating by e-mail."

"Why does that Cameron woman care about messing with you, Dad?"

"She's a traitor, kid. We linked her to terrorists and forced her to resign. We also relieved her of all the ill-gotten gains she received for selling her country out. Di must have all her feelers in the wind trying to find any way she can exact revenge."

"What do you want to do, Muerto," Johnny asked.

"Discredit Dorsett with anything we can find linking her to Cameron, including payoffs. Di couldn't have done all this in one day. She's had Dorsett keeping an eye on me, awaiting an incident within her jurisdiction she could get me with. Let's make sure her boss, District Attorney Daryl Atherton isn't in Cameron's pocket too."

"At what point do you make sure Cameron doesn't put you in prison," Rachel asked. "She's already ignored your warnings."

Nick took a deep breath. "One thing at a time. First, we find out how much help Di is getting locally to haunt me. We'll fix this episode now. Cameron's lesson will have to wait until after Pilot Hill. We know where to find her when the time comes. Johnny's been tracking her movements. She's also on the FBI's radar, thanks to Harding's FBI friends Sam and Janie. I read them in on what we did behind the scenes to make her resign."

An hour later, while enjoying the view from the balcony watching the fog move in and sipping Bushmill's with his friends, Nick was satisfied they had Dorsett's number. Combining all the networked information the 'Unholy Trio' found concerning real estate deals, botched cases involving Cameron's friends on two occasions in the Monterey area and payment from Cameron for no apparent service, Nick assembled the case with timeline. He couldn't bother with formality but Nick understood he couldn't make what he had public himself, due to the way Dorsett's information had been gathered.

"How does DA Atherton look, Gus?"

"He's clean of Cameron. She was hired on Cameron's recommendation, but that would not be unusual. I have his office computer gateway open for anything you want to do. I can put Dorsett's file on his Desktop."

"Nope. We can't take a chance like that. I'll call Paul on my secure line. I haven't updated him on the Pilot Hill mission. He can officially approach the DA with the file, letting him know I work as a consultant with CIA, FBI, and Department of Justice. Atherton will be confused at first, but once he knows what's going on, this may clear up fast."

"Good," Rachel said. "Do it now. It's not that late in DC."

Nick considered it. "Okay. I'll be right back."

"I'm going down and make a veggie tray and dip."

256

"And order pizza?"

"Yes, Daughter of Darkness," Rachel agreed, walking out with Nick. "I'll get a couple of big ones with everything but anchovies, right gang?"

A chorus of affirmatives rang out. Nick's phone beeped on his way out. It was Grace.

"I couldn't meet with DA Atherton, but Dorsett stonewalled the video. The police chief consented to see it and hear our explanation. He advised us unless we can convince Atherton of what's going on, he already received notice the DA's office wants you brought in for further questioning."

"Thanks, Grace. We have it covered."

"You're going to nail Dorsett to the wall, huh Muerto?"

"Absolutely."

* * *

"Sorry to call you after regular working hours, Mr. Atherton."

"Who is this and how did you get my private number?"

"This will be a little hard to explain. I am Paul Gilbrech, the Director of the CIA. This is not a prank. If you would like, call this number back. It is my direct line at Langley."

Atherton shot out of his seat at the dinner table, waving off his wife. "No Sir. That won't be necessary. How can I help you?"

"I sent you a folder just now concerning the incident at Fisherman's Wharf. It contains a video record of what US Marshal McCarty witnessed along with his actions in the matter. The other file contains dealings between former disgraced Senator Diane Cameron and your Assistant DA Dorsett. No one in public knows this but Cameron resigned under pressure because of evidence found by Marshal McCarty tying her to terrorist organizations. I wager Dorsett didn't show you the video Marshal McCarty put in her hands, did she?"

Atherton's features tensed. "No... she didn't. I'm beginning to understand your point here. Is McCarty an asset of CIA?"

"I can't tell you specifics, but Marshal McCarty because of his combat experience and logistics training consults with CIA, FBI, and Department of Justice. He has thwarted numerous terrorist cells and attacks on the homeland. He was asked in to assess the hostage situation because of his skills as a sniper. The situation was handled incredibly well without civilian or police casualties. The reason we have the file connections between Dorsett and Cameron is because anyone dealing with Cameron gets added to the terrorist watch list we have on the former Senator. May I ask that you view the folder and call me back here?"

"Of course, Sir. I will do so immediately."

"Thank you." Gilbrech disconnected.

* * *

The knock on Atherton's office door halted the conversation in progress with another Assistant DA, a retired Navy Commander with a grim featured persona spread over his ebony features. Assistant DA Dorsett waited at the door. Atherton motioned her in. Dorsett walked in with a smile that disappeared when confronted by the dour looks on her boss and co-worker's faces.

"Sit down, Emily," Atherton said. When Dorsett was seated, Atherton continued. "I won't make this long and drawn out. You've committed some grave errors which cannot be ignored. I told you to keep me updated on the hostage situation that happened at the Wharf."

"It was a domestic dispute, Sir." Dorsett could see the aggravation building in Atherton's body language.

"I have the video in my possession of the incident you withheld. I also have a file containing your dealings with former Senator Cameron and her pursuit of US Marshal McCarty. Her reasoning was revenge for his ending the Senator's selling out of the nation. Your reasoning was obviously financial... and oh my, you certainly received that."

Dorsett leaped to her feet. "Where the hell do you get off spying on my personal life?"

"I didn't. When you continued dealing at Cameron's beck and call even after her forced resignation from office, your name showed up on the terrorist watch list for consulting with her. The authorities tracked your dealings under Homeland Security auspices. Nothing would have happened to you but in choosing to pursue Cameron's vendetta on Marshal McCarty, you committed a number of felonies. They will be recorded in your file. We will not be implementing legal proceedings against you. Pack your things and clear out of your office. There are two policemen waiting for you there to make sure you don't commit any other crimes."

"I'm being set up! You see what's going on here, don't you, George?!" Dorsett turned to her fellow district attorney for support.

Retired Commander, George Whittaker, stood too. "I was given this case because I still have a Top Secret clearance from my naval career. Former Senator Cameron is a traitor. You conspiring with her to frame Marshal McCarty proves you're no better than she is. My advice is this. Don't say another word. This meeting has been recorded. I will be prosecuting those two bastards Gayle and McKinley on so many felonies, they won't see the light of day for fifty years. Anything else you have to say will be used against you in a court of law and by God I'll be the one doing the honors. If not for Marshal McCarty, the wife, kids, and probably numerous civilian hostages would have been murdered."

Atherton waited until Whittaker finished before standing. "If I hear even one word of bullshit from you either here or in public I will have George pursue every single felony against you. I will have you frog-marched in handcuffs from wherever you are, directly into a jail cell. Now get out of my office."

A terrified Dorsett left the office without a word as ordered.

"I still think we should have charged her, Daryl."

"I know. The only reason I'm not pursuing her is I don't want any distraction from putting those idiots away for as long as we possibly can. That video scared the shit out of me. They were on the verge of executing everyone on the pier."

"I will get them. Don't worry about that. I'll update you at the end of the day." Whittaker left the office.

Atherton dialed the number he had been given. When Paul Gilbrech answered, Atherton said, "it's done, Sir. Thank you for bringing this to my attention."

"Thank you for dealing with it, Mr. Atherton. If you ever have need of Marshal McCarty's services, call me. I know he will help if he can."

"I will indeed."

* * *

Nick escorted Sonny and Jean to school along with Gus. The greeters from the other morning arrived as Nick walked toward the car alone. They awaited him away from the school front. As usual with the traffic dropping off kids, Nick parked half a block away from the school. Nick smiled as the man and his friends approached. Sergeant Neil Dickerson and his partner, Cheryl Rossdale stepped out of their unmarked car to intercept the men. Neil's arrival with his partner in full uniform caught the three men by surprise. The big man Nick had run over the morning before tried to lead his companions across the street. Neil stopped them.

"Excuse me, Sir," Neil said. "Do you have children attending this school?"

The man answered in Arabic, shrugging with a fake smile, pretending he didn't know English. Nick stepped in and repeated Neil's question in Arabic.

"That is none of your business."

"If you wish to avoid being arrested with me as your interpreter, you should answer the question," Nick said. "I know you speak English. It would be best if you did so now. You will not be going anywhere until I find out why you tried to stop me yesterday."

"I do not have children in this school," the man told Neil in English. "This is a free country… correct?"

"Yes… if you're a citizen," Neil replied. "Also, you tried to stop Marshal McCarty yesterday in front of the school. If you don't have a very good reason for doing so, you'll be coming to the station with me in handcuffs along with your friends. We don't allow people to stalk others outside our schools."

The man behind the big guy reached inside his coat, only to have Nick draw his .45 caliber Colt with the barrel pressed against the man's temple. "Move, and I blow your brains out."

Neil and Cheryl had drawn their weapons in the intervening seconds. Nick reached into the man's coat. He retrieved a Walther 9mm and handed it to Cheryl. "On your knees with fingers locked behind your heads."

The three men did as Nick ordered them. Each man carried a Walther 9mm and two extra clips. They had no identification on them. Nick spoke only after they were secured. "Tell us who you are and what your business is with me."

"We will tell you nothing."

Neil smiled as Gus strode next to Nick. "I release custody of these suspects to US Marshal's McCarty and Nason."

"Thank you for the assistance, Sergeant. I know you and Officer Rossdale prevented a violent incident in front of the shool. Marshal Nason and I will take charge of the prisoners now."

"Wait! We demand to be taken into custody by the police!"

"I'm sorry, Sir," Neil said to the big guy. "That ship sailed. We were called to assist the Marshals in carrying out a federal warrant. Besides the felony of carrying guns near school grounds without permits and identification, you and your friends have no identification period. We have officially transferred custody."

Officer Rossdale passed the evidence bags to Gus containing the weapons. "I hope you can find out what this weird influx of armed Middle Eastern men into our area means, Marshal McCarty."

"So do we, Cheryl. We'll be in touch once we identify these men," Nick replied as he and Gus moved the prisoners toward Gus's Ford SUV.

When they had the three men restrained in the backseat, Nick attached the silencer for his .45 caliber Colt. He stuck the silencer end under the chin of the man on the driver's side. Gus stuck a syringe into his neck. The big man began to yell. Nick used his stun-gun on the man's groin for thirty seconds of ultra-agony. He smiled at the last man as Gus moved to the other side of the vehicle to reach him.

"It would be best to stay quiet or I light you up," Nick said in Arabic. "Understand?"

The man nodded. Gus used a syringe on him and the big man in the middle still shaking from the stun-gun discharge. "Would you have let Neil have these guys, Muerto?"

Nick shook his head as he entered the passenger seat while Gus slid behind the wheel. "The fix was in. Neil didn't want them. He had a hard time believing another troop of whackos were seeking a meeting with Muerto, the angel of death."

Gus chuckled. "You had cover with the federal warrant Paul sent by courier."

"He's worried. We're still playing catchup. After the string of atrocities across the country, Paul wants a message delivered at Pilot Hill. Bring your costume, Payaso."

"Don't worry about that," Gus replied. "Johnny would hound the shit out of me if I didn't. He knows Lynn will want to join us in the movie. He's been dying to make another movie with Crusader Crue. We better put the Cleaner in a costume too or she'll be pissed."

"You're right. We'll have to invent a name for her too. Hey... how about Scourge?"

"Oh man... that's really good. She'll go nuts over that one. We have to keep her happy. We need Cleaner Cala. She's much more efficient than you were. When you help her, Johnny and I think of you as the assistant."

"Good one," Nick allowed. "A backup helicopter pilot is a winner too. Have you gotten Issac settled somewhere?"

"Tina found him a house near us. Until we get the papers settled, he's staying at the Martine Inn. He loves it, but he wants his own place. With the amount of money we've confiscated lately, it was petty cash. Speaking of confiscated money what do you have planned for former Senator Cameron? That was one convoluted frame job she tried to play on you."

"I'm thinking of asking Crue's minion, Sylvio, to make me one of those portable acupuncture foot heel devices. It leaves no mark and a forty minute session of treatment will teach Di a lesson she'll never forget."

"She deserves it. I doubt Cameron will stop trying to get you one way or another. That prank should have cost her the deal she made to resign without prosecution."

"I'm thinking we'll take care of Kader in New York and stop by Maine to see the former Senator," Nick replied. "It's a nice thought to reeducate Cameron but I'm afraid we'll need to save her for another time. She'll be busy answering for her minion, Dorsett."

"I used to think I'd like to lie low, keep out of trouble, and live the good life without thought to the destruction of a nation. Never again. After all the Isis attacks and attempted attacks coupled with a resurging Al-Qaeda, I want to be one of the violent men allowing other more peaceful souls to sleep at night without worry."

"Amen, brother. Pilot Hill will be our first actual offensive against these Isis mutants."

* * *

"Hello there," Nick said in his device altered voice. The Unholy Trio and the newly named Scourge ringed the gurneys with strapped in captives. "I'll save you some time. You three are new illegal Muslim mutants arriving from our porous Southern Border. We researched your pictures and fingerprints. You're wanted by Interpol pussies who couldn't catch a cold. The US Marshals decided we could help you three into the light once we found out everything you dunces came here to do. We know you originated from Saudi Arabia. Omar Kazir. You're up first, big guy. Tell me what you're doing here looking for Nick McCarty."

"I will tell you nothing!" Omar and his companions stared at the black-light illuminated horror scenes on the ceiling above them. The creepy theme from the 'Exorcist' movie played in a hushed accompaniment.

"Oh my… I was hoping you'd say that." Nick walked toward him with scalpel in hand. "I don't have the new tools yet so we're going old school today. You're probably wondering why we stripped you munchkins down to your underwear. Let me show you."

Nick cut Omar from his breastbone to his groin. Johnny sprinkled bleach into the screaming Omar's wound over his bulging intestines. They allowed Omar to scream on until he passed out from the pain three minutes later. Nick gestured over the other two terrified men.

"Now that I've cleared any notion in your tiny minds about whether we take no for an answer, let's get started. You're next, Solomon Didi." Nick pointed at the thin man with thick black beard on the gurney at the opposite end from Omar. "Yes, we know your name too. First, tell us where you and your buddies are staying, where the room key-cards are, where the vehicle is you parked near the school, and then get talking nitwit or I start cutting. We have the Ford keys from Omar's pocket."

"The Monterey Hotel. The green Ford Explorer we rented is parked a block in the opposite direction from where you left your vehicle. Our identification and hotel keys are in the glove compartment. We…we were sent to hire McCarty before Al-Kadi could reach out to him. Saudi Prince Rabiah Al-Saud sent us. He wishes to have McCarty kill Saran Al-Kadi. On the Dark Web it is rumored McCarty was approached to kill the Prince. We were either to hire McCarty or kill him," Didi confessed, realizing he would never see the light of day again anyway.

"Very good, Mr. Didi. Why approach McCarty at his daughter's school?"

"We knew about an incident where a very rich man, Milton Formsby, approached McCarty in a restaurant setting. He and his men were never seen again after that night. Omar... thought if we approached McCarty at the school he would hesitate to shoot before we had an opportunity to try and hire him."

"But then you three would have executed him if he refused?"

"Yes."

"I like you, Solomon," Nick said. "I have some technical questions for you. We'll be recording so answer in detail. Tell us everything about Al-Saud's whereabouts, guards, and favorite places he goes in public. Don't leave anything out because we'll be torturing the truth out of good old Omar. If he has another version different from yours, I'll be very unhappy with you."

"I am a dead man. I do not wish to die screaming. I will tell you everything I know." Didi did exactly that for the next forty minutes.

"He is telling the truth, Muerto," Cala said.

"I think so too," Nick agreed. He nodded at Gus. "We'll keep Omar for a few moments longer."

Gus administered the syringes to Omar's relieved cohorts. After they expired, Johnny and Nick put them into body-bags held open by Gus and Cala. By then, even with the cleansing Nick did and salve he put over the wound, Omar screamed his way into consciousness. Nick bopped him in the head.

"Shut the hell up! You're in luck. I'm sick of looking at you. Your friends were most helpful so we have a great baseline to determine the truth of what you'll be telling us. They passed on to the great virgin hunting ground peacefully without pain. If your factual input checks out, we'll give you a hotshot to hell where you belong. Would you like to start reciting what you know or would you like another dose of intestinal cleaning?"

Omar sobbed and cried real tears. "Can't you… give me something for the pain?"

"Sure. Once you finish testifying you won't feel any pain, at least until you reach hell. I don't know what's there for you. In finding out your real identities we also found out what you did for the Prince. Your two buddies were simply a couple of ex-Saudi military dupes. You Omar have been a very bad boy. Al-Saud used you as his enforcer. I bet you never thought you'd be on the receiving end of what you used to dish out. If you don't start talking, nothing's going to buy you a peaceful passing. You know quite a bit more about Al-Saud than your pals."

"I know all of his places where he goes into hiding!" Omar suddenly became excited. "Yes…yes… I know every one of them. I was also his personal bodyguard and the only one he truly trusted. That is why he sent me here to hire the devil, McCarty. Better he had sent me to kill Al-Kadi! Can I buy my life with this extra information?"

"Ah… no, but thanks for giving me some guidelines about what you do know. Get started."

"But… all I can do is buy death."

"That's where you're wrong. Show him again, Johnny."

Omar yelped and pleaded he was ready to talk. It did him no good as he received another bleaching. Before he could pass out, Nick warned him. "I'm going to relieve you of the worst of the pain. You'd better get talking when you can speak again."

With the wound bleach washed away and more salve applied to the wound, Omar gasped out everything he could think of. Johnny and Gus worked with their satellite laptops to pinpoint all the places mentioned. Nick guided him to numbers of men Al-

Saud always had with him and if there were any nightspots such as casinos or nightclubs he frequented when traveling to his favorite hideaway in Dubai.

"He...he loves Nasimi Beach. There are always many tourist women there where he may act out his part of being a playboy sheik. Al-Saud gets a luxurious private cabana where he stays all day and night. He gets a suite at the Atlantis which is part of the waterpark there."

Nick smiled. "Does he have any plans to go there soon?"

"Al-Saud must leave Yemen very soon or the Americans will find him with their damnable drones. He can never stay in one place for longer than a month. When he stays in Dubai, Al-Saud has enough people in authority bought off he can remain quietly for sometimes two months."

"How many men does he travel with? I would imagine it's difficult not to be tracked with a huge retinue," Nick pressed.

"He has a dozen men who travel with him, but not on the same flights. It is but a short distance from either the Kingdom or Yemen. Al-Saud always has two personal guards with him. I am one of them. I was supposed to be back in Yemen before he left for Dubai. I...I could guide you. It would be easy to-"

Nick injected him. Omar tried to gasp something before the fast acting poison injected into his carotid artery worked, but failed before the light faded from his eyes with lips still quivering. "Every moment with Omar produced a new vision of his past exploits to mind. I think I'm getting soft in my old age."

"Yeah, right," Gus snorted out his pronouncement with a headshake accompaniment to Johnny and Cala's amusement. "I agree with you on the atrocities the guy has committed. Damn... I thought the Saudis were slightly more civilized."

"Only on the surface," Nick replied. "I know the Nasimi Beach establishment from a past job in Dubai. My contract was for a Syrian General who thought he was a playboy. He stayed at the Atlantis too and he loved the waterpark."

"Did you kill him at the hotel," Johnny asked.

"No. I killed him on a fishing excursion about ten miles off shore. I acquired a small fishing boat, fished in the area he liked to frequent, dressed like a nomad on the water."

Nick remained silent while he and Johnny carefully lowered Omar into his body-bag.

"Do not leave us hanging, Muerto," Gus admonished. "You shot him in the head from five miles away, right?"

Nick chuckled. "Nope. He had his boat captain try to capsize my boat, laughing and drinking… until he saw me stand in the boat with the XM307 25mm grenade launcher. I guess you could say I had the last laugh."

"Weren't you afraid they would catch you," Cala asked.

"I didn't leave a thing other than tiny pieces of debris on the water surface. Then I moved away down the coast to my safe haven in Ajman. I traveled from there across the peninsula to Khor Fakkan where Frank had a boat waiting for me. We had a hard time getting paid for the job because they didn't find the debris for weeks. Someone in Qatar issued the contract. It established me as one of the top five private hitters in the world."

"So that general was a bad guy, huh," Cala continued with interest.

Gus laughed, remembering a similar question Rachel told him she asked. "He was to someone, right Muerto?"

Nick shrugged. "Yeah, we didn't really look into right and wrong on contracts in the sand. They were all bad to us except the

Israelis. The Mossad agents helped me out of a number of tight jams both in Europe and the Middle East. We had similar interests. Anyway, I guess I'll have to add the Prince onto my list. I have a rather unusual idea about how to do it. I'm thinking of taking the contract on Al-Kadi and confirm it with my usual upfront funds transfer."

"You dog! You're going to see Al-Kadi with the ploy to take the contract on Al-Saud as an ice breaker," Gus finished his thoughts with certainty. "What will you tell Al-Saud when you turn around and take a contract on Al-Kadi? We did just put his messenger boys in body-bags."

"Very observant, Payaso. I'll tell Al-Saud he should have approached me in the regular way. Then, I'll tell him the truth – I tortured his men until I found out his plan and then killed them. He'll think about that for a few moments and ask how he can make things right. I'll tell him no hard feelings and I'll take the Al-Kadi contract for double my usual price. He'll laugh like the rich pirate he is in reality and cough up my upfront fee, asking when he can expect completion. You've been around me too long to have figured out my twisted plot so quickly."

"Show of hands," Gus addressed the amused Johnny and Cala. "Did anyone not figure what Muerto planned the moment he mentioned taking the contract on Al-Kadi?"

No hands. Nick chuckled. "Does this mean you'll be converted to the entertainment of Kabuki dancing too since you know me so well, Payaso?"

"Just because I can decipher a sicko's plans does not mean I want to be one."

"Understood. We'll put our room temperature guests in the freezer and then I'm going home to do some Dark Web contracting. Johnny, can you and Cala collect the ID's, return the Ford, and retrieve all their gear from the hotel?"

"Absolutely," Cala answered for Johnny.

"Drinks, conference, and dinner afterward at your house, Muerto?"

"Yes. I should have word about Pilot Hill by then, Johnny. Can you and Tina come over too, Payaso?"

"We wouldn't miss it. I want to hear about your conversation with Al-Saud. That will be one interesting interaction," Gus replied. "You'll have to return to the sand in order to get him. Are you sure it wouldn't be better to settle with killing Al-Kadi, and collecting the fee?"

"Better for whom," Nick asked as they loaded the bodies on the gurneys again for transport to their freezer. "Al-Saud knows me too well. He sent men to Jean's school. I'll have to repair that break in my security net just like I'll deal with the New York Kader. Eliah Kader will have to be tracked while we're on the Pilot Hill mission, so everyone bring your iPads with you on our trip. We know all his hotspots in New York, thanks to Lynn. If he runs, we'll have to find out where. As I explained, I did a job in Dubai before. I can't expect Al-Saud to go fishing, but there are a number of easily approachable places at the Atlantis Water Park in Dubai."

"We will go with you, Muerto," Johnny said.

"No can do, Kabong. You and Cala are too valuable here. I'll have to do Al-Saud alone. It will all be easier that way. I have contacts there and a Mossad agent I collaborated with. He couldn't figure a way to get at the Syrian General without an international incident. Frank put me in touch with him. We shared intel and I completed the contract at sea without a trace. He'll help me if he's still stationed in Dubai."

"I can go with you, Muerto," Gus said.

"No you can't. You don't speak the lingo. If I have to take Al-Saud at the Atlantis Hotel, I'll have to infiltrate as a worker or something. Besides, you have to assume leadership of the Unholy Trio in my absence, Payaso."

"I don't like it."

Nick shrugged. "I'll be careful. It will be an important message to establish about coming anywhere near me in the future without an invitation."

"I hate to mention this, Muerto," Johnny said, "but although the Saudi Royal Family squabble and back-bite, they will take it badly when finding out about the assassination of an Al-Saud."

"I'll make sure they know it was an Al-Kadi contract – just business, nothing personal, Johnny. It's just business."

Johnny immediately lowered his head. "Yes… Godfather."

* * *

On the balcony, Nick finished writing the scene in his new Diego novel with a satisfied flourish of dark humor. Leo and Jed discovered their femme fatale partner, Fatima, planning yet another behind the back ploy to betray Diego while hiding out in their Caribbean safe-house. Knowing his lover intimately both in mind and body, Diego listened with amusement to Leo and Jed's warnings. Diego explained how the trap backfired already, with local authorities on his payroll tipped off in time to nab both Fatima and her accomplices.

Nick leaped out of his chair, spilling Deke off his shoes, as Rachel slapped him in the back of the head while Jean giggled. Sonny, sitting next to her, studiously looked away. "You betrayed Fatima! How could you? She's the best thing that's ever happened to Diego, you jerk!"

Putting aside his angst at how he had allowed his wife to ninja approach him, read over his shoulder, and attack him, Nick made calming gestures. "It's part of the story. I don't deserve to be slapped around for writing pulp fiction. You do understand these people are not real, right?"

"I thought 'Blood Beach' would be a deepening romance between Diego and Fatima," Rachel replied, folding arms over chest. "You have imagination. Use it, you block-head."

It took both Nick and the kids a few moments to recover composure after Rachel's verbal smack-down. Deke sat uneasily, watching his two human companions with furrowed canine brow, face tilted in questioning pose. "I'm the writer. If you don't like my story, write your own, shrew."

Rachel gasped. "You called me a shrew! That's it! Put 'em up, Muerto. It is so on. I'm going to kick your ass right in front of the kids."

Rachel dropped into fighting stance, her hands in boxer like position, ready to punch or defend. When Nick started laughing, she launched a respectable jab towards his head. He caught it in one fist. When she couldn't pull it back, Rachel tried a right cross with her other hand. Nick caught that one too with Deke yipping next to him. He glanced down.

"She started it."

Deke 'grumpfed' and nudged Nick's leg.

"Okay... okay." Nick forced Rachel into a chair while she unsuccessfully tried to yank free of Nick's hold on her fists. "I'll let her go, but only because you asked. Want a beer, Deke?"

Deke leaped from side to side as the awakening Quinn squealed in delight from his swing chair. Rachel relaxed as Nick released her. "Brute."

Nick retrieved three beers from the refrigerator and poured Deke one in his bowl. He took the other two over to the table. "Want a shot to sip with it, babe?"

"I might as well. That's how abused women handle their lot in life, right?"

"Absolutely." Nick served the shots. He sat down, holding his in toasting pose. "I'm not killing Fatima off. It's all part of a larger plot. You can't critique me on content until you've edited to the end. I'm not even there yet."

Rachel toasted with him as Jean and Sonny smirked in quiet observance. "I'll wait until I finish. You're not giving Fatima even a hint of trustworthiness. Now you have Leo and Jed distrusting her."

Nick shook his head slowly from side to side. "That's because she is untrustworthy. Fatima will have to earn their respect again. They will forgive but not forget."

Deke's ears perked as he looked toward the balcony entrance a moment before the doorbell chimes announced visitors. Nick checked his security screen on the balcony. "I'll get it. Our guests have arrived. Think about what we'll order for dinner."

"Can we have Chinese tonight, Dad," Jean asked.

"That sounds good to me. I'll run it by our guests. Start writing the stuff down you'd like to order while I let my cartoons and T-Rex in. I'll send T-Rex up for a moment while I update the cartoons about Pilot Hill."

"Intercom me about the food so we can order while you talk."

"Will do, Hon."

At the door, Nick ushered everyone to the kitchen while pointing upstairs for Tina. "Rachel and the kids are upstairs, Tina. They're picking out Chinese food to order if that sounds good to all of you."

"Oh yeah, it does," Tina stated. The others agreed to Chinese with enthusiasm. "I know just what stuff to get."

In the kitchen, Nick poured Bushmill's Irish for Gus and Johnny. "You're designated driver again, right Cala?"

"Yep. I'll have some of Rachel's iced tea though."

Nick served the iced tea. Once seated, he recounted where the operations they were involved in stood at the moment. "John told me we go tomorrow night. Can Issac go on that short of notice, Gus?"

"Are you kidding? He's so pumped, he can hardly speak. What about the 'Red Dragon Security' guys?"

"Chuck and Sal will be there. We needed extra perimeter troops. Even with all of us, it will be good to have Cala, Samira, and Issac along as armed extra drivers. Laredo and Jafar will be updating us with satellite shots and troop numbers. If all goes well, I'll own the main house before anyone needs to be inside. Final tweaks will have to be done after we fly into Oakland."

"What about Al-Saud?"

"I made overtures for a communication at my drop. I see you have your laptops with you. Did anything on the electronics you retrieved from the hotel room reveal anything of note?"

Cala held out an iPhone. "I went into their rooms dressed in a burka so I couldn't be filmed. We checked them out of their room electronically after I gathered everything in the room. Johnny loaded it all in a hat and hoodie. Omar has a direct line to Al-Saud on his iPhone."

"We will go through everything at home later," Johnny added.

Nick waved the iPhone. "This is outstanding. It will save us time if Al-Saud thinks it's Omar calling. I have an added idea to discuss with him. If he agrees to the contract terms, I'll let him know I'll be in Dubai soon, and ask him if he would like me to look for anything in particular to bring him from Al-Kadi's compound."

"That is very devious… and delicious, Muerto," Cala said.

"I think I'll sip one down here and call our buddy Al-Saud. I'll have to wait until eleven tonight. With the time difference it will be 9 am where he is. I don't want him to be irritated because I woke him. He may have received word of my greeting on the Dark Web by now but I doubt it. This phone call will be fun. I guess we'll talk later after I contact Al-Saud. We'll be flying to Oakland tomorrow at 10 am so it would be best to get a good night's sleep."

Gus and Johnny booted their laptops into networking operation. They spent the next half hour until the food arrived briefing Nick on everything Omar and his cohorts stored on their electronic devices. Johnny made a file with everything, except the Al-Saud phone number, and sent the digital fingerprints to Paul Gilbrech, including pictures of the dead men. Nick added a brief on how he planned to handle the Isis/Al-Qaeda rivalry. The food arrived and the friends adjourned to the balcony.

"What kind of mischief did you cartoons invent down there," Rachel asked.

"How many have you had, Rach?"

"Never you mind, Muerto. I only sipped one other after you left. Quinn has been entertaining us with facial contortions."

"While you're gone, we don't have to stay in the safe-room, do we, Dad?"

"Not if I can trust you and Sonny to be as observant as you two were at the Point when the hoodies tried to get your Mom and me. Both of you take your knives, stun-gun, and spray with you everywhere. Pretend while I'm gone we're back on the road with

276

the mobsters chasing us. By the time I get back from this outing, I'll have a lead on our safety factor here at home."

"We're on it," Jean stated, bumping fists with Sonny. "Nobody better mess with Viper and Cracker. Let the cuttin' begin!"

Rachel's head dropped to the table. "Oh my God!"

* * *

At eleven o'clock Nick used Omar's phone and direct line to Al-Saud. He answered irritably in Arabic. "You were supposed to call me the moment after you met McCarty. Is he dead? I saw a vague notice to me from him on the Dark Web. What is going on?"

"I am not dead, Prince," Nick replied in Arabic. "Your emissaries confronted me at my daughter's school. They are dead. You could have contacted me on the Dark Web. Why throw away your men's lives in so wasteful a manner?"

Silence.

"I realize this is just business, Prince," Nick continued. "Did you wish to present a business proposal to me?"

"I must apologize for my men. They misunderstood their orders. I wanted them to make contact with you the moment they reached your city, but they were to call you first. They were not told to confront you."

Lie to the infidel, huh? "I understand. What were they to contact me about?"

"I wished to hire your services to erase a man near where you are who seeks to kill me. Would you be open to such a contract?"

"Who is the target?"

"Saran Al-Kadi. It will not be an easy task. He lives at a guarded compound north of you. There will be many soldiers there. I have already survived two attempts on my life orchestrated by Al-Kadi. I need the contract completed as soon as possible."

"I have heard of this Al-Kadi. He contacted my drop on the Dark Web trying to hire me to kill you. I turned him down because I did not wish to take any more contracts in the Middle East. I have a plan though if you know where I can find Al-Kadi."

"My intelligence on his location is correct."

"It will cost you one million dollars."

Silence.

"Do not waste my time, Prince."

"I will pay it," Al-Saud agreed after a moment more. "Will half in advance suffice?"

"Yes. I have a transfer account in Belize." Nick gave Al-Saud the transfer instructions. "Make the transfer. Once confirmed, I will call you back."

Nick disconnected. He checked his Belize account set for only receiving funds. The money appeared in his account after half an hour. He transferred the money to another account and called Al-Saud.

"Very well. I will begin preparations. Send me everything you have on Al-Kadi's location."

"How will you approach him?"

Nick smiled. "I will contact him and tell Al-Kadi I will take the contract to kill you. If he agrees to terms, I shall get money from him for his own death when I visit the compound. Once he is dead I will blow the place up to cover my escape."

Silence and then laughter. "You are a very bad man. I will send you the information within the hour."

"Omar told me you will be visiting Dubai soon. I will be meeting a colleague there on an arms deal he would like me to protect. Is there anything of Al-Kadi's you would like me to bring you in Dubai?"

"Yes!" Al-Saud's excitement was palpable in his voice. "Can you bring me everything of an intelligence nature from his computers?"

"Certainly. I can copy the drives and bring them to you. They will cost you another one hundred thousand dollars if I can successfully clone them. I will contact you when the contract is fulfilled with proof. We can make arrangements to meet in Dubai once you have proof of Al-Kadi's demise."

"May I ask how you found out about my visiting Dubai?"

Nick thought of Omar's initial introduction to pain which loosened his companion Solomon's tongue. "The hard way, Prince."

"Understood."

Chapter Eleven

The Compound

John met Nick with a big smile at the Oakland hangar. They shook hands. "Hey, brother, how are things in paradise?"

"Oh… you know… a snake here and a snake there," Nick answered. "I guess you know from my notes on the New York Kader and Al-Saud, I'll have a busy time after our Pilot Hill venture."

"We've taken a vote here in the north bay. We're coming with you." John shook hands with all of Nick's crew. "You are all a welcome sight. We need everyone we can get on this caper if we hope to confiscate Al-Kadi's compound in one piece."

"I appreciate the offer, brother," Nick replied, "but I'll have to do Al-Saud on my own. It's a tricky mission with too many questionable outcomes. I have some assets in place there I can count on. Unfortunately, the New York Kader gig is the same way. Both are narrow hits. If I go in with the forces of darkness, either one of them could explode into an incident with far too many unintended consequences. Either one could jeopardize what we're trying to accomplish. If we can handle the Pilot Hill operation to our benefit, I believe it will ease a lot of matters in our peripheral view."

"Clint said you'd say that… very nearly verbatim," John said with a grin. "I'm not your Mommy, and I sure as hell ain't in line for the number one assassin in the world race. If you get into trouble and you need our help, we'll try to get to you in time, in spite of you disrespecting our original offer, so call us if you need us."

"I will, my friend. I hope to plot out my endeavors with Kader and Al-Saud so they will not be missed. Did you get the outline I sent you for my plot?"

John Harding led Nick's crew to the converted EMT van. "I did and I think it's entertaining as hell. Your call to Al-Saud was a work of genius. You do know once you're overseas in Dubai, they may just shoot you in the head, right?"

"Did you just insult me, John?"

Harding laughed. "Have it your way. I hope the assets overseas are as dependable as you think they are."

"That makes two of us," Nick replied, holding the rear van door open for his crew.

"Are the two going in with Muerto at Pilot Hill primed for their part," Gus asked as he entered the van behind Johnny, Issac and Cala.

"Believe me, Fernando and Senta have only one purpose in life – to please Cruella Deville," John replied. "You'll see when we get to Pain Central. It's good to see you again, Issac. I'm glad you were able to come on mission."

"It is good to see you too, Sir," Issac said. "I am very excited to be a part of this. St. Lucia is experiencing an influx of Muslims. A hundred Isis recruits from the other islands have flown to Syria."

"I heard about that. Nick told me you have a house now in Pacific Grove. How are you adjusting to the weather?"

"I am freezing my ass off, John." Issac replied in a hushed voice, avoiding Nick's smiling glare. "I was promised the sun and all I have been given is an icy wind."

"Nobody promised you anything, Cheeto breath." Nick handed Issac his large equipment bag. "You're going to clean my helicopter when we get back, young man."

"So, you have a Cheeto addiction, huh Issac?"

"I have a weakness for them, John," Issac admitted. "They are so plentiful here. It is mean though to call me 'Cheeto breath'."

"You'll survive. Get in the van. I'm riding in the front with John," Nick said.

* * *

Carone and Bulgar sat on chairs with heads bowed near the meeting table. Nick didn't need more than a glance to tell the two were broken. Everyone, including Sal and Chuck from Red Dragon Security, sat at the meeting table at Pain Central. Lynn's personal assistants Dannie and Amara watched Clint Jr. and Mia in the theater room. Tonto had already sniffed out the newcomers and escorted them to the table for heartfelt greetings.

"I see what you mean about our helpers." Nick walked next to Fernando and Senta. They immediately became attentive. "Hello there, Fernando. John tells me you and Senta are well rehearsed in what we will be saying at the compound."

"Show Muerto how well prepared you both are, my good little helpers," Lynn said.

The pair stood. They took stock of their movements and facial expressions before standing next to each other as if standing on the compound's doorstep. Their absolutely perfect dialogue, delivered without tremor or wavering tone, impressed Nick so much he clapped the cringing Fernando on the back.

"Outstanding! How did the introductory call to Al-Kadi go, Fernando?"

"Al-Kadi acted supremely interested," Fernando answered. "The Mistress of the Unimaginable made a recording, Sir."

Lynn started the audio call in to Al-Kadi to set a time for their visit. Nick listened intently, hearing the relief in Al-Kadi's voice. Fernando discussed the need and reason for his moving the Tempest to a new anchorage. Al-Kadi agreed with all of Fernando's suggestions about keeping the ship's position and radio silence for the time being until it became safe to reposition the Tempest.

"You are incredible, Lynn," Nick said. "I may be able to do a lot of damage inside. If this works the way I hope, I will kill the guards with Al-Kadi, pick a spot for an ambush within the room I meet him in, and have Saran-wrap scream for help. The number of guards answering his distress call may reduce the number of soldiers inside significantly."

"Damn good, Dead boy," Lucas said, getting nods of agreement around the table. "We could move then on the perimeter in full force. Clint can spearhead the house entry with Tonto when we clear it."

"What happens when Nick tells you to get down, my darlings," Lynn asked Senta.

"We drop to our faces on the floor with fingers locked behind our heads, Mistress," Senta answered without hesitation. "We do not move until ordered to."

"Very good, Senta. I believe we're as ready for this as we can be, Muerto."

"Yep. They've activated too many lone wolf attacks, probably orchestrated right out of a cell training center like Pilot Hill. It's payback time for the lives lost while our leaders busily tried to strip us of the weapons to defend ourselves."

"Thanks for a part in this," Sal said. "Chuck and I have been going nuts watching these chicken shit attacks."

"What are you using in the big house for weaponry, Nick?"

Nick hesitated a moment which furrowed Lucas's brow. "I'll show you, Chuck. I read the reports on when Senta was with Al-Kadi. She was required to wear a burka at all times. Isn't that true, Senta?"

"Yes, Sir. All women moving around the premises where Saran lives must be fully covered. Even when he used me for an assassination I would have to be covered until given into my target's control."

Nick reached into his equipment bag, retrieving a spandex belt with a quick release holster made specially to hold an MP5. It had slim pockets on each side to carry extra clips. "This will fit tightly to Senta's waist with weapons within reach at the rear. After they frisk me head to toe at the door, I'll keep Senta close by me when moving to our meeting with Al-Kadi. If they try to separate us, I will go for my weapon immediately. The party will have to start then. I can have my com gear clipped to the belt too so I can get into contact with the network the moment I begin eliminating inside opposition."

"Nice," John said. "I like it."

"Wait a damn minute." Lucas bumped into Nick, rooting around in the bag. He brought out a grenade. "I knew it! You're fixing to blow the hell out of my vacation cottage in the mountains. I ought to shoot you right in the head."

Nick sighed as everyone enjoyed Lucas's Marine drill sergeant face-off with Nick while waving the grenade under his nose. "Look Ahab, this isn't a suicide mission. If I need to blow the shit out of something to save my ass, I'll do it. Don't let whale-shit confiscate my backup plan, John."

It took a few more moments before Harding could speak to the issue of confiscation after the whale-shit comment. "Leave... the grenades alone, Pappy. I'm not losin' Muerto. Especially after he has that 'Spaghetti Western' ploy going between Al-Saud and Al-Kadi, getting paid by both sides with his own extermination plan for both in effect."

Nick grinned. "You recognized my 'Clint Eastwood' plot, huh?"

"Oh yeah," John answered. "It's the plot of a 'Fistful of Dollars' where Eastwood as 'the man with no name' plays off the murderous Rojos and Baxters against each other while getting paid by both."

"I used it in Florida when I helped my wife Rachel and daughter Jean out of the mess they were in. It's nice you recognized it, Dark Lord. I'm going to play my part inside the compound until Al-Kadi pays my upfront fee for killing Al-Saud if I can." Nick shook hands with Chardin. "Fenric Ballesteros is dead, Claude."

Chardin looked surprised. "Thank you. I crossed him one time and he held a grudge. He's tried four times to kill me. I figured if anyone nailed me out of the blue it would be him. Fen wasn't a bad sort for one of us psychopaths. I received bad intel on a job. Fen was nearly captured by the Egyptians. That's a bad bunch to be captured by, especially when they believe you know something they want."

"Don't you use those damn grenades unless absolutely necessary, meaning you can sacrifice all your body-parts first until you only have one hand to pull the pin," Lucas ordered.

"On a more serious note, Cheese told us about ex-Senator Cameron trying to get you outed and hung up to dry during the hostage situation you fixed," Tommy said. "How'd you do getting clear of that?"

285

"I had to have a little help from my friends on that, but I did learn who instigated the assistant DA and practically owns her ass," Nick replied. "I will have to deal with Cameron, not in a permanent way, but I am considering using Lynn's foot massage method to get her in line if Sylvio can make a portable one for me."

"I will make you one the moment we return from Pilot Hill, Muerto," Sylvio stated. "It is a very good teaching tool for recalcitrant students."

"Thanks, my friend, I will use your teaching method sparingly. I'm glad to see you and Jess in on this too, Dev. We need all the drivers and perimeter guards we can get. I wish this were a lock as far as how Al-Kadi's terrorists in training will react, but the truth is, at the first shot they might take to the woods. We can't have that."

"Agreed," John replied. "Before we send you in, we'll move everyone into position. We will have our snipers and assault force ready on the outskirts. I'll go in with Clint, Tonto, Johnny, and Lynn. Lucas and Casey will be in the sniper's nests we've already picked out for a crossfire that should be deadly for anyone near the house. That leaves the perimeter for the minions, Sal, Chuck, Dev, Jess, Claude, and Achmed. Denny and Samira will handle networking and satellite surveillance. Gus, Tommy and Issac have armored vehicle duty, ready to drive us out of danger or to hunt down escapees. Laredo will fly the stealth for air support. After the recent Isis media tagged lone wolf killings across the country, we're making a statement once again. Like all of you, I thought the 'Starlight of the Seas' mission would help here on home soil as it did overseas."

"We needed to force the bastards out of hiding anyway," Lucas said. "This way, the American public can get a clue, and understand this is war, kill or be killed."

"Exactly," John said. "Except for Al-Kadi if Muerto can get him out alive, this is a kill mission. Lynn can find out everything Al-Kadi knows or has learned from birth to death after we get him back here. He dies then and Muerto gets proof to take with him to the sand for the hit on Al-Saud. Denny had our armored vehicles transported to a place outside Pilot Hill. We're taking no chances. If worse comes to worse, we'll drive the armor right through Al-Saud's house. The only casualties I want to see are the terrorist trainees."

"One other item while we're hashing this out." Denny had been silent through the whole briefing. Paul Gilbrech made the 'kill mission' call already. Denny would only have Al-Saud for a short time. "This attempt by an already known traitor, ex-Senator Diane Cameron, to mess with Nick cannot be swept under the rug. They have enemies' lists in politics. We need to start watching our congressional leaders with a more proactive approach. They're being elected by promising entitlements and many have never held a real job in their entire lives. This is a dangerous time. They've allowed our deadliest enemy to infiltrate our country in the hundreds of thousands."

"Do you mean assassinate these people," Tommy asked.

"No. That won't work. It would end badly for us no matter how much good we did," Denny replied. "I mean to establish a way to discredit these parasites who get elected promising freebies and then sell out their country for a buck. We have ways to get to these people without killing them. Nick took out Cameron that way. He made a sitting Senator resign or face prosecution. We can do the same."

"What about the ones who stay below the radar legally but who we find selling influence to foreign countries," Clint asked.

"There may be some who will have to be taught like Nick plans to teach Cameron," Denny answered. "She obviously didn't learn her lesson the easy way. I know from Nick's report to Paul

287

Gilbrech that Cameron deserves to be shot by firing squad. We can't do that at this time without the liberals going on a suicide watch. Nick may do her a favor this way, because despite her plea deal to resign, we'll send her to prison on some other charge. In any case, keep what I said in mind. We will be watching these jackals more closely."

"Let's get loaded," John said. "We have a final lesson to teach at Pilot Hill. I wish we could do it with music but this one has to be silent death."

* * *

Nick checked Lucas and Casey's nests in the trees opposite the main house nearly four hundred yards away. He climbed to each perch in the darkness with his night-vision range finders at their request. The kill zone area fronting the main complex, within full sight of the two nests, made the positioning perfect for a bloody crossfire. He grinned at how the guards patrolled the grounds and the stationary spots on the upper levels of the building. It was obvious they thought their assignments of guarding the compound to be demeaning and unnecessary. Not one of them had night-vision oculars to scan the outlying areas. The perimeter was left unguarded completely. With the thick walled ornate barrier and solid steel grated gate, Al-Kadi's men felt obviously safe.

"This is damn near perfect, Lucas," Nick said. "Casey's angle crosses your fire zone with as deadly a field as I could have pictured."

"Thanks for taking a look, kid," Lucas said. "With an op this touchy at night, I didn't want to miss something. Another set of eyes is welcome. I'll bet you'd like to be in my place."

Lucas knew his former pupil very well. "You got me," Nick admitted. "I live for this nest setting and kill zone. My part in this will be loud and exciting but this… this stirs my blood."

"You had your fun on the 'Starlight'. When you blew the heads off the captain and bridge crew on the first attacking boat before blowing it to pieces with the XM25, the rest of us nearly forgot what the hell we were doing. It's my turn."

"And mine," Casey said in their ears. "I've been watching the troops deploy around the perimeter. We're nearly ready for your big performance, Muerto."

"I'll get down and calm my assistants. They're a bit nervous about their parts, especially after the last minute pep talk by the 'Mistress of the Unimaginable'."

"I heard that," Lynn said. "Get to work. I promised my toys if they did a great job helping you I'd allow them to attend camp with Denny. Senta worries me, Muerto. She's a high caliber actress. I'm usually sure of my creations, but in this instance, I'm a little uneasy."

"I hear you, Lynn." Nick climbed down from Lucas's nest. "I will keep your reservations in mind when we get inside. Hey… if this was easy… anyone could do it, right?"

"That's right, Dead Boy," Clint said. "Pay attention and watch your six."

"You never used to be this touchy/feely, man from nowhere."

"I grew in stature while you were shrinking, Dead Boy."

Nick had to stop on his way to the entry vehicle while enjoying Clint's reply along with the rest of the network in his ear. "Okay then… here we go."

John Harding waited for Nick. Jafar waited at his side. Jafar volunteered to drive the three in, pointing out how it would look to the guards and Al-Kadi if they didn't have a driver. He also mentioned the captives would have to be watched closely on approach. The fact Jafar would not be searched because he would

289

stay with the car was the deciding factor. An MP5, hidden under the driver's seat, would be Jafar's go to weapon although he also packed a Walther 9mm handgun. Jafar said he would drop Nick and his companions at the door. Afterward, he would drive the BMW used in the approach to the side where he would await the outcome and action calmly near the car. He was dressed in a black suit with tie and Kevlar vest underneath the clothing.

"You're certain you want to do this, Achmed," Nick asked as Jafar held the door for him.

"Absolutely," Jafar answered with a grin as John put away the .45 caliber Colt he watched Fernando and Senta with until Nick joined them.

"It's a solid plan," John said. "I transfer custody, Muerto."

"I have them, Cheese. I'll see you on the other side. If anything goofy happens, I will take care of Achmed."

"I know you will. Do not be a target, little brother," John said to Jafar.

"I will be good, John. Lucas would never let anything happen to me. He'd never be able to turn his laptop on again."

"Why you little... turd," Lucas muttered to much amusement. "You are dead to me."

"Am not," Jafar stated with confidence while getting behind the steering wheel. "Here we go. I will pray Ahab's sight doesn't fail him before the mission is completed."

Nick listened to the outrage from Lucas and amusement from their comrades with deep appreciation. He had been so long on his own, Nick hearkened back to his days with Delta Force when his brothers in arms meant everything to him. After the 'Starlight of the Seas' mission, Nick thought of Harding's 'Monster Squad' as family. He glared over at his traveling companions with distrust as Jafar drove away. Senta worried him

290

as she did Lynn – not in a fragile sense, but in a methodology of how to kill her once he was betrayed. If he could stay close to her until gaining an audience with Al-Kadi, Nick felt everything would be fine. With his writer's imagination, he could contemplate all possible actions with clinical perception. Nick felt after a few moments rehashing the coming action in his mind that he had anticipated every conceivable happening.

"Take deep breaths," Nick instructed Lynn's helpers. "We'll act our parts as rehearsed. When it comes time, get on the floor face down and cover. Stay there until I tell you it's okay to get up. Any questions?"

Fernando and Senta kept their heads down while shaking them in the negative. Senta glanced at Nick after a moment. "Why are you doing this? You are the foremost assassin in the world. Even Claude Chardin acknowledges that. I heard you tell him you killed Fenric Ballesteros. We knew from Al-Kadi you had killed Felix Moreau. You could have anything you want. Why participate in this stupid spy game?"

"Shit! She's going to fuck you, Muerto," Lynn muttered through what Nick thought was probably fist clenched rage as she listened. "Abort this."

"Easy." Nick addressed Senta, while also answering Lynn, without giving away the fact he was in constant contact with his friends. "We're going through with the mission, Senta. Calm yourself and play the part given to you. Don't volunteer anything other than answer as you have been instructed. I will handle the rest. Why I do what I do means nothing in your mind, so why talk about it. Focus on your job."

"It's your funeral, but she's been acting the whole time," Lynn said. "I can't believe the little tool fooled me."

"She didn't," Nick whispered.

Jafar entered the open gateway. It closed behind them. "That wasn't nice."

"It won't matter, Achmed," Nick said. "Proceed with ceremony, my friend. Remember, we're the guests of honor."

Jafar slowly rounded the ornate circular driveway. He stopped in front of the lavish front entrance where four armed guards approached to greet the BMW occupants. Jafar leaped out with professional quickness to open the rear door for Nick, Fernando, and Senta.

"Put on your game faces, kiddies," Nick whispered. "You stay close to me, Senta as we rehearsed.

After leaving the vehicle, Fernando took over the vocal interaction with the guards. "I am Fernando Carone. I am here to see Saran Al-Kadi as planned. Come now. You all know me. What is this game all about?"

"You were to be stopped until we make certain Mr. McCarty is unarmed. Your host is most anxious to speak with you and McCarty, but his reputation must be taken into consideration." The lead guard spoke in Arabic.

Nick guided Senta in full veiled robes to the guard's side. He spoke with the guard in Arabic. "I understand the precautions. What would you have me do?"

Surprised at Nick's fluid Arabic, the guard gestured to his companion. "Momar will pat you down, Sir. Please do not be offended. We are merely taking precautions necessary in these times."

"Of course." Nick allowed the guard named Momar to thoroughly search him for weapons, all the while lightly grasping the sleeve of Senta's burka. She made as if to move away, but one glance into Nick's eyes and nearness caused her to hesitate. Momar finished his frisk, shaking his head in the negative. *Oh boy... Senta's ready to bust our dress rehearsal.* Fernando, on the other hand was broken and anxious to finish his part.

"Please. I must get back to the Tempest as soon as possible. I have no way of knowing if I was tracked to my new anchorage."

"Of course," the lead guard acknowledged. "Follow me. The Bulgar woman's presence has been ordered also. I see she is dressed appropriately."

"I think I should wait here until the main meeting is over before seeing my master," Senta stated.

Nick grabbed her arm painfully enough to evoke a yelp from Senta. "You will do as Saran Al-Kadi orders. I have no patience for your hesitation, nor do I care for your input! Be still and do as you are told!"

Nick's Arabic guttural toned rebuke silenced Senta into a head bowed pose as the guards stifled mirth at the way Nick handled her. Fernando again took lead, also surprised at Nick's adlibbed interaction with Senta. Fernando made a slight hand gesture at the guard who greeted them, but was staring at Senta uneasily. "Lead the way. Let us meet with Saran quickly. There is much to discuss."

Fernando looked toward Jafar as agreed upon beforehand. "Drive the car out of the way and remain here until we complete our meeting, Jafar."

"Yes, Sir," Jafar acknowledged. He reentered the BMW and drove it around the circular drive until it no longer blocked the front entrance.

As requested the guard led the three visitors inside. Nick, well versed with the plans and pictures of the interior, recognized they were being led to Al-Kadi's private quarters. That fact did not bode well in Nick's imaginings of outcomes. They should have been brought to the ornate meeting room Fernando had described in detail. The guard glanced over his shoulder at Senta. She gave him nearly an imperceptible head shake Nick would have missed if not for his excellent peripheral vision. For his part, Nick checked to see the other guards following them. They were ten feet further to the rear and not paying attention.

Nick waited no longer. He ripped the rear of Senta's burka upward, drew out the silenced MP5, and fired a round down through Senta's back. Her screams of agony as she fell to the floor in a writhing heap drew everyone's last moment's attention. Nick fired into the lead guard's head, dove to the floor, and stitched each one of the guards following them before they could bring their weapons to bear. Nick then fired a shot through Senta's head, stilling all sound from her forever. Fernando had dove to the floor as trained, locking shaking fingers behind his head. Nick drug him to the side of Al-Kadi's doorway.

"Did I just hear screams and silenced MP5 firings, Muerto," Lynn asked.

"One of the toys is broken, Lynn. Sorry. No one else enters, Lucas. We are mission engaged," Nick stated.

"Understood. Stay clear of the front, Dead boy."

"Will do."

* * *

Nick's pronouncement needed no further discussion. Lucas and Casey went to work. Both sides in the conflict surprised each other. They didn't expect us to have snipers and our asses covered on the perimeters. We didn't know this was a trap. If Nick hadn't noticed something inside, it would have been a pitched battle at close range. Because of his warning, coupled with our snipers' work on the guards at all levels outside the house and front grounds, our skirmish line was prepared. Lucas and Casey scrambled down from their nests on the approaching enemy's side of the woods to join our Monster Squad. Al-Kadi's small army of men moved on us from the wooded area across Plum Drive.

The moment we began to take fire from woods across the way, our armored vehicle drivers streaked in from their positions to give us spaced cover. They left the vehicles and joined us with weapons and ammo, including XM25 airburst 25mm grenade launchers. Gus brought along Nick's XM307 they used to blow the Mexican fighter jet out of the air. Issac and Tommy split at my direction with combat experienced Jess and Dev to hold our line. I helped Gus with the XM307, while Clint, Lynn, and Claude spread out to provide cover fire with Chuck and Sal on our M2 .50 caliber machine gun. We barely had enough time to finish our skirmish line when I saw the rocket streak from the woods. It blew our middle armored vehicle onto its side.

"Fire!" My one word caused ecological damage across the road for I would guess a couple years. Between the airburst grenades and M2 machine gun fire, I doubted the likelihood of survivors. "Cease fire!"

A few screams and other sounds of wounded men could be heard above the eerie din of silence falling over a battlefield after the weapons fire ceases. "Hold the line. Put out our armor car fire. Clint, Tonto, Johnny, and Lynn come with me. We're on the hunt. Laredo! We need you with the heat vision in the air over the woods. Denny! I need whatever satellite shots you can give me. Lucas and Casey gather Achmed to hold the house perimeter until we can help Muerto.

Tonto the werewolf led our hunting party. We fired into every body as Tonto worked point. We worked tediously but carefully with our night-vision equipment. The task needed to be done in quadrants with our werewolf guide. I had no intention of sending Tonto on a seek and find in the woodland unless I received Laredo reports on hot imaging, or Denny came through with updated satellite images Samira could relay to us. Laredo flew the

Stealth UH-60M over the hunting zone, also by quadrants, relaying clear areas to us.

"How many accounted for, DL," Denny asked.

"Twenty-two in the woods. Never mind the dead. Are you getting any satellite feed yet?"

"We're repositioning as quickly as it can be done from Langley. I-"

"Hostiles at your two o'clock, DL. Six lying in wait, only slightly spread. Five more at eleven o'clock. They think we can't see them. Oh baby... let me have them, big guy. I want the 'Ride'!"

"Toast 'em, Laredo. We have Werewolf with us."

"Back off and do the long approach, Laredo," Lynn added. "Make sure you have the front cams on!"

"Oh yeah!"

We waited in the darkness, spreading slightly with Agent Tonto slightly in front on guard duty. Johnny knelt next to him. "I wish I was in the Stealth with Laredo."

Lynn sighed. "I hear you, Kabong. So do we all."

A minute later, from far off, the 'Ride of the Valkyries' grew in volume, mind, and body as Laredo flew the Stealth down onto our enemies. By the time he passed over, the entire earth shook with sound. The M75 grenade launcher disintegrated the ambushing squads before they even knew what was happening. Laredo did flybys all across both sides of the road with the music blaring from every speaker. It was a good time to be a Monster. Our Werewolf, Agent Tonto, crept about the devastated region left by the M75 firings. He walked back to us calmly, snorting with reassuring Tonto promptings for pets and hugs. It was time to check on our interior agent provocateur: Muerto.

* * *

Nick patted Fernando's back. "Easy, Fernando, we're okay.
I could tell you didn't notice Senta's connection with the guard.
The 'Mistress of the Unimaginable' will know you acted on her
behalf in a good manner. Stay quiet. Your part is done. You can sit
next to the wall with me. I will have to work the rest of our in
house extermination on my own. You'll be fine if you don't
interfere in any way. Can you do that?"

"Yes, Muerto… I will stay quiet and not interfere with your
operation. I have only death or the Mistress in my future. I…I am
yours to command. I know your people will win. We have been
lied to from the very beginning. Your people are not soft for the
taking. If I can get into a prison cell, it will be better than death or
the Mistress's displeasure."

Nick recognized Lynn owned Fernando. It didn't matter
what his fortunes were before or in the future. He would act in
accordance with whatever he felt Lynn would want him to do.
"You're doing fine. Stay quiet while I interact with your former
cohorts."

Fernando bowed his head as he leaned against the wall and
clasped his hands. "Understood, Sir."

Nick waited as he heard the battle outside, enjoying each
and every comment on the network. The acolytes of Al-Kadi began
their approach shortly after, moving to follow orders from Al-Kadi
directly or becoming nervous because of the outside sounds. Nick
scooted Fernando to the side, his MP5 at the ready. The interior
darkness leant itself to Nick's remaining undetected. None of the
approaching men incorporated night-vision capabilities. They
moved carefully toward Al-Kadi's room. Nick shot the one in the
rear position of the approach with his smilingly delivered silenced
MP5 hollow point round.

The man's startled last grunt of death as he pitched
backward to the floor attracted his companions' attention. Nick

stood as they glanced back at their fallen comrade, delivering short deadly bursts they were too late to do anything about. Nick changed clips, moving in on the dead and dying with finishing fire, whispering '*say hello to my little friend*' the whole time. Eight dead soldiers lie at his feet before he swiveled away to the side, waiting and listening for any further approach.

"We're right outside the front door, Nick," Lucas said. "Say something, kid."

Nick collected the grenade and a small leather envelope from Senta's belt pouch. "I'm in the hallway of Al-Kadi's quarters. All are dead in the hallway. I'll stay here if you wish to bring Tonto in for final check. I have not moved on Al-Kadi's room yet."

"I'm on my way with Tonto now," Lynn said. "Everyone else is combing the woods for survivors, but I think Laredo took care of that."

"Understood. I have cross view of the hallway passing through the front entranceway. No movement so far. I have no eyes on the rear of the house. A large party came after me here so I'm not sure if there's anyone left."

"Hang tight. We'll make our entry in five minutes," Lucas said.

"No rush. This hallway is the only way out. I remember from the pictures of the house outside that he had bars put in over the windows. Just in case he has a tunnel, can you keep surveillance of the surrounding area with the heat screen, Laredo?"

"Will do," Laredo agreed.

"The call's been made to steer clear of the area no matter what," Denny said. "The locals have not made any calls into the cops, despite the noise. Oh shit! Jesus, Lord in heaven… the satellite photos are streaming now. The damn woods across from the house looks like a World War I no-man's land. Did anyone leave even a bush or dandelion standing?"

"It was combat, you turd! We weren't harvesting corn, moron," Lucas barked onto the network. "We have an armored vehicle blown over on its side by a rocket launcher. We just killed over thirty of the enemy outside with another near a dozen inside by Muerto's hand. It was a trap! Muerto sniffed it out. What happened in there, Nick?"

"Senta and the guard gave it away. I couldn't take chances. She must have found a way to warn Al-Kadi when our backs were turned. We're lucky Al-Kadi figured we were easy pickings. On the other hand, by the sound of it, you combat troops had your hands full."

"It was outstanding," Sal said. "We blew the shit out of that bunch in the woods."

"What Sal said," Chuck added. "How's Achmed? He was stuck on the front grounds."

"I am well, Chuck. I kept my head down. Lucas and Casey killed everything living in front of the house. Lynn is here now with Tonto."

"We're coming in, Nick," Lucas said.

Nick had moved to a point where he could cover their entry. "I have sight on all threats. Come in."

Tonto rushed in first, low to the floor, sweeping from one side to the other. He stopped near Nick, sniffed, and moved on. The squad of deadly killers fanned out behind with John Harding in the lead. He grinned over at Nick's small salute. The team with Tonto sniffing for threats cleared the lower floor. Each room, searched in order, produced nothing of an informational or human presence. They moved on to the stairs and the upper floor. It took only ten minutes to rejoin Nick. Tonto sniffed out the dead bodies and blood. He approached Al-Kadi's entranceway, growled, and returned to Lynn. She and her companions moved to the hallway sides.

Nick knocked on the door. "Hello. Come on out, Saran. We're ready to talk. Your army's dead. If we have to come in and get you, it will cost you in pain."

"You will kill me anyway!"

"There are so many ways to die, Saran. If you make this hard, your dying will be bad."

Silence.

Nick shot apart the locking mechanism and doorjamb. The door swung slightly open. Automatic weapons fire in what Nick could tell was 9mm blew through the door. When the firing stopped, Nick waited a moment before speaking. "That wasn't very nice. I'm going to throw a grenade inside your room and blow you to kingdom come. I'll count to three. If you're not out here next to me, your pieces will be. One... two..."

"No!" The door slammed open. Al-Kadi rushed out with his hands up. Tonto ran him over, continuing inside to check the room while Nick restrained and helped Al-Kadi to his feet.

Lynn walked past to get in with Tonto. "I'll check the room."

John Harding joined Nick. "I'm not sure if we can spare the time here in interrogation, Nick. There was literally a small army. If not for bringing the heavy weapons, we might have gotten our heads handed to us. As it was, Laredo had to finish them off. Denny's working on a collection team. This was a mess... a damn successful mess... but a mess none the less. We'll need to move Saran to Pain Central. Can you wait for a few days while we make sure of his story?"

"Sure, John," Nick answered. "He'll have considerable funds here though."

"I'll leave the minions here to watch the house and interact with Denny's cleaning crew. I'm sorry your 'Spaghetti Western' plot didn't work out for you."

"That's okay. Al-Saud wants only his network information. I figured we could clone the drives, make sure all relevant info is off them, and then I'll take what's left to Dubai for my meeting. We can take the photos of Al-Kadi now, and I'll get on the road. Samira drove a confiscated vehicle to Pilot Hill with my tools. I have to go see the Kader in New York. If everything works out there to my satisfaction, I'm going to the sand."

"What? You are going to kill me now?" Al-Kadi's outrage began to seep dumbly into his features, the full black chin beard bobbing with his mouth. "I knew it! You bastards were sent by Al-Saud! We can make this right. I will double what he's paid you!"

"Do you need him unmarked, John?"

"Nope."

In a split second, Nick pistol whipped Al-Kadi to the floor. He then pounded him unconscious. Nick retrieved the small leather envelope he'd taken from Senta's belt. Taking the scalpel from the small leather pouch, Nick slit Al-Kadi's throat with a shallow slice so the blood welled thickly, soaking the bottom part of his beard grotesquely. Once there was a small pool of it around Al-Kadi's head, Nick turned to Johnny, who had accompanied the house assault team. Johnny nodded. Without another word, he began snapping pictures from different angles. Johnny finished by taking digital fingerprints and a DNA swab.

"Done, Muerto." Johnny looked over his pictures. "These are very good."

"Thanks, Johnny." Harding and his crew had been chuckling over Nick's adlib of making Al-Kadi appear dead. They remained silent as Nick tightened Al-Kadi's shirt around the shallow neck wound tightly. Nick straightened to his feet. "Good as new."

"That was very cute, Dead Boy," Lucas said. "Does this mean you'll be leaving for New York right away?"

"If I can, I'd like to duck out of here with my crew. We're heading for New York. I believe Kader will be getting word about the people he's lost and head for the sand. We're through playing with the Kaders. Eliah and all the male Kaders we find with him are going bye/bye. If you learn how the hell Al-Kadi knew we were coming I'd sure like to know who tipped him."

"We'll call you once Lynn gets him in the mood," Harding said. "There's really nothing more here for any of us to do before the cleaning crew finishes. Be careful in the sand. If you get into trouble, don't hesitate to call."

Nick smiled. "I won't, brother. The only other thing I could use is a letter, written and signed by Saran. Do you think we can get Agent Tonto to talk him into writing it, Lynn?"

Lynn smiled. "Absolutely."

* * *

"I'll admit to one thing, John," Denny said while inspecting the grounds across the road from the compound, "if this doesn't set those Isis bastards on their heels, nothing will. I put a team to work on our escrow papers. The compound will be ours once Al-Kadi signs it over to us with Lynn's help. I know a construction company in Sacramento that will build and repair the compound without any questions asked. We have a lot of small cosmetic repairs to be made but nothing real bad. It could have been a lot worse except for the vegetation across the road. Can I still have Fernando?"

"He's been my good little helper," Lynn said. "Muerto took care of my other toy. If not for him needing her to be a weapons carrier, I wouldn't have let her go in. She was a little too polished for my taste. It all worked out in the end. We decimated the pricks. It was definitely a killing field across the street. Do you want to take Fernando with you now?"

"Yes, if I can," Denny replied. "Does Muerto know you're giving Fernando to me? Carone did send men after Nick."

"Fernando would already be dead if Nick thought he wasn't broken. Nick kept him alive here in the house," I answered for Lynn. "I don't blame you for being careful. You know what happened to that rogue NSA boss, Frank Richert."

"Yeah. I do. I'll take Fernando with me when I leave. Did Nick get what he wanted off of Al-Kadi's computers?"

"Jafar, Johnny, and Clint worked to redact anything we didn't want given to Al-Saud. The rest they doctored and gave to Nick. If we're clear then, we'll take Al-Kadi and go, Denny."

"This is a beautiful place. Once we get a nice landing zone built, this could turn into a regular weekend retreat."

"Our thoughts exactly," I agreed. "We've never dumped this many bodies on you, Den. How tough is this situation?"

"They ain't getting Muslim burial rites if that's what you're askin'," Denny joked. "They'll be lucky if we don't cremate them in pig fat."

"That's very civilized of you, Den."

"It's a better fate than what they did to Ambassador Stevens in Benghazi. We don't ever forgive and forget about that travesty."

"We won't. We'll chalk up a bunch more notches on this op and move on to the next. Maybe we'll get enough shit off those

303

computers, coupled with the sheer number of soldiers in this Isis training compound, to finally get the idiots in DC to stop importing them."

"I'm not that progressive in thought," Denny sarcastically pointed out. "Seriously. This op might make the difference. If we could report this incident in its entirety, I think there would be a day of reckoning for Islam. If I hear one more word about moderate Muslims, I'm going to puke."

"Hey, the cleaning crew's picking up a whole bunch of moderates as we speak," Lynn pointed out.

Chapter Twelve

Kader Finality

Nick relaxed in their suite at the Trump Soho Duplex Penthouse with Gus, Johnny, and Samira. He normally would have done everything differently, but this way Nick knew he could find a way to get Eliah Kader under the radar. His crew sharing the straight through drive helped considerably. Gus rented the Penthouse under his name. They would enjoy a couple of days comfort while Nick worked through the information gathered from the flash drive Ishmael Kader's wife had given him. Nick planned to hit this nail with a hammer rather than his usual detailed operation.

"You're really serious about this, Muerto?"

"It's the best solution, Gus. Think about it. We can make Eliah disappear with us and take our time questioning him on the road back home. I don't want to do a hit here in New York. A missing person works much better for us. If I manage to take Eliah in secret, no one will be in any rush to look for him. We know his address. The old prick lives in a one bedroom condo on East 85th."

"Let me go in with Cala," Johnny said.

"No! Let me do this with Muerto." Cala hugged Johnny sitting next to her. "We will get this man I am related to in blood only. Seeing he has me, we can gain entrance. I will sell my part at the door. I will wear a hijab so he can see fear on my face. Muerto has a rough black gray beard. With ball cap and hoodie and speaking Arabic, he will be perfect as my deliverer from Al-Kadi. The letter Tonto made Al-Kadi write will get us inside for sure."

"Cala's right," Nick agreed. "Not this time, Johnny. We have to keep you on the down low for the time being. We've worked the Ebi Zarin identity too many times lately. I don't even want to do this with Cala but with the letter and my disguise, all will be well. I will not let harm come to the Cleaner, but I leave the final decision to you, brother. If you have any reservations we'll find another way."

"I want this, husband," Cala added.

Johnny nodded. "It will be as you wish. I trust Muerto. Payaso and I will be ready with the trunk open for my in-law to ride in. Those satellite feeds Paul tied us into show Eliah moving around with two other men in suits and beards. They look like pros. That is a tight fit in a one bedroom walk-up condo. They are undoubtedly not fine law abiding citizens."

"If they stay with him when Cala and I visit, that will work out well for my plan. I will call Lynn a half hour before we knock on the door. She told me Al-Kadi would be ready to receive calls if need be from Eliah."

"That will make your door greeting nearly foolproof with Cala acting unhappily," Gus said. "I wish we could chance having a cam on you, Cala. They will be very surprised when you faint to the floor. Muerto has pulled that prank before. All eyes will be on you a split second before they gain a .45 caliber created third eye."

"I will perform brilliantly and we will finally be rid of my Kader curse. Do you believe Eliah is the last one doing this, Muerto?"

"According to Ishmael's wife, Eliah has been responsible for everything that's happened. He's the one who blocked the payoff I offered to leave us all the hell alone. Eliah threatened Ishmael's family because he tried to change the other elders' minds." Nick lifted his glass. "Let's have a toast to Ish. He was born into the wrong family, but maybe now his wife and kids can escape Islam's curse. I wish he had called us."

They toasted Ishmael.

Cala sighed and sipped her wine. "At least I had one decent male relative."

"Lynn's assistant, Amara, had the same family problems. I believe the Monster Squad has made a severe reduction in the number of male Nejems. They were tied into our Pilot Hill bunch. I don't think there was an Ishmael in their family reunion in hell."

"I wonder if Lynn cured Florence," Gus said.

"My guess would be it's a guarantee," Nick replied. "There's something about the way she breaks someone down in interrogation. I'll bet Senta resisting the cure gave Lynn pause for thought. I know they'll have Chuck and Sal keeping a close eye on Flo. This is a dangerous business leaving enemies alive at your back."

"I figured you would have killed Flo," Johnny said. "Did Senta really turn on you or did you seize the opportunity?"

"A little of both. I needed to distract the gunmen. We'll know what happened when Lynn finishes with Al-Kadi if she hasn't already."

* * *

Claude asked to sit in on Al-Kadi's interrogation. He helped Clint and Jafar sift through the mountains of information to judge what could remain for Nick's visit with Al-Saud. He earned the time. I could tell he wanted to ask a question when Saran became pliable. I noticed something bothering the assassin from the moment he heard our operation involved Saran Al-Kadi. Although Al-Kadi wanting to have Claude killed I'm sure was enough reason for Chardin to want Saran dead, I knew it wasn't the only reason.

Saran pissed Lynn off on the way home. He thought because he was still alive that we planned to let Al-Saud or someone have him. No one explained what Nick had done to him. Saran figured we were suddenly scared of lawyers and lawsuits because Nick beat him like a red headed stepchild. Lynn listened to him whine and threaten us with everything under the sun. It was amusing at first. Then it dawned on Lynn that Saran didn't know his men were all dead. That's when the fun began.

Lynn clapped her hands together with delight. She took Jafar's iPad over to Saran. We record everything we do with video and audio. It's sick in a way, but we're monsters. Anyway, Lynn sat next to Saran and said, "I bet you'd like to know what happened to your army of misfit Muslims, don't ya'?"

"They will be freed soon," Al-Kadi stated with confidence. "We merely defended our land against invaders. You will all end your days in prison for this outrage. I will never be handed over to Al-Saud."

Lynn was amused to no end as were we all. When she managed some breathing control, she stated with some excitement, "oh, Saran, you're right on all counts… except about us ending our days in prison. First off, your soldiers are all free. They did defend what they thought was your territory. It wasn't, but that's neither here nor there. Thirdly, you're right – you will not be handed over to Al-Saud. That letter I dictated to you was for another reason I'm sure you have suspicions about. Let me show you this to fill in some of the blanks."

Oh boy… the look of horror on Saran's face as he watched the bloody annihilation of his men, their screams, and Laredo's cockpit video of the survivors in the woods blown to bits – priceless.

"Murderers! My men were trying to surrender!"

"Really?" Lynn grabbed the iPad as if she cared, squinting at the screen and replaying the section that offended Saran. "Oh damn. Look at this, you guys."

We put sad frowns of concern on our faces as we scooted to a position in the UH-60 where Lynn could enlarge the part and put it on replay. It was hilarious. We oohed and awed, shaking our heads, seemingly heartbroken over the fact that murderous swine, without a uniform or country, tried to give themselves up when they knew we were going to kill them all. Lynn threw the iPad into my lap. It was a tight fit for all of us. Lynn glared at us with hands on hips.

"You monsters!"

Once Lucas lost it and started braying, we were lost. Then it was the monster mash for the next few minutes with Saran gasping in outrage. Lynn sighed finally and took a deep breath.

"Look at this from our point of view, Saran. Your men were ambushing us, with full intention of doing a Benghazi on our asses. We didn't rape your guys, burn them alive unarmed, or drag their bodies through our streets. We killed them. Now you... you're different. We goin' to teach you, sucker! I have questions for you when we get to the place we call Pain Central. If I were you, I'd start thinking of anything to tell me from your birth on that will make me happy. I don't have a hard-on for you yet, but you give me a bad time in interrogation, and I'm going to show you the new rules of engagement for handling the Muslim horde, pussy!"

Lynn's speech, complete with Cruella Deville death stare, shut Saran up for the rest of the trip. No more protests or any other nonsense. He realized the facts in evidence. We didn't care about his feelings and he was going to die at some point: screaming or sighing. So, here we were with the minions and me handling strap and equipment duty, while Claude looked on. In a half hour, Saran Al-Kadi was in love with the thought of death. He called for it like a lover. He didn't get it though. Lynn introduced him to our 'Truth or Consequences' game with Denny, Clint, and Jafar crosschecking everything using the intelligence gathered from his computers at the compound.

We left Saran for a time to allow his brains to seep back into place. Lynn gestured at him. "I don't want to go too far. Muerto may need an introductory phone call for that Kader guy. We have to make sure Al-Kadi's voice returns somewhat to normal. He'll be calling shortly if he needs the call done. I know you want something answered, Claude. Would you like to ask it after the phone call?"

"Yes. I did not want to interrupt. Do you think it's promising that he knew nothing of any other major network or cell compound?"

I exchanged glances with Lynn and the minions. We'd been through this before. "I don't think so. They are smart enough to keep most of their operations compartmentalized for this reason. Importing thousands more of the Muslim horde is insanity for just that reason. Many may be already secretly in cells transported as refugees. They will have only to affiliate with a mosque wherever they are injected into a community. We know for certain the Muslims are stockpiling weapons in the mosques. What was it you wanted to ask?"

"It's not important on the network scale, but I would like to know what happened to a woman I knew in Paris before the Arab Spring. The good guys nearly killed me. I took a contract on a French diplomat. It didn't go well. I fled to Paris with a bullet in my leg. The woman I knew there from long ago named Felicia Martel is a cousin on my Mother's side of the family. We met as children for a time when my Father was killed in Morocco and we needed to live in Paris for a time with relatives. Felicia and I became friends. We stayed in touch over the years. She became a nurse. Felicia helped me until my leg healed enough to make my way to England."

When Claude paused while glancing over at the moaning Al-Kadi, Lynn became impatient. "Very cool story, but what does it have to do with Saran-wrap?"

310

Claude smiled. "She lived alone. Men in Al-Kadi's employ took her during the riots. Felicia was very beautiful and only twenty-eight at the time. I didn't find out the story until months after the Arab Spring travesty. My Father was a Saudi national, but he was not an Arab dog filled with hatred. He left to live in Morocco where he met my Mother. He was a common laborer but a good man. I would have followed his example. I took many contracts from Muslims to kill other Muslims because they killed my Father for leaving the death cult. This is the first chance I have had to get close to Saran-wrap as you call him. I would like to know what happened to Felicia."

"No problem. If he knows, he will tell me."

"I'll get us some coffee," I volunteered. "C'mon, Quays, you can help me."

"We spend so much time in here, we should install a Cappuccino machine," Quays suggested.

"Good idea, my treasured minion," Lynn said. "Make it so."

* * *

Nick and Cala looked good approaching Kader's walk-up. Nick wore blue jeans, black windbreaker, black Giants baseball cap, and had his hood up. Cala wore an ankle length, dark blue dress with a light blue headscarf. She had practiced her terrified scowl and dialogue to match with Johnny until even Nick thought he was a bad guy. They knew from satellite imagery Eliah was home with two of his men. Nick prepped Lynn to set up the call with Al-Kadi if necessary. Saran was ready. Nick rang Kader's condo.

"What is it?" A gruff voice sounded ready to descend the stairs and mug them.

"I am Momar Bata," Nick said in fluent Arabic. "Saran Al-Kadi sent me with the woman Eliah Kader has asked for: Cala Kader. We know you do not wish to take chances. Here is the phone number Al-Kadi gave me for you to call and confirm."

The voice grunted while taking down the phone number given. "Wait there."

A few minutes later, a higher pitched voice, brimming with excitement came on. "I have called Saran. He says you do indeed have Cala Kader with you and the McCarty is dead. I will buzz you in. Come up quickly. Mine is the first on the right."

"As you wish, Sir." The buzzer announced the unlocking of the outside door. Nick gripped Cala's arm. "I can feel your excitement, Cleaner. Take deep breaths and get your scowl ready."

"Yes, Muerto."

The door opened and a bearded man with white Kufi, carrying twenty pounds too much weight at his belt motioned them in happily. "I am very pleased. Saran has given me a gift I can never repay. Did you see the McCarty die, my friend?"

Nick smiled while shaking his head. "Unfortunately, I was already traveling with Cala Kader by then. She has been a problem but is now safely in your hands."

"Yes… she and Dimah Kader have caused much loss to our family." Eliah circled the trembling Cala, her face a mask of terrified obedience, staring only at the floor in front of her. "If she is lucky, I will find another rich suitor. She has been defiled and will fetch only a fraction of what we could have gotten for her."

Eliah reached to take Cala's arm. At his touch, Cala gasped and fell faint to the floor. Eliah and his two men standing to the side of Cala snorted in amusement at her collapse. The twin hollow point .45 caliber slugs from Nick's silenced Colt tore into the heads of Eliah Kader's personal bodyguards, pitching them to the

312

floor. Cala straightened and punched Eliah in the groin. He screamed, falling with both hands over his injured part. Cala jumped atop him but Nick pulled her away.

"Kick's only, Cleaner. We don't want blood all over your clothing."

"Of course, Muerto... sorry." Cala went to work on Eliah, rage at the long deadly pursuit of her by the family she shared DNA with charging each kick with added power. She backed away at a gesture from Nick.

"Nice friendly hello." Nick handed her the small bag with hooded plastic rain cover inside and a pair of surgical gloves. "Here you are, Doctor Cala. Do you still want to retrieve my slugs? If not, I'll do it."

"I want to do it. I bet I could be one of those forensics pathologists."

"I bet you could to0. Make it your major. We'll send you to any college you want to attend."

Cala finished covering herself. She took out her probing kit and scalpel set. "I like what we do better but I might take a few classes. I liked college. It's just that I love being with Johnny and our Addams' family. We do everything. We're detectives, assassins, soldiers, killers, pathology experts, coroners, and computer pros. Not to mention we feed the fish."

Nick bound the groaning Eliah while enjoying Cala's recitation on their skills. "You are a very sick young lady, Cala."

"Yes... I have been corrupted. You said you had a plan for our scene. Will it still work?"

"Oh yeah. We're on our way out, Payaso," Nick finished his call for their ride and propped Eliah against a wall. He dipped his finger into the blood of a dead man nearest the wall. He finger painted: As-salamu alaykum in Arabic script. He added 'Isil is jihad, Al-Qaeda is the devil!' - all in bloody script.

"I have the slugs." Cala made a face. "These two men stink. Perhaps we should pepper spray them before we go."

"Good one." Nick lifted Eliah onto his feet. He fired off an arc from his stun-gun where Eliah could see it. "I will have this pressed against your ball sack. If you make one sound while I'm guiding you to our vehicle, I will burn your balls off. Understand?"

Eliah nodded fearfully as Nick held a plastic bag open for Cala to dump her protective clothing into. Nick went to Eliah's closet, picked out a light windbreaker, and threw it over Eliah's restrained hands. He then wiped down everything they touched with Cala's help. They bagged the electronic devices to take with them. Nick held the door for Cala so she could walk in front of Eliah with a solemn pose while wearing her headscarf. Nick locked and closed the door behind them. At street level, Nick held the door for Cala before jamming the stun-gun into Eliah. Johnny held the door open for them to get into the back. In seconds, they were on their way with Eliah blubbering between Nick and Cala. Nick stripped off his gloves.

Nick elbowed Eliah in the ribs. "Silence!"

Eliah quieted, glancing fearfully at Nick. "You are McCarty."

"Yes. You've called for me by sending killers after my family and friends, including your own niece. Here I am. I tried warning your family many times. Most of them are all dead now. Ishmael knew you sent him to his death by blackmailing him into trying to kill me. He left a last message with his wife, naming you, and telling me exactly where to find your stupid ass. He reached out to pay you back for sending him on a suicide mission. I promised his wife I would make sure you never caused another death. Besides, I wanted Cala to have a chance to beat the shit out of you."

"Let me go! I will make sure… I give you my word… no one will bother you again!"

"Lying to the infidel, huh?" Nick smiled as his three companions enjoyed Eliah's pleas which they all knew to be false. "I'm afraid that ship steamed out of port. Your family surprised me with the depth of its stupidity. Did you ever wonder why so many of your idiot relatives disappeared when sent after me? I figured when I killed that old zombie who turned down my five million dollar dowry, Ishmael might be able to make you all see the light, and leave me the hell alone. I called the old zombie, Yoda. What the hell was his first name?"

"Mohammed," Gus answered.

"Yeah, that's it," Nick acknowledged. "He looked like a raisin baked in the sun on a hot sidewalk. Anyway, that was your family's chance to be reasonable. Soon, your family will be reasonable. We have business to discuss though before I send you to join the rest of your missing family in hell."

"But…but is there no way I can live in this deal? Why would I help you if I cannot buy my life?"

"Heh…heh… I don't think you understand," Nick said. "We're going to stop somewhere quiet for a question and answer session. Cala will be our visual lie detector while her husband will be transferring funds and checking your information. Unfortunately, on a road trip like this one I'll have to use my old school interrogation method. I wanted to try my new acupuncture technique on your feet, but frankly, I don't want to cart your ass all the way to California. I have a spot in Pennsylvania where we can have our talk. It's in the Allegheny Forest. If you'd like to start being cooperative now, maybe by the time we get to your final resting spot, I'll simply put you to sleep for good."

Eliah began to sob. "I…I don't know anything."

"There's no crying in terrorism! Cut the crybaby crap. Sure, you know all your accounts and passwords. We have your laptop, tablet, and phone. You're going to help us transfer everything to us. These trips cost money, and I made sure Ishmael's wife received a substantial amount of money to free the women and children from the Kader curse."

"Wha…what curse?"

"That would be me. Are you fired up and ready to go, Johnny?"

"Yes, Muerto. He can give me his account numbers and passwords now. I have his laptop booted to the desktop too. We can make all the transfers. We have a clear satellite signal. He has Norton 360 Security System with an identity safe. If I get in there, I can take care of everything."

"Okay, Eli, get talkin'. Most people, even terrorists, have one of those password vaults, Johnny mentioned. Do you keep all your account places listed with passwords in your identity safe?"

Eliah nodded. He knew these people would torture him to death. Anything could happen between now and when they stopped, he thought. If he could stay alive long enough, he might somehow be rescued. The transfers could be reversed in his mind if he stayed alive. Eliah Kader recited his password for the security vault, and the file listing his account numbers and banking information on a spread sheet.

"Oh my, Muerto," Johnny exclaimed. "Eliah has done very well for himself even though he's never held a real job in his life. He has nearly eight million dollars in accounts I do not think his Kader herd know anything about. I have been able to lighten this monetary burden from his shoulders. That was a good investment with Ishmael's widow. His main financial additions have come from… wait for it… Saudi Arabia and Qatar. The deposits, funneled through a corporate account linked to both nations under a joint venture fund titled Al Alef Global have made Eliah Kader a partner with Saran Al Kadi. Imagine that."

Nick pinched Eliah Kader's cheek. "Why you little conduit, you. This explains the merger you were planning with Omar Fontaine. You bunch of cockroaches launder money, influence, and serve as halfway houses on both coasts for infiltrators. No wonder you could scoff at my dowry offer for Cala. Does Al-Kadi have the largest money holdings?"

Eliah cringed but remained silent.

"Don't be afraid. Saran won't be alive much longer. Why do you think he helped me out with a phone call to you as backup? My friends convinced Saran to help me in a very painful way I hope to help you avoid."

"You… have Al-Kadi?" Eliah lowered his head, shaking it negatively from side to side slowly. "We are lost. How has this been done? He had a near army of the faithful built to strike. It…it does not seem possible."

"Yeah, we've been busy repairing breeches. Some of us darker elements of America decided to act on behalf of our citizens instead of the Islamic ass kissers in DC. Our efforts are beginning to make some major inroads, such as annihilating that army Al-Kadi was building."

"No!" Kader jerked upright, staring with horror into Nick's smiling face. "They…they are dead… all of them?"

"All but Saran, whom my friends are questioning. I heard he was shocked all of his troops went virgin hunting too. I found him hiding out in his bedroom hoping the ambush he planned for us worked."

"You people are monsters! You cannot just execute us like dogs!"

"We don't execute dogs. I like dogs. I would never hurt a dog. I have a dog named Deke. He's worth a hundred of you asswipes," Nick lectured. "You wouldn't like him though. He drinks beer, never hurts children or women, and he hates the followers of the death cult. That last discriminatory feeling is my fault. I told him Muslims think dogs are unclean. Deke was very incensed over my revelation. Excuse me for a moment. I have to call the Monster Squad and make sure they know about Al-Kadi's funds. Johnny… entertain Eliah with the compound video or as I like to call it: the Isis Snuff Film."

Johnny chuckled. "Yes, Muerto."

Lynn answered on the third buzz. "Muerto? How you doin'. We were wondering if you'd be checking in."

"Everything went well, Lynn. That phone call was priceless. We have Kader with us now. He's been very helpful. It seems Al-Kadi was the main money launderer and financier of the funds funneled into the states from a joint venture between Saudi Arabia and Qatar called Al Alef Global. I wanted to make sure you had that information."

"Did you just insult me, Muerto?"

Nick laughed appreciatively. "Sorry… just checking."

"I'm glad you called. We have a problem Claude clued us in on. It's an important personal matter with him. It seems a cousin of his was kidnapped in Paris during the Arab Spring riots. Al-Kadi had a hand in the Arab Spring debacle and he knows where the cousin is. I don't know where you are, but she was sold to a man named Haris El-Amin. He lives in Schenectady on Union Street near Union College in a very nice looking multi-story home. I'll text Johnny the address in case you're interested."

"I'm interested. We'll be nearing Schenectady in a couple of hours. Is Al-Kadi capable of another phone call on our behalf?"

"Great minds think alike," Lynn replied. "He is indeed. Claude and I think this El-Amin would allow a phone call between Felicia and Claude if Al-Kadi asks him. It would mean telling El-Amin the truth about the connection between Claude and Felicia, but also make it a trade for Claude's services by Al-Kadi. We'll have him call right away to introduce you to the meeting."

"Nice plot, Lynn. That might work very well. Let me talk to Claude."

"Absolutely."

"Nick?"

"Lynn explained a little about your cousin. I'll be glad to look in on her but maybe you better spell it out for me as to the parameters of the visit. I like the phone call ploy."

"Of course, my friend. Her name is Felicia Martel. She would be in her late thirties now, nearly a decade in El-Amin's control. Al-Kadi hosted them in New York two months ago. Felicia wore a black burka, so he could not tell what condition she was in. She kept her head down and trailed El-Amin like a dog. I just need to know if she can be rescued or if she has been turned into a forever slave. Lynn thought I should ask for your help instead of going myself. She believes you could perhaps find out if Felicia is okay without making things worse for her if we force Al-Kadi to make a personal plea to El-Amin before you arrive there."

"I will find out. What would you like done if she appears willing to leave her life?"

"I would leave it to her. If you are willing, I would be grateful if you could carry out any fate she would like for El-Amin."

"That's plain enough. If I have a question when I've investigated Felicia's situation, or she does, I would like it to be on

Facetime so you may see her. Keep your iPhone with you. If our ploy works, I will have her Facetime with you."

"I will await your call. Thank you, Nick. This means a lot to me."

"I hope the visit will be a good one for your cousin. I will talk to you soon." Nick disconnected. "It appears we have further business in New York. Can anyone think of anything else they'd like to ask our buddy, Eliah?"

Silence. Nick gave Eliah Kader a pat on the back of the head. "I think you did quite well. Do you have anything else you'd like to tell us, Eli?"

Eliah began to speak, but the syringe Nick stuck into his neck worked quickly. "There you go. We need to have you go sleepy time for a while, Eli. Pull over in a quiet spot so we can put Eli in cargo and cover him, Gus."

Nick explained the situation after they deposited the sedated Eliah in the back cargo area with a tarp covering. "I'm thinking me, Johnny, and Cala, all dressed in our Muslim costumes, could ring the doorbell, check on Felicia, and proceed from there. If we get a lot of flack from this El-Amin, I may have to insist. This is volunteer only. Claude is no saint. John Harding stopped him from assassinating Samira and maimed him while doing it. They recruited him from the dark side. We can agree Johnny and I have monster credentials from our past. If we're allowed to see Felicia and the years belonging to this El-Amin have put her beyond our reach mentally, then we'll just leave. She may have six kids and be happy as hell for all I know."

"I'm in," Johnny stated.

"And I," Cala added. "She was kidnapped from her home and sold into slavery. As you say, Muerto, if she wants out, we should help her."

"What about El-Amin," Gus asked.

"We have room in the cargo area for one more. Eliah will have company on his Allegheny resting place trip."

"I want you to do a Kabuki dance with my Uncle, Muerto."

"Cala!" Gus nearly drove off the road as Nick and Johnny enjoyed Cala's request.

"He deserves it, Payaso," Cala stated. "I hope Felicia is okay. I can only imagine what it was like for her. I am glad Lynn has punished that Saran Al-Kadi who stole Felicia's life."

"Remember to keep your feelings in check. Lynn will have Al-Kadi make a very enticing phone call introduction I'm sure. We have to be calm through this no matter how it comes out. This has to be Felicia's decision without our input, whether she's brainwashed or not. This will be either a visit or a rescue. It will not be an intervention. Is that clear, Cala?"

"Yes, Muerto."

Nick's phone buzzed an hour later. "Hi Lynn."

"The phone call worked. I had Saran state he needed Claude for a contract in Yemen and the call was the only way Claude would consider it. We learned during the interrogation that El-Amin has participated in the money laundering enterprise Al-Kadi worked with his overseas conduit. It was suggested by El-Amin, Claude could talk with Felicia immediately. We anticipated that and had Saran tell him Claude demanded people he trusted see her while he was calling."

"Interesting. I will let you know how this proceeds. Tell Claude we will not make things worse for Felicia no matter what. With Al-Kadi gone, we can put this El-Amin on our watch list to make sure he doesn't hook up with another cell."

"That's our thoughts on it too, Muerto. Talk again soon." Lynn disconnected.

"We're on," Nick said.

* * *

Nick and Johnny wore their white kufi head coverings with clothing neatly arranged. Cala, again with conservative clothing and headscarf, walked demurely behind the men as they approached the door to El-Amin's huge well maintained home. Nick rang the doorbell, stepping back slightly with hands clasped in front of him. A thin bearded man in a dark three piece business suit answered the door with a scowl. Without a word, he motioned the visitors inside.

"I have been told to greet this intrusion on my life," El-Amin muttered in guttural Arabic. "If not for my business associate this meeting would never take place. What name do you go by?"

"I am Momar Bati, sent by Saran Al-Kadi," Nick stated in Arabic when they were inside the house. "My companions are trusted friends of Claude Chardin. They will be observing the phone call and will speak with your wife, Felicia."

"She is my property, not my wife," El-Amin retorted suspiciously. "Saran knows this. Why do you not?"

"I am merely an emissary on behalf of my employer. I did not wish to offend and I have no knowledge of your personal life."

El-Amin grunted. "Let us get this farce over with. Follow me."

In the spacious living room, a woman wearing a black burka knelt near the leather couch. El-Amin walked over and sat down near the woman. "These are the people I spoke to you about.

322

They wish for you to speak with a cousin of yours. Do you know this Claude Chardin?"

The woman kept her eyes on the floor. "Yes. He was my cousin. I have not seen him in many years."

"Saran wishes for you to speak with him. This man will put you on the phone with him."

Nick Facetimed Claude. When he established a good signal and audio, Nick handed the iPhone to Cala. She went over to kneel next to Felicia, put the iPhone on speaker, and held it where the two could see each other on the screen.

"Felicia? I am so happy to see you alive. I tried to find you after Paris."

"It matters not, Claude. I am dead to you now. I...I am glad you are well. You look much older, my cousin, and thin."

Claude chuckled. "Yes. I had an accident which forced me into a healthier lifestyle. What of you, my dear one. Do you have children?"

Felicia hesitated, glancing up at her now scowling companion. "I had something happen after Paris... which prevented my ever giving birth. I wanted... I mean..." Felicia began to sob. "I'm sorry... my cousin. I cannot-"

"Enough!" Haris El-Amin reached for the iPhone, only to have Nick's hand snatch his. A second later Haris was on his knees. The bones in his hand began to crackle.

"I do not think you understand the purpose of this call, Haris," Nick continued in Arabic, unsure at the moment if Felicia was upset because she didn't want to talk with someone from her past life, or upset that she couldn't speak plainly.

"Let go of me, dog! I will have Al-Kadi kill you for this outrage!"

"I doubt it."

"Please!" Felicia clasped her hands together as she dropped the phone in pleading fashion. "Let him go. He will surely beat me to death after you leave if you go any further with this!"

"No… he won't." Nick snapped El-Amin's wrist. When Haris fell forward with a scream, clutching his wrist, Nick stungunned him into unconsciousness. He picked up the iPhone as Felicia cringed away from him into Cala's arms. "Did you hear all that, Claude?"

"Yes! It is as I feared."

"Here's Felicia again." Nick handed Felicia the iPhone again. "You can take off the face covering to speak. No one will harm you again. Are there any others in the house?"

Felicia took off her face covering headdress with shaking hand. "Yes. There are two other women upstairs. One is only twelve."

"We must repay this man, Muerto," Cala said. "He needs a good cleaning."

"I think you may be right." Nick gestured at Johnny. "See to the others, Johnny. Take Cala with you. Take no chances until the situation is clear."

"I shall enjoy helping you with the cleaning on this one, Muerto," Johnny said as he took Cala's hand. They went upstairs.

"Speak with your cousin, Felicia. Then, we will work out a plan."

Nick watched the tearful but excited conversation. He cringed at the news she and the two others in El-Amin's control had gone through female genital mutilation. Thinking about Jean being only a couple years younger than El-Amin's youngest slave fired the rage he had been holding in check. Felicia handed him the iPhone. Nick stayed watchful with El-Amin.

"Claude said you would handle his…his disappearance. Is that true?"

"Yes. You go upstairs and help my friends with your house companions. I will discuss things with Claude. Do not worry about this butcher. Is there anything special you would like me to do with him?"

Felicia shuddered. "Claude said I could leave this monster to you. That is what I will do. I do not wish to think about him anymore."

"As you wish. Go on and assure your friends." Nick waited until she was out of earshot. "I'm here, Claude."

"Can you help El-Amin turn over everything to Felicia? Clint has been creating an account in a local Bank of America right on Union Street. I've already texted you the details. Clint said if you'll bring the property statements with you, he and Jafar will transfer the title to Felicia with all the papers needed for identity and everything. My wife and I will book a flight to go there immediately to help. I can't thank you enough for this, Nick."

"No worries, my friend. I am happy to do it, and so are my cleaning assistants. Guess what? They have a nice cellar here. It will be perfect for discussing property and bank accounts with Haris. Would you like a video moment?"

"No Nick. I leave the creature's ending in your capable hands. I am sure he will pay for his sins."

"Yes… he will. Talk at you in a while."

* * *

Haris El-Amin awoke groggily, his knees aching from kneeling on the cement floor of what he recognized as his

325

basement. He felt the cold house stanchion at his back. Duct tape was wound around his chest and under his arms. Another winding around his shoulders and chest held him securely, coupled with windings around his forehead. He couldn't move his legs at all. Haris assumed rightly they were secured to the stanchion too. Some material crackled under him. The two men from earlier walked in front of him with big smiles.

"Hello there, Haris. In reality, I am Dr. Muerto, and this is my assistant, Dr. Kabong. We specialize in a treatment called intestinal cleaning. It's rather old school but effective. Here's a demonstration." The man showed Haris a scalpel while the other man pinched his nostrils, forced a rubber ball in his mouth, and put a strip of duct tape over his mouth. A mirror from his basement was positioned so he could see what was happening. Haris screamed.

* * *

"Gee, Dr. Kabong, he's screaming already and I haven't even started."

"I imagine the little girl he had mutilated screamed too, Dr. Muerto."

Nick took a deep breath and slapped Haris into silence. "Right you are. Okay, Haris, here's how this works. The demonstration comes first. When you get a taste of that we'll uncover your mouth. You have one minute to begin telling us all your bank account passwords. Dr. Kabong already has your laptop open on the table with your three bank accounts windowed on the desktop. We also need to know where you keep your house papers. Felicia showed us where your safe is. We'll need to know the combination for that too. Okay, here's your demo, shit-head. After it's over you'd best not be bashful about telling us what we want to know."

Nick sliced El-Amin from breastbone to groin, just deep enough so the intestines began to bulge. Johnny poured bleach over the wound. They watched the effect on Haris with clinical interest. "It's a good thing we did so many duct tape winds, Johnny. Otherwise, I think Haris might have bucked right out of them."

"He seems to be enjoying this as much as I had hoped."

"Indeed. Did Cala mind escorting the girls to dinner?"

"No," Johnny answered, glancing at his watch before neutralizing the bleach with warm water and salve. "She will keep them away for a couple of hours. Gus will make sure they stay safe. We should then arrive at the Allegheny Park at about exactly the right time. Is the cutoff you're familiar with safe enough for us to dig for a while without being observed?"

"Oh yeah. I'm sorry about having the digging become part of this. It's a hell of a lot easier throwing them out of the helicopter."

"I don't mind. Cala's not too crazy about dark woods. I was thinking maybe we should leave her at a town until we finish." Johnny readied his iPad for recording.

"Sure, Johnny. That would be fine." Nick leaned over and pulled off the duct tape from Haris's mouth. "Are you ready to speak? Remember you only have one minute to speak. Otherwise you get a second demo. Ready?"

Nick pulled the rubber ball out. It was off to the races. When they acquired all the information requested, Nick went upstairs to the safe while Johnny transferred funds to Felicia's new Bank of America account. Nick found thirty-nine thousand dollars in the safe and all the house documents. He made copies of the house documents on the house printer and made a printing of the safe combination. By the time he finished, Johnny was receiving confirmation on the new account transfer.

"Haris had over two million dollars. It's all been transferred and the accounts closed," Johnny told him. "How did you make out?"

"Thirty-nine grand and I have the papers. We're good to go."

Nick stuck the final eternity syringe into El-Amin's neck while Johnny readied the body-bag Haris had been kneeling over. They cut the bindings and lowered him into the bag. There was very little cleanup needed. Gus had taken one of El-Amin's vehicles to escort Cala and the others. When Gus returned with his charges, Nick had already finished off Eliah Kader and loaded El-Amin beside him with Johnny's help. When everyone was together in the living room, Nick explained everything about the financial side.

"When Claude comes to visit, he'll have the property in your name, Felicia. If there's any kind of a glitch we've missed addressing, Claude will straighten it out when he visits. I've already sent copies of the papers to our IT specialist. He'll get them ready before Claude leaves. Will you be okay here?"

"Now that the beast is gone, we will be fine." Felicia took Nick's hand in both hers. "Thank you. I know I can never repay you. It is good Claude has friends like you. He was very lost for a long time."

Nick patted her hand. "I've programmed the phone Gus bought for you. It has my number, Claude's, and John Harding's. If ever Haris's friends or business people stop here looking for him, remember what I told you to do."

"Yes. Be polite. Tell them Haris left without telling us where he was going. Take down their names if they wish to leave them with us, and pepper spray them if they try to force their way in."

"Use the stun-gun I gave you as a follow up. Stun them until they stop moving. Then call me and the police."

"And tell the police they tried to force their way in," Felicia finished. "We will do it. I'm glad Claude and his wife are visiting for a time. This will take some getting used to. It…it has been many years since I have been allowed my own thoughts. I hope to return to Paris and see my surviving family. The identities Haris had made for us are very good as are the passports. When he went overseas, he never left us alone. If he had to go away on business, he had a man come and stay at the house with us. We were always afraid. We are cowards."

"Don't think about that at all. I have experience with men like El-Amin. They are brutal nightmares to common people. It takes monsters to handle monsters, Felicia. Think no more of this time of captivity. You and your friends are now part of our extended family. We can and will be here within hours if you need us."

"You are not a monster."

Nick smiled slowly. "Yes, Felicia… I am."

* * *

"The young one still fears somehow El-Amin will return," Cala said from the backseat. "Perhaps we should have allowed her to see his body."

"She's already seen enough for now," Nick replied. "Living at her age with a slaver like El-Amin, it will be all Felicia can do to bring her around to civilization. It may never happen. Johnny and I probably should have cleaned him a while longer. I have an idea I should have thought of with the first Kader I killed secretly. We're going to stop at a butcher shop on the way to the woods when we drop Cala off for a while."

329

"It is too much inconvenience, Muerto. I'll be okay in the woods."

"We have to backtrack to get on the freeway again anyhow. We'll hit the butcher shop, drop you at a nice coffee shop, and go tuck Kader and El-Amin in for their long dirt nap."

"What's with the butcher shop?"

"We're going to get pork pieces, hopefully something the butcher normally throws out. Uh oh," Nick said, seeing the twisted look forming on Gus's face. "Too much?"

"That's gross," Gus said. "What the hell will you tell the butcher you're going to use them for?"

"I'll tell him I'm burying devout Islamic monsters in the woods and they need a shroud."

Johnny and Cala enjoyed the exchange, but Gus shook his head with unconcealed disgust. He suddenly straightened. "Damn, Muerto... you're going to take pictures, aren't you? That's just disturbing."

"Nope. Mutilating and preying on a twelve year old girl from the time she was nine is disturbing. El-Amin's burial rites will be a little justice. I'll send Felicia a digital file to show the girl if she still has nightmares about Haris coming back to haunt them. I'll send whomever takes over the Kader family, if they have anyone left, the final resting place of their deceased leader. They say a picture's worth a thousand words, right?"

Gus took a deep breath. "I concede your point. What will you tell the butcher?"

"I'll tell him I've got a dog that eats burnt barbeque and loves it. I'll say I can't afford to barbeque the spoiled brat real meat as a treat, and he likes pork guts barbequed in cooked pork blood."

"Yuck," Gus replied. "I'm telling Deke on you."

"Where'd you think I got the story from?"

* * *

Having driven off road on a fire trail, Nick remembered from a past contract, located near the Allegheny National Forest, the Unholy Trio proceeded to the burial site with backpackers' headlamps. The weather, drizzling in a light steady mist, created perfect conditions for the burials. The ground was soft but not so wet it couldn't be excavated. It didn't take the trio long to create graves deep enough not to expunge their contents at an inopportune time. They posed each of the deceased at the bottom of their grave with hands folded over their chests. Nick poured the contents of the two large plastic bags over the dead men up to their hands. He then added a pig's head to each grave on the shoulder of each corpse. Johnny moved in with digital camera and flash, taking stills of each grave from different angles until satisfied he had more than a few keepers in the bunch.

Johnny viewed each one with professional expertise, having learned many trade basics while on location with Director Lynn when she filmed the 'Hollywood Bounty Hunters'. "These are incredible, Muerto. I'm glad the butcher actually had a couple heads. They project nightmare into the scene."

"Good job. Let's get them covered." Nick and Gus worked the shovels filling in the graves easily while Johnny packed their body bags for disposal in another place. Nick moved rocks, leaves, and branch debris over the filled in graves until the site looked as natural as it could.

Nick moved away in the darkness, checking the scene with reduced light. "The rain will blend a lot of it quickly. That's it. You two head single file back to the SUV. I'll brush our trail sign."

"Who the hell do you think might do a ground check all the way out here, Muerto?"

"I don't think, Payaso. I do the job and pay attention to the details. Quit yappin' and get moving. I'd like to hit a real nice place somewhere before Illinois to stop for the night with a nice Bushmill's Irish nightcap... or morning cap."

"Get moving, Payaso," Johnny ordered. "Now, all I can think of is a hot shower and a nightcap."

"I can't believe I'm saying this," Gus replied as he led off in the direction of their SUV, "but I'm starving. I need food."

"Your wish shall be granted, Payaso." Nick used a thick branch with still green leaves on it to brush debris over their many foot prints around the graves, stirring the moist dirt.

His job along the trail proved more difficult because of footprint depth while carting the bodies, especially Nick's own. He had led with a gloved hand on each of the body-bags while Gus and Johnny packed the shovels and other ends of the bags. He used the heavier leafed branch to poke and prod until most indications left would only be discoverable by a professional tracker. Seated finally, Nick leaned comfortably in his seat.

"Maybe we should have said something over the bodies," Nick said. "You know... rot in hell or something."

"It would have just been redundant, Muerto," Gus said. "Man, I'm glad you thought to buy the Bush in town when we dropped Cala off. I'll bet everything's closed. Maybe we should eat there if anything's still open. We don't look too bad. The pine scent Fabreeze is working in the SUV. It should work on us."

"Good input, Payaso," Nick said. "I don't know why but I have a real hankerin' for pork chops."

Chapter Thirteen

Loose Ends

"Check these out, Cheese." Lynn showed me her iPad with pictures in our general lounge area while Clint and Jafar worked on the paperwork for Claude to take with him on his visit to see his cousin in our computer room.

I set aside the laptop with final touches on our Pilot Hill compound plans. The feasibility of what we planned for a landing zone with room for vertical jet takeoff would need input from engineers Denny had tapped for the project working for the Air Force. I grinned at the two sets of grave pictures, recognizing the pictures we had seen of Eliah Kader and Haris El-Amin. "Oh my, the pigs' heads are a nice touch. I bet Claude liked these."

"Oh yeah, he did. Since we can close the books on all our loose ends here in the states, I'll feel better about going down to LA to direct the 'Hollywood Bounty Hunters' in their season opener. Everything's ready to shoot the final takes."

"I liked your idea about keeping the bond skip secret until the drama and love scenes were filmed. When Chuck and Sal called to tip you about Nardo Sirapio returning to the states soon, I figured it would be a disaster trying to entrap him. He troops around Europe dancing the global warming jig with all the limousine liberal jet set, avoiding any place he can be extradited from."

"It's a tough one," Lynn admitted. "I directed the kids to do their continuing romance scenes, combined with some small sub-plotting in case we don't get our hands on Nardo. He hasn't been in the states for years. They live by a separate law structure. As long as they're celebrities making movies, anything they do is okay. I'm surprised Nardo didn't try to simply turn himself in, buy everyone off, and flit around with street cred. He should have paid more attention to the identity of the girl. The girl's parents sure made that difficult."

"Yep. The family of the sixteen year old girl he roofied at a charity benefit for the 'Climate Change' con ruined all Nardo's hit and flit plans. Her Dad's a cop and a friend of Sal's that was working security at the event. Red Dragon Security works contracts overseas. They've tried bagging Nardo when in the same place but missed him. Here in the states, they're hesitant about kidnapping a celebrity like Nardo, even on a legitimate bond."

"We're in the same position." Lynn paused, thinking about the entire episode as she had learned of it. "Sal did tell me about Nardo drugging the girl, taking her to the hotel he was staying at, and then leaving her a day later without a trace. Her parents nearly tore apart the city looking for her, only to have her show at the homestead, bruised and raped. Sal said Nardo tried to tell the authorities through his lawyer that he wasn't even there because he'd used an alias when signing in at hotels. He claimed to have left for Europe right after the benefit. The Dad screwed him on that move by collecting videos of him from security cameras both at the event leaving with his daughter and at the hotel. A rape kit was done. Nardo wasn't as careful with his condom as he thought."

"Exactly. Sal wants to get him before the Dad does. He thought of 'Hollywood Bounty Hunters' immediately. Both Chuck and Sal loved the way we handled Michael Moronas, but he didn't know if we could handle Nardo the same way. I told him we couldn't. We could kill him and make him disappear but then we can't use him on your television show. It's better if we can convince Nardo to act in a scene of his own arrest and transfer."

"I was a little too flippant about the cop's daughter. What's the family names again?" Lynn took out her iPad. "I need to make notes and do some research. We'll have to do this high profile with our FBI team, Sam and Janie. I'm thinking we'll do a run through with the Russells explaining exactly what Nardo did, combined with our Bounty Hunters episode, translating it into a warning to other girls to be extra careful when in a strange environment."

"Their names are Carney and Phyllis Russell," I told her. "The daughter's name is Carmen. Chuck and Sal believe they have enough proof to go through any trial with a slam dunk conviction, but with Nardo's money, who knows."

Lynn asked the important questions. "Where's he at? Does Sal know where he's headed?"

"That's where Chuck and Sal's network really came through. Nardo's traveling incognito by cruise ship from Lisbon to Bridgetown, Barbados. He arrives in Barbados tomorrow after a twelve day cruise. Slick has a couple favorite aliases Red Dragon is familiar with. Although Interpol refuses to arrest a celebrity or anyone with money, they keep track of the expats that can be blackmailed. Nardo has passports under two other names, James Baldwin and Clarence Fellow. Nardo paid a hefty price to make his way to Lisbon but he left a financial trail under the Clarence Fellow identity. Chuck knew the only way he could get into the states would be by private jet. This Clarence Fellow alias owns an out of the way ranch in Carson City, Nevada."

"So Red Dragon put a watch on any Clarence Fellow on a private plane arriving from Barbados? Damn... that's good work. Don't leave me hangin' Cheese."

I grinned at Lynn's impatience. "From Barbados, he's booked a private plane ride from Grantley International Airport in Barbados and destination Carson City Airport three days from now."

"I have to make a call!" Lynn had her iPhone out a moment later. She put it on speaker as Nick answered.

"Hey, Lynn. I guess Claude loved our funeral arrangements, huh?"

"Absolutely. Where are you at?"

"Hastings, Nebraska, sipping Bushmill's by the pool before we drive across the eternity that is Nebraska."

Lynn and I enjoyed that swipe at driving across a very hypnotically brutal route across the Midwest. "Excellent. I have a mission for the cartoons. If you and your cartoons decide to accept this mission, as always, if it is unsuccessful, we will disavow any-"

"Cut the Mission Impossible crap, Dr. Deville. I've had two big Bushmills already and you're killing my buzz," Nick interrupted as his companions could be heard laughing in the background.

"Take me off speaker, Nick."

"Sure. Okay, what's up?"

Lynn explained the situation and who the mark was. "He'll be at his hideout in Carson City two days from now. Could I talk you into collecting him and transporting Nardo to my reeducation camp at Pain Central? If it all works out, I'll want my assistant director Kabong with me for an episode involving Nardo's transfer into FBI hands."

"Text me the address for the hideout. We'll look it over. You're figuring the place is unattended, but looked in on by one of those property management firms. Do you have any info on how often they check it over?"

"Damn… good thinking. I'll get that info from Sal and text it to you with the address. It sounds like you have a plan already you little rascal."

"I do, but I need to confer with my associate cartoons. We'll get it done. He does have a legitimate warrant out on him though, right?"

"Yes. He's been wanted for a long while. The prick's still hired for movies filmed on location and finished before any kind of extradition can be arranged. That would make it legal for you as a United States Marshal to arrest him without a snag, right?"

"Yeah, it would. I don't want to be included in the apprehension credits though. This cross-country trip has been completely under the radar successfully so far. I'd like to keep it that way."

"We can do that. Once we have him here, I'll confer with our Fed friends Sam and Janie as to how good our case is for an episode of Hollywood Bounty Hunters."

"Doesn't he have to act a part willingly to be turned over to the FBI?"

"Did you just insult me, Muerto?"

"Oh… ah… sorry, I didn't think you were really going to fix Nardo. Sucks to be him as Casey would say. I'll call you when the deed is done or I have a question. Text me the info, including if his ranch gets looked in on by a property management firm."

"Will do," Lynn agreed.

"Thanks for this, Nick," I told him. "I know we're piling up favors on our end."

"Doin' right ain't got no end. Talk at you later, John."

After Nick disconnected, I grinned at Lynn. "I noticed you didn't tell him not to break your toys."

"Nick's not as ham-handed as you, Cheese. He's cold and efficient without your flawed emotional side."

"That's hurtful, Crue."

* * *

Nick finished his explanation of Lynn's request after a swim and sipping another Bushmill's Irish with his friends. "What do you think of my plan?"

"It's a workable monstrosity, cleverly done. A true serial killer's methodology," Gus stated with clinical flair which immediately evoked amusement.

Nick hung his head comically. "See… I get a task of righteousness assigned me in a moral cause, and past indiscretions haunt everything I do in penance for my many sins."

"Poor baby," Gus replied in false sympathy for Nick's amusing drama note. "I'm in. This Nardo guy… I can't stand the sight of him. When Tina mentions him, I call him 'Nardo de Pussyface'. He looks like a baby in need of a pacifier, especially since he's put on a few pounds. I've heard him rant the environmental whacko clichés and I figured that environmental foundation he funded with all the hoopla was a preplanned ticket to reenter the states legally. Apparently, in the world now, if you're green, you're clean, even if you drug and rape a sixteen year old girl."

"Cala and I are with you, Muerto," Johnny added. "I like having the extra day after we arrive to simply take stock of our surroundings before he arrives."

"That's the key, Johnny," Nick acknowledged. "I've done numerous contracts where establishing a place the mark would eventually return was essential to completion of the contract. Yes, I know I'm a monster. We're doing good with Nardo. We're not killing him. We're simply delivering him to a place where within hours of his arrival, he'll wish he were dead."

Gus snorted. "You'd kill him in a heartbeat if Lynn asked you to."

"Yeah… so what's your point," Nick asked to much hilarity.

* * *

Nardo Sirapio opened his garage door by remote and drove into his garage, attached to the two story dwelling in Carson City he thought of as his 'Hole in the Wall' hideout. No one knew of its existence. He could sneak in and use it as his base of operations to see people on the sly, work deals, or relax for a few months in between movies. He closed the garage door and walked toward the connecting entrance to his house. Nardo smiled with self-satisfaction concerning his ease in bypassing all laws pertaining to travel with a fake passport. It was so easy.

Unlocking his door, Nardo stepped inside a few feet, closed the door and walked toward his kitchen. He wanted a drink. He felt the Taser needles embed into his arm. The jolt, pain, and disoriented feeling of dread raced through him at hyper-speed. He fell to the floor, vibrating to the electronic impulses sent. As blackness descended on him, Nardo saw the black robed figure smiling and waving at him.

* * *

"He's really out of it, Muerto," Cala said, pinching Nardo's cheeks.

"Damn it! I knew I should have eased off the juice," Nick admitted. "Finding all the shit he has on his computer was too much input. I'm happy it's not us interrogating him."

"He's special, Muerto. Nardo is a famous celebrity." Gus gave Nick a shaming gesture with left hand index finger extended in brushing movement over his right hand index finger. "Thou shalt not kill'."

"Stuff it, Payaso. We have most of what we wanted. I'm glad Grace was able to get a federal warrant to search his premises and fax it to us. Maybe we should rethink this. Let's abandon him somewhere around here. We'll fix him real nice and then bury him."

"I must object, Muerto," Johnny cut in, slapping Nardo's cheeks lightly. "I will be helping Director Deville by special request to produce the Hollywood Bounty Hunters episode. She will be very upset if you simply bury her star. You also have to consider loyal Kabong missing out on a new filming opportunity."

"You're right." Nick took a deep breath as Sirapio regained consciousness in sputtering and gasping increments. "Once he's awake, I'll do the arrest part with Miranda while Director Kabong films it to send Lynn."

"Thank you, Muerto," Johnny said. He and Cala helped Nardo get to his feet shakily. They sat him down on a straight backed chair from the kitchen. "Are you coherent, Mr. Sirapio?"

"Who... are you people? I'll have you arrested if you don't leave my house immediately." Nardo tried to stand but Nick shoved him down.

"Stay right where you are unless you'd like to be Tasered again," Nick told him. "Are you ready Kabong? How do I look?"

Nick wore black jeans, black t-shirt, and black windbreaker. He had shaved for the takedown of Nardo, knowing he would be doing a formal arrest.

"Very ominous," Kabong told him. "It is a somber look for the scene. I'm ready. Begin."

Nick turned to Nardo, showing his US Marshal's badge and ID to the camera and then to Nardo. "I am United States Marshal Nick McCarty. You, Mr. Sirapio, are under arrest for the drugging, kidnapping, and rape of a sixteen year old girl, Carmen Russell."

Nick formally read the Miranda warning to Sirapio, who became more irritated with each passing second. "Do you understand these rights as I have read them, Mr. Sirapio?"

"This is a mistake! I wasn't even there."

"That will be determined in a court of law. Do you understand your rights?"

"Yes! I want my lawyer right now!"

"As you wish. I will be transporting you to the proper authorities in California. Thank you for your cooperation." Nick received a nod from Johnny who turned away to send the video for Lynn's approval. They waited for the confirming call which came a few minutes later. Nick put Lynn on speaker.

"Outstanding arrest, Nick," Lynn said. "That's perfect. Kabong sent me the takedown too. You nearly ruined my film star."

"My apologies. Wait until you see what this asshole has on his computer."

"I will correct all sins of the past here. Remember, he has to be prepped for the episode. Sometimes that can be very painful."

"Understood, Lynn. We're on our way. I'll see you when we get there."

"Until then, Marshal." Lynn disconnected.

"You can't break into my house, take my computer, and zap me! This is illegal search and seizure!"

"You'll have your day in court, right after we take you to your holding area." Nick pulled Nardo to his feet. "Put your hands out. I'll restrain you with your hands in a comfortable position for transport. If you cause any problems I'll have to restrain you in a more painful manner."

Nardo hesitated. No weapons were on display. He knew karate.

Nick smiled. "Go ahead and resist arrest, Nardo. You'll have to travel with two broken arms but it's your choice."

Nardo stared into Nick's eyes and stuck his hands out. Gus put on the handcuffs. "I'll have your badge for this."

"Yeah… I know. If I were you, I'd be worrying about how you plan on explaining those videos on your computer of seven other underage girls you drugged and defiled."

"Those…those were taken illegally. They'll never allow them into court!"

"I have a federal warrant to search your place, idiot." Nick held the warrant so Nardo could see it. "Your fleeing the trial was the deciding factor for the judge to issue a blanket warrant. You're cooked, pal."

"I'll give you a hundred thousand apiece to let me go. These were victimless crimes. I-"

"Don't, Nick!" Gus moved in front of Nardo with his hands in a stopping gesture.

Nick hesitated for a long moment, staring around Gus at Nardo before putting away his Colt .45. He grinned and shook a finger at Nardo. "Oh… you so lucky. You'd better be good on the way or I am going to toast you."

Nick's phone buzzed a moment before he entered the SUV for the trip to Oakland. "Hi Rach."

"Where the hell are you, Muerto? You were supposed to be home yesterday."

"The Unholy Trio and Cleaner have been on a 'Magical Monster Tour'. It's completed now so I'll be home today. We're stopping in Oakland to drop off a prisoner, but after that we'll be heading home."

"I miss you. I'm going on all your missions from now on."

"I have to go to the sand next."

"Except that one."

* * *

"Johnny Five," Clint greeted Johnny at the door as he led Nardo into Pain Central with a curious Tonto at his side. "Where are your partners in crime?"

"They're bringing our computer evidence collection. Nick decided to be extra careful with them. I now pass Nardo Sirapio over to you."

"On behalf of Agent Tonto and myself, I accept." Clint made a hand gesture at Tonto. "Agent Tonto. Please escort Mr. Sirapio into interrogation. Follow Agent Tonto, Nardo. Show Nardo what happens if he doesn't follow you, Tonto."

Clint made another gesture. Tonto went werewolf crazy, snarling, snapping his jaws, and instantly terrifying the cringing Nardo. Clint gestured again and Tonto tugged on Sirapio's leg. "Follow him now, Nardo."

Sirapio dutifully followed Tonto who didn't even look around. Nick, Gus, and Cala walked in with a variety of electronics equipment from their three stops on the Monster Tour. Clint led them to the storage area.

"Do you need any of this back, Dead Boy?"

"No. I copied the stuff off the Kader gadgets. Say hello to everyone for us. We're hitting the road home. Johnny and Cala would like to stay if Lynn thinks she'll need them for the LA filming. Johnny's excited about the new director gig."

"I think that's what Lynn has in mind. We only have a short window of time to get the episode done. Sam and Janie will be available in two days for taking custody of Nardo. We're returning Lynn's experiment, Flo Nazari, to her parents in LA. We don't know how that will work out. Lynn reeducated her for sure, but it's a hit and miss as we found out with Senta Bulgar. You and Cala can stay at our house, Johnny."

"Great! Thank you. I'll get our bags."

Cala gave Nick a hug. "Thank you for bringing me along, Muerto."

"You did wonderfully, Cala. We needed you at Felicia's house. Have a good time on location with Director Deville. C'mon, Gus. We've already received enough warnings to get our asses home."

"Thanks for helping out with our enemies list."

"No problem. They were right on our way, Clint."

"Want some company on your trip to the sand?"

"I would but I have Al-Saud set nicely to see only me. He will undoubtedly have men watching for my arrival in Dubai. He's staying at the Atlantis. I'm very familiar with the place."

"Call us if you get into a jam there, brother."

"Will do. See you on the flip side, Clint."

"Before we go," Gus said. "How's work coming along on the Tempest."

"Real good. We have a team working on her from the mainland," Clint replied. "That reminds me, we're working on ownership papers. We liked your suggestion of adding the 'Lone Ranger' theme to our music selection. Since Ranger is okay with all of you we'll have the name changed on the boat."

"I like it," Nick said.

"I liked Johnny's suggested name: Infidel's Revenge," Gus added, "but like Nick said, we might as well blow her up ourselves."

"Yep. It was our favorite too," Clint replied. "We could add one of those skulls with an American flag on its forehead too. We're having some nice armaments installed on her. We could probably have a huge black flag to display, if we want to piss off someone, featuring a skull and the Infidel's Revenge moniker."

"That would be great, Clint," Johnny said as he joined the group with his and Cala's bags. "I hope we have an opportunity to do another Crusader Crue video. The cat videos are kicking my butt on YouTube. I must get something of substance uploaded soon."

* * *

"What will we do without Kaders screwing with us," Gus asked as he drove toward Pacific Grove.

"Enjoy walking to the school again," Nick replied. "This road trip was chock full of surprises. I'm ready for some mornings at the beach, days and nights writing on the deck, and walking the Dekester."

"How long will you take off before you go to the sand?"

"I'll know more about that when Al-Saud responds to my report on Al-Kadi's ending. Clint fixed Saran nicely inside a body-bag with a perfect .45 caliber hole between his eyes for me to send Al-Saud. It was better than my quickie pictures at the compound with a slit throat. He will be letting me know when he wants to meet in Dubai. He's already paid me for the hit. I gave him the opportunity to look over what I have from the Pilot Hill compound before paying for what he asked me to retrieve for him."

"I bet Rachel would like you to hang around for a while. You have a book signing too, don't you?"

"I promised Pilgrim's Way Books in Carmel I'd do another signing. I half expected them to cancel because I had to kill that book killer outside their establishment."

345

Gus chuckled. "After the headlines you received with the US Marshal McCarty Shootout in Carmel, I'll bet they had plenty of demands for your return. Did you get much writing done on the trip? I saw you typing away but you never mentioned anything about progress."

"I managed fifteen hundred a day. 'Blood Beach' will be a hit I think. Diego's romance with Fatima despite her constant betrayals have Jed and Leo frustrated as hell. They can't believe Diego hasn't shot her in the head yet. Did you get a chance to read the copy I put on your Kindle?"

"Yep. It's your best one yet. Johnny thinks so too. He's read through your whole series already. He'll be pissed about missing a book signing."

"Johnny's so pumped about learning the ropes making movies, I doubt he'll give it a thought. I wonder if Rachel will allow Jean to go with me. I know she'll ask if she can go along with her minion, Sonny."

"Those two are inseparable," Gus said. "I've tried not to think about what kind of devilment they cooked up while we've been gone. Issac told me everything's been quiet. After he returned from Pilot Hill, he patrolled our neighborhoods. He shadowed Rachel when she took the kids to school."

"Issac's our extra utility player we've needed. Rachel said she appealed to Jean one on one and Jean reacted to being treated like an adult very well. I'm glad you and Johnny will be around while I'm playing in the sandbox."

"I hope Johnny stays in touch. I want to hear how Nazari looked to him. I thought Senta was reprogrammed but she damn near got you killed. Speaking of writing. How did you do on 'Blood Beach' today? Will you be writing on the deck or can Tina and I come over?"

"I wrote my fifteen hundred on the ride to Oakland. I'll get in another five hundred words. Jean will be working on homework with Sonny or throwing knives. I'd like you to come over with Tina. It will be a nice night on the deck."

"We'll be there. When will you do the book signing?"

"I have to let them know when I get back. I think it would be good to do a book signing without a book killer visit, but it would be really nice not to get a grammar Nazi. Pilgrim's Way ordered a bunch of my entire series. In addition to taking questions about 'Dark Interlude', I'm supposed to give a short talk on my progress with 'Blood Beach' before the signing. My agent Cassie e-mailed me that the publisher is ecstatic about my doing more signings."

"Have you figured out what you want to do in Dubai?"

"A lot depends on my interaction with Al-Saud. I've been in touch with my contact you met when I came out of retirement and we went to the sand. I wired Khalil a hundred grand to make his way to the Atlantis in Dubai. He's acquired a vehicle and Denny helped arrange a safe-house for me. I may have to take Al-Saud to a place more private where I can negotiate with him for all of his ill-gotten gains."

"How do you know this Khalil won't sell you out and keep the money?"

"I promised him a million more if he helps me with the many aspects of the mission. It's not all about the money anyway, although I could tell from our correspondence he wants in on this in the worst way. I saved him and his family. They were caught in a roundup of Kurdish Christians in Afghanistan at a time I entered the area with a CIA team to get the Taliban leader in the area. My way of doing things was find someone getting stomped on by peaceful Islam and fix their situation. I saw Khalil, his wife, and two sons ushered into a mosque in Herat with a few dozen others, kicked and whipped into a holding area there. I went in at night against orders, slit the throats of the guards and freed the people inside. Khalil helped me while I set charges inside the mosque, which was nothing more than an armory. I blew the mosque to kingdom come. I booked safe passage for Khalil and his family to Dubai. I convinced him to pretend he and his family were Muslim refugees, willing to work doing anything to stay. Anytime I've had a job in the sand, Khalil coordinates everything."

"Didn't you get screwed going against orders?" Gus showed intense interest in yet another McCarty past event.

"Nope. Khalil knew where the Taliban leader lived. I killed him the same night during the chaos after I blew up the mosque. The CIA team were following the book. They loved my improvisation. The guy who ordered me to stand down was demoted to shit-land."

"Damn, Muerto, you should be in charge of CIA ops."

"We have the right guy in charge now. Paul Gilbrech and Denny Strobert make a great team at the Company if we can keep them alive. Anyway, in answer to your question about Dubai, I have the puzzle pieces in place for when I hear from Al-Saud. Khalil has smuggled some tools for me at the safe-house, thanks in part to Denny's assets in the area. Khalil contracted the same cleaners he helped us out with before at a price undeniably a blessing in that sand pit. I took care of them pretty well before, but I'm making them rich enough this time to go somewhere nice."

"Then you are going to need cleaners."

"Maybe…maybe not, but I believe so. It's better to have them in place if I do need them. If I can get an audience with Al-Saud in his room at the Atlantis, I plan to kill his hired help, and take Al-Saud for some conversation. He's high in the ranks of Al-Qaeda in Europe. If I bring home information gifts for Paul to use, I will get to continue my rogue operations. I'll possibly need a top notch cleaning crew to ease the rough edges on my plan. We'll talk more about the specifics when I hear from Al-Saud. It would be nice if I can take them outside the Atlantis."

"I don't envy you going back into the sand. Don't think I forgot about the Nazari name. That's why I'm so interested in the Florence Nazari experiment. It's obvious her husband didn't know you probably killed one of his relatives, Sheik Abdul Nazari."

Nick liked the fact Gus remembered the Nazari name. "I'm glad you remembered the name. Nazari chose the Isis side. Al-Saud sided with Al-Qaeda. I'm not expecting any Nazari relative interference over there if you're worried about that. I won't know, of course, until I get to Dubai. One stipulation Al-Saud made was I have to travel under my real name. That's the main reason I have to retain first class cleaners on the job."

"Are Khalil's cleaner team trustworthy?"

"They're his sons, Asim and Ghazi. With the guards Al-Saud always has near him, I have to cover the aspect we'll need to clean the Atlantis rooms before leaving. I've paid for the list of goodies I had Khalil import for me. He's stockpiled a Colt .45 with silencer, an M107 sniper rifle with silencer, and an XM25. Leaving Dubai may get messy. Khalil has the same pilot on notice we used to get out of the sand last time."

"Why not shoot Al-Saud in the head too and forget the negotiations."

"That's very shortsighted of you, Payaso. I have expenses. You know how frugal I am. Besides, Denny has inquired as to whether I can bring Al-Saud."

"I think I know some sand people who will very shortly enjoy more opportunity than they ever dreamed possible," Gus replied.

"Khalil is indeed as frugal as I am. He will have a chance to apply for citizenship elsewhere. He went with me on a job in

Switzerland once. I believe he has an eye on immigrating there where he'll be able to become a practicing Christian once again."

"He doesn't want to come to the United States?"

Nick smiled. "Whenever I've mentioned it, Khalil reminds me that Chicago is the murder capital of the world. They read the death list news for Chicago over there. He has mentioned we have more deaths in Chicago on any given weekend than in the Iraq warzone most of the time. I told him I could help him move to Texas where they love guns, Christians, and hard workers. He says it's cooler in Switzerland and they love all the same things. I couldn't argue with him about that. He's greased a lot of hands at the Dubai Atlantis hotel in preparation for my arrival. I will know Al-Saud's whereabouts at all times along with his men. It's my key ace in the hole to keep from being ambushed."

"What if they do set an ambush?"

"Then I ambush them instead. They're cheap buying information and help. I'm not. Khalil knows how I operate. He also knows to look for honest disgruntled helpers."

"You do have a way of drawing in a loyal following of people. Has your method ever backfired?"

"A couple times, but only here in the states, and nothing real bad. I had to go with plan B in those instances."

"Grenades?"

"How perceptive of you, Payaso."

* * *

"Oh... baby... you really did miss me." Nick stroked Rachel's side as she lie gasping in the aftermath of an intense interlude. "That was sheer genius tricking Jean into taking her minion to the 3D Imax showing of the new Star Wars episode."

"We better… get a shower. We have to pick them up in an hour." Rachel attempted to rise but fell back on the bed. "God… I don't think I can move. Go get your shower first and get Quinn ready while I take a bath in the downstairs bathroom. Help me out of this bed, Muerto. They're at the Cinemark in Monterey."

"You'll have to take a quickie bath, baby," Nick said, scooping Rachel off the bed with Deke joining his journey with her in his arms down the stairs. "Quinn must have sensed his old man's needs. He didn't make a peep."

"I timed everything perfectly," Rachel replied, her arms tightening around Nick's neck, "and damn if it wasn't worth every moment of planning."

"Do you mind Gus and Tina coming over in a couple hours? They'll probably bring Issac over with them too."

"I don't mind. I got what I wanted. I'll have seconds later."

"You will indeed, my dear."

* * *

"We tracked you Dad," Jean announced while leading Sonny into the backseat. "You went on a rampage without a single headline. I heard you had to make a couple of unexpected stops. My informant Al came through with a scoop on your rescue of Mr. Chardin's cousin. You even had a chance to kidnap a famous movie star for Lynn's Hollywood Bounty Hunters."

"It sounds like Al is as big a sneak around the Harding household as you are in mine, Viper. I hope you don't get her into trouble with her Dad."

"I won't if you don't rat us out to him."

"Jean!"

"She's still sore about me acing her extortion bust. Nice to see you too, kid. How are you doing at home, Sonny?"

"About the same, Sir. I think my folks have some kind of scam in the works. When I know more details, I'll be able to figure out if I need advice."

"Anytime. I thought your Dad was tending to his passport office job more diligently."

"He is, but I think my Mom wants him to take her back to DC and appeal his exile. If they move back to DC, can I stay with you?"

"Absolutely. I think it would be a bad idea for those two trying to get another gig in DC. They nearly ended up in prison the last time. They have the wrong sort of ambition for DC."

"I mentioned that fact but they told me I was too young to understand. I told them I wouldn't go to DC with them no matter what."

"I'll talk to a few of my friends in DC. They'll whisper a few words of wisdom in your parents' ears. Phil is still on a probationary list of people who can go to prison over the passport office terrorist thread. They might travel to DC but the doors will all be closed."

"Thank you."

"I'll keep it very quiet. I don't want them suspecting you had anything to do with it."

"You look like your head's going to explode, Mom," Jean observed.

"I will speak no evil of Sonny's parents even if I pop a vein holding it in. Don't you think it would be a good idea if Sonny at least found out what plan they're hatching?"

"I'll keep listening… I wasn't going to say anything until I was sure, but I heard Nick's name mentioned a couple times. They heard me move and shut up. I haven't forgotten though. I know my folks can be dangerous," Sonny explained. "I don't want them involved in something so deeply you have to kill them. They're so stupid!"

"Easy, kid," Nick said. "I'm not going to kill them. That's off the table. We'll make sure they don't go off the cliff of ignorant actions. Pilgrim's Way Books wants me to do a signing tomorrow. Saturday is a big tourist moment so there will probably be a big crowd even though it's a short notice signing. Johnny Five can't come this time but Gus will be there. Would you two like to come? Remember, it's strictly voluntary."

"Yes!" Jean pumped a fist. "Sonny hasn't seen you drill a book killer right between the eyes yet like I did."

"Jean! Oh my God… one more word and you'll never see the inside of a bookstore again. I'm glad Gus is going. I have to work or I'd bring my Ruger over there too. I've noticed you're getting some hostile reviews over the Muslim targets Diego has been dealing with, reflecting your real life jaunts into danger against the religion of peace."

"The fans ripped them apart," Nick replied. "I think the gloves are off as far as the actual blue collar citizenry are concerned. They know what's in the Quran now, thanks to not only researchers, but also historians, who know the bloody truth about fourteen hundred years of pedophilia, inbreeding, slavery, female subjugation, and conquest. I'm certain they're not fans of my novels so the only way they'll ever protest a book signing is if they come with at least a hundred of their murdering mutant brethren. It won't go well for them."

"Hey… let's not do a major battle with Jean and Sonny in the middle of it, Muerto."

"Not in my plan. Believe me, Rach. I don't want anything to happen at a book signing. I was just letting you know I've noticed the new book killing reviews from the 'outraged' Muslims. I can tell within a sentence they haven't read the book. They do have the premise of their negative comments right. I know who the enemy of the world is: Islam and its acolytes. Therefore, my avatar Diego also reflects my current feelings about the Islamic scourge trying to stuff Sharia Law and No-Go zones down my throat. I can't let anything get in the way of this reality where our existence as a free nation depends on us making the right decisions to save our nation."

"I'm with you, Dad! Doin' right ain't got no end."

"Jean!" Rachel bumped her head into the passenger car window. "I'm going to hell."

Nick was enjoying the comment so much while trying to drive the car, he earned a head slap from his mate. "Hey… no hitting. I have Gus and Tina coming over later. Issac is busy so it'll just be Payaso and T-Rex. I have five hundred more words to write in 'Blood Beach'. Let's get home, figure out drinks and snacks, and enjoy our deck time. I'm sure you two young buggers have weekend homework. This will be an excellent time for your assignments to get done under adult supervision and help."

"We need to train, Dad," Jean stated. "Sonny and I will practice with the knives and after the book signing we'll go to the range for firearms training."

Nick didn't look around. "You'll get your young butts up to the deck, do the entire weekend's homework, and then we'll talk about other training."

"Okay… but our participation in a homework marathon is under protest," Jean replied.

"You're cruising for a time out from all input, girl," Rachel jumped into the conversation immediately at that point. "Speak ill of the homework completion and you'll not only complete your homework, but you will be without an electronic device for two weeks."

"This is like being under Sharia Law!"

Nick grinned back at Jean. "Nope. If you were under Sharia Law, you wouldn't be able to learn how to read, much less go to school and travel a block without escort and burka."

"Not fair! You pulled the Muslim reality card on me, Dad."

"Yeah... I did."

* * *

"Gus and Tina... my two most welcome guests," Nick said as he opened the door.

"Oh my, Gus... someone has been sipping a few before our arrival," Tina said.

"After all we've been through the last week, I'm hoping to join him in short order. Lead us to the sustenance of lost souls, brother," Gus directed.

"Right this way, brother. I'm cutting Deke off though. He was a little wobbly coming down to meet you two. I'll counter his lust for beer with treats. Watch this... 'bacon, bacon, bacon'!"

Deke streaked up the stairs to the deck.

It took a few moments before Tina and Gus could follow Nick to the deck.

"I'll bet that sobers him up," Gus observed.

"It makes him drink water, but it adds a walk for me this evening," Nick replied while leading the way onto the deck. He opened a new bag of treats and sat down with them. Deke hovered at his side in patient sitting position. "Easy boy. I know the beer makes you frantic. Easy does it, buddy."

Nick fed him a small piece at a time rather than put out a bunch for him to devour. "The kids are throwing knives so we can talk. That's it, Dekester. Small bites."

"You and Deke are so comical, Muerto," Tina said as Rachel gave her a glass of wine. I think that damn dog feeds off of everything you do."

"We are drinking buddies. He understands me."

"You mean he knows you're a serial killer?"

"That's just mean, Gus," Nick said, lowering his head in serial killer penance. "Deke loves me. He doesn't care if I arrive here from the dark side."

"That's only because you entice him with beer," Tina noted.

Nick took in a deep breath with a spreading of his hands. "That may indeed be a factor but animals know things beyond human perception. Deke and I bonded immediately the moment I met him."

"Has Al-Saud contacted you yet, dog whisperer?"

"Yes. He and I have interacted digitally. Rabiah and I will be speaking in another fifteen minutes as a matter of fact. He loved the picture I sent him of Saran Al-Kadi in the body-bag Clint supplied me with. I explained I only gave him a fraction of the info I took from Saran's abode. He was hot to get everything at any price. I told him I would meet him in Dubai with samples. The game is afoot."

"It seems like a damn trap, Muerto," Gus said. "You're never this trusting. Do you know something we don't?"

Nick smiled. "I spread enough money in Dubai to be the all omniscient Wizard of Oz if I want to be. I have human intelligence Al-Saud was far too cheap and arrogant to buy. Otherwise, I'd abort the mission. I'm not doing a suicide mission, Payaso. That arrogant bastard will be landing in a hostile environment built with money he's too aloof to spend. Relax. Let me handle this the way I know I can. Remember Felix Moreau. He thought he was on top of the food chain too."

Nick began dancing around to everyone's amusement. "I am the great and powerful Oz!"

"Damn," Gus muttered. "I think Muerto's in the tank."

Nick stopped. He shrugged. "Sorry. I was having a little fun. I do have many pieces in place to help me with this mission. I didn't treat it as an assassin. I know I have backup but I've covered all avenues of disaster my active imagination could think of. I'll speak to Al-Saud and see if I detect anything amiss. I spoke to Khalil today. He has been hard at work spreading wealth."

"Those people don't know what your plans are, do they," Gus asked.

"No. Only Khalil and his sons know what I'm doing in Dubai. Our paid informants were told we need to be apprised of Al-Saud's wherabouts at all times because of a business dealing. Rachel gave me the okay to take the kids with me tomorrow to the book signing. Do you still want to go, Gus?"

"Sure. I'm surprised you're letting the kids go with us after that last gun battle outside the bookstore, Rach."

Rachel breathed in deeply. "They finished their whole weekend's worth of homework. Jean would torture me all day tomorrow if I didn't allow them to go. I know you and Muerto will watch out for them. I bet after that shooting last time, the bookstore will have more security at this signing."

"They can't afford it so I'm paying for extra security guards," Nick replied. "We sold so many books after my last signing ended in a street battle that Cassie joked about my shooting someone every signing."

The four friends were still enjoying Nick's adlib when his special phone rang. The green light on its side indicated no one was trying to trace the call when he answered in Arabic. "I received your payment. Everything is in order for my Dubai trip if you would like to look over the rest of what I took from Al-Kadi's compound."

"Very much so. I made inquiries about Al-Kadi's compound through contacts in the area. They told me the place is under guard by federal authorities."

"My business with Al-Kadi was by circumstance somewhat messy." Nick wondered about Al-Saud's contacts in the area. "After I left the area, the FBI and Homeland Security moved on the place. I don't know what happened after that, nor do I care."

"Understood. You will be traveling alone as we planned, correct?"

"Yes. When would you like me at the Atlantis?"

"One week from tomorrow if possible."

"I will be there," Nick agreed. "Do you wish for me to join you in your room?"

"No. I believe we should meet somewhere public first. Let us meet at the Neptune's Retreat in the waterpark."

"Good choice," Nick said. "What time would you like to meet?"

"Three o'clock in the afternoon."

"Agreed. I will see you then." Nick disconnected. He smiled at Rachel. "I have five days before I need to travel, babe."

"I'm going to the range with you and the kids tomorrow," Rachel said. "I want to make sure we spend every minute together until you leave."

"Good. Then you want to go with us to the book signing too, right."

"I take that back… not every minute."

* * *

The line moved along with very little interruption after Nick's talk on his new novel. He explained the new Diego adventure with emphasis on Nick's romance with the conniving Fatima and answered questions from the fans of the series. Gus, whom the fans knew of as the model Nick created Jed from, answered a multitude of boating questions, many of them addressing sailing in the Caribbean. Jean and Sonny searched the line of people for book killers and grammar Nazis. It wasn't until three quarters of the way through that Jean spotted a potential candidate.

"Bearded guy, seven people back, Dad."

Nick and Gus both glanced at the one Jean indicated. The man had a full black chin beard with no mustache. Lean and over six feet tall, he wore a black kufi head covering, black slacks, and a loose fitting pullover drab green top, covered somewhat by the partially zipped windbreaker. The man glared at Nick without blinking. Nick smiled at him.

"Oh yeah," Gus said. "I think you're right, Jean."

"He doesn't have a book either," Sonny added.

"Yep," Nick agreed, focusing on the next man in line, a darkly tanned gentleman in his sixties with white hair. Nick shook the man's proffered hand. "Hi. I see you have 'Dark Interlude'. Did you enjoy it?"

"Good action but repetitive. I think you may be getting lazy, Nick," the man said, grinning to take the sting out of his critique.

"Writing an action pulp fiction series can seem repetitive," Nick replied. "The romance with Fatima, and the subplots involving Jed and Leo discovering her antics behind Diego's back didn't stimulate your interest, huh?"

"My name's Ted by the way. It actually read like you threw in the romance and Leo as filler with snappy dialogue."

"At least you thought the dialogue was snappy," Nick said as he signed the inside. "Thanks for stopping by."

"You missed the part about being filler."

"No, but honestly, I write stories as I imagine them happening, including dialogue interactions between characters."

"You should be more open to criticism and change, Nick."

"I don't write to please readers, Ted. I write to please me. If when I'm done with a novel the readers are pleased with the product, I'm happy. If they're not, they need to find another author."

Ted frowned. "Maybe that's what I need to do."

Nick smiled. "No hard feelings, Ted. Take care of yourself."

Ted took the book from Nick. "Thanks."

"Not a killer, but touchy," Gus whispered.

"His points are probably legitimate but I wouldn't enjoy writing if I couldn't do it the way I wanted to."

The next people between the bearded man and Ted were big fans who mentioned reading his entire series of Diego novels more than once. Nick noticed his security guards watching the bearded guy too. The man walked to the desk with his fists clenched. In his peripheral vision, Nick saw Jean and Sonny trying to edge closer to the conversation.

"Hello, Sir. Did you have anything you would like me to sign?

"Yes." The man reached inside his coat, pulled out a knife while diving toward Nick and shouted, "Allahu Akbar!"

Nick blocked the knife arm and struck the man's nose with his palm in a vicious, full force strike, driving his attacker's nose bone upward into his brain. The knife clattered to the floor a split second before its owner collapsed lifelessly, doing a boneless dead cat bounce on the floor. Screams, commotion, and security guards with weapons drawn to cover the dead man followed the action. Nick looked over to see Gus with weapon drawn and both kids with their knives in hand.

"Put the knives away, kids," Nick whispered. Jean and Sonny did as they were told. Gus holstered his Glock.

"Why the hell didn't you shoot him," Gus asked as silence in the aftermath became nearly palpable.

"Even my Colt may not have stopped him from using the knife. He was too close. Watch the crowd, Gus. We don't know if he's the only one." Nick held up his hands while moving around the desk to address the crowd. "I'm sorry about this. I'll come to you and sign your books until the police get here. I'm afraid we'll all have to stay until they get this sorted out."

There were cheers and applause while Nick talked with the security guards. "We didn't expect anything like this obviously."

"Hell of a move, Nick. I called it in. We thought this was just a book signing. Imagine our surprise. How many agencies do we call in on this? You have more experience than us Carmel cops."

"Just locals until the suspect is identified. I'll work the crowd. Might as well sell some books. It will relax folks a little."

"Are you armed, Nick?"

"Yeah, I am, Ben. You and Dick deserve a bonus for this gig. I'll take care of you."

"That's not necessary."

"I know, but if you only knew how many novels this incident will sell, you'd know the bonus will be well worth it." Nick shook his head. "This is going to be a mess."

"Yep."

Chapter Fourteen

Al-Saud

"Some book signing," Rachel said as everyone sat on the deck together eating pizza. "I should take the rap for this since it was me who mentioned Muslim nutso attacks."

"You should have seen it, Mom! Dad smashed him in the nose and he was dead," Jean said with much excitement. "Sonny saw it too."

"I've seen it close and personal," Rachel said. "Is it over, Nick?"

"All we have right now is it was the media manufactured 'Lone Wolf' attack. Word is it's my fault for portraying murderous Muslims as murderous Muslims in my novels. I'm supposed to be informed about his identity the moment they know who the guy is. He's not on any database in this country. They've sent fingerprints and pictures out on the wire overseas. If they had let Gus and I get near the body, we'd have learned who it was in an hour if we'd been allowed to take his fingerprints and picture. Once we're updated on the details, we'll find out if he was just another whacko Islamist. He put a new definition on the tag 'book killer'."

"What about Pilgrim's Way Books," Rachel asked.

"They don't want anything to do with Muerto's book signings," Gus said. "I'm betting when they make a tidy sum selling his novels that Muerto will be a welcomed guest once again."

"The book signing was the best," Jean said. "Everyone wanted books. No one even cared about the dead body."

"Oh boy…" Rachel began when Nick's phone rang.

"John?"

"Hey, Nick," John Harding greeted him. "Kabong told us about your book signing just before the news broadcast hit. Anything further on the mutt who attacked you?"

"Not yet. I think it's a solo crazy, but they're all being brainwashed to kill at any provocation. I had Jean and her friend with me so I'm not real happy."

"I can imagine. If you learn it's a wider threat count us in."

"I will, brother. I forgot to tell Kabong when Gus and I called him earlier about going to the sand later this week. Gus and Rachel have your number. If something bad starts here, I'll have them speed dial you Monsters."

"Absolutely. The Pilot Hill landing zone has already been constructed. Denny said it's large enough for a Harrier jet landing. Laredo says it's been a while since he flew a Harrier. We're signed to get a refresher course. It starts in a month. Want to join us?"

"I sure do. Denny didn't waste any time getting the LZ installed. I guess he wants the secret Monster Launch Pad running ASAP, huh?"

"That's the plan. They're finished with the armaments for the Ranger too, including a 'Faraday Cage' shielding all electronics. We may have to plan a cruise soon."

"Count us in. I'll tell Gus. How's the filming going?"

"Very well. Reeducation camp for Nardo proceeded as planned. Lynn and Kabong will be doing final takes tomorrow. Sam and Janie will be there to accept transfer of the prisoner. Call me before you leave for the sand, brother."

"Will do." Nick disconnected, turning to his family and friends. "You probably heard parts of that. They have the Ranger armaments finished, Gus. We may be doing some cruising soon."

"It will take all of us unless we sign on a crew to help. If we all go, we can cruise in safety if everyone pitches in. Issac has experience in the engine room as I do. I'll go over the engine room features. I'll create a list of provisions for possible breakdowns, maintenance, and repairs. I'm not handling the food."

"That's the bad part," Rachel said. "Once you go cruising on a ship like 'Starlight of the Seas' with people waiting on you hand and foot, it's difficult thinking about doing all the work required to keep everyone happy."

"They had everything on the 'Starlight'," Tina agreed. "Count me out. I'm not going cruising with the pirates. We'll be in a war zone I'm sure and it won't be only meals and cleaning we'll be pitching in to do."

"Sonny and I will go," Jean said excitedly. "We don't care about food. We'll clean and do chores. When do we leave? We'll need to board our captured ships with knives in hand!"

"Jean!"

* * *

"We're glad to have you back, Kabong. I have to leave soon." Nick greeted Johnny and Cala at the door. "Thanks for speeding the identification process with Jafar. Did the rest of the filming go okay?"

"Yes, and Lynn says it's the best episode yet. She really listened to my suggestions and acted on them. I have learned much about dialogue from your novels, Muerto."

"Thanks. I'm glad Lynn liked your input."

"As to our targets, Jafar thinks those other three will leave for the Mexican border soon. The one you killed, Gibril Salib, was last listed and seen in a Syrian refugee camp in Jordan, along with his cohorts Chahid Oda, Larbi Ajam, and Malik Naifeh. They left the camp hours before the Jordanian police arrested them for instigating treason against the King. The police in Jordan have since connected them with Isis. The four of them came here from the East Coast to be resettled in San Jose. Jafar believes they picked you as a high profile target. There is a new tactic since the stabbing deaths of the Paris policeman and his wife."

"I've read about it," Nick replied, leading the way into his kitchen. "The lone attacker stabs his target before randomly stabbing bystanders until escaping in the melee. So far, the bastards have gotten away with it. In the bookstore, our security guys would have been afraid to fire in a crowd. They never found the prick's car. That means he had a driver, Johnny, and I think you and Jafar found him."

"Jafar thought of hacking into Pilgrim's Way Books security. All we needed after that was to plug in the time frame through the security company's feed."

Nick chuckled as he served his friends coffee. "They stopped right in front of it with their faces hanging out. We go tonight. You and Cala researching all the known and secret masjids in the area previously sure helped us now."

"Yes. We simply made the rounds when we returned from the north," Cala replied. "We found the van at the second fake masjid near Lover's Point. When Johnny and I first checked it out, we marked it as a terrorist halfway house."

"We won't worry about electronics," Nick said. "We'll use the EMP gun before I go in. I bought a car off of Jerry for this job. When I finish, we'll load them in their own vehicle, drop them off in the valley for prep work before disposal, and give the van and extra car to Jerry for recirculation. He's in all the way and will be awaiting the arrival of both vehicles."

"How do you do these type of break-ins, Muerto?"

Nick shrugged. "I'm an expert locksmith, Cala. Once inside, I kill everything with a heartbeat. Mistakes happen only in hesitation. I wish I could take prisoners tonight for Denny but we can't take the chance this close to my trip to the sand. If I get Al-Saud in a position overseas at my safe-house to do a conference call with Denny, I'll do it. Otherwise, I take care of business and get the hell out of there. Every extra minute I spend on peripherals endangers my helpers. C'mon upstairs. Everyone's up there reliving the bookstore signing through Jean's eyes. We have veggie tray and snacks."

"If all goes well, will we have a morning at the beach with the Irish before you go, Muerto?"

"Absolutely, Johnny."

* * *

Malik Naifeh stirred uncomfortably. He sweated profusely, soaking the sheets around him. Sitting up groggily and throwing off the covers, the light on his nightstand turned on. A masked figure waved at him.

"Hello there. I'm Muerto." Nick sighed while taking off his mask. "Okay... I'm Nick McCarty. Your friend Gibril came to my book signing event with violence in his heart. I drove his nose-bone into his brain. You and your buddies, Chahid and Larbi, must have partied tonight. You all smell of booze. I guess you were all having a wake for poor old Gibril. It made things so much easier for me. I've already fixed them without any bloody mess. I gave you my slower acting liquid killer."

Malik dived for his nightstand drawer only to be stun-gunned to the floor.

"That was stupid, Malik. Did you think I hadn't already found and confiscated all of your weapons?" Nick stun-gunned Malik's groin, causing screams so high in pitch, they only disturbed the dog next door. When Malik could speak again, Nick patted his head. "I really don't want to do that again but time's a wasting. Who put you idiots on me at the bookstore?"

"Fuck you! Arrest me, I-"

This time Nick applied the stun-gun until the already dying Malik passed out. Nick slapped him until he vibrated slowly into shuddering consciousness. Nick switched to Arabic. "Not very smart, Malik. You are dying. You have a couple of hours left before my injection kills you. If you want to spend the entire time having me caress your nuts with the electrodes on my stun-gun then keep playing dumb. Who sent you guys after me?"

Malik began to cry. Nick stun-gunned him again.

"Hello there again," Nick said in Arabic when Malik regained the ability to speak. "Do not bother crying or whining. You are dead. How you pass the next couple of hours is up to you."

Nick lit off the stun-gun, causing a heartfelt yelp of terror from Malik. "Blue arc or peace. Your choice."

"Gibril hated your novels! He suspected you killed Mohammed Dafar in New York!"

Nick laughed. "I get it. He was a Dafar acolyte. Tell me about how you four connected with this shit-hole masjid to hide in. By the way... I did kill Dafar."

"We...we trained in the woods up north," Malik replied dejectedly. "A man named Saran Al-Kadi sent us here to await orders for what we were to do."

Nick relaxed. "Saran's Pilot Hill compound trained you assholes and sent all of you here. Good to know."

368

Nick killed him with a wrench of his head, breaking Malik's neck with a sickening crunch. "We're good to go, guys. Let's load 'em."

Acknowledgement followed Nick's order. Nick dragged Malik down to the entrance, wrapped in his bedding as he'd done with Malik's companions. Minutes after Gus and Johnny entered the house, they carted the three corpses out to the Chevy van, owned by the Elm Masjid. Everything after proceeded as planned, complete with Cala the 'Cleaner' taking charge of the bodies. They delivered the two vehicles marked for cleaning and recertification to Jerry. In the morning, Nick flew their UH-60 stealth helicopter out over the Pacific Ocean where they deposited the remains of their terrorists from the freezer.

Cala handled the controls on the way back as Nick continued her flying lessons. "I am doing well, huh Muerto?"

"You're a natural, Cala, and you have no fear. As Laredo often says, that's a key to piloting anything. Are you ready for lessons, Johnny?"

"No," Johnny admitted from the back next to Gus. "I will stick to learning how to captain our various boats. Gus is going to teach me and Issac maintenance and repair on our different engine configurations too. Laredo has databases and intricate check lists for all the aircraft. He hopes we can be a self-contained strike force without outside help."

"That's a good plan," Nick replied. "In the coming years, I see a need for being under the radar with nearly everything we do. I think we put a dint in the Islamic Trojan Horse. If we could get the government to quit importing the Muslim horde, we could actually make some headway in this war."

"Were you ever tempted to make a hit on an American President," Gus asked.

"Nope. I don't think any tried to kill me like a couple of senators did. Presidents have term limits. I'd rather see regime change at the ballot box, if we can keep the dead people and illegal aliens from voting. I used to think America couldn't be harmed by even a bad President in eight years with the system's checks and balances. I'm not so sure anymore."

"I think you should reconsider having Cala and I come along with you. We both speak fluid Arabic," Johnny mentioned.

"I need to do this alone. I don't want anyone else from here over there, especially you, Johnny. We have you in the clear in the USA, but over there Ebi Zarin is wanted by Interpol and a handful of other law enforcement agencies and secret police. You don't want Cala caught in a dragnet meant to nab the dangerous Zarin."

"True," Johnny admitted. "That would not be good."

"Does Paul know you're doing this," Gus asked.

"Yep. He loaned me a CIA safe-house through Denny's auspices in Dubai for Khalil to stay at until I get there as I told you. I don't want Khalil and his sons to be seen at the Atlantis until they're needed. Khalil believes he can get one of his contacts at the Atlantis to make a keycard to Al-Saud's suite."

"Is this a fact finding mission too?"

"It depends on circumstances, Gus. I agree with what Paul suspects – that Al-Saud knows how the network operates that keeps smuggling the numbers of recruits in at cell compounds like Pilot Hill. He and Al-Kadi were rivals, but I'd wager it has to do with Al-Saud wanting to take over a place like the Pilot Hill compound for his own purposes. He was none too happy about my hint that the federal authorities were all over the compound. There's something I'm missing in all of this. Paul would like to confirm there's not a conduit from Europe we have no clue about. Those recruits at Pilot Hill had first class papers and passports. Paul and I are hoping the same outfit running an identity mill for

Al-Kadi may be supplying Al-Saud's people. Lynn bled Al-Kadi dry. He told Lynn the recruits already had their papers when they reached him. Al-Kadi received his orders anonymously on the Dark Web. His cell was to remain compartmentalized so they couldn't expose the entire network if caught."

"But what about this 'Lone Wolf' attack crap," Gus persisted. "Think about thousands of these bastards spread all around the country after leaving terrorist training depots like Pilot Hill, with no orders or connections once they leave the training compound. They're free to cause havoc like the one trying to kill you, or on a larger scale like San Bernadino."

Nick hesitated, concentrating on Cala's flying. "That's damn good, Gus. They could play into this insanity of stripping away the Second Amendment and disarming the populace in the face of a much larger threat. It's already working after the Orlando massacre. You'd think the idiots running the country and the media would stop playing right into their hands. I like your thinking, Gus. If what you surmise is true, I'm not sure how valuable Al-Saud is, other than a spoke in the terrorist wheel that facilitates whatever he's asked to do."

"It makes sense, Muerto," Johnny agreed. "Would you still like to go down to the Point this morning?"

Nick leaned back in his seat, the enormity of Gus's theory blanketing his imagination far into the future. "I sure would, Johnny. We could be in the middle of this stupid war forever."

      * * *

Nick checked into his suite at the Atlantis without incident. Khalil called him on the satellite phone he brought along for communication only from Khalil. It could not be monitored. "Hello, my friend. I'm checked into the Atlantis."

"We have an opportunity, Nick. Al-Saud has a meeting at the Bab Peshawar Restaurant in Sharjah, after which he will be traveling along Maliha Rd. His destination is the Galb Al Gamar General Trading building."

"Damn! I know that route." Nick closed his eyes picturing from memory the nearly deserted stretch of highway. "There is a Gulf Dynamic Services building along the route. If I can get atop the building with my M107, I can take Al-Saud at a barren spot along the route. How certain are you of the information."

"Very sure. One of my contacts servicing Al-Saud's suite overheard the plans made on the phone. You are very impressive remembering the route and buildings. I could not get the keycard made without suspicions raised. I have our cargo pilot from your last adventure killing people. I promised him a hundred thousand US dollars to fly us out of Sharjah International Airport. Is that satisfactory?"

"You are amazing, brother. It will be perfect if the route pans out. I will meet with Al-Saud tonight and conduct the meeting in a business as usual persona. Tomorrow morning at 2 am, I will position myself on the roof of the Gulf Dynamic building."

"I have a taxi to use. I will be out front in fifteen minutes. Will that be acceptable?"

"With this new information, I would like you to stay away until I need to get into position, unless it is possible for you to bring my Colt to me. What are the chances of taking my Colt inside the Atlantis?"

"Not good, Nick," Khalil answered. "Another problem is that Al-Saud's bodyguards will be armed."

"Then stay away from here until you pick me up at 1 am out front. I will be fine meeting with Al-Saud. He would have no reason to suspect me of anything other than business here in the Atlantis. He'll be okay with the change of plans because I arrived early. I'll convince him the waterpark meeting would be bad for future business. I will go over my plan with you under the new circumstances when I see you later, brother."

"I will see you then, Nick. Good luck."

Nick called Al-Saud immediately after disconnecting from Khalil.

"You are in the hotel. My man saw you arrive," Al-Saud said by way of greeting. "Will you come to my suite or will you require rest?"

"I slept on the plane. I'm actually glad to skip your waterpark meeting. I will shower and be at your suite in twenty minutes."

"That is acceptable. How long will you be staying at the Atlantis?"

"Only until after my business with you is completed. I must travel to Abu Dhabi tomorrow. Do you require me to stay any longer?"

"No. I had hoped to suggest you leave here as soon as possible. Your Arabic is excellent. I can understand why you move so easily in the Middle East. I will see you shortly." Al-Saud disconnected.

Nick took a shower, shaved, and dressed in black slacks and short sleeved black pullover shirt. He prepared himself for anything, knowing he would be with armed enemies, and no way of knowing their intentions. Nick slipped the flash-drive he had made for Al-Saud in his pocket.

* * *

A burly bearded guard in kafi head covering and white robes met Nick at the door with a metal detector wand. Nick lifted his arms, allowing the man to check him for metal, glad now he did not have his Colt. Another guard, similar in stature and appearance to the first stood inside the suite with a smiling Al-Saud near the room's elaborate bar. Nick motioned the guard with him to walk in front of him. The guard looked toward Al-Saud who nodded. The moment they reached the bar, the guard leading him spun with handgun in hand. Nick took it off him before it could be pointed as if the guard was a child. Nick slammed him into the other guard while wrapping an arm around the throat of a very startled Al-Saud with the guard's weapon pointed up under Al-Saud's chin.

"That was not very nice, Rabiah," Nick said. "Do you have a death wish?"

Al-Saud waved off his men in a halting gesture. "You... you are every bit as impressive as I had hoped. Please do not kill me. I will add another hundred thousand dollars to your account for this inconvenience."

"Tell your men to sit on the floor with their backs to the wall and their hands interlocked on their laps. Once they do that, I will shoot you and them in the head if they move. Do you understand, Rabiah?"

"Do as he says! Quickly!"

The guards did as ordered. Nick guided Al-Saud onto a bar stool between him and the bodyguards. "I see you have a laptop on the bar, so you must have thought to check the information I brought you."

Al-Saud shrugged. "I had hoped to speak with you in a more in control position. I know you are now thought of as the most dangerous assassin in the world, especially after killing Al-Kadi. Has his compound truly been taken over by the authorities?"

"It appeared that way from what I heard." Nick retrieved the flash-drive from his pocket, placing it in front of Al-Saud. "Check the drive. Let me know if it is more of what you wanted like the sample I already gave you."

Al-Saud booted the laptop with shaking hands. He inserted the flash-drive. Ten minutes later as he examined the contents, he relaxed, smiling at the screen. "This is excellent, worth every dollar. How shall I make good on your payment?"

"I will contact you when I return to the states. You realize how imperative it is that you make good on the payment if we are to do any future business."

"Yes! Of course. I would never betray a valued professional like yourself. I may have much work for you in the future, Nick. May I call you Nick?"

"Sure. I believe that concludes our business. I will be keeping your guard's weapon. Please walk me to the door, Rabiah."

"It...it is my pleasure and yes... keep the weapon." Al-Saud walked Nick to the door and opened it for him.

Nick stepped around Al-Saud and outside the suite. He put what he recognized as a Caracal 9mm handgun inside his belt under his shirt. "I need not tell you to stay away from me and keep your men away too, do I?"

"No, Nick. We will stay away from you completely. Good day to you. May Allah bless you."

"Good day." Nick closed the door. He smiled and walked quickly back to his room. It was time to rest for his task ahead.

* * *

Nick greeted his old friend with a hug. "It is good to see you once again, brother."

Khalil beamed, his features an open book as to how he felt about Nick. "My sons will see you after the chore. Let us drive toward our destination while you explain everything you have in mind for this ambush."

The two men entered Khalil's taxi. As Khalil drove away from the Atlantis, he glanced over curiously at Nick. "How did your meeting with Al-Saud proceed? I feared for you."

Nick quickly explained what happened with Khalil enjoying the interlude immensely. "Al-Saud I am sure needed to change his pants after your meeting, Nick. Is it true you killed Felix Moreau?"

"Yes. It led to a complication I had to take care of too."

"Moreau was a bad one. How is it you wish to do this?"

Nick took out his iPad from the small bag he brought with him. "Park at the roadside when it is convenient."

Khalil did so and Nick showed him the map of Sharjah. "I like this spot. It is barren of anything at the roadsides. I want you, Asim, and Ghazi a hundred yards before it. When I stop Al-Saud's vehicle, you will need to move quickly. I have learned it may not be necessary or even prudent to take Al-Saud prisoner. If you get to his vehicle and he is still alive, leave him so, and drive to me with both your vehicle and his. I will be off the roof in short order. We will then drive to the safe-house. Is Vinny waiting for our call at the airport?"

"Yes. He awaits our arrival no matter how long it takes. Al-Saud's vehicle will be bullet proof, my friend."

Nick grinned. "Nothing is bullet proof. The loads for the M107 I sent you are high velocity, depleted uranium .50 caliber hollow point slugs. His vehicle will be stopped."

"This will be a very long shot," Khalil pointed out.

"It can't be helped. All will be well. Did you bring the grappling gear I asked for?"

"Yes. It is old school though. You will have to leave it behind."

"Understood."

* * *

Nick checked his field of fire after positioning the M107 tripod stand solidly overlooking the Maliha Rd. His night vision scope, set to the coordinates he determined from his range finders, focused on the small stretch of road he had in mind. He then checked where Khalil and his sons were parked at the roadside.

"You are perfect there. Mark it, and you three can leave until it is time for Al-Saud to do his final drive."

"We will stay, my friend," Khalil said. "This is our last adventure before our move to be Swiss citizens. All is set in place. I do not want the unexpected to ruin everything."

"Understood. We wait then, my friends – predators in the dark."

Khalil chuckled. "You cannot resist the turn of phrase even when not writing."

"I guess so," Nick admitted. *I'm becoming a caricature of myself – what a rube.*

* * *

At nearly 9 am in the morning, the Malihu Rd. was still clear. Nick heard Khalil in his ear.

"He has rounded the bend onto Malihu just now, Nick!"

"On it. Rest easy and be ready."

Nick settled in behind the M107, the air around him beginning to heat but with no wind or even a breeze. Al-Saud's limousine grew in the cross hairs of his scope. The moment the vehicle reached Nick's chosen spot, a straightaway section of barren road, the first pad of Nick's index finger tightened on the trigger. He fired a three round burst through the driver's seated

377

form and a three round burst into the man next to him. The limousine slowed, drifting to a small crevice at the roadside.

"Clear, Khalil! One person in the back. Both men are dead in the front. I will watch but arm yourselves."

"Understood."

Nick watched Khalil's taxi streak to a halt next to the limousine. Khalil and his sons approached the vehicle with weapons drawn. Nick grinned as Al-Saud stumbled out of the backseat, blubbering and begging, with his hands bowing into the dirt. They restrained him and threw Al-Saud into the backseat once again with Asim next to him. Khalil and Ghazi rearranged the front seat. A blanket was thrown over the bloody seat. Khalil drove the limousine while Ghazi followed in the taxi. *Denny's going to be pleased with this.*

At the safe-house, Nick cleaned the limousine while a terrified Al-Saud was watched by Khalil and sons. When Nick was satisfied, he went inside to shower and shave. He joined his companions where they sat at the kitchen table. "That went very well, my friends. Did you contact Vinny?"

"Yes," Khalil said. "He filed the flight plan as requested for Doha in Qatar. Are you sure we can get out of there, Nick?"

"Absolutely. My boss is so happy, he's deploying the fifth fleet near enough to send a plane for us. It's time for your family to immigrate to Switzerland. Your family, due to being Christians and well off, along with the USA's recommendation, will be accepted."

Khalil hugged Nick. "God bless you!"

"You have my number if there's any problems. I look forward to visiting one day, my friend."

"You will be most welcome!"

* * *

Denny met Nick as he exited his plane ride aboard the USS Truman aircraft carrier with a restrained Al-Saud. The two men shook hands while walking toward the island structure.

"Damn, Nick… this is incredible. Al-Saud will be invaluable within my cloistered group of terrorist advisors."

Nick gestured at the now arrogant looking Al-Saud. "He thinks this is picnic time where he can remain quiet while waiting for special treatment, halal meals, prayer rugs, and servants to wipe his ass. This is what happens when there's no instant training. He was on his way to meet someone when I nabbed him. Rabi didn't want to tell me who and we didn't have time to play together in the sand. I have no dog in the hunt because I don't think he knows much about whatever I'd be interested in. I figured everyone can share in the fortunes he's stashed away. He's all yours."

Denny grinned. "I brought along the cure for his reluctance, just in case there's something near on the horizon."

Lynn Montoya Dostiene walked out of the hatch at the side of the island with a big smile and her three minions alongside. "Nick! You look good after your sandbox excursion."

Surprised, Nick hugged her and shook hands with the minions: Sylvio Ruelas, Gus Denova, and Quays Tannous. "It's great seeing you all. I'll leave my buddy, Rabiah in your capable hands. I'm a little tired of his company."

Lynn pinched the red-faced Al-Saud's cheek. "We're going to have such fun!"

Nick patted Al-Saud on the back as the minions took charge of him. "Sucks to be you."

The End

Future Nick and Jean Bonus Story IV

Connecting Threads

Benny watched the approaching gangbangers near his high school's front gate with regret. He understood everything within his new world of family, friends, education, love, caring, and best of all: hope. Benny also remembered what put him in a crack-house as a young teenaged victim. He knew the young men approaching him shared his similar origins and race, but they shared nothing else within his soul. Benny felt empathy for doomed souls as he had experience with hopelessness. He had been practically raised in a crack-house before his new family plucked him out of it. The reason he fit so well with his new family drew from many deep wells, but lack of fear topped the list. Beaten, starved, used as a sex slave, Benny had done everything requested for his own survival. When rescued from his putrid former life with matter-of-fact extreme violence, kindness, and people he could count on, the life changing event allowed the real soul of Benny to surface. Like his new Dad told him when he adopted Benny – 'I offer you only a chance at a life with honor but you'll have to work for it, Benny'. Benny remembered smiling at Nick McCarty, the most dangerous living entity he had ever met, with hope and saying, 'I will do anything for such a chance, Sir'. Nick had shook his hand with firm promise, 'welcome to the family, kid'.

Benny waited for the 'bangers because he knew this would have to be taken care of. Otherwise, kids at his high school, and innocent future victims of these vicious young thugs would be part of an unending list stretching into the future. Benny waited for them with relaxed patience as his new Dad had taught him. He knew the punks approaching couldn't hurt him worse than he had been hurt in the past without killing him. He smiled and waved as they stopped in front of him.

"Hi, guys."

Benny's greeting, met with the clichéd derision of young male predators without guidance, honor, respect, or more importantly human compassion or empathy. It went on for a few moments of snickering laughs and hand gestures of dismissal. Benny waited with patience and awareness as taught by his Dad. He watched for disappearing hands or sudden motions with relaxed watchfulness.

The leader of the underwear showing crew pranced from side to side towards Benny with shoulder popping smoothness, making condescending hand gestures at Benny. "I get it... I get it. You too stupid to know not to face up with us, Benny. We don't make exceptions for retards. Your sissy ass ours now! I warned you!"

Benny decided instantly there would be no avoiding of this interaction. "I have a tag name like you do now, Squiggy."

Hearing the laughs at his expense from his own crew, Squiggy denied and deflected as imagined. "Man... I ain't no Squiggy, you cheap ass 'ho! Shut the fuck up! I plan to make you scream, pussy!"

Benny smiled without moving as the aforementioned Squiggy jived in front of him with arm, hand, and finger gestures gone wild. Benny held up his hands in a placating fashion. "Calm down. What is it you guys want anyway? I know you hate my guts for some reason. Let's negotiate. I want to go to school and do well. If you let me, we can all just get along."

"See!" Squiggy stabbed Benny with a forefinger. "We told you to find another school, B! We don't want your 'stick up the ass' shit in our school! You feel me, rocket?!"

"My Dad wants me to go to school at Pacific Grove High School. My sister graduated from here."

"Too fuckin' bad. We heard about your ol' fuckin' man. He supposed to be a bad dude. We got that covered, homey. We pop him like a bad pimple. You reported us. That means a death sentence!"

Knowing you're wasting your time reasoning with someone did not enter into Benny's consciousness. He had no fear, and he had no hesitation to speak his mind. "My Dad would like you to also stop dealing drugs in and around the school. I asked him to let me convey the message to you so as to avoid violence."

It took many minutes for Squiggy and his gang to stop enjoying Benny's declaration.

"So...so... you come here to face off?" Squiggy launches into another snorting, jiving appreciation of Benny. "You stone cold dumb, B! You think you a loner bad ass, huh?"

Benny shrugged. He gestured at the approaching people at his back. "I'm not alone. This is my sister Jean, and brothers Sonny and Quinn. That's our dog Sammy next to her."

It was then Squiggy and his crew noticed the scarred blonde woman approaching with two huge guys bracketing her. A lean, white, longhaired dog strode panther like at the blonde's side. Squiggy glanced back and nodded at one of the guys in the rear. He reached into his hoodie. The dog streaked into him, jaws clamping and tearing at the reaching arm, while crushing him to the pavement. Sammy glanced at Benny who held a hand in a leveling gesture. Sammy held in place.

"Anyone else reaches, I pin their hand to their chest," Jean said.

"With what, bitch?" Squiggy reached.

No one saw the knife emerge or take flight with power. Squiggy felt something thud into his hand. He staggered backward, glancing down to see a knife handle protruding from the back of his right reaching hand, pinned into his chest. He screamed. Jean strolled forward and yanked the knife free with a vicious arm and hand movement, leaving Squiggy to fall on his rear end in shock. Squiggy clutched the wounded hand in place at his bleeding chest. Jean, Sonny, and Quinn moved amongst Squiggy's crew.

"On your knees, kiddies," Jean ordered. "We're not the cops. Do as you're told or we shoot you all in the head."

Quinn flipped Sammy's takedown victim over as if he were a ragdoll and frisked him with professional thoroughness. Sonny threw other reluctant members of Squiggy's crew onto their faces if they didn't get on their knees. Jean focused on Squiggy holding his damaged hand tight against his chest wound.

"We were asked by a police friend of ours to look in on your drug operation here at the high school, shit-for-brains. Our brother Benny attends here. My Dad wants this stopped. We're going to call the cops to pick you idiots up. We'll be filing charges according to what they find on you thugs at the entrance to a school."

Squiggy sat straighter, sweating and feeling the pain. "Bitch... you better-"

"Shut-up, stupid!" Jean grabbed Squiggy's hair, shaking his head violently. "Don't make threats, shit-head! We take them personally. I'll carve the nose off your face if you're still stupid enough to make dumbass statements!"

Squiggy saw death appear as Jean flipped open the knife that had taken him down. He began rubbing his inner right leg. "I...I'm done."

The fifty caliber hollow point slug splattered Squiggy's compatriots behind him with blood, brain, and skull material. Jean straightened, her arms gesturing at the sky above. "What the hell, Dad?"

"Check the inside of his right leg he was rubbing, Daughter of Darkness."

Jean's mouth tightened as she stayed silent while checking Squiggy's right leg while enduring her siblings' suppressed amusement. "Damn it... I... oh crap."

Dead Squiggy strapped a hideaway .32 caliber automatic at his ankle. The .50 caliber shot had scattered the crowd forming to check out the confrontation. Squiggy's crew knelt unmoving with hands locked behind their heads as ordered. The kill shot removed any rebellious behavior they had been contemplating. Jean frowned as her Mom's chuckling enjoyment of the missed firearm sounded loud and clear over their networked coms.

"You didn't need a spotter for this, Dad," Jean mumbled as they stripped weapons and drugs off the kneeling gangbangers.

"Apparently, I did. I'm sure you would have beat him down before he shot you in the head, but I couldn't take the chance," Nick replied.

"You were toast, you scarred up little turd," Rachel zapped Jean. "What did you think the guy was doing, counting his toes?"

"If things were like when I was a kid, Dad would be in prison, Trailer-trash."

"We wouldn't take a gig like this under those rules of engagement, Viper," Nick said as sirens sounded in the distance. "Neil will be there himself. The school's been terrorized by those punks for a long time. We can't have Benny caught in a crossfire at the school. Don't forget to show your ID's if Neil isn't first on scene."

"We will," Jean said. "Thanks."

"That's why I'm here, kid. Good job."

Benny finished taking pictures and digital fingerprints with Sammy at his side. When the first police cruiser drove onto the scene with sirens blaring, Jean, Sonny, and Quinn had their FBI and US Marshall credentials out. The police were briefed about the operation by their Chief, but as Nick surmised, it would be a mistake not to make sure the first on scene police officers did not see any weapons in evidence. The two officers kept lights flashing but turned off the siren. The young woman police officer left the passenger seat, saw Squiggy's corpse and went for her weapon. Jean sighed but kept hands in the air as did her companions. Benny kept Sammy behind him. The woman's older partner, a man in his mid-forties, called out to her.

"Suz! These are the FBI agents the Chief explained would be handling this sting. Don't draw on them!"

"This is nuts, Jim! They blew that kid's head off! What kind of crap is that?" Suz moved around her door with weapon now pointing at Jean. "You four get on your knees. I don't give a shit what kind of ID's you have!"

Jim looked closer at the dead Squiggy before moving over to Jen with a cautioning hand. "They didn't kill him, Suz! They have backup."

Suz glanced at her partner. "What are you talking about? They're-"

"We have a sniper in place, Officer Bently," Jean interrupted. "The perp on the ground went for an ankle gun. Our sniper killed him. You know how dangerous this area is nowadays. We don't take chances when asked in on an operation."

"Get on the ground." Bently walked in on Jean.

With a twisting hand grip move too fast for Bently to see, Jean was holding her weapon. Sonny made a calming gesture at her partner who nodded. Jean popped the clip and cleared the chamber. She then jammed it into Bently's holster with attitude before handing the stunned officer the clip.

"Put this in your breast pocket and don't touch your weapon again." Jean patted Bently's shoulder. "I made a mistake today too. I didn't frisk the dead guy like I should have. That's why he's dead. My companions and I are with a special branch of the Justice Department. We have credentials with the FBI and the US Marshal's office. Your Chief knows us very well. Let's wait for him, huh? I'm US Marshal Jean Salvatore. This is my husband, US Marshal Sonny Salvatore, and my brother, US Marshal Quinn McCarty. I've worked with you before, haven't I, Officer Furlough?"

"I think so," Jim Furlough held out his hand to Jean who shook it. "The 'Posse' gang bust, right?"

"That's the one," Jean acknowledged.

"Your Dad... ah... Nick McCarty. He's a good friend of the Chief's and he's your backup sniper, isn't he?" Furlough turned to Bently. "Jean saved your life, Suz. Her old man holds badges with every agency in existence. He's like his kid here, he prefers US Marshal McCarty. The 'Posse' drew down on us with automatic weapons. McCarty killed every 'banger that reached. His two partners, Nason and Groves arrived with a woman they called 'Cleaner' to take the gang into custody. I think they were illegal aliens because I never heard anything about the gang after that. Did they get extradited?"

"Ah... yeah, they did," Jean lied. *To hell maybe and Cleaner Cala's freezer.* "Listen, we don't have to tell the Chief about Bently's misunderstanding, right Jim?"

A look of relief flashed over Furlough and Bently's faces. "Nope. Thanks for your understanding, Jean. I see you've corralled this lot with weapons and drugs."

"They confronted our inside source, my brother Benny. He has all the weapons bagged with the drugs each perp had on him. They've all been digitally fingerprinted and recorded with what they carried along with their pictures. It's all been sent to Chief Dickerson's private e-mail file. Benny will testify at any trial if the DA doesn't get them to plead out. We'll back him."

"How do you people get away with this?" Officer Bently, still stung by the way Jean easily disarmed her, couldn't let the incident fade. "You could be charged with-"

"Shut up!" Jean held a cautioning hand in Bently's direction. "A thank you would have been fine, but since you're too stupid to put this into perspective, just hold your tongue until Chief Dickerson gets here. You're beginning to bore me."

Red faced, Bently surged toward Jean. Her partner missed his holding attempt. Jean finger locked the officer to her knees, exerting pressure until Bently cried out. Jean smiled. She decided a more impressive lesson was needed.

"Jean," Sonny murmured quietly. Jean paused at the sound of her husband's voice, but incrementally increased pressure while trying to calm the heat inside.

"Daughter of Darkness!" Rachel's voice ended Jean's lesson. "She's a cop. We don't hurt cops, you ninny."

Jean released Bently and helped her up, wishing she could mouth about ten insults on her Mom while doing it. "Chief Dickerson will be here shortly. Go over by your patrol car, Officer Bently. If you stay here, I will arrest you for impeding a federal investigation and case."

Bently eyeballed Jean, rubbing circulation back into her hand.

Sonny walked forward with a hand in cautioning manner. "Please do as Jean says. Your meat wagon and the Chief will be here shortly. We're not your enemy. The only action Marshal McCarty had was to kill this young man before he turned his hideaway weapon on us. Quinn? Escort Officer Bently over to her patrol car."

Quinn grinned at Bently as he moved to do Sonny's bidding. "C'mon, Suz. The only thing that could happen here is Jean kicking the crap out of you. We're here to help, not get into fights with police officers."

Quinn's voice had a soothing effect on Bently, who looked up at the six and a half foot tall Quinn's lean features with an acknowledging nod. She let him lead her over to the patrol car. Furlough moved nearer the still kneeling gang members who Benny had motioned Sammy over to watch.

Furlough gestured at Squiggy's crew with exasperation. "This shit happens on an increasing basis here. Pacific Grove was a tourist's favorite destination, where we literally used to only have a mild theft arrest or disorderly conduct charge. For the last decade gang intrusions mixed with the escalating terrorist refugee problems have turned a simple tourist city into a small war zone at times. Ah… here comes the Chief."

Chief Neil Dickerson had already left his vehicle and driver with the Monterey County Coroner's vehicle and an incarceration arrest vehicle right behind it. Neil walked with an annoyed persona straight for Officer Bently, standing next to Quinn by her squad car. She straightened as Dickerson neared them.

"What the hell didn't you understand about aid and assist these federal agents, Bently?! Marshal McCarty called me on the way over here to let me know you aimed a weapon at his daughter. You're damn lucky she took it off you before he blew your head off! From now until the end of time you make sure you follow my orders to the letter when I ask in a federal intervention. We have these scum now that have been terrorizing the school and surrounding area. Marshal McCarty's son, Benny recorded the entire event as bait to draw this gang in front of the school with weapons and drugs."

Dickerson put a hand over his head in a thought gathering process while Quinn grinned at the mortified Bently. The Chief waved a hand finally in dismissive fashion. "How close, Quinn?"

"With Mom spotting, probably a heartbeat. She doesn't take kindly to Jean getting drawn on. I think Officer Bently understands we don't exactly operate within local police guidelines, Chief. We all make mistakes. Jean didn't frisk the leader, having already wounded him. Dad had to kill him. The little gangster went for a hideaway at his ankle."

"Oh shit! Rachel was spotting for Nick. Good Lord, Bently! I should put you on administrative leave. You've used all your luck up on this one. Stay here with Quinn until I sort the rest of this out."

"Yes, Sir," Bently answered.

Chief Dickerson walked over to the scene where the last of the gangbangers were being loaded into the detainee vehicle. The coroner worked quickly around the aforementioned Squiggy, completing his analysis quickly before his two assistants loaded the body for transport. The coroner, Donald Waverly, gave Dickerson a small wave of acknowledgement.

"He's dead, Neil."

Dickerson enjoyed that pronouncement for a moment. "Thanks Don for arriving so quickly. I'll get the first responder reports and my own observations to you before the end of the day."

"No hurry. I've handled Marshal McCarty's sniper backup operations before. A head shot with his .50 caliber M107 leaves very little need to puzzle over cause of death." Waverly knelt next to Sammy, stroking the dog's head. "Damn. I remember this big mutt when he was a small ball of fur yapping around your ankles, Benny."

"Yes Sir, Sammy's all grown up and super-smart," Benny said.

Waverly moved toward his vehicle with a wave. "Good seeing you all. Tell your Dad and Mom hi for me, Jean."

"Will do," Jean answered. "Take care, Don."

"Take Bently and follow the meat wagon, Jim," Dickerson told the officer.

Jean turned her attention to the Chief then. She shrugged. "I screwed up a little, Uncle Neil."

"So I heard. Thanks for not ending Bently. I heard from Quinn it was close."

"Yeah… it was. The second mistake we made was not just following her order to kneel until you arrived. She pissed me off. I nearly got her killed and I did get Squiggy killed."

"The right one got dead, kid. I asked you all in on this. Thanks to Benny, we'll be ending this damn invasion of the school. I didn't know what else to do. Everyone griped and complained but no one had the backup to bring this bunch down. Did Gus and John observe?"

Jean pointed over at a window tinted SUV across the street. The driver's side window opened and Gus Nason waved at Dickerson. "Cleaner's in the back too. We weren't sure if we could pull this off the way we hoped."

Dickerson gave Gus, John and Cala a quick smiling salute before Gus drove away. "I will let your Dad know if the DA screws this bust up in court. Any ideas on your newest venture with Harding's crew from the Bay?"

Jean glanced at Sonny, trying not to let the startled feeling at Dickerson's words reach her features. Sonny shrugged. She turned again to Neil. "Dad briefed you about that, Uncle Neil?"

"Nick knows I'd cut my own tongue out rather than betray him. He informed me because Santa Cruz County is in the neighborhood and no one is certain when they will strike. Your Dad told me… hey… do you have Nick in your ear?"

Jean shook her head. "Mom and Dad know Gus, John, and Cala are with us. They packed it in. We're meeting at Otter's Point when we finish. You're invited."

"I can't. I'm staying on this gangbanger bust to the end. Anyway, Nick told me there are as many as a hundred Middle East refugees operating in a hidden compound behind a ranch front along Glen Haven Road, building a small town with new arrivals every day. It's meant to be one of those No-Go Zones where they plan to install their own guards and Sharia Law, complete with training facility. He put me on alert in case I get word of anything happening suspiciously down here. I put out a vague alert to the Carmel and Monterey departments so we could exchange any hint of attacks or suicide bombings. It's tough though. We're hanging on by a thread as tourist retreats. I hope to hell you all end them. I'm sick of this shit."

"I hear you," Jean replied. "We're discussing finalization on our joint action. John Harding, along with Clint and Lynn Dostiene are meeting us to discuss a way to proceed. As usual we have to map out the collateral damage in some politically correct format. It's either that or a kill mission. You're not the only one sick of this Sharia Law No-Go Zones like Dearbornistan. Dad and Harding tackled a No-Go Zone near Santa Clara when I was a kid. The Muslims of the Americas tried to begin an enclave there with Sharia Law posters and copied Dearborn, Michigan's creeping jihad idea of incrementally seizing control of an area."

"Nick said this bunch have kept their recruitment completely under the radar," Neil replied. "He told me they built the gated community with armed guards."

"During their undercover building project, some of the Santa Cruz County's stranger inhabitants began disappearing," Sonny said. "Since it has happened in that area before, it took multiple disappearances before anyone in authority paid any attention. Inquiries to the Santa Cruz County Sheriff's Department drew Clint and Lynn's attention. They're the early warning system for Harding's crew involving Muslim jihadist activity."

"Dad found out from Clint that they plan to keep expanding separating walls, along with making the inner compounds impervious to most conventional weapons. Once Clint alerted Harding's tech guy, Jafar, they coordinated an attack on the so called community of Ramoi until Jafar infiltrated every communication sent, received, and shared there. Those creepy munchkins, as Cala calls them, think they have the makings of a new Caliphate out of the public eye."

"The Michigan militias are still fighting to control Dearbornistan and the surrounding enclaves there," Quinn said. "At some point we're going to need a more substantive action in the big Muslim population zones. Half of their population are still playing the wait and see card. They aren't assimilated Americans. They're waiting for the opportunity to jump on the dying corpse of America the moment their brethren lie and murder their way to our destruction. The government won't intercede on a large scale, nor will the authorities in charge locally."

"Jean, is it okay if I walk Sammy down to Otter's Point from here," Benny asked. "He needs a longer outing and walk."

Jean hugged her adopted brother. "You did great today, Benny. Sure… go ahead. I'll keep my com unit in. You do the same. Dad would bite my head off if I didn't take precautions like he used to."

"Absolutely," Benny said with a grin. "Nice seeing you, Uncle Neil."

"Take care, Benny." Neil watched Benny and one of the most savage dogs he'd ever seen in action walk away. "Great kid. What the hell ever got into Nick to suddenly adopt a child of the abyss? That place you all hit to get Benny and those thugs was a hell-hole."

Jean shrugged. "Same as Dad adopting Sammy the Werewolf. His hunches are scary good."

Neil chuckled. "Sammy the Werewolf, huh? It fits him. I knew Nick would miss Deke's passing too much not to adopt a replacement. Benny and Sammy are like they're joined at the hip."

"More true than you think," Quinn agreed. "If we ever wanted to discipline Benny, we'd have to shoot Sammy with a tranquilizer dart."

"You're right about Deke's passing. It hit Dad harder than Mom and me. Deke was his beer buddy for over a decade. You saw the contraption Dad made for Deke when his hind legs gave out to arthritis. Dad would still carry Deke upstairs to our ocean viewing room he writes in."

"Yep. The damn dogs thread into our lives so tightly we can't think of them as anything else but a family member. Call me if you need anything on this new venture. I will call Nick if I hear anything related to the latest menace created by idiot politicians."

"Will do, Uncle Neil." Jean hugged Neil. He shook hands with Sonny and Quinn. "Tell Bently no hard feelings, okay?"

"Sure thing. I think she wants to have Quinn's baby, so it may all work out anyway." Neil walked away chortling over his Quinn zinger.

"What were you doing over there with Officer Bently, young man?" Jean posed in her Rachel imitation with hands on hips.

Quinn watched Chief Dickerson walk away with a contemplative look on his face. After Jean bopped him in the back of the head, he returned his attention to his sister. He held a torn paper in his hand. "She gave me her phone number. Neil must have noticed, although I thought we were alone when she did it. Uncle Neil hangs out with Dad too much."

"Maybe Harding's daughter Al is coming with them to visit," Jean said. "She's still single. You've always had a crush on her."

"Yeah... when I was five," Quinn replied. "Al's engaged. You've seen the pictures. If she comes it will be to hang out with you and Sonny. After all the adventures you three had, she has a great time showing you her knife skills, or spotting and sniping, that improve from each succeeding visit. After she got her law degree and became an FBI agent, Al likes to rag us with the fact we were issued our credentials."

"Let's go hit the beach," Sonny said. "I doubt Al will want to be around any talk of a black op, kill mission. Enough about Al. Who shadows Benny from here? He's out of sight."

"I'll do it," Quinn volunteered. "I haven't jogged yet today. I'll pace him down to the beach. With Sammy, I'm not sure tailing him is even necessary, but if something happened to him after an op like this, Dad and Mom would beat us like monk penitents."

"Okay, but you keep your earwig in too, Kong," Jean ordered.

Quinn smiled. "I will. Do you think I should call Suz, Sis?"

"We could use a police contact. One that's banging my brother would do."

"Nicely put, Hon," Sonny said as Quinn laughed and jogged off. "I bet you're anxious to see Lynn again. She's going to be a Grandma soon when Clint Jr. and Mia have their son this month. I bet you're wondering if it will mellow her out or not."

Jean snorted in derision. "Grandma Cruella mellowing out? That'll be the day. She'll have the kid doing knife tricks before he's two. Lynn and Mom have been friends ever since the 'Starlight' op. Clint Jr.'s Godfather Lucas nearly came unglued when Clint Jr. joined the Corps. He's in the reserves now same as Quinn. That was a shock when Clint Jr. and Mia fell in love. They married right after high school when Jr joined the Corps. When he asked Jafar and Samira's daughter Mia to marry him, it turned out to be the 'Monster' event of the year when they got hitched. What a party. Mia's like John Harding's wife Lora, she wants no part of the 'Monster' squad work."

Jean and Sonny walked over to their vehicle, hand in hand. "Have you been taking much heat from Rachel about grandkids?"

Jean shrugged. Nearing thirty, Jean's biological clock only recently kicked in a little. "Is the sky blue? Is water wet? I give Mom purpose in life. I'm not ready. I know Lynn did it in her mid-thirties, and killed people the night Clint Jr. was born. She's a legend. I don't know if I'm ready for legendary status. Are you getting antsy?"

Sonny made Jean stop, launching into a kiss beyond passion, love, and petty problems about other people's perspective on their lives. When he pulled away gently, Sonny saw everything in Jean's eyes making all life matters a small thing. "That's what I'm talkin' about. I don't get anything, including antsy, when I'm around you, you scarred up little turd."

Jean giggled at her Mom's familiar taunt. "I'll keep it in mind. I wonder how many Irish Dad will have before we get to the beach."

"None," Sonny answered, slipping into the driver's seat. "He won't have a taste before we're all together on the beach."

"Yep. His favorites, Benny and Sammy, are out in harm's way."

* * *

A half dozen young teens Benny recognized blocked his progress down the sidewalk with Sammy out of nowhere. Benny immediately signaled Sammy down with the flat of his hand. He tried a smile.

"Hi guys. Nice day to tool around after school, huh?"

"We heard you Narced some friends of ours, Benny boy," the lead guy said, pulling a knife out. "We was watchin', home boy. That can't go down. We need product at the school and you just shut our asses down."

Benny measured the teens in front of him with the same perceptive eye he gauged any confrontation in life since being trained by his Dad. Except for the leader, the others were run-of-the-mill high school thugs. The leader, Bart Crowelly, did his best each day to provoke Benny, but failed to get more than a smile.

"Don't even think about putting your mutt on us," Bart warned. "We'll kill him."

"No, you won't," Quinn said, jogging into the middle of Bart's crew. "If Benny gives Sammy the attack order, there won't be anything left of you punks but pieces."

The crew backed away from the huge Marine. One at the rear tried to stab Quinn after stepping to the side. Quinn caught the hand and broke it at the wrist with a side-hand strike, leaving the hand to hang by skin and the knife clattering to the pavement. Quinn smashed the knife wielder across the face with the back of his hand, sending him catapulting to his back. Quinn pointed at Bart. "Benny wants you, prick. I'm going to frisk you. Move, and I have Sammy frisk you. You don't want that, partner. The rest of you lock your hands behind your heads. Anyone that doesn't gets what Mack the Knife got."

Bart's crew did as instructed. Bart stood stock still, looking down at Quinn's gasping for breath Mack the Knife, trying to get enough breath from his meeting with the pavement to breathe and grip his useless hand. Quinn relieved Bart of everything, throwing the cache into a pile. Bart carried a 9mm Taurus automatic at his back. All the new colored pills being hawked to the young and clueless were in a plastic bag in Bart's hoodie, along with a switchblade knife. Disarmed, Bart tried the outraged attitude.

"You can't do this! A lawyer would eat you alive over this."

Quinn smiled, while Benny made a hand gesture to Sammy. The dog leaped to guard the crew with teeth bared and drooling growl. "I'm not a lawyer. Benny's talked to me about you, shit-head. He worked the sting to get your suppliers. We have them in custody. Benny had it in mind to fix you after finishing with the bust. He's all yours, Benny."

Grinning, Benny moved around Bart with the sudden look of a predator. "I've listened to you porking me at school all this time, Crowelly. Here I am. My brother Quinn won't interfere. He knew I dreamed about a meeting between us once we busted your suppliers. When I get done with you I promise you won't want anymore."

Crowelly began crouching into a fighting stance, but Benny moved with lightning speed to drop and leg whip Bart to the pavement. He rolled atop the prone Crowelly with devastating elbow strikes turning Bart's face into bloody mush. Benny didn't quit until Bart began sobbing and crying. Benny straightened away from his foe.

Quinn watched with an older brother's pride. "Nice. Feel better, Ben?"

Benny nodded, never taking his eyes off of Bart. All the school hallway baiting and bullying had left a mark. They called Crowelly 'Black Bart' at the school because of his color and tactics. Benny was black too, but he cared not at all for the race rage at the school. He knew Crowelly to be one of its prominent instigators. Benny kicked Bart in the side, cracking a rib, and eliciting a scream from Crowelly. Benny remembered the first lesson Nick taught him – never let your adversary up. Make sure if you get him down, he stays down, and if he lives, he remembers the moment for the rest of his life.

Quinn turned to the rest. "Strip down to your underwear and do it quickly. Anyone still clothed when I count to ten gets their faces rearranged."

Quinn began counting. In seconds the crew were again standing with fingers interlocked behind their heads in their underwear. Quinn gathered weapons and drugs from each stack of clothing. He moved over to Mack the Knife and finished the gang frisk. Benny and Sammy watched his back every moment. Quinn stood in front of the crew after stashing the weapons and drugs in Benny's backpack.

"Our business is done, kiddies. Here's the deal. Take your drug dealing crap the hell away from the school and never look cross-eyed at my brother Benny. Break the deal and we come for you one final time. We will blow your houses up and kill everything you've ever known. This isn't a police action. We'll turn your lives into a kill zone. This is your only warning. Help your asshole friends to their feet and get the hell out of my sight. I don't care if you have to drag them. Do it or die!"

The crew hurriedly dragged their leader and knife wielding cohort to their feet. They never paused as they half dragged and carried Bart and Mack the Knife along the sidewalk.

"Thanks, Quinn," Benny said. "I thought I'd have to let Sammy kill someone."

"Sis sent me as you and Sammy are Dad's favorites," Quinn joked, shoulder hugging Benny.

"She said exactly that... didn't she?"

"Yep."

"Why do you think Dad does kind of go easy on me and Sammy?"

"He loves projects. Once he takes them on, he rides the wave into the rocks. Make sure he never reaches the rocks, kid."

"I hear you, brother." Sammy fell into line next to Benny with nose near his hand. "School will be interesting after this."

"We'll be there for patrol, Ben. Sis knows follow-up has to be done for a few days until we scope out the situation. If we left anything to chance we'd have to deal with Trailer Trash Momma."

Benny laughed, clapping his hands. "Oh my God... Mom had Dad this morning. Every time she pins her hair back, opens her blouse, and does the Trailer Trash opening... oh my... I start laughing so hard I miss what the heck she's going off on."

"Clarice Salvatore is running for city council. She asked Dad for a donation to her campaign fund. Sometimes I think Dad makes this stuff up so he can get Momma going," Quinn replied. "Unfortunately, I checked at Sis's insistence. Clarice is running."

"Oh God," Benny came to a stop, shaking his head. "Mom will have a stroke if Clarice gets on the city council. Dad's one of the most dangerous men alive, and even he wouldn't have the balls to donate to Clarice's campaign fund."

"If you hadn't run out of the kitchen you big girl you would have heard Dad calming Mom down with the promise to donate to anyone with the most chance of beating her. We can't get involved in this. We'll have to rally around Brother Sonny."

Benny started walking again. "Sonny would never back his Mom or Dad in anything. I believe like Mom. I think they stole Sonny out of a baby cart at the hospital. We know Phil and Clarice. Those two are the most toxic human beings I've ever seen and I was raised in a crack-house."

This time it was Quinn who had to stop as he was enjoying Benny's statement with Benny grinning at him. "Don't... don't repeat that ace, Ben."

"I won't. Sonny's the best. I feel uncomfortable when Mom goes off on Sonny's parents. I know he shares her feelings about them as people. I think they do love him though."

"I don't know about that." Quinn walked along shaking his head. "They tried to use him in everything under the sun as a prop. You're right in that Phil and Clarice probably love him as much as two sociopaths can love anyone."

"Dad claims he's a psychopath. He's tough to figure."

"Like Sis always told me, 'don't figure Dad, and don't ever ignore his advice'. I never have and never will."

"That's because of her scars, huh?"

"Yeah. She ignored him and paid for it."

"Dad, Uncle Johnny, and Uncle Gus got him though," Benny said, hoping to hear more about the incident than Jean's simple 'he's dead' answer.

Quinn was silent for a few more steps, looking around at how close they were to Otter's Point. "That guy didn't go gently into the night, Ben. They kept him alive until he paid for his sins. Cleaner chopped him up for disposal from our helicopter for the fishes."

"I guess it's best to remember Dad can blow the heads off three guys and walk into the Monte to short order cook for Mom without missing a beat."

Quinn nodded. "Good one. That's exactly the picture of Dad to remember."

They reached Otter's Point at the bottom of the steep street in another ten minutes. Benny pointed. "That Mr. Harding is scary."

"John's a great guy. That's Lynn Montoya Dostiene between Harding and Clint. She's the scariest woman on earth, Ben. Harding's Monster Squad call her Cruella Deville. They just show videos of her past interrogations to prisoners and they puke and spill their guts. Uncle Johnny and Aunt Cala have been helping her direct and make films for a long time. She's a famous director now."

Quinn took a deep breath watching some of the deadliest killers in the world laughing at another killer, his Uncle Johnny, feeding the birds with them flocking around him in a cloud. "Yep. They've acquired a huge fortune but never quit doing what they do best."

"We're going to do the same thing, huh Kong?"

"With Sis prodding us, I doubt we'll have a choice. Don't rule out being a doctor or something else in the medical, engineering, or restaurant business. We do own a restaurant. Your grades are super. You'll be able to do anything you want. We could use a good medic, although our luck has been holding."

"Do you really think I could be a doctor?" Benny had come to a dead stop at the rock wall bordering Otter's Point.

Quinn was surprised at Benny's question. "Hell yeah. Dad and Mom would send you to Harvard if we can get you in with grades. Dad would probably donate an entire wing to some college to get you in. You excel in biology, chemistry, and all the math courses past analytical geometry and calculus. Keep it going, Ben. The sky's the limit."

"Could I still learn to fly our fleet like all of you?"

"Sure. Cala's a great teacher. Sonny's the one you want though for flying our jet. If he didn't love what we do he'd be flying as a commercial pilot. Cala mostly loves the stealth copters we have."

Benny laughed. "Fillets for Flipper, juice for Jaws."

Quinn sighed. "Yeah, the Cleaner is a bit graphic when jettisoning our recalcitrant bad guys for the final time. Uh oh… Mom's giving us the Trailer Trash Momma evil eye. We better get down there."

"Want me to take the weapon pack?"

"No… I got it. Best give Sammy his freedom. He looks ready to shoot off like a rocket."

"Shit!" Benny knelt down to take off the unnecessary leash. "Sorry, pal. Go play."

Sammy streaked at the cringing party of family and friends, sliding to a stop before prancing into their midst for pets and hugs. Sonny, Jean, and Al joined them at the steps. Jean hugged Benny.

"Now that was entertainment. The streaming live scene of the attitude adjustment for that Bart prick was enjoyed immensely. Trashy wanted to buzz kill the beat down to make sure you didn't get hurt. Dad said, 'the boy has Kong and Sammy. Calm the hell down'. It was hell-a-funny with everyone watching down here."

Benny embraced Al with affection. "I'm glad you came with your Dad, Alice. It's good to see you."

Al patted his face. "It's nice to see nothing's changed down here in Grove-Land. You bunch are more active than my whole FBI department. You're a junior this year, right Benny?"

"Yep, and I'm in the star program to graduate a year early. Quinn says I could go on to pursue being a doctor."

"Hell yeah," Al replied. "Nick and Rachel would be in heaven to see you go through med school."

"I'll do it in conjunction with the Marine Corps though," Benny stated. "I'm going to be a Marine like my brothers and sister."

"Damn, kid… you don't have to be a Marine," Jean said. "The way we've been training you, the Marines would be a letdown in the skill department."

"Sacrilege! Don't let Mr. Harding's friend Lucas hear you say that. I hope he visits soon. I want to tell him I'm going to serve my country in the Marines," Benny stated. "The best surgeons in the world served in support positions where they handled the wounded. Quinn's right though. I can be a doctor."

"No doubt about that," Sonny said. "C'mon. Mom will be over here yanking us along by our ears in another minute."

Al put an arm around Benny's shoulders while they stepped carefully in the sand. "That would be wonderful if you could get to be a doctor, Benny. I guess that Bart guy you clocked has been riding you hard, huh?"

"I was working undercover to set up the bust, but yeah, Bart led the pack at school taunting me," Benny admitted. "I may have let a little too much feeling seep into the payback."

"No such thing," Jean stated as they moved amongst the adult group.

Quinn shook hands with John Harding, Clint and Lynn Dostiene, and then faced his Mom. "There was no danger, Ma."

"Don't you disrespect Momma, Kong!"

"Bart boy decided to stake out our bust, Ma. Sis sent me to shadow Ben. It turned out great. Ben didn't have to let Sammy rip apart everyone in Bart's crew. We'll keep track of them, right Ben?"

Benny hugged Rachel. "Quinn's right, Ma. We were fine. Sammy was perfect."

Rachel's lips tightened, but she nodded in agreement. "You all did just right. I'm glad we ended that fuckin' Squiggy."

"Ma!" Jean did a for shame gesture at Rachel, with forefinger of right hand brushing over the forefinger of her left with everyone else enjoying the interaction with vocal appreciation. "The Marine Marauders oversaw all action with care and dedication."

"I like your new trio tag, Viper," John Harding said. "Lucas of course loves it, as do those two ancient Marine coots, Chuck and Sal from Red Dragon. They all should have retired together to a pond where they could fish and exchange memories. That damn Lucas has busted my chops so much lately I'm thinking of retiring before him."

"Yeah... that'll happen," Al scoffed. "We're all here, Dad. Can Clint and Lynn get to it before Johnny goes out for more bird treats? Do something with your husband, Cala. Gus says he's been pulling this bird shit for over a decade."

Cala Groves couldn't speak. She was laughing so hard at Johnny's gasping reaction to his private bird interaction, it took many moments while avid appreciation of Al's critique was enjoyed by all, for her to voice a response. "My husband is very addicted to his bird friends. It is a blessing. We give him scraps for the flying rodents. He distracts them from us if we are eating – very useful."

Johnny shrugged, having run out of bread scraps, he joined his friends and family. "It is as Cala states, my disrespectful life's partner to be punished later for her transgressions."

"Oooohhhh… you are so forceful." Cala embraced Johnny with stilted speech to much amusement. "I am so scared."

"Should we stake out Bart's crew," Gus asked, holding tight to his wife Tina in the chilling wind breezing across the beach.

"Let me follow the situation in school, Uncle Gus," Benny replied. "It may be that the serious ending of Squiggy, and the arrest of his crew, will quiet this situation. I'll be able to tell. If the police can keep the suppliers in jail, the thugs like Bart and his gang should fade."

"Want to sit with us, Benny," Nick gestured at the ring of lawn chairs.

"Is it okay if I walk Sammy down to Lover's Point with the kids?"

"Sure. We have you on audio," Nick replied. "You watch out for Little John. He thinks he's sixteen instead of six."

"His older sister fusses over him so much I doubt she'll let him near anything," Cala said. "I can't believe Lila will be a teenager soon."

"Go on, Benny," Johnny said, giving his wife a shoulder hug. "Dan takes orders from Lila, so Little John will be fine."

Benny and Sammy went to gather Johnny and Cala's kids for the long walk.

"How old is Dan?"

407

"He's ten, Lynn," Cala answered. "He's quiet, but the one we keep an eye on all the time. He has taken to the knife like a kid in the candy store."

"Really?"

"Oh Lynn," Jean said. "He's better than Sonny and I were at that age. Dan has the bug. He loves the throwing knives."

"I saw you pin that Squiggy creep's paw to his chest. You put some snap into that toss, girl. Maybe we'll get some sparring time this visit."

Jean hid the absolute adoration she had for Lynn Montoya Dostiene with effort. "I'd like that very much. Sonny, Quinn, and I spar constantly. I'm hoping we've gotten at least near to you in skill."

"I'm certain of it, kid," Lynn declared as the adults sat down together for the more serious subject of a massive kill mission. "I'm losing a step. I need a replacement, right, babe?"

"Not hardly," Clint answered.

* * *

"That was a great visit, Dad."

I looked over at the spitting image of my wife Lora with a nod of acceptance as I drove the stretch limo toward our North Bay base. "Yeah, it was. I liked Johnny's idea of infiltration with Cala into their midst for confirmation. I don't like them continuing to do this crap. We all know what they'll find. The bastards don't congregate in secret except to establish their damn No-Go zones."

"You know Kabong, Cheese," Lynn said. "He'll be filming the hell out of everything. Jean's going in as their daughter. She speaks the lingo like a native. They've done this crap before. We need to find out if the place is a hive training center, or a congregation community geared as usual to provide the chicken-shit assholes with kids and women to act as shields."

Clint chuckled at my silence. "I think Cheese is at the point he wants to start doing some Hiroshima drops."

"I admit it. We've been allowing this seeping poison for over two decades. We now have whole American cities under unannounced Sharia Law. That all of us citizen dupes are now armed to the teeth is the only reason they haven't moved on us as they have in Europe. While we're cleaning this nest out, we should go to Washington, DC, and take care of some traitors there selling us out on a daily basis."

"Comment, Al?"

My daughter grinned back at her Aunt Lynn. "I'm done with right and proper. That we have Paul Gilbrech and Denny Strobert still in charge at CIA is a miracle. With Janie appointed FBI Director, I figure we at least control law enforcement to the point we can react. Nick's friends Tim and Grace are as high in the Justice Department and US Marshal's office as we can get anyone. I transferred to the West Coast because Janie's partner Sam Reeves runs the San Francisco office. I have a newbie's long view, but I never forget what you all have battled over the years. It helps to remind me with friends like Jean and Sonny too."

"I was just ragging you, kid. You know the situation. We work from under the log in the woods, where it's wet and icky. When we get the call, it ain't to preserve anything but the Union."

"Amen to that. We'll survive all this... I pray to God... but why do they make it so damn difficult?"

"Nothing happens in a vacuum, Al," Clint said. "We've taken care of more than a few power players who have corrupted the entire system. When it became standard operating procedure to get elected and become a coin operated commodity for sale to the highest bidder, the legislative branch of government became the enemy of the people. Forget all that. We're glad to have you in on this. Being in contact with Sam and Janie is hell-a-important."

"Clint's right," I added. "We need attention directed away from our forces of darkness. Believe this, if Johnny, Cala, and Jean find a male Muslim infestation of terrorists, we're going in thar' and set things right. If they find terrorist families, we'll have to do the surgical strike we all hate. We'll be deporting the families we find there. They won't be innocents, but since we're not allowed to do a 'Harry Truman' on them like he did to end WWII with the Japanese, we'll hand them over to you and Sam. With Janie's support, we can get them sent back where they came from. The first hint of asylum from our leaders and we go postal."

"At least we have people in place who know the game we've been in the midst of for the past decade, Dad," Al stated with some frustration bleeding through. "They never assimilate. They lie, cheat, and litigate. They constantly strive to jam Sharia Law down our throats. I can understand how all of you feel. We've been fighting inside a war zone on our own soil with the enemy creeping inch by inch no matter how many battles we win."

"It's agreed then," Lynn stated. "We move our assets into place for a kill strike. I'm as sick of this 'Whack-a-Mole' game as Cheese. At least the government was forced to quit granting them citizen's rights just because they slimed onto our soil somehow. Rounding the so called innocents for deportation sucks. No use opening that wound. At least they'll be wailing together some place in the sand. It seems right the pricks call themselves the French translation since France is nearly belly up to them."

"They take on whatever term the media whitewashes for them," Clint said. "I bet you're not real happy risking your best assistant director."

"Johnny and Cala are like us. They can't stop flirting in the danger zone. Sonny and Jean are the same. Rachel's been spotting for Muerto for a long time. Anyway, Laredo won't fly anymore missions, so it's a good thing the kids are all picking up the slack from that old coot. After Laredo and Dannie's Mom, Sybil, married, he went all in on the family. Our whole crew has an oddly incestuous type thing going. Clint Jr. marries Jafar and Samara's Mia. Dannie married Nick's buddy, Clyde Bacall, after getting her doctorate degree. I'm glad Sybil doesn't mind Dannie's kids calling me 'Ma. With Dannie's kids, I've gotten to practice my Granny persona. It's nice to have Laredo flying us anywhere we want to go. He has Clint Jr. only a little time away from his pilot's license."

"Achmed would fly us anywhere too. With all the money we've confiscated from murderous Muslim hate groups and their enablers, we have quite the air force between Nick's bunch and ours. I'm a little pissed Jafar wants us to stop calling him Achmed the Dead Terrorist. Just because he's fixing to be a young grandpa doesn't mean we should have to knuckle under to his demands as Jr's father-in-law."

"It's a small thing," I said. "He'll never get Lucas retrained though. It's getting hard keeping all the 'Monster' extended family straight in our heads. I like your idea about keeping this op simple, Lynn. We move our tools into place and wait for Johnny to give us the final observation. If they refuse to admit him, there will be collateral damage."

"Agreed," Lynn and Clint said. Al knew better than to assume a vote in Monster decisions.

Al turned to Lynn. "How do you like Rachel running against Sonny's Mom for City Council?"

"If Trashy doesn't win, there will be blood," Lynn replied.

* * *

The adults enjoyed the cooling October breeze after the Harding contingent left, sipping beverages of choice while waiting for Benny and the kids to return from the long hike. Nick assumed Benny would have a rider on his shoulders on the way back.

"I forgot to tell Benny to stop and get a treat at Mandos," Nick said.

"Are you kidding? Sammy won't budge after getting to Lover's Point without turning right for Mandos. Benny walks him along to Mandos so many times, they store scraps for the big beggar," Rachel said. "He knows better than to pull that crap on Momma."

"Oh good... you've scared our dog into submission, Trashy... you must be very proud."

"Shut-up, Scarface, before Momma puts a hurtin' on you!"

"Are you really going to run for City Council against Clarice, Mom," Quinn asked, trying at Nick's raised brows at him to change the subject. It worked.

"You're damn right I am. We're going to the mattresses!" In a split second, Rachel did her entire 'Trailer Trash Momma' transformation to much amusement.

"Easy, Hon," Nick urged. "You've had a couple of wines."

"Oh no! Oh no you didn't just call Momma a lush, Nicky Pooh!" Another split second passed as Rachel turned on Nick with fists up, but lost her balance.

Nick had her in a heartbeat, easing Rachel down on her chair again. "I'm designated caretaker today, Momma. You know that. Calm down. We have another month before the election."

Nick kissed his soul-mate with momentary passion so as not to elicit the usual disparagement from their adult children. Rachel melted in his arms, briefly stroking his face. "You're still hell-a-fast, Muerto."

412

"I want your knees and hips all in good shape for the election, my love."

"Oh shit!" Tina motioned with a head movement toward the beach's stone steps. "It's Phil and Clarice. Oh joy. Can anyone tell me why those two risk life and limb to trek down here to interrupt a great 'Momma' performance? Stay calm, girlfriend."

"I'm good," Rachel said, glancing over at Sonny's worried expression. "Calm down, Cracker. I'm not going to beat your Mom senseless right in front of you."

"Yeah, but I know you have your sidearm with you," Sonny replied, only half joking. "I really don't want you to shoot either one of them either."

Rachel smirked, leaning over to pat Sonny's hand. "I have to tone this down somehow with your folks. I just haven't figured out how yet. It's a process."

Sonny sighed. "Tell me about it."

Phil, potbellied now, with obvious hair implants, stared at Nick with abject fear of something you don't understand that could kill you without a tremor of remorse. Nick smiled at him and waved.

"Hi Phil. Hi Clarice. What brings you here on an until now wonderful October afternoon?"

"Oh sure, Mr. Big-time Author!" Clarice had once again forgotten past interactions with the McCarty family. "How dare you even hint at running against me for City Council! You may have big time money from God knows where, but-"

Jean squeezed her Mom's hand on the way out of her chair. "Calm down right now, Clarice! Phil knows better than to do this, even down here on a public beach. Choose your words carefully. I can tell from your red-faced features you don't like my Mom running against you. Since you can't stop her, and there's no way in hell you'll ever change her mind, why journey down here into the danger zone? Do you think you're safe to say anything you like because it's broad daylight and your son is here? Think again. Ask Sonny."

Jean's words chilled Clarice as Phil's had failed to do. She darted a glance at Sonny. He was smiling in the usual way he had when no matter what she did or said, it would have no effect on him. "Oh sure… I see where his mind is… I-"

Jean darted forward to grip Clarice's nose in an unbreakable grip. Sonny leaped to intercept Phil. "Stay out of this, Dad!"

Clarice knew instinctively she had crossed a line. Jean release her nose. She gasped dramatically for breath.

"I warned you! Ask Sonny. My Mom and Dad raised him. They love the shit out of him. No one knows what you two love besides power and money. Ask him if you dare. Otherwise, you both need to wave and go on about your day."

"Sonny!" Clarice cast an award winning feature filled face of victimhood at her son.

Sonny released his Dad, patting him on the shoulder. He moved over to his Mom without hesitation, putting a comforting arm around her shoulders. "Mom… I love you and Dad. I know what you two are, but I still love you both. Doesn't that mean anything to you? Nick saved my life and yours, yet you two still treat him like shit. I spent more time at his home than anywhere on earth while growing up because I love everyone in the McCarty family. I allowed this discussion to go this far so I could at this point tell you and Dad my loyalty and honor are with the McCarty's, not with you."

Clarice gasped, stepping back with her hands covering her mouth in award winning form. "We love you. These people are killers! They would slit-"

Jean grabbed Clarice's mouth in an unbreakable squeezing grip. "Don't finish that, Clarice. You and Phil are not in touch with reality. We take that into consideration, but there is a limit to that allowance. As I said, be careful of your words. I see Phil understands."

Phil, who had been watching the rise of retribution on Nick and Rachel's faces, jerked Clarice away from Jean. "We have to go now! Don't say anything else!"

Rachel took a deep breath and stood up. "It's okay, Jean. Listen Clarice. I'm running against you. Nick has already filed for me. We have nearly every business in the city wanting me on the City Council. My next stop after that will be Mayor. Don't come around throwing tantrums. It's all a done deal. We love your son like our own. He's with us because he has a heart and conscience. Be proud of that. Go ahead, Phil. Escort Clarice off the beach. If I were you two, I'd stay the hell away from here."

Phil yanked Clarice toward the stone stairs as she mumbled something about electioneering and fraud. Rachel sat down, gesturing for Sonny and Jean to sit. "I hope we can get them to stay away from Otter's Point. They must check the house and then come straight down here."

"I doubt it," Sonny replied. "They want a meeting in public with cars driving by when they decide to confront us about something."

Amused by most of the Salvatore visit, Nick grasped Rachel's hand. "We're going to get her elected. We could probably get her into the Governor's mansion if it weren't for El Muerto."

"I want to beat Clarice," Rachel replied. "I don't want to turn our lives upside down."

"Maybe if we propelled you into the Governor's mansion, you could do 'Trailer Trash Momma' for a nationwide audience," Jean said.

Rachel laughed, pointing at Jean. "Good one, Scarface. I could imagine the news conferences when I got a crap question and I bring 'Momma' out. Let's beat Clarice. She and Phil are relatively harmless right now. They aren't money strapped are they, Sonny?"

"I put them on a budget, Ma. They don't like it but I know they'd find a way to get into trouble otherwise. The extra money I gave them went for this whacky run for council I'd bet. Uncle Johnny? Are you sure I couldn't go in with you. I speak the language very well. Even Dad said so."

"I wish we could," Johnny said. "Hell, I'd like to go in dressed as El Kabong with Muerto, Payaso, and Cala the Cleaner at my side, guns blazing. We'll only have one chance of getting in there, one guy and two supposedly helpless women. We're copying the method those dolts used Muerto sanctioned on the Fisherman's Wharf pier long ago. The woman tucked automatic weapons in her burka. Viper and Cleaner can do the same thing. They'll be suspicious enough as it is, Sonny. I'll be lucky if they don't turn us away."

"We're lucky Kabong's Ebi Zarin identity is still working on a careful basis," Nick added. "Zarin is an Isis legend. He appears out of nowhere, claims to have a cell forming, and everyone who comes into contact with him dies. Besides, ever since Clint streamed me the surveillance footage from satellite, Gus has been studying the compound."

"It's built like a small town," Gus said. "They're not stupid. They have streets, housing, and stores. The largest building is the mosque. One of the reasons the Monsters came to see us was for confirmation on what I saw, and finalize the infiltration without anything passed even on a secure line. Clint and I agree the mosque acts as their armory as always. It's shielded. One of the ways we've been able to stay a step ahead relies on unavoidable building costs and plans. They can't get away with any structures utilizing water, electricity, and gas without filing plans. Their lawyers are useless against California's tax collectors. This Daesh sect we've handled before bought many properties in impoverished out of the way areas all across the USA."

"We have to get inside the mosque somehow," Jean said. "You said you saw some burka babes running around that for sure weren't women, right, Uncle Gus?"

"Yep. Too tall and too hairy and rough handed. I could tell from the small opening they have for their eyes, with only what I could see of their features, they were male goons. Plus… there are no children at all. I'd bet money if they ever get wind of an inspection, they'll bus in real women and kids to wail about discrimination in the street."

"It wasn't that long ago when we ran across this spinoff Daesh bunch and extracted Tim and Grace's relation, Kelly Brighton. They were dopey enough to use visible armed guards. You never mentioned the place again, Dad."

Payaso and Kabong started laughing, as did Cala the Cleaner.

"Okay… I get it… what happened, and why wasn't I told about it?"

"You went back to college when Paul called me with a kill mission. He wondered if the 'Unholy Trio' could erase the compound from existence," Nick answered. "I told him sure, but we'd need massive cleanup. Paul agreed to have a bulldozer team ready to smooth things over after we finished. The Monster Squad was on another gig. Otherwise, we wouldn't have done it alone."

"It was my first kill mission as pilot," Cala said. "It was glorious! We struck in the dead of night with the Stealth UH-60M. At a mile away, we blasted 'The Ride of the Valkyries' so loud the buildings in the compound shook. They didn't know what was coming. I fired off the M139 Volcano dispenser on the first pass."

"Good Lord," Jean whispered.

Cala smiled, nodding her head. "Yes, it was quite impressive. I nearly obliterated the compound with all forty of the mine canisters. The second pass we fired AGM-144 Hellfire missiles. The third pass, we used the XM25 rocket launcher and GAU-18A .50 caliber machine gun to…to… ah-"

"Salt the earth," Nick finished for her.

"Yes! I was very good at piloting our 'Death Star'."

"We have our own AC-130J 'Ghostrider' now though, as does the Monster Squad," Johnny said. "We will employ both and have the 'Death Star' on hand if we need to do a gentle cleansing."

"I have the exact coordinates for three snipers' nests, Muerto has already been over," Gus said. "We did a recon of the area last night before the meeting as we explained before you came, Quinn. Nick and Rachel will be at one, Lucas and Casey on another. There's an opening for a third, Sonny."

"I'll take it." Sonny paused, wondering if he should go on. Jean jarred him with a shoulder. "Benny wants in. He's perfect for my spotter, Dad."

"No damn way!" Rachel stood, staring right at Jean with hands on hips. "This is your doing, Scarface!"

Jean waved her off. "Sit down, Trashy. Benny's been training constantly. He's begging for a chance in combat. Quinn started off as a spotter. Give him an opportunity. We'll have him covered."

Nick yanked gently on Rachel's arm. "Benny deserves a shot, babe. You've seen him. He's as good a spotter as you are, with a sixth sense for wind and air change, not to mention he's a genius at math."

"Ben wants to be a doctor," Quinn added. "He wants to do it in combination with joining the Marines."

"Jesus…" Rachel whispered, sitting down again in slump shouldered defeat. "We're doomed."

"You must have missed the part about Ben wanting to be a doctor along with being a Marine, Ma," Quinn said.

"That is great," Nick said. "Your Mom needs a little time to absorb the reality part. We could use a medic. We're all okay at field dressings, but a surgeon would be a real plus, right Rach?"

Rachel shrugged as Tina handed her a glass of wine which she drank half of before speaking. "I guess so. Benny's gone through so much… why the hell do we have to adopt him into our combat wing?"

"He's Ben McCarty now, Trashy," Jean stated. "Okay… he's in as Sonny's spotter. We're set for this, Dad. When do we move the pieces into place?"

Nick smiled. "Tomorrow morning."

* * *

Quinn grinned as he heard Clint Jr. and Lynn trading barbs as they waited in place near the terrorist community of Ramoi with a strike force of Quinn, Clint, Lynn, and Lynn's minions: Gus Denova, Quays Tannous, and Sylvio Ruelas. They also deployed armored vehicles in strategic spots near the entrances into the Daesh training camp with Tommy Sands, Jess Brown, and Devon Constantine as drivers. Jess and Tommy would block the approach, ready to move in for quick extraction. Devon was the secondary force's ride inside to support Johnny, Cala, and Jean. Jafar and Samira waited in the UH-60M helicopter. Also at the ready near them Laredo Sawyer remained at the same hangar and private air field with extended runway Nick had purchased near Gilroy. Laredo flew the AC-130J Ghostrider with Gus Nason in the copilot's seat, working weapons. John Harding piloted the other UH-60M with Issac Leon next to him.

"Get your damn head in the game, Jr!"

Clint Jr. glanced at Quinn with a big grin. He was six foot, three inches of ripcord tough, crew cut killer. "Hey Ma, your vagina is showing. Maybe you better sit this one out, Betty."

Clint only managed to grab his wife in a last second clutch as she launched toward her son. "Easy…easy, Lynn. He nailed you again. You're giving him combat instructions when he's Marine Recon like Quinn."

Lynn relaxed in Clint's grip, pointing at her offspring. "There will be blood, you know-it-all little shit."

"I learned from the best, Ma. Calm the hell down, Betty," Jr. sparked her with the term he'd been bombarded with ever since he was a kid, listening to his Mom bait unsuspecting Snow Whites. "We get the order. We move in and kill anything that has a male heartbeat, including any burka babes with hairy hands, reaching for weapons. Why don't you do some knife tricks until you get comfortable, Betty."

The only person able to make such a statement smirked while everyone around him moved away as if near a detonating mine. Jr turned back into position, weapon at the ready, even though if everything worked out as planned, the fake community would be in ashes. Quinn watched his brother in arms crouch in comfortable silence.

"Recon!"

They all heard Lucas's term of endearment for his Godson at the expense of Clint Jr.'s Mom. Lynn chuckled. "Shut the fuck up, Ahab."

"We're all on the network, Betty," Lucas jabbed her. "We know you're worried. It's best to do this as Jr advised – either get ready or sit it out. None of us would think any less of you."

A chorus of grunting acknowledgements agreed with Lucas's assessment.

"I'm in," Lynn stated. "I'm done mommying. If there's any more Betty digs from anyone, I'll have my foot massage gear ready to go. That includes you, know-it-all."

Clint Jr. locked eyes with his Mom. "Understood, Ma. We'll be fine."

"I wouldn't be worried if Cheese hadn't used up all our good Karma and luck with all his near disasters."

"I heard that, Crue," Harding said. "We're flying into position now."

Quinn gripped his weapon, ignoring any further banter. Their support aircraft were in the air, minutes from positions already decided on. He needed a moment to gather his thoughts for combat. His sister would be in a place, if things went wrong, where there would be little to shield her from harm, other than the rain of death exacted by the sniper teams. Quinn had made peace with the fact he would kill everything without thought or hesitation until he reached her: men, women, and children. Let God sort them out at the end. He knew any of them could be wearing bomb vests.

* * *

Johnny approached the gated community's entrance with tired realization he would once again be forced to dredge up his Ebi Zarin identity, although he disavowed and detested every aspect of his long ago dead identity. He drove a late model BMW, steeling himself to interact with the guard in a completely nerveless manner, without any indication of what churned inside of him. He well knew one mistake could rob his children of ever seeing him and Cala ever again. Cala gripped his arm momentarily.

"It is a small thing, brother," Cala echoed, reading his expression, with a long ago reference to his favorite movie: Thirteenth Warrior.

They reached the outer gate with Johnny patting Cala's leg with acknowledgement of her intuitive grasp of his emotions. The guards at the gate were only armed with holstered weapons. He made an instantaneous mission decision as the guard drew near with a sneering look of animosity. Johnny knew the mosque would be the key to their report.

"Give me my MP5," Johnny told Cala. She and Jean hid the old but very reliable silenced machine pistols under their burkas. Cala instantly slapped it into his hands from underneath her garb.

"Uncle Johnny?"

"Be ready, Viper."

When the two guards reached the car, Johnny lowered his tinted window and shot both men in the head with two short bursts. Jean instantly disembarked from the car, running toward the guard post, but there were no more men inside the guard shack. She held ground, watching for any kind of notice. Johnny dragged the two bodies out of sight. Cala smiled at her husband as he reentered the BMW's driver's seat.

"I'm tellin'," Cala joked as Jean joined them.

"No need," John Harding said. "I wasn't thrilled with you three trying to get past those guards and leaving them at your back either.

"We're watching the compound," Rachel added. "Clear so far, but you'll have to recon fast if the guards had check in times."

"Clear from our nest," Benny said.

"Clear," Casey acknowledged.

"Are you headed for the mosque, Kabong?"

"No change there, Muerto," Johnny replied. "The guards' body language as they approached did not look promising. We will go directly inside the mosque and need time for a thorough search."

"Absolutely," Nick said. "All snipers' nests have a viewing of the mosque entrance. We will maintain a clear escape zone even if we have to let the 'Ghostrider' loose on everything around. You copy that, Laredo?"

"Understood," Laredo said. "We are in support distance right now. Gus fed the mosque coordinates into our weapons system. We're ready."

Johnny backed in beside the mosque, the hands on his watch reading a little after one in the morning. The three kept dressed for the time being while approaching without weapons showing. Before nearing the mosque's entrance, Jean fired their wide range EMP weapon at the approach while Johnny and Cala took positions on either side of the approach. By prior agreement, if they could talk or shoot their way past the guards, the armory they were certain had been placed in the mosque would be target one. Jean threw the electromagnetic pulse weapon in the car again. She then ran past her two guards to the front with a hand held battering ram, tried the door, determined the locking mechanism, and smashed through with one stroke of the ram.

Automatic weapons fire sliced through the opening as Jean slipped to the side, dropping the ram, and readying her weapon. Johnny and Cala ran to the other side with Johnny pulling the pin on a grenade. They knew the armory would not be on the main floor of the mosque. He tossed it in. It made a spectacular explosion inside with fire and debris shooting out the open entrance. Johnny waited twenty seconds and threw another one in harder. Jean smiled as the second one exploded with screams of agony.

Shouting, running figures firing wildly approached, only to be cut down immediately from above. Sirens sounded on the highest tower which also acted as the call to prayer for the murderous cult. Johnny, Jean, and Cala crossed paths firing in short bursts after slipping on their night-vision helmets with breathing filters. They fired indiscriminately into every body alive or dead they found. The damage from the grenades appeared ancillary rather than structural. Firing outside increased every minute, but the three knew the mosque had to be cleared before proceeding to look for the hidden armory.

"Main floor secure," Johnny stated.

"Secondary force on the way," Clint said.

Devon zigzagged through the compound's streets with the two UH-60M helicopters in support with 'Ride of the Valkyries' blasting from both helicopters' sound systems. They fired the Yak-B Gatling guns, making sure everything in front of secondary force died. John shot ahead as the armored vehicle neared the mosque and blew the prayer tower and siren to pieces. Devon whipped the armored vehicle into a slide bringing it around to face the escape route. Secondary force deployed around the mosque. Quinn and Clint Jr. halted at the entrance.

"Kong and Cutthroat at the door, Viper. Secondary force deployed."

"Come ahead. We're at the access to the underground part, we-"

As Quinn ran toward the access with Clint Jr. watching his back the rear of the building exploded. He spotted Jean, Johnny, and Cala diving to the floor. Quinn ran through the exploded section, taking the force of five rushing at it completely by

424

surprise. He smashed through them like bowling pins. Close order combat followed unlike anything the attacking men expected. Quinn and Clint Jr. drew their K-bar knives without hesitation, knowing from experience the lethal shock their vicious stabbing attack would cause. Only one of the enemy who had been at the back after firing the rocket launcher broke free. He stood to shoot down into the milling mass of warriors. Jean's MP5 burst blew his face apart.

The bloodied Marines finished off the other four enemy with killing strokes up through their chins. A larger attacking force moved toward them from the maze of buildings behind the mosque, firing as they came.

"Get down, Kong and Cutthroat!" Nick's sharp order was obeyed instantly by the two Marines. M2 Browning machine gun fire cut through the rear assault party with devastating accuracy. Bodies nearly cut in half pitched all around until John Harding landed the UH-60M into the street's rear, firing the Yak-B Gatling guns in a tight rotating fashion, clearing out everything in their path. "Sorry, Kong. We saw the threat, but couldn't move into position with the M2 until a moment ago. Thanks, Cheese."

"Combat… the inexact science, right Muerto? I didn't see anything move down there when I took out the tower. One more inexact science moment and we back out and let the 'Ghostrider' turn this place into dust."

"Agreed," Nick said. "Anyone hit down there?"

"Cleaner's wounded." Johnny worked to staunch the blood oozing around the wooden stake from the rear debris explosion, knowing better than to extract it.

Quinn and Clint Jr. arrived at her side a moment later. Quinn gathered her into his arms and headed for Harding's stealth. Issac helped him ease her into an emergency gurney on board the UH-60M. Johnny dived in with her.

"Achmed! Move into support position," Harding ordered. "I'll fly Cala to T for transport."

"On it," Jafar acknowledged.

Quinn and Clint Jr. joined Jean. Lynn and Clint ran toward them from the front to take Johnny and Cala's place. Quinn smashed the access door leading down with one kick, slipping to the side in anticipation of weapons' fire. His three companions fired bursts down into the underground facility for a moment.

"Damn it!" Jean hesitated for a moment. "We can't throw stuff down that hole without taking a chance of blowing ourselves to kingdom come. Do you think there's anything worthwhile down there?"

"Only one way to find out," Lynn said. "We fire a coordinated burst. Then Kong drops down with Cutthroat backing the play."

Jean reached out to smack Quinn on the back of his head. "You two warts fire the moment you hit the landing. Hear me?"

Quinn grinned. "Wow, I'm glad you came, Sis. Cutthroat and I would never have guessed we should fire when we hit the landing."

Muffled laughter sounded uneasily in their ears from the networked assault group. Jean nodded. "Good one. Fire in the hole!"

Jean, Clint, and Lynn took turns firing bursts down into the void below. Clint gestured him down and Quinn dropped down the staircase barely touching a step with Clint Jr. right behind him. He hit the landing hard, swinging toward the interior, firing as he turned. Quinn's burst riddled the unwary man readying to fire upwards again. Clint Jr. joined Quinn to concentrate their bursts at moving and firing targets.

"Landing clear! Bad guys here!"

Quinn's words brought Clint, Lynn, and Jean individually with cover fire to the landing and outwards to join Quinn and Clint Jr. They held position. Each enemy who popped up to fire absorbed a .45 caliber hollow point slug through his head as Clint switched to the weapon least likely to explode anything hidden in the underground facility. So deadly was Clint's fire, the last one hiding raised his hands shouting he was surrendering. Lynn clutched her husband's hand before he could execute the last one.

"Don't break my toy. He can help."

Clint smiled and nodded at his wife, the premier interrogator of all time. Quinn and Clint Jr. had already secured the prisoner by then.

Lynn took off her helmet, sniffing distastefully at the cordite in the air. "Okay, porky, let's get this over with. Take us on a tour of the armory. Miss something and you get one of these."

Lynn jammed her stun-gun against the man's groin, his scream echoing while he landed hard on the floor. Lynn bent down to pat his face. "Ah... so sweet... you think that hurt. You ain't seen nothing yet, sweetie. Do you understand the rules of the game or would you like another demonstration?"

Still clutching his groin in the fetal position, the prisoner nodded his head in violent affirmative acknowledgement until he could speak. "I...I will show you anything... anything you want to see!"

"That's my good little helper. Get him on his feet, boys. Let's get the tour over with before we make this town into a crater."

With Gatling guns blazing, Jafar's voice sounded over the com unit. "Taking fire. They are regrouping, Crue."

"Wait one." Lynn turned with a triggered arc of blue to get her prisoner's attention. "I'll only ask this once. Do you have any women and children here? If you lie to me I'll cut your dick off and choke you with it."

"No! They are held near here in case of an inspection! Please… it is the truth."

Lynn smiled. "Thank you, my little helper. Turn up the music, Achmed. Laredo?"

"Here Crue."

"Once the UH-60's are clear, lay waste to everything until there's nothing but smoke and flame left."

"Understood. You copy, Dark Lord."

"Understood. Holding position after Cleaner drop off. T speeding for med help."

"Understood," Jafar acknowledged. "Clear of area now."

"Plug your ears, kids. Ghostrider raining death and destruction."

With 'Ride of the Valkyries' blasting, Laredo's AC-130J Gunship made passes of which nothing survived on the surface. The UH-60M's killed everything trying to escape the apocalyptic gunship fire. Nick and Rachel retreated with the M2 machine gun and sniper rifle, watching as Laredo and Gus literally erased everything from existence around the mosque. Rachel kept moving toward the extraction point. Nick stopped, setting up again for cover fire.

"Hold on, Trashy. We have work yet to do. I could use wind, heat, and fire readings."

"What the hell do you think is going to be down there, Muerto?" Rachel began spotting again, letting Nick know the alterations in wind current, temperature flux, and wind direction at varying distance ranges.

"You'll see, my love."

It did not take long before Laredo turned the area surrounding the mosque into rubble.

"Movement!" Benny's voice sounded for the first time. He called out coordinates, zeroing in on an area where a hatch flipped over amidst the chaos. The first combatant rising out of the opening dropped sideways and fell back inside.

"Nice work, Cracker," Nick said. "Good job spotting, Killer B."

"Oh man... I like that, Dad... I mean, Muerto."

The amusement couldn't be hidden as Nick called out to air support. "We have a hive hole at last called out coordinates."

"On it." Laredo flew in the A130, and Gus hit the hole with a Hellfire missile. Nothing but a smoking crater and some debris survived the impact.

"Shit!" Rachel called out coordinates as another hatch opened, this time with four armed figures streaming out of it. Nick and Lucas killed all four instantly. Without being told, Laredo moved in and sanctioned the hole for all time.

* * *

The waiting game continued for the next fifteen minutes before Lynn came on-line again. "My little helper took us on a tour of the facility. We need Denny in on this with Hazmat teams as well as bomb disposal units. They have stuff best not discussed. We'll have to stay in place to guard the area, Cheese."

"Issac's making the call out right now." I looked over at my copilot. Issac turned his pad my way. Denny's grizzled face stared back at me. "Hey, Den... how's it hangin'."

"So much for the quiet kill, huh Cheese?"

"On the upside, we may have barely stopped a bio attack. I guess the politicians will have to man up. They won't be able to whitewash this episode. They have a reason for an armed conflict."

Denny sighed. "Agreed. Issac said Crue has a survivor. Would you please ask her to keep him for me? I will be on site in two hours with requested teams."

"Will do. Cheese out." I switched back to the network. "Denny requested your helper stay alive, Crue."

"No problem. He was very helpful, including leading us to a jackpot of gold and bearer bonds. These missions cost money. We're taking payment now. Trashy will need campaign money too."

"Thanks, Crue," Rachel said. "I'll probably get cut off on my way to the Governor's mansion though. Muerto doesn't want to expose the cartoons to public life. Have you heard how Cleaner is yet, Dark Lord?"

"T says they arrived at the hospital emergency room only a few minutes ago. They have her on the table now with Johnny by her side. We'll secure the area until Denny gets here and then go see her. Are you good for a couple hours, Ahab, or do you want me to fly in a gurney?"

"You're lucky you have a copilot, Recon. Otherwise you'd be in imminent danger of a friendly fire incident."

"Heh…heh… I'll bet."

* * *

Nick sat at a table drinking coffee inside their campaign headquarters at the Monte Café with Rachel next to him. The results trickled in at a turtle's pace for local elections in a tourist town like Pacific Grove. Johnny, Cala, Gus, and Tina sat with them. All their kids watched the election result program on the screen set in place for the election. Sporadic cheers rang out in relation to the slow numbers coming in a couple hours after the polls closed.

Jean popped out of her chair with all kids, including Little John, turning to salute the adult table. "Councilwoman Trashy. Would you like to make an acceptance speech to the Marine Marauders?"

Rachel took a deep breath as Nick hugged her. Everyone at the adult table applauded. Rachel stood, waving at the now saluting kids. "I would like to say thank you for all your dedication to my small time election. I'm sure your Mom will be calling to congratulate me any moment, right Sonny?"

"Oh yeah, Ma... anytime now... the moment they begin passing out ice cream and cake in hell, pigs fly, and she stops throwing temper tantrums at my Dad."

"You'd better take Jean over to visit her," Nick replied. "She'll probably need an intervention or a suicide watch."

"You're right." Sonny grabbed his coat. "C'mon Viper, we have to save my Mom."

"I'll pass. Use your stun-gun."

The End for now.

Thank you for purchasing and reading Cold Blooded VI: Red Horizon. If you enjoyed the novel, please take a moment and leave a review. Your consideration would be much appreciated. Please visit my Amazon Author's Page if you would like to preview any of my other novels. Thanks again for your support.

Bernard Lee DeLeo

Author's Face Book Page -

https://www.facebook.com/groups/BernardLeeDeLeo/

BERNARD LEE DELEO - AUTHOR'S PAGE -

http://www.amazon.com/Bernard-Lee-
DeLeo/e/B005UNXZ04/ref=ntt_athr_dp_pel_pop_1

AMAZON AUTHOR'S PAGE (UK) -

http://www.amazon.co.uk/-/e/B005UNXZ04

Made in the USA
Lexington, KY
15 June 2017